THE IRON HOUND

ALSO AVAILABLE FROM TIM AKERS AND TITAN BOOKS

The Pagan Night
The Winter Vow (August 2018)

BOOK TWO OF THE HALLOWED WAR

THE IRON HOUND

TIM AKERS

TITAN BOOKS

THE IRON HOUND
Print edition ISBN: 9781783299508
Electronic edition ISBN: 9781783299515

Published by Titan Books
A division of Titan Publishing Group Ltd
144 Southwark St, London SE1 0UP

First edition: August 2017
2 4 6 8 10 9 7 5 3 1

Visit our website: www.titanbooks.com

A CIP catalogue record for this title is available from the British Library.

Printed and bound in the USA.

This book is dedicated to the readers who have followed me from the earliest days of Veridon, into the city of Ash, and finally onto the mad and rolling hills of Tenumbra. Here's to a thousand adventures, and a thousand more.

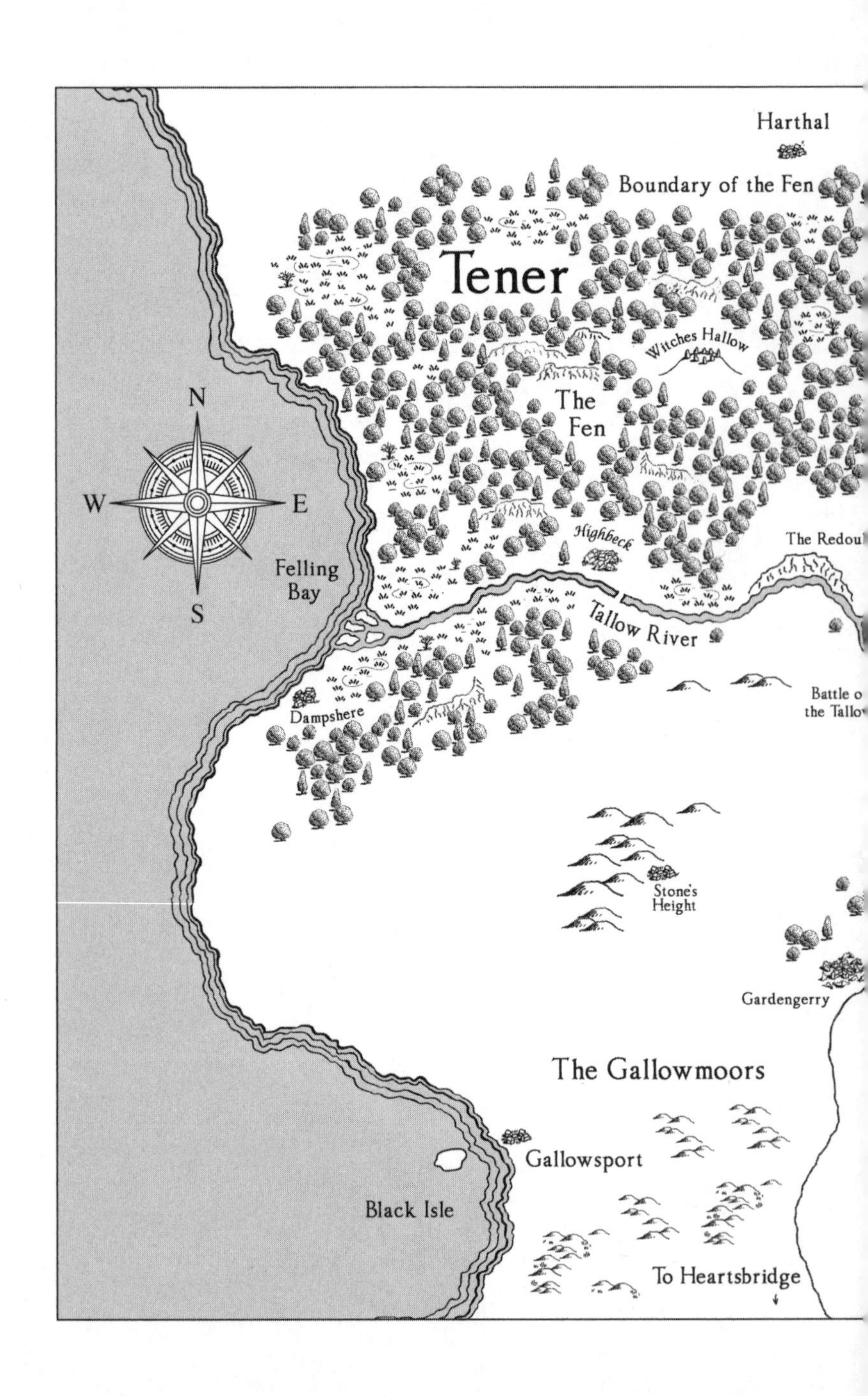
Harthal
Boundary of the Fen
Tener
Witches Hallow
The Fen
Highbeck
N
W
E
S
Felling Bay
Tallow River
Dampshere
Stone's Height
Gardengerry
The Gallowmoors
Gallowsport
Black Isle
To Heartsbridge

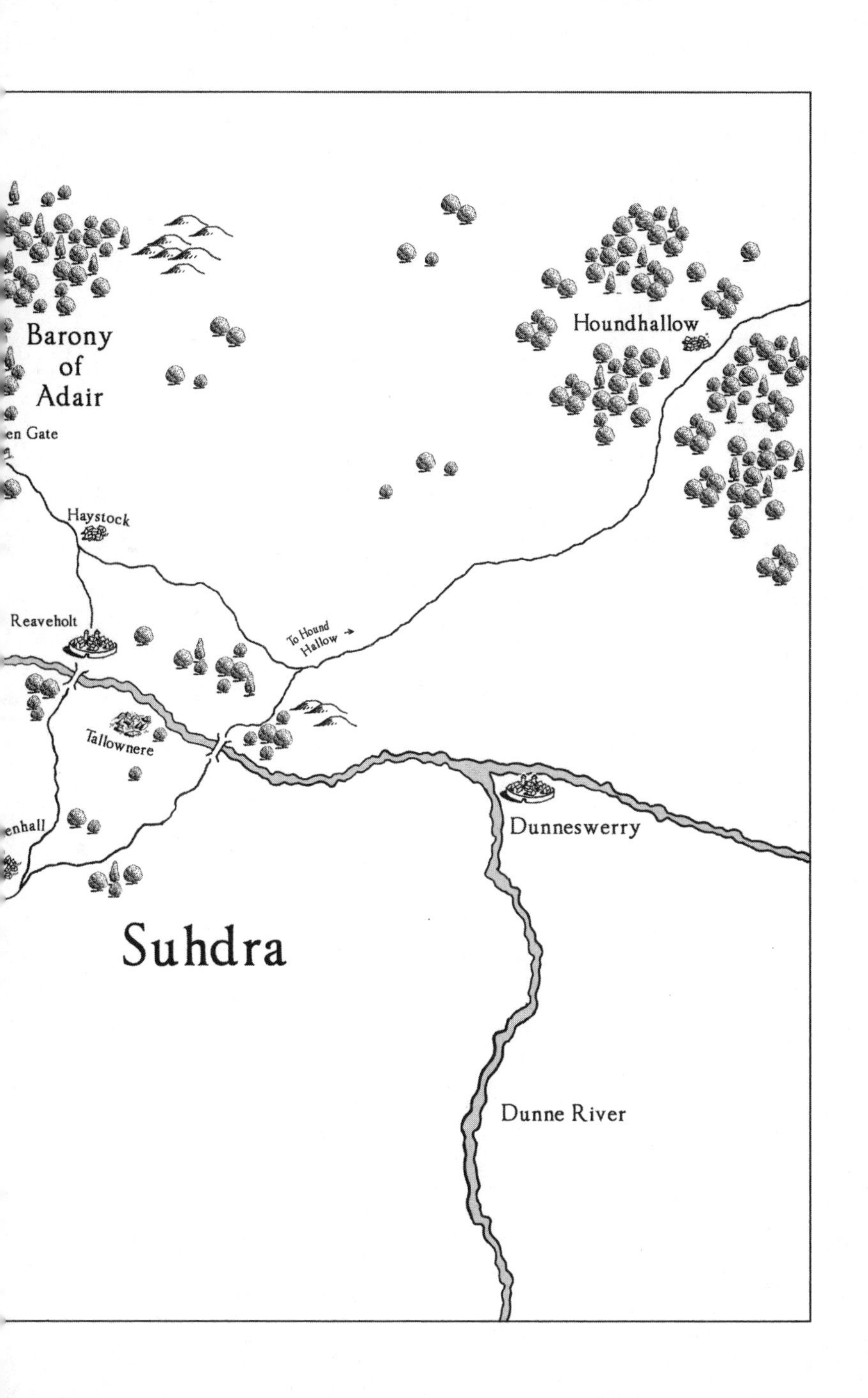

Barony of Adair
en Gate
Houndhallow
Haystock
Reaveholt
To Hound Hallow →
Tallownere
enhall
Dunneswerry
Suhdra
Dunne River

1
LOST CAUSES

1

THEY FELL LIKE a pair of suns, black and amber. Their tails curled with smoke and the burning cinders of autumn leaves. Their fall tore a wound in the sky, and in the world itself. The impact shivered the trees with a wall of air that thundered down the valley, whipping branches and stone and earth.

The river that bounded the witches' hallow hissed with steam and frost, and the stones that formed a dozen henges scattered throughout the forest rang like bells beneath the hammer. Where they struck, their landing left a deep gash in the ground.

Gwen Adair climbed out of the trench.

Her hair was a wild mass of orange light, with sparks of red and black shimmering throughout, and her skin flickered gold and amber. She dragged a black mass behind her. Its talons dug at the earth, scraping wounds in the grass that bled shadow. The creature screeched in frustration. Gwen turned and gave it a solid kick.

"Shut up," she hissed. "You've caused enough trouble. Just shut up for a moment so I can think!"

The gheist responded with a growl. "I am not your tame dog, mortal. I am the grave, the sunset, winter's fury and summer's fear! All mortal life ends in my embrace, just as day ends in night! I will never..."

"Shut! Up!" Gwen howled. She bent her will toward the gheist, summoning the power of the Fen god coursing through her blood to send a wave of glittering light into the mass of shadows at her heel. The gheist shivered in pain, squealing as sparks of glowing energy danced through its bones. Gwen withdrew the lash, and the demon's cries subsided. It settled down, collapsing into a slowly swirling darkness, the bright tips of its claws clicking quietly together. An eye, slate gray and endless, blinked open.

"You can not hold us forever, iron girl," it whispered. Its voice was like a whetstone, sharpening the air. "Already I feel you dying. Whatever you have become, whatever understanding you have with Fomharra, I will be free once again."

"We'll see," Gwen muttered. The name was unfamiliar to her, though the spirit in her bones thrilled at the word. She gave the gheist another kick and started dragging it forward once again. The broken hill at the center of the hallow loomed in front of her, its peak a ruin of stone and torn sod. Her feet dug into the grass as she pulled the gheist uphill.

There was something else holding her back. The god bound in her heart recognized this place, and did not want to return. She didn't blame it. The witches' hallow had served as its prison—or sanctuary, or tomb—for generations. Silent centuries spent in darkness. She could feel its isolation in her blood.

Gwen reached the crevasse that led into the hill, and paused. Sunlight drifted peacefully into the tomb. The body of one of the inquisitors lay halfway down, his skin dry and leathery, his life consumed by the power of the god's awakening. There was no sign of the others. From her perch,

Gwen was able to see the distant shimmering of the river, and the blooming fields of flowers that marked the final resting spot of the hallow's guardians.

Something moved among the trees, a herd of creatures very much like deer, only made of wicker and stone. They pranced nervously among the shadows. The scattered henges, once used to focus the wards that protected this place, lay abandoned.

The hallow was a ruin, its power fled. Hopefully there was enough of its ancient force left to perform one final task.

She started down into the tomb. The death gheist gave one last mighty struggle, wings flapping and talons scrabbling at the stone, its voice silent in the effort. Gwen dragged it under, and as soon as they landed among the scattered stones of the Fen god's cairn, the death gheist collapsed into silence. Gwen dusted her hands—purely a habit, as her sun-bright skin seemed impervious to dirt—and looked around.

A lot had changed, and yet nothing. Here the Fen god was once buried. Here the pillar that held its spirit, cracked like an egg, Gwen's bloodwrought dagger still embedded in its heart. The smooth stones of the cairn lay tumbled around the sanctuary. The air smelled like dry leaves and wet roots. The crystals that had illuminated the tomb flickered dimly in the sunlight.

"So this is your plan," the gheist whispered as she released her grip. "Bury me as they buried Fomharra. Hide me away from mortal eyes, that my power might be contained." The demon curled in the dark corner, eyes and claws glinting in the bare light. "It did not work before. It will not work now. Especially with your house fallen."

"I'm not a fool," Gwen said. "The witches' hallow was only able to shelter the Fen god because of the wardens. Now the wardens are all dead."

"You could replace them," the gheist said. "You could become my true guardian, and stand eternal watch at my tomb. Your family served that role. You could assume it, become the true guardian of the pagan watch."

"Given eternity, I'm sure you'd find some way to trick your way to freedom," Gwen answered. "Hells, given eternity, I might let you go just to get some peace from your damned whispering. No, that would never do."

"Then what? Will you raise an army of pagans to hold me here? Negotiate with Heartsbridge to imprison me? Surely the inquisition can't be trusted again?" The gheist slithered away, the coiled strands of shadow that formed its body tightening into a fist. "Face it, huntress. You have no plan, and no hope. Release me, and spare yourself the corruption I will bring."

"I don't have a plan... yet," she allowed, strolling to the cairn and starting to arrange the stones. "But I figure there's enough power here to hold you for a while, and in the meantime I can come up with something. Or someone will. You really—"

The gheist struck her from behind. A swirling cloud of shadow-tipped claws spun out of the boiling mass of its form, clattering off the stones before cutting into Gwen's back. Black wounds appeared across her body. She fell forward, skinning her hands so that they bled on the stones.

"You are as soft as all the children of blood," the gheist hissed. It rose, its snapping tendrils looming against the hollow shell of the hill. "So wise. So clever. So bright... but you all die, eventually. You all come to me, no matter how fast you run."

"You will find more than blood in my veins," Gwen answered. She pushed herself up, her hands slipping on the blood-slick rock. She turned slowly, drawing the autumn gheist around her like a cloak. Her eyes turned to gold, and a mantle of sun-bright leaves settled across her shoulders, turning her skin the color of beaten copper. The dark wounds filled with glowing light. The darkness leached away, spattering to the floor like burning pitch.

"I will let others run," she said. "I mean to stand against you."

"Stand and fall. *Run* and fall," the gheist said, slate gray eyes narrowing into slits. "It matters not."

They crashed together. The impact sent sparks flying through the empty tomb, sizzling out in the damp earth, leaving only the flashing light of their struggle to illuminate the damp air. The gheist struck, fell back, struck again, each attack a sweep of talons that appeared out of its shadowed body and then disappeared just as quickly. Each time Gwen turned to face the demon, its form melted into the surrounding shadows, only to reappear somewhere else in the damp confines of the tomb. Every time she blocked its attack, a small fragment of her divine light dissipated.

Suddenly the assault ended, leaving a musty silence.

"You will not escape, demon," Gwen panted. She turned slowly in the center of the room, gathering her strength and her courage. "I won't let you."

"Let me?" The gheist's voice slithered in from the shadows. "As if you have the strength to oppose the god of death!"

"Sacombre held you. A mortal man, and without ancient rites." Gwen drew herself up. The mantle of the autumn god glistened around her shoulders, shining brighter, filling the tomb with light. The dark gheist crouched in the corner. "If that fool can contain you, surely the huntress of Adair, holding the power of the god of autumn, can do no less."

"I was invited by the gray priest, not compelled, and when he was used up, I discarded him," the gheist replied. "For all your piety, you are no shaman. The autumn god is not yours to command, any more than the ocean bows to the will of the ship, or the storm to the fluttering leaf!"

"Test my strength, and you will see your error, demon!" Gwen shouted, her voice echoing off the walls. She reached out to the autumn god, drawing light into a bright spear of power that materialized in her hands. Something stirred beneath her soul, beyond the ken of her mind. She pushed it back, and howled her fury. "I will bind you, or destroy you, or both!"

"She flinches from your touch, child," the gheist said. The pool of shadows that formed its body spread thin, leaking out into the cracked walls of the tomb. "Your tame god will burn her leash, and taste the blood of her master."

"Do not think to flee!" Gwen shouted. She whirled around, trying to keep her attention in every corner of the damp room, burning still brighter to illuminate the lurking darkness. "Do not make me hunt you."

"I have never been prey," the gheist whispered. A column of barbed shadow launched out from the darkness, crashing into Gwen's bright shield. She resisted for a moment, then the gheist's oil-black body lapped around her defenses, cutting deep.

With a sudden impact the demon threw her through the crumbling shell of the hill, punching her body through stone and sod until she flew free of the tomb. Gwen rolled as limp as a rag through the rough grass of the hallow, coming to rest among the poisoned flowers where Frair Lucas had nearly died. She lay there, the autumn god swirling around her. The spirit that was pinned to her soul thrashed like a fish on the line.

The death god blossomed from the hill, rising into the sky on shadow-torn wings. It swept down the hill to where Gwen lay, settling on the edge of the clearing and grinning with its legion of teeth.

"It will not need you much longer," the gheist murmured, cocking its head curiously. "Your precious god will discard you, as I discarded that fool Sacombre. Give in to it. Surrender. Why would you hold a god you don't understand?"

"Not understanding is part of it," Gwen muttered. "I have Elsa to thank for that." She struggled to her feet. The bright red petals of the poisoned flowers burst at her touch.

The autumn god fought to get free. She could feel it pulling at her deepest flesh, at the tattered shards of her soul. Nevertheless, Gwen faced off against the swirling darkness at the edge of the field, wondering if it had been a mistake, bringing death to this place. Maybe it would be her last mistake.

"Poor, foolish child," the gheist hissed. It grew over the clearing, its thin limbs weaving together into a canopy of night. "You were not this god's chosen avatar. It must have been an act of true desperation, for the witches to sacrifice one so dreadfully unprepared. Have they fallen so far?"

"You talk too much," Gwen snapped.

"I've been caged far too long, and that priest had nothing interesting to say. All damnation and vengeance and war." The gheist continued to uncoil, reaching dark arms around the clearing, occulting the forest and cutting Gwen off from the rest of the hallow. "There is plenty to enjoy, certainly, but butchery is bland. Tasteless." It crept closer, black tendrils drifting into the clearing like drops of ink in water. "Nothing as exquisite as the cultivated murder."

"It's clear why you and Sacombre got along so well," she responded, "and surprising that you left him behind."

"Death is not meant to be leashed, child," the gheist answered. "Sacombre should have known that, but you mortals, always dancing away from the darkness, thinking you can cheat the final tally. Summer always becomes winter. Birth is only the first step toward death."

"As winter becomes spring," Gwen hissed. "You seem to forget that, demon."

"Demon? You should name me god, not demon." The gheist swelled to its full height, glaring down at Gwen. "Have you abandoned the faith of your house so quickly? Has the death of your family shaken your beliefs?"

"Death of my..." Gwen shrank away. "What are you talking about?"

"Oh, yes. Yes, of course. You suspected, didn't you, but that is different from knowing. Here," the gheist whispered, withdrawing a little, drawing a spindly arm back as though pulling aside a curtain. The air split, and shadows filled the sky. "I brought them with me, so that you might say good-bye."

A door opened in the shadows, and through it walked Gwen's father. He was fractured, like a statue roughly hacked apart and then haphazardly rebuilt. Colm Adair's face was bloodless, the wounds that crossed his body puckered and raw, the skin peeling back like a toothless smile. When he saw his daughter, Colm tried to speak, but no words left his mouth. Only a painful, grating sound.

"What have you done to him?" Gwen demanded. Something began to break inside of her, a pain as real and cold as a knife wound. She took a step forward. "What have you done to my father?"

"What have I done?" the gheist echoed. "Nothing. This is Sacombre's work... and yours, as well." It waved another sinuous arm, and two more figures appeared in the shadows. "Your mother and brother fared no better, I am afraid, though their deaths were quicker. Lady Elspeth barely had time to scream, I think."

Elspeth and Grieg looked much as they had the last time Gwen had seen them, except for scarves of crimson blood that spilled from their throats and onto their breasts, the wounds in their necks still weeping. Young Grieg looked startled, but there was only fear in Elspeth's eyes.

"The silence is the worst part," the gheist said, motioning to Elspeth's flopping lips, the only sound a wet gurgle that bubbled from her severed throat. "Hardly fair. But I can remedy that, and give them voice. Here."

The gheist floated behind them, the inky tendrils of its body caressing Lady Elspeth's pale corpse. A shadow passed through her skin and stitched shut the wound in her neck. Gwen's mother twisted around and took a startled breath, blood dribbling from her lips. Then she turned to Gwen and raised her hands.

"I could do nothing," she said. "Nothing! Sacombre stepped from the shadows and snatched my son up like... like... as if to hug him. He turned my boy toward me and ran a blade across his throat." Elspeth's eyes turned wet, tears spilling down her cheeks. She bent to Grieg, who stood swaying in the field, staring up at Gwen. Elspeth ran lily-white fingers over the sticky wound in her son's throat, as though she could close it with her touch. Her fingers trembled. "He killed my boy. He killed my son."

"Stop it," Gwen hissed. Her voice failed her, and she

realized tears were streaming down her face. She backed away from the phantoms of her dead family. "Stop doing this. You're mocking them. You're mocking me."

"I am showing you what you face," the gheist answered. It rose up, sliding to the side of the three dead bodies. The wound in Elspeth's neck reopened, and her breath disappeared in a bubbling torrent of sobs. "They are mine now. Their bodies, their lives. Every memory you have of them, every happy moment you spent in their company, every hope you had for their future. Mine. Dead. Buried. In the grave. Mine is a blade that will never stop cutting, and from which no one can escape.

"Not even you."

"You're a terrible god," Gwen muttered through her tears. "A god of misery. I will never serve you."

"No, but you will bow to me." The gheist drifted closer, its slate eyes narrowed, the wicked whisper of its claws dragging through the grass. "Everyone does. I am nothing like that tame bitch you're riding."

Something stirred in Gwen's bones, a torch of rage that whispered up from her soul. The autumn gheist moved around her shoulders, quiet and angry. Gwen struggled for a breath, but then the god that was stitched to her bones broke through her skin, seizing control and speaking through her, its anger humming through her bones.

"You have had your fun, Eldoreath," a voice said, ringing with golden bells and fury. "The mortal child is broken, and my season is passing—but before I go, I will show you tame." The words were not Gwen's, their meaning risen from a soul that had never known flesh. "The conclave was right to bury your madness. Now I must finish their job."

"Which of us is truly risen, child?" the death gheist

asked. "And which of us slept her way through the wars?"

"Mad dogs don't rise. They merely slip the leash for a while. Now put away your toys, and face the rage of an endless god!"

Like puppets whose strings had been cut, the dead of House Adair fell to the ground. Colm Adair came apart like a puzzle that has been dropped. Grieg and Elspeth fell together, their arms folding over each other in a final embrace, mother comforting son, son seeking the sanctuary of his mother's love. It broke Gwen to watch, but she could do nothing.

The autumn gheist filled the clearing with sunset light. The poison flowers wilted, their petals breaking into new growths that squirmed between the grasses like snakes.

Eldoreath burst forth, squeezing the clearing with the domed darkness of its limbs, trying to crush Gwen and Fomharra in a web of night. Like a coal smothered in ashes, Gwen burned hotter and hotter, brighter and brighter, until the flames of the autumn gheist slowly started breaking through the death god's trap. The tangled web of its attack started to give. One night-dark strand snapped, and then a second, and then Gwen rose, and the god through her.

She rose into the sky on a spear of light, a pillar of golden leaves that shuffled over her flesh like velvet. At the base, the death gheist lay in a heap, like a rubble of broken trees. Slowly, it patched itself together, gathering the shattered bits of its body together.

Fomharra laughed, and the sound shook the forest.

"Nothing clever left to say? No more promises of death, or exquisite murder?" Gwen looked down at the death god and laughed again. "Well, I'm glad to have shut you up, once and for—"

Gwen started to fall.

2

THE DIM LIGHT of dozens of campfires stretched to the horizon, their flames flickering beneath the banners of the south. Tents creaked in the stiff autumn wind, and laughter drifted up from the Suhdrin camp. Above them, the sky was crowned in glittering stars, and Cinder's pale face hung like a coin in the sky.

A second camp clustered inside of the Fen Gate's ruined walls. The Tenerrans were a somber lot, staying close to the castle walls and talking quietly among themselves. The guards that roamed the perimeter were deadly serious, as scared of the Suhdrin army as they were of the coiled shadows of the forest. The season of mad gods was at hand, and only a fool would walk the night alone, especially in a castle as haunted as the Fen Gate was purported to be.

The center of the castle was mostly ruin. The famous towers of Adair's keep lay in shambles, the shattered doma and attendant halls haphazardly repaired. The only buildings that were untouched by the Fen god's assault were the stables, the kennel, and the lonely splinter of the huntress' tower.

"Will they ever go home?" Malcolm muttered. He stood on what remained of the Fen Gate's battlement, cloak clutched tightly to his chin, the chill of the coming winter sharp in his bones. Castian Jaerdin stood beside him, along with a handful of guards. Jaerdin stomped his feet against the wall, trying to hammer some warmth into his toes. The duke of Redgarden sighed.

"They have no taste for winter. A good frost will drive them back to the Burning Coast," Jaerdin said.

"Somehow I think their spirit will not be so easily broken," Malcolm answered.

"Half their number has already retreated to Suhdra. The rest will follow, in time—and gods bless it's soon, so that I may join them and leave this miserable land," Jaerdin said unhappily. Malcolm chuckled. His friend was bound temple to toe in fur and misery.

"You are welcome to return home, Redgarden," Malcolm said. "Roard has joined his banner to our cause, and Sacombre's heresy has taken the fire from the Suhdrin host. This war is all but over."

Jaerdin grunted. He nodded toward the two opposing camps and the slow orbit of guards.

"This does not look like a field of peace," he said.

"No," Malcolm said. "It does not."

"We must be careful, Malcolm. This was a short fight, a short season of war. These armies are merely what Halverdt was able to draw to his cause in a few months, bolstered by Sacombre's support." Jaerdin paused for a moment, weighing his words. "There are many spears in the south, many that have not yet stirred. We must play our cards carefully to keep them there. It is good that Roard stands with us, but not enough."

"*You* worry about Suhdra," Malcolm said. "I get messages from the north every day, promising support should Halverdt's host push further in their direction. Promising spears and horses and the full fury of Tener. We were lucky to keep them out of the fight so far. If Suhdra escalates, we will not be so fortunate." He gestured down to the camps clustered below. "The smart ones have gone home. Only the stubborn remain."

"The stubborn and the zealous," Castian answered. "Those who travel south carry stories of Adair's heresy, along with the bodies of their dead. Their families will mourn, and then perhaps they will march. To avenge those deaths."

"May aye. May nay," Malcolm said. "Gods will know soon enough."

Jaerdin didn't answer. He just stood there, beating his feet against the stone and muttering. A messenger picked his way up the tumbling stairs to approach the two dukes. One of the guards intercepted the man, checking his identity and searching for weapons among the bundled bulk of his cloak and armor. Castian and Malcolm watched.

"This weather really is foul," Castian muttered. "I don't know how you stand it."

"There is a reason we invented whiskey, Redgarden. It keeps winter at bay."

"Last time I was at the doma, the frair sang the autumn bell," Castian answered. "We are barely out of summer, Houndhallow."

"Winter has come early," Malcolm agreed with a nod, "and sharp."

"My scouts say that a dozen leagues to our south the weather breaks. Gentle autumn still reigns in most of Tenumbra, Malcolm. It's only our little ruin that suffers," Castian said, hopping lightly from foot to foot. "If there was any doubt this place was cursed before..."

"Enough of that talk," Malcolm said sharply. "My men already jump at every shadow and mouse. No need for them to hear their lords discussing curses." He raised his voice to the guards. "Let the man through, Aine. If he has a hidden blade under all those layers, it will take the better part of the night for him to draw it."

The guard grudgingly obeyed, but kept a close eye on the messenger. Malcolm saw why the man mistrusted the newcomer—he was dressed in the black and gold of the church.

"News from Heartsbridge?" Malcolm asked.

"Aye, my lord," the man said. "His holiness Gaston LeBrieure, celestriarch of the Cinder and Strife, sends his greetings and deepest thanks for your role in uncovering the heresy of the high inquisitor."

"And the heresy of dear Colm Adair, I imagine," Malcolm muttered. "Gods know what they'll make of that in Heartsbridge."

"Such matters will be left in the inquisitor's hands, I am sure," the messenger said with a bow.

"Inquisitor?" Malcolm asked. "Listen, the celestriarch may be a little behind in the proceedings, but Frair Lucas left us some weeks ago. There's no other representative of the inquisition at the Fen Gate."

"Precisely," the man said. "Which is why a new inquisitor will be here shortly. I left his company a day ago to give you fair warning, that his chambers might be prepared."

"A day ago?" Malcolm asked.

"Yes," the messenger answered. "He should be here—"

"In the morning," Jaerdin finished.

"Well," Malcolm said stiffly. He turned to Castian and nodded his farewell. "I have preparations to make, I suppose. Aine, see that this man is given something to eat and a blanket to sleep on."

"My lord," the guard said.

"Where will we put them?" Castian asked. "It's not like the keep's fit for habitation. It wouldn't do to have the roof fall on their heads while they pray. Gods know what the church would make of that."

"No, and I'm not sure I want to put him in Gwendolyn's tower," Malcolm answered. "Not until we know the depth and craft of her heresy. It could be dangerous."

"Dangerous?" Castian said. "I sleep in the huntress's tower, Malcolm!"

"And you're a braver man for it," Malcolm answered with a smile. "But no, we can't have them in the keep nor in the tower, and there's no more room in the courtyard—even if the frair was willing to take a tent. I must think of something."

"Perhaps the Suhdrins could serve host to the inquisitor," the messenger said sharply. "If you can't find a bed worthy of the celestriarch's chosen envoy..."

"The inquisitor did not come all this way to sleep outside the walls," Castian said. "Last I checked, the Suhdrin host was out there, and we are in here."

"And they haven't the numbers to shift us," Malcolm said. "That much we've proven."

"Not yet," the messenger said. Malcolm and Castian grew still, staring at the man. "They haven't the numbers to shift you *yet*." He glanced up from his stiff bow to crack a smile. "How many would it take, do you think?"

"What have you seen?" Castian snapped. "You traveled here from Heartsbridge. What did you pass along the way?"

"Again, I will leave that for the inquisitor." He turned to the guard. "There was talk of a bed? It has been a long day."

Malcolm kept his eyes on the messenger. After a moment he

nodded stiffly to the guard, watching as the man was led away. When they were alone on the parapet, he turned to Castian.

"What was that about?" he asked.

"A threat? A warning?" Castian ventured. "Perhaps the inquisition will stir up trouble as they come north. I would not put it past them. They won't want the Circle of Lords to focus on Sacombre, not for too long. Better that the dukes worry about the threat of Tener."

"The threat of Tener," Malcolm said. "The threat of the pagan night."

"Whether real or not," Castian agreed. "Best we find the inquisitor a comfortable bed."

"I'd hoped to have the doma repaired before anyone from Heartsbridge arrived," Malcolm said with a sigh. "I wanted them to find us faithful. Singing the evensong. Observing the rites."

"They know of your faith, Malcolm," Castian said.

"Do they? Perhaps." Malcolm stirred himself and started toward the stairs. "I leave you to this miserable view, Redgarden. If there is a Suhdrin army marching north, I must speak with my fellow lords before news of it reaches the camps."

"Good night, Houndhallow," Castian said, turning back to stare uncomfortably over the vista. "And godspeed."

Malcolm hurried down the stairs, nearly tripping on the broken stones of the stairwell. Morning didn't give him much time. And there was much to do.

Grant MaeHerron was waiting at the base of the wall. The big man was dressed for battle, his axe cradled loosely in his arms like a child. The heir of the Feltower—still presumptive until his father's death could be confirmed—was never far from his axe. The edge shone as bright as silver in the torchlight.

Malcolm nodded. "We have guests coming, Feltower."

"Sir MaeHerron, if you please," the man rumbled. "My father may live."

"You must accept his passing, Grant," Malcolm said quietly. He had known the boy since his birth. Grant MaeHerron was a few years older than his own son, and had always kept himself apart from the rest of the children of the Tenerran court, but it was hard to think of him as the duke of the Feltower. "You must accept your father's death, and his title. Your men need you. We all need you."

"He may live," Grant repeated stubbornly, hugging the weapon closer.

Malcolm sighed, but shook his head. "We will discuss this another day. For now, there is news from the south, and preparations to be made."

"I saw the church's messenger when he arrived," Grant said. "His horse was near dead. The inquisition is coming?"

"They'll be here in the morning," Malcolm said, "but that is not our greatest worry. Are the other lords awake?"

"Roard and his whelp watch the gate. Dougal and Thaen take some rest. Jaerdin was with you. I don't know where the others are."

"Gather them. The Tenerrans only. Leave Roard at his watch," Malcolm said. "What of Rudaine's host? Who commands the men of the Drowned Hall?"

"His master of guard, a man named Franklin Gast. Word has been sent, to ascertain the will of Rudaine's heir," Grant said. "They may leave us."

"Go wake them, and bring them to what remains of the doma. We have much to discuss."

"Are we finally breaching the subject of surrender?" Grant asked.

"Wait for the doma," Malcolm said. "We will have a friar bless the meeting, and then we will see what is necessary."

Grant MaeHerron nodded gruffly, then left, still clutching his axe. That man would not surrender easily, Malcolm knew, either his hope or this castle. He turned and slipped into the shadows of the ruined keep.

Hurrying through the corridors, he nodded imperceptibly to each of the dozen hidden guards who protected this part of the castle from curious eyes. They were dressed as stablers, cooks, pages shirking their duties in the abandoned halls of the castle, but each wore chain under their disguise and kept sword and spear near to hand. They let Malcolm pass without comment.

He came to a door and knocked. There were muffled voices inside.

"Who goes?"

"Her husband," Malcolm answered, careful to not use his name or station. Anyone trying to impersonate him would surely draw on the duke's authority to bull his or her way inside. "Let me in, Doone."

He heard someone pull aside the cloth that was jammed beneath the door, a dim light filling the corridor as soon as it was clear. Locks were thrown. Sir Doone eased the door open, her eyes flicking past Malcolm to the corridor beyond. Once she was sure things were safe, she urged Malcolm inside and closed the door. The locks were in place before Malcolm's eyes had adjusted to the gloom.

His wife provided the only light in the room. The witch's touch that had saved her life and cursed her flesh had changed Sorcha into a creature of strange light and stranger mien. She sat in a chair of fitted stone, its surface weeping with condensation. There were no windows in the narrow chamber, but Lady Blakley still stared wistfully to the west, the direction her son had traveled weeks ago. Her veins glowed with murky light.

Sorcha's blood was gone, transformed into clear, bright liquid that flickered with an inner light. When she glanced at Malcolm, her eyes were deep pools of shimmering water, and her hair shifted restlessly around her head like a crown of seaweed. Malcolm went to one knee beside her.

"My love?" he whispered. "We must go."

3

GWEN FELL AND didn't stop. Whatever strange link held her in the pillar of light was coming loose. Panic welling up, she could feel her soul snagging on some unseen line as she tumbled through the leaves, struck the ground with a thump, bounced, crashed down again. Her breath left her, and her skull rang like a bell.

As she lay there senseless for a moment, her vision swam with the forest and the sky and the towering body of the autumn gheist. Gwen tried to stand, but the strength was gone from her limbs. She tried to cry out, but could only gape like a beached fish. Her breath began to come back to her, when an unspeakable force grabbed her and dragged her along the forest floor.

Gwen bounced from tree to mossy stone, digging a rut in the damp sod whenever she thumped back to earth. She lurched, jerking along for a dozen yards and then stopping. Pulled forward again, going through bracklebush and grassy field. Finally, between crashing jerks, she was able to reach her feet and look around.

The autumn gheist had been dragging her like a forgotten toy. A fragile net of amber light trailed from the god's body, tangling among Gwen's limbs, disappearing into her flesh and emerging again. Before she could say or do anything, the gheist took another massive step, jerking her off her feet and crashing through the forest.

Fomharra stopped again, and Gwen was able to quickly regain her feet.

"Wait!" she shouted. "Where are you going? Come back!"

"You do not hold me, child," the gheist breathed, its voice humming through Gwen's skull. "And my season is done."

"But I need, we must… the demon!"

"We must nothing," Fomharra said, then turned away and continued its journey. Gwen fell, tumbled, and was dragged through a field of raw stone before coming to rest on the pebbled beach of the river that bounded the hallow. From her knees, Gwen could see the bluffs beyond. She was about to cry out when the gheist moved again.

Gwen tumbled into the river.

The cold took her breath and her sense. She fought against the current, but no matter which way she thrashed, she was dragged deeper under the surface. Her lungs burned, already empty from screaming and the constant, thudding impacts of her journey. The strands of light that tied her to the towering gheist pulled her forward. By the time she reached the far shore, Gwen was limp as a rag.

River water poured clear and cold from her mouth as she was pulled up the beach. The sky and stones rolled over her. Her mind drifted. She would be shattered against the stone cliffs, or dragged into a lake, or left to freeze somewhere in the wilds of the Fen. She was dead. She was ruined.

Gwen tumbled against something stuck into the stones of the beach. It was warm to the touch, and when she folded over it, it cut her like a knife.

Like a sword.

Gwen opened her eyes.

Sir LaFey's lost blade stuck like a mast from the ground. When the gheist moved forward, the skeins of light that bound it to Gwen strained against the blade. She thought she might be cut in half, and blood poured dark and hot from her wounds, but she stayed put. She wrapped her hands around the hilt and pulled her belly away from the cutting edge. The gheist tugged again. The lines pulled taut, humming with the strain. And then they snapped.

As she collapsed to the beach, Gwen's blood mixed with water that was still streaming from her nostrils. She whimpered as the injuries crashed through her mind, lay there as the amber light of the autumn god dimmed on the horizon, and then was gone. Her hands had been cut deeply by the blade, and the wounds inflicted by the death gheist festered with wicked shadows.

The first footfall was nearly silent, the practiced stride of a woodland hunter, taught by the wolf and the whisper. A shadow lurked among the trees, bright eyes staring at the fallen huntress. It was joined by another shadow, and then a third, and then the forest was full of silent spears.

Cahl stepped from among the trees, followed by a cadre of pagans with their cloaks and spears and crowns of willow. He walked to Gwen and knelt beside her broken body. He glanced at the sword, Gwen's blood leaking into the runes of Strife, remnants of heat curling off the blade.

"It is the huntress," he said finally. He gathered her into his arms and stood. Her arms hung limp, trailing ribbons of blood. "There is still time for her soul, if not her flesh."

"She has lost the god," one of his companions said sharply. It was a man tattooed with a mask of leaves. "Fianna said she would fail us. What good is she to us now?"

"You have lost too much of yourself, Aedan. She is not a forest to be burned for our warmth." Cahl stretched his cloak to cover Gwen's unconscious body, then nodded to his other companion. The young boy, little more than a child, stepped forward eagerly. "Taeven, stay here. They will come looking for her, or for what happened to her. Warn them that the god of death has slipped its chains, and that the autumn god is lost as well." He started to turn away, paused, glared at the sword. "And see that the vow knight gets her sword back, but be sure that she knows the cost of that blade, and the weight of the death that goes with it."

"I will," Taeven said seriously.

Without another word, Cahl slipped among the trees. Within moments the beach was empty of all but the young pagan, and the blade, and the sound of shadows in the forest.

4

IAN BENT HIS head close to the charger's neck and spurred the beast on. The forest whipped past them, branches scoring bloody tracks across his cheeks. The only light was the dim image of Elsa LaFey's fleeing form, sunlight leaking from her armor, briefly illuminating the narrow path before surrendering to the shadows. The sound of his horse, the whistling passage of trees, the hammering of his heart, all filled Ian's head and drowned out any other thought but flight and fear.

Behind them, a mad god followed. It brushed aside the trees as though they were bowling pins, roots popping out of the soil with dull squelching sounds, trunks groaning as they fell. The earth shook.

Ian spared a glance over his shoulder. The gheist's back writhed with a thousand barbed quills that rustled drily as they slithered together. Its head was a thick lump, mouthless, bristling with smooth black eyes. The creature was falling back, however, until only the mosaic of its eyes was visible in the scant light that shone from Elsa's invocations. Ian smiled, turned back to the trail...

...and had to react quickly. Elsa was stopped, her mount pulled up and stomping sideways on the path. The vow knight was leaning over the saddle and looking down. Beyond her there was nothing.

Ian pulled hard on his reins. His horse complained, skidding on the damp ground as it dug iron-shod hooves into the earth. He came up just short of a ravine, its edges sharp with rocky debris. Water crashed far below.

"This way," Elsa said quickly, then she set off along the ravine's lip. Both directions looked the same to Ian, a jagged cliff that stretched into the darkness. He briefly considered abandoning the vow knight, counting on her holy glow to draw the gheist, but he would be lost without her. And even if he survived this attack, Ian would be helpless against the next. So he pulled his horse in line and spurred forward, trying to keep up. He glanced back again to see if their pursuer would pick up their scent.

The gheist skidded to a halt, large stones clattering over the edge of the ravine, to drop loudly into the noisy river below. It looked around, its coat of barbed quills undulating silently, and saw them. It was terribly still for a heartbeat, watching them with its multitude of eyes. Then it followed, moving faster now that it was clear of the trees.

Ian turned toward Elsa. "We should get back into the forest!" he yelled.

"Gheists have boundaries," Elsa replied. "Even ferals have rules."

"You think we'll be safe across the river?"

"No idea," she said, "but we weren't safe in the forest, and the horses can't keep this up much longer. We need to find a place to cross!"

She was right. Ian's mount was quivering under his thighs. Between the constant riding and frequent pursuit, these horses didn't have much left in them. The last thing he wanted was to have to walk out of the Fen. He had done it once, but that had been in the company of a witching wife and her shaman. There had been fewer gheists that time, too.

Fewer by far.

The barbed, bristling god came closer, and their mounts were slowing. Ian pulled up next to Elsa, the vow knight's mount trembling at the verge of collapse. LaFey's scarred cheeks were bright with embers. She was burning her blood to keep the horses going, but there was only so much Strife's magic could do. The pair exchanged a look. Elsa shook her head.

"No further," she said.

Ian looked around. This far from the forest's edge, they were on a broad ledge of stone and moss. The horses stumbled to a halt, and Elsa slid from her saddle. She started adjusting her armor, cutting the buckles on several heavier pieces and throwing them away to clatter on the rocks.

"So, here then," Ian said.

"Keep going," Elsa said. Her voice was ragged. "I can hold it for a while."

"No," Ian answered. He slid to the ground, twisted, and cracked his back, staring down the ravine at the rapidly closing gheist. "Even if my horse could go another step, no. This is my death as much as it is yours."

"Have a little faith," Elsa said smartly. "I may yet live. I'm wearing armor, at least."

"Ah, but I'm faster on my feet."

"Just fast enough to die fancy," she said, holding her sword at arm's length, frowning at the blade. It was plain and gray, without the bloodwrought runes of the winter vow. Elsa had lost her sword at the witches' hallow, when Gwen's magical presence had swept her miles away in the blink of an eye. This blade came from the Fen Gate's armory. "If only I had my true sword."

"Always making excuses," Ian said. "You don't see me complaining."

"No one expects much of the half-heretic son of Houndhallow," she replied. "Once I'm gone, this forest will swallow you whole. You're fucked, Blakley."

And then the gheist was on them. It leapt into the air, its broad limbs going wide, claws extended, the barbed cloak of its back bristling against the night. It grew larger and larger as it jumped, its eyes twinkling brightly, and then its chest split. An ebon slash ran from throat to groin, widening as it fell toward them, until pure darkness filled the sky.

The creature's form dissolved into the air. Its quills flaked away, becoming motes of sharp light that fluttered down like snowflakes. Its eyes scattered and became stars, twisting into unfamiliar constellations in a moonless sky. Its body dissipated into inky smoke that curled between the trees. Talons clattered to the ground.

The river was gone.

The horses were gone.

They were somewhere else.

"So," Elsa said, still in guard position. Her sword leaked molten light, the metal of the blade popping as it fried in Elsa's hands.

"We seem to have found a new and interesting way to die," Ian said. He slid his blade from its scabbard. "Though I don't *remember* dying. Is this the quiet?"

"I'm not the sort of priest who could tell you," Elsa said. "Though I think not." The ground around them turned into soft loam, sprouting with tufts of pale grass that bore a disturbing resemblance to the creature's quills. The forest was there, but at a distance, and a thick fog swirled around them, as black as night.

"Your light is dimming," Ian said.

"I'm tired."

"No, I mean..." he stepped closer. "It's as though the air is eating it."

Elsa looked down. The cloak of sunlight that wafted off of her armor was evaporating like cobwebs touched to flame. She grunted.

"This is more than darkness," she said. "I can see the stars just fine."

"Yes, though they are no less disturbing," Ian said. While they watched, the constellations disappeared in an undulating wave, to shine brighter as they reappeared.

"I've heard tell of gheists like this," Elsa said. "They are a place, rather than a deity. A realm."

"So it... *ate* us?"

"Absorbed, more like," Elsa said, creeping carefully forward. "But not the horses."

"Lucky horses."

"May aye, may nay." Elsa clenched her shoulders, straining against the darkness. Her sun-touched aura flared briefly and then flickered out. The vow knight staggered, and Ian reached for her. She shrugged his hand away. After a few heartbeats of silence, she shook her head, her voice rough.

"We will not be burning our way out of this."

"Is that always your first instinct, Sir LaFey?" Ian asked gently.

"First and last and always," she answered. "Come, there must be a way forward."

Despite the darkness they could see where they walked, though the view bore no distinguishing landmarks. There was the distant forest, which never seemed to get closer, the barbed grass that clattered peacefully in the slight breeze, and the sky of unfamiliar stars that occasionally blinked in horizon-spanning waves.

They walked aimlessly.

"There is something among the trees," Ian whispered.

"Yes," Elsa answered.

He could just barely see it, out of the corner of his eye, a cloak flickering between branches, eyes the color of distant stars. A pack of predators—perhaps wolves—followed the apparition, stepping lightly through the forest like a fog.

"The god, do you think?"

"Or his demons. You're the one steeped in pagan lore, young Houndhallow. What is this place?"

Ian kept looking around, stepping carefully among the tufts of grass, straining his ears for any hint of the river they had left behind. The trees were filled with strange sounds, like dry bones rubbing together, and the rattle of insect song.

"This is the night," he said, finally.

"That is close enough."

A voice came from in front of them, sounding like velvet carefully cut by the sharpest shears, as quiet and soft as a sigh. Abruptly they were at the tree line. Part of the darkness solidified, and a hunched figure stepped out. His face was smooth and dark, and his hair was pale. It was difficult to focus on his features. Ian's gaze kept sliding away from the man's glittering eyes, though his mouth hung in Ian's vision like an afterimage, teeth and lips set in a grimace, the corners cracked and wet.

"Why are you crossing through my realm?"

"Crossing through?" Elsa asked. "You brought us here. We'd be happy to leave."

"That cannot be." The man twitched, his head shifting like a king settling his crown. A palsied hand appeared from behind the figure to briefly touch his heart. "All come to me. All are gathered to this realm. I have never sought another to bring them in. You must be mistaken."

"And yet, here we are," Ian said.

"Indeed," the man said, bowing slightly at the waist. "And so I ask, what has brought you and the others to my realm?"

"The others?" Ian asked. He looked around, saw nothing but the stars and the forest and the darkness. "What others?"

"Men of steel and ink. There is a familiar taste to them, but I am a stranger to their hearts. They have forsaken me." The man looked Ian over, lingering on his face, as though trying to recall him from some memory. "There is something of me in your heart, however. Who are you?"

"Ian Blakley, of Houndhallow," Ian replied. "I am—"

"The hound hunts through my forests during the day, but cowers at his master's fire when I come to him." The man looked from Ian to Elsa, smiling as though he had made a joke. "My realm is for wolves, Ian of Hounds. Best you get going, before they find you."

"This is worthless," Elsa spat. She strode forward, her gait stiff, blade swept back and ready at her thigh. The loamy ground swelled beneath her feet, wrinkling into ridges that absorbed her steps. She stumbled on, but with each step her feet sunk deeper and deeper into the ground, until thick moss was churning around her waist. She shouted in frustration, and a wave of flickering light washed over the ground. The grasses crisped and turned to ash. The ground shrank away from her.

"That was hardly proper," the strange man said. He was no longer close to them, his still form standing off to one side, fingertips lightly brushing the cracked flesh of his lips. "I know your kind, summer-child. You have your own realm. Leave me to mine."

"Then return me, or I'll cut my way through!"

"Hardly proper," the man repeated, then he began to fade into the trees.

"Wait!" Ian shouted. He ran forward, and the world seemed to tilt, causing him to drop his sword. It disappeared in the darkness. He found himself running uphill, though the ground remained steady. Ian pressed on. "You can't leave us here!"

The man looked startled at his approach, and shrank back. Ian reached the trees and used them to pull himself forward. The world tipped again, and he was suddenly hopping from trunk to trunk like the rungs of a giant's ladder. He glanced behind, and Elsa's light shone dimly in the fog. From this distance it looked as though she were trapped in a cage of branches, her blade flashing back and forth.

Ian struggled on.

His hand came down on something cold. Instantly a wetness spread down his arm, to drip from his elbow. His hand was wrapped around the blade of a sword, its tip buried in the trunk of a tree. He jerked back, blood trailing from his split palm, pain reaching his senses. Shaking his fingers he examined the wound, a narrow cut, not deep enough to reach muscle, but bleeding like a split wineskin.

He looked up at the tree and saw that it was a collection of arms and armor. Spears rattled against branches, broken helms hung like rusty fruit, and bodies. A half-dozen bodies dangled, their faces cloaked in mist, their limbs twisted as if in some final spasm of horror.

"The others," Ian whispered to himself. He crept closer, careful where he placed his hands and feet, until he was alongside one of the bodies. It turned slowly on a length of chain, its limbs wasted and thin. The corpse wore the black tabard of House Thyber. The sigil of the earl of Cindermouth, the pale hand seared with a crescent moon on the palm, hung in tatters from the dead man's chest.

Again the forest changed. It became vertical, the ground a sheer cliff from which the trees emerged like arrow shafts. They shifted and formed a thick web of stone-hard wood, their canopies lost in swirling fog, their roots pulling free of the earth until there was no ground, only the directionless maze of branches and trunks—wiry limbs that snarled together. And still Ian climbed. There was a light ahead.

It was Elsa. She hung in the middle of a tangled ball of wicker, limbs bound and skin scratched raw. A steady flame flickered from the blade of her sword, and the branches around it were charred black. Then the steel, untempered in the holy forge of the Lightfort, began to fail. On seeing Ian, she struggled to turn toward him. The trees resisted, groaning as she twisted in their grasp. Her face was clutched by whip-thin branches that burrowed into her flesh. The blood that leaked from those wounds was stained with ash.

"I have no power here," she whispered. "I burn, and the tree falls away, but eventually it returns. And this blade will not last much longer. Where have you been?"

"Climbing," Ian said. "I just left your side."

"Hours ago," she said. "Where is our friend?"

Ian looked up into the maze of tree, and then down. Fogs swirled all around.

"I don't know," he admitted, "but I think I found the others he was talking about. Men of Thyber, long dead. I wonder what they were doing in the Fen?"

"An interesting question for a later time," Elsa said. Ian raised his brows.

"Do you want me to cut you free?" he asked.

"No, Ian. I want you to leave me to die," she said tightly. "You idiot."

Ian reached for his sword, then remembered. There was a knife in his boot, though, so he drew that and started working on the tangle of branches that held Sir LaFey in place. The wood was tough, the bark cutting his knuckles as he sawed through it, and the flesh beneath was dense and fibrous. Still he cut and cut, his own blood running down his fingers until the handle of the knife was red and slick.

The first branch snapped, and then another. He burrowed deeper into the tangle of wood, grabbing handfuls of branches and putting them to the knife. The tree creaked around him.

"Careful," Elsa hissed. Ian glanced up with a smile.

"Don't worry. It's not like you're going to fall or anything."

"No, you idiot! The tree!"

Ian looked back down at his hands. Thin branches were cradling his wrists, and as he jerked his arms back they looped as tight as a snare, trapping him. He yelped, and started cutting at his restraints, but other branches coiled closer, hooking into his elbows, twining between his fingers, drinking the blood of his wounds.

He dropped the knife and watched as the tree pulled it away, wrapping it in wicker until it disappeared. Ian fell backward, winning free of the trap but barely catching himself before he fell. Elsa watched with a frown as he scrambled to find his footing.

"My hero," she muttered.

"That didn't go as planned."

"No?" she said. "And here I thought your goal was to be caught here with me, that we might spend eternity in this nightmare." She closed her eyes and leaned back, sighing mightily. "The horses had the right of it."

"I'll find the gheist," Ian insisted. "I'll get him to let us go."

"Without so much as a knife? Perhaps you can trick him with your clever wordplay."

"I'll think of something."

"Yes," Elsa said. "I'm sure you will."

He grimaced, and started climbing again. Quickly the fog hid Elsa from his sight. He climbed for what felt like an eternity, and then he climbed some more.

Elsa's tangled cage came into view again.

He looked around and there, just to one side, was the tree of dead Tenerrans, looking more wasted than before. He was going in circles, and time was moving in ways that made no sense. Ian settled against the nearest trunk and closed his eyes. He wondered why he wasn't tired, or if maybe he was so tired that he couldn't tell the difference. He stared at the swirling fog where the tree's canopy should be, and then he realized that his eyes were closed, but he could still see.

He opened his eyes. Nothing changed.

"Night," he whispered to himself. "Night and the land of dreams... and so the logic of dreams."

Ian shimmied along the trunk toward where the canopy should be, getting closer and closer to the fog. The tree branched, the limbs getting thinner and thinner until they creaked under Ian's weight. A crown of dry leaves shook free, spinning down into the distance. He reached the tip of the tree. There was nothing beyond it but fog.

So he jumped.

5

THE STONES WERE stained with the blood of the choir. Rough rows of barrels and broken wood served as pews, while the altar had mostly survived the attack of the feral god. There was still much work to be done.

The shell of the doma was shattered, patched with canvas and clapboard, the air still raw with the stink of massacre. Most of the repairs had been done by volunteers, faithful soldiers and stewards who wanted to return the sanctuary to a place of worship. Malcolm had served more than one shift among the rubble, dressed in simple linens, lending a hand where he was able.

The room was silent when he entered, though not empty. Duke Lorien Roard sat next to the altar, sleep still heavy on his face, wrapped in a cloak of black leather that was apparently insufficient against the cold. Castian Jaerdin, still dressed in his furs and misery, stood at his side. The Suhdrins were separated from the rest of the lords of Tenumbra.

Grant MaeHerron, along with Ewan Thaen and Manson Dougal, lingered among the ruined pews. Those three were the last Tenerran lords who had sworn to the Fen Gate's defense. Another man stood nearby, his back to the wall, dressed in simple mail and resting his hands on the hilt of his battered sword. When Malcolm came in, this man started and nearly drew his blade. Malcolm gave him a nod.

"You must be Sir Gast, Rudaine's man," Malcolm said. The knight grunted and offered a hand for Malcolm to shake. "It is good of you to offer your leadership at this time. It is more than your lord could have asked."

"He can't ask me anything from the grave," Gast said, "and it matters little enough. I was brought up to lead men in battle, and this is close enough to battle to not make a difference."

"Is there any word from the Drowned Hall? Rudaine's heir must have heard of his fate by now?" Malcolm asked. "I sent a rider with his helm and my sympathies."

"Aye, and we thank you for that. Lady Mariah wasn't happy to be left behind. She may command us back, or she may join us here. Or neither. Or both." Gast shrugged mightily. He had scars all along the back of his neck, and more on his scalp and hands. His hair, gray-black and bristly, was patchy around the white skin of old wounds.

Malcolm thought that they must be of an age, he and this grizzled knight. He couldn't help but wonder if he looked as roughly handled. When he took Gast's hand and shook it, there was great strength there.

Turning toward the rest of the gathering, Malcolm walked to the center of the room. They watched him nervously. Other than the handful of torches that flickered throughout the chamber, there was no heat among the stones, and little light.

"So, you have us here, torn from our beds and our duties," Lorien Roard said. The duke of Stormwatch looked miserable, and he made no effort to keep it from his voice. "To what purpose, Houndhallow?"

"I have a guess," Castian muttered. "Though I doubt it will bring us any joy."

"Yes," Malcolm acknowledged, "we've had a messenger. Duke Jaerdin was with me when I received him. Heartsbridge has sent us an inquisitor. He will be here in the morning."

"Couldn't be soon enough, as far as I'm concerned," MaeHerron said. "It will take more than our narrow faith to cleanse Adair's curse from these stones."

"Do we trust the inquisition to do that?" Manson Dougal asked. "It was Sacombre who brought a god of death to our walls, and stirred Suhdra to war under false pretenses."

"Hardly false," MaeHerron said, giving his fellow Tenerran a sidelong look. "There can be no doubt as to Colm Adair's heresy."

"Nor Sacombre's," Roard answered. "Though I don't imagine those wash each other out."

"If we're not going to trust the inquisition, then who *can* we place our faith in?" MaeHerron snapped. His lands sat in the shadow of Cinderfell, the shrine of Lord Cinder and heart of the inquisition in the north, so his reaction could be anticipated. But it made Malcolm uncomfortable, especially considering the troubles to come. "Sacombre will face his crimes, as Colm Adair never will."

"Because he's dead," Malcolm said. "Listen. There is fault to be found on both sides of this fight. I will welcome the inquisitor when he arrives, and keep an eye on him as he works. A little more discretion on Lord Halverdt's part might have prevented this entire war."

"As a little more discretion on *your* part might have unearthed Adair's heresy before now. That it took a heretic to reveal a heretic does not speak well of the north," Roard said from his place by the altar. The rest of the room bristled—even Castian Jaerdin. He placed a hand on Roard's shoulder.

"Let's not be casting judgment around like seeds to be sown, Stormwatch," Jaerdin whispered. "We are here as allies, after all."

"Let's not forget that this man marched north at Halverdt's side in the first place," Dougal said sharply. "I'm not sure why he's included in this council."

"He's here because when our other defenses had fallen, he and his son held the gate against the Suhdrin charge. Without him, most of our host would be dead," Malcolm said. "Including my son."

"Where *is* your son, Houndhallow?" Dougal asked. "I haven't seen him since the battle. Has he returned to your castle to prepare your defenses, should we fail here?"

"He travels with the vow knight, Sir Elsa LaFey, seeking Gwendolyn Adair," Malcolm answered. "Against my urging, of course."

"And your wife?"

"She is still recovering from her wounds," Malcolm answered smoothly, shooting MaeHerron a glance. "I hope to return her to Houndhallow before winter."

"Hopefully the inquisitor will be able to help with that," Dougal said. "Though healing is more Strife's domain."

"Hopefully," Malcolm said. "But that is not why I called you together. The church's messenger also brought word from the south."

"From Heartsbridge?" Roard asked. "A declaration of the church, or from the Circle of Lords?"

"No declaration of the Suhdrin circle will hold weight in these walls," Ewan Thaen muttered. "Not while there's Tenerran blood in my veins."

"The Circle of Lords is our greatest hope," Roard snapped. "There is an army outside these walls that is overburdened with grudges. Marchand will stand by Halverdt's quest, especially now that his accusations against Adair have proven true! And with Emil Fabron dead by your hand, Blakley, his men aren't going to skulk back to the Black Mountain—not without a taste of vengeance."

"LaGaere returned south, but probably to raise more banners and stir the hearts of Suhdra," Jaerdin interrupted. "He left most of his men behind, with orders to keep us bottled up until he returned."

"Exactly, and it's not like any of you are going to surrender the Fen Gate without a fight," Roard continued.

"These are Tenerran stones, and this is Tenerran soil," Thaen said simply. "Tenerran lives will defend it."

"Tainted with Tenerran heresy," Jaerdin muttered, but Roard ignored him.

"Which is why we must put our hope in the Circle of Lords," Roard said. "If cooler heads prevail in Suhdra, they can convince those who remain here to come home."

"For now at least, it would be a false hope," Malcolm said. "The messenger spoke very loosely, but it seems as if the hosts of Suhdra are marching north."

"We've faced many of their number already," MaeHerron said. "How many could remain?"

"Many of them scattered when the..." Roard paused, looking uncomfortably around the ruined doma. "When Lady Gwen appeared. Those banners would need to be gathered again, and if the Circle has committed to deciding this matter by force, they could call many more swords from their vassals. There wasn't time to draw more than a small portion of our strength when Halverdt made his plea."

"And now they march into the teeth of winter," Jaerdin muttered. "Better to have waited until spring, or at least tried to negotiate a peace that would have let them withdraw to Greenhall."

"Perhaps they will come no farther than Halverdt's border," Dougal said.

"Not if they intend to maintain a force here," Roard answered. "Right now their supply line crosses at White Lake and travels through as much forest as it does over roads."

"Aye," Thaen said with a smile. "The Reaveholt still stands." On the road from Greenhall and the Fen Gate, that castle defended the only true bridge across the Tallow. It was still manned by vassals of House Adair, though word of the heresy had thrown their loyalty into question. For the moment, they had denied passage to the Suhdrin forces determined to lay siege to the Gate. "Any battle there will be bloody."

"Unless they surrender out of faith to the church, and to keep the inquisition from laying Adair's sins at their feet," Dougal said glumly.

"They've been true to their watch so far," Malcolm said. "Let's not doubt them just yet, nor seek out reasons for them to die, either."

"What do you mean by that?" Castian asked.

"Simply that we must decide what to do with the Fen Gate. Not tonight, not immediately, but soon." Malcolm did a slow march around the room. "Stormwatch is right. There are deep grudges on both sides of this fight. They are going to be difficult to untangle, and bloody, as well. Worse, the fate of this castle itself must be known." He paused, letting the idea sink in. "House Adair is destroyed. Only Lady Gwendolyn remains, and she will not be sitting the Sedgewind throne anytime soon. If she's ever found.

"The barony may pass to another of Adair's kith," he continued, "but who among them will be trusted by Suhdra? Or their fellow Tenerrans, for that matter? Who among us doubted Colm's faith, and the faith of his family? And yet here we stand, in the wreckage of his heresy."

"Would you claim this holding for your own, Malcolm?" Ewan Thaen asked guardedly. "Not that I have any problem with that, but there will be other claims."

"No, I would not. Even if Tener wanted to give it to me, there is too much trouble in the Fen. Trouble I don't want," Malcolm replied. "And even if I did claim it, would the people of the Fen accept me? Can they be trusted? How broad was Adair's sin? How many witches make their homes in Fenton, or the forests beyond?"

"We can't very well put the entire holding on trial," MaeHerron muttered. "Putting a good Tenerran lord on the Sedgewind throne would do much to ease my mind—though I think the claims of Finnen or MaeGallon might carry more weight."

"Where are Finnen and MaeGallon?" Dougal asked. "When Lady Blakley called for banners, did they come? If this matter isn't going to be settled by inheritance, then shouldn't it be won in battle? Of all the dukes I see in this room, I am the only baron who would benefit from the holding."

"And so it begins," Sir Gast said sharply. "The cake topples from the table, and all the dogs come running."

"Who the fuck are *you*, anyway?" Dougal snapped. "I don't remember asking a servant's opinion on the matter!"

"My lord died holding this border," Gast answered smoothly. "I will not see it handed over to the first baron who chooses to speak up."

"We're not handing anything over to anyone," Malcolm said quickly, "and keep in mind, this is no boon. Anyone who holds these walls will suffer the endless attention of the inquisition and the mistrust of all Suhdra. Greenhall isn't going to become a friendly hearth, simply because Gabriel Halverdt has died."

"If anything, Lady Sophie is going to want that death atoned," Castian said. "Though gods know whether she will seek payment from the church, or from the north."

"Perhaps the church could assume command of the castle?" Roard suggested. "See the walls made holy and the border calm." At that the entire room tensed up. MaeHerron and Gast spat dismissively, while Dougal laughed. Even Jaerdin covered his face with a weary hand.

"That may have worked when you had a king who needed usurping, and the church was the best answer," Malcolm said. "But it will never be tolerated in the north, not even in a holding as troubled as the Fen." He shook his head. "Tenerran blood for Tenerran thrones."

"And look how well that has worked," Roard snapped. "You can't turn a tribe into a great house just by giving it a name and a motto. Nobility does not sit well on the shoulders of savage men!"

At that the blades came out—MaeHerron first, then Gast and Dougal and finally Malcolm, if only to keep the peace. Castian Jaerdin backed away from the altar, drawing his sword reluctantly.

Roard only laughed.

"You would butcher a Suhdrin duke who chooses to join your cause?" he said. "Fine, then spill my blood, and see what becomes of that army that is marching to your door."
Roard stood abruptly. "Malcolm, I have had enough of this discussion. I will stand at your side because of our friendship, and because Sacombre's war was built on lies and fear. Yet you can't solve this with threats. Send word to the Circle of Lords. Sue for peace. Or find your help in the church. But I don't think you want the kind of war that Heartsbridge can wage."

"No, my friend, I don't," Malcolm agreed. "And neither do you." Roard stood stiffly for a minute, then sighed and collapsed into his chair.

"Fatigue sharpens my tongue, but not my mind," he said. "Forgive me, gentlemen. I misspoke."

There was silence, finally broken by the rasp of swords returning to sheaths. Malcolm was about to continue when the door opened. Sir Caris Doone entered the room. She was dressed for war, as she had been every day since the Fen Gate fell. She nodded around the room, then turned to Malcolm.

"Lord Blakley?" she asked, then motioned toward the door. "The inquisitor is here."

6

THE WIDE, MUDDY track the Suhdrin army had ground into the earth ran from the Fen Gate straight south. It overlapped the road, stripping the forest bare on either side for half a mile.

Frair Lucas and his escort followed this devastation until the road turned southeast toward the Reaveholt. The army's path continued south, crossing open fields and ruined brush like a scar. In retreat, the elements of the Suhdrin forces that had fled from the attack of the Fen god had followed the same path in reverse. There were signs of their predation, in ruined wagons and burned homesteads all the way to the horizon.

Lucas paused at the intersection of the two trails. Sir Torvald, his constant companion and frequently miserable host since their departure from the Fen Gate, rode up next to him. The clatter of wagons followed behind.

"The road or the ruin," Lucas muttered. "Neither an inviting choice."

"There will be no food south—the army has seen to that," Sir Torvald said. The big knight sat awkwardly on a dray that was much too small for his bulk, his own horse having died during the siege of the Fen Gate. "We lost a lot of supply wagons to pagan raiders as we came north. We had to forage our meals."

"And had to burn down the farms while you were at it, just to be thorough," Lucas said.

"It was war," Torvald answered.

"Yes, yes, there's no better word for it. War," Lucas said. He looked mournfully across the horizon, holding back a sigh. "We will keep to the road."

"Beg pardon, frair, but is that wise? The Reaveholt is still in Tenerran hands. Adair hands, if you believe the stories. One of his heretic knights is still holed up behind those walls, succoring gods know how many witches!"

"Then it's best we follow that path, speak to these witches, and see their justice done," Lucas said. Torvald perked up at that, forcing the frair to shake his head. "We are not bringing war to the Reaveholt, Sir Torvald. We escort the wounded and condemned, not to mention the heretic Tomas Sacombre. Our business is for the church, and the church's writ will be honored. Even at the Reaveholt."

"They will not let us pass easily," Torvald answered.

"Not if we come to them with sword and fire, no," Lucas said. He looked back at the tangled column that followed them. Wagons full of the infirm, spottily guarded by Suhdrin knights, many of them nursing wounds even as they patrolled. They were a sorry lot, those too broken by the gods at the Fen Gate to face battle, or overwhelmed by the betrayal of the high inquisitor, in whom they had placed their trust. This was not a fighting force. It was a rout, of the spirit if not the body, and somehow Lucas had ended up in charge of it.

At the center of the column sat an iron wagon, barred and guarded. It held two prisoners—the witch Fianna, handed over by Malcolm Blakley in the wake of the battle at the Fen Gate, and former high inquisitor Tomas Sacombre. There was the source of Frair Lucas's authority, and his greatest burden. For he was the man charged with bringing the high inquisitor to trial, to justice, and probably to death. The column followed his word, out of some kind of awe or fear or just sympathy.

A familiar figure rode beside the wagon, dressed in the bright red of his house. Facing Lucas, Martin Roard raised an arm in salute. The boy had insisted on following the caravan south, leaving his father to treat with Malcolm Blakley back at the Fen Gate. Lucas suspected he was ashamed at having betrayed his lifelong friend, Ian Blakley, or perhaps intended to set his honor right by seeing Sacombre brought to justice.

Lucas turned back to the cross-country scar.

"The men and women who fled along this route will be desperate. They are far from home, stranded in the pagan north with its feral gods and blood-hungry raiders. They burned any possible shelter on their way up, so we can't imagine them seeing much hospitality from those they left behind," Lucas said. "We cannot count on their loyalty. They will be more interested in their safety than our duty."

"Isn't it our duty to see them safely home?" Torvald said. "They are Suhdrin brothers after all." The big knight sat slumped in his saddle, the wispy ends of his moustache drooping nearly to his elbows.

"Some questions have a spiritual answer. Questions of duty and faith and honor," Lucas responded, turning to Torvald, then back to the ruin to their south. "Others, however, have a practical answer. We don't have the food to spare, sir. If we follow that path, we will starve before we reach Greenhall."

"And if the guardians of the Reaveholt refuse us?" Torvald asked.

"They will not," Lucas answered, and hoped it was true.

The walls of the Reaveholt were ancient and strong. The bluffs along the Tallow were steep, the river a roaring whitewater that couldn't be crossed. The castle perched like a hawk on the river's edge, overlooking the Holtspan, the great bridge that joined north and south.

Halverdt's army had bypassed this stronghold out of desperation and zealous speed, instead crossing at the fords at White Lake following the rout of Malcolm's army. Even if the siege of the Fen Gate had continued, the garrison here would have proven an insurmountable thorn in the side of the Suhdrin army.

Lucas ordered the colors stowed, all save the black and gold banner of the church and the white flag of peace. High Elector Beaunair had ridden under the church's banner. His body was among the wagons, along with Duke Halverdt and the rest of the honored dead—those noble or wealthy enough to justify carrying home for burial.

They formed into columns to emphasize the thinness of their ranks, and let the wagons of dead and wounded wind down the road. Frair Lucas rode at the head, with Torvald and the few Suhdrin lords who accompanied them. Only Duke LaGaere rode in full regalia, his armor shined and his lance hung with the favors of the inquisition. Martin Roard left his distinctive copper armor in the wagons, opting for simple linen and a tabard of red and yellow. The young man looked out of place among the grizzled knights who followed close behind. That lot was armed and armored, but their numbers weren't enough to pose a true threat to the castle.

The defenders watched from the walls. The only banner to fly from the towers was that of Sir Bourne, a red waterwheel with a leaping fish above, all on a field of black.

"At least he has struck Adair's colors," Lucas said. "That's a positive sign."

"As Adair struck his pagan colors following the crusade, and we can all see where that led," LaGaere muttered. There was a murmur of agreement among the knights, but it died as soon as Lucas turned to face them. The Duke of Warhome shrugged. "We must judge our enemies by their actions, frair," he persisted defensively. "I have seen enough Tenerran betrayal to fill a tome. I will not soon forget that."

"What of Sacombre?" Lucas countered. "Was his betrayal any less, and that while wearing the colors of the inquisition? I am wearing an inquisitor's robe, and answer to the inquisitor's title. Do you suspect me of the same heresy, Warhome?"

"That would be a dangerous game, frair," LaGaere answered. "Besides, without Sacombre, we would never have uncovered Adair's heresy. Perhaps he led us true, despite his failing."

"That is for Heartsbridge to decide," one of the knights said quickly. She wore Fabron's colors, but with a crest of circled antlers on her breast. Lucas remembered her from the last Frostnight tournament he had spent in the south, five seasons past. She had been an ace in the gentleblade tournament. He was surprised to find her in an army of invasion. Her name was Chloe Horne, if his memory served.

"Yes," Martin Roard agreed. "We must not allow the faithful of Suhdra to doubt the high inquisitor's sins. Malcolm Blakley was very insistent on that point."

"Is Malcolm Blakley your lord?" LaGaere asked. "Or do you

act in the interest of Stormwatch, as your father commanded?"

"The needs of Stormwatch and the needs of Houndhallow are often joined," Martin said shortly. A round of mocking laughter went through the knights, starting and ending with LaGaere's sneering face. Martin remained unswayed. Sir Horne stepped to his aid.

"It is best to judge before we act," she said. "Isn't that what Cinder teaches us?"

"A battlefield does not allow such luxury," LaGaere said.

"We are not here to do battle, my lord," Horne answered. "Else we would be flying the flag of peace dishonestly."

"No," Lucas said, "we are not. Warhome, you stay here. If Sir Bourne decides to cut us down in a hail of arrows, you have my blessing to wage whatever battle you see fit. Sir Torvald, Sir Roard, Sir Horne, if the three of you would come with me." Lucas turned to face the closed gate of the Reaveholt. "Let us see what sort of peace we can find."

The approach to the Reaveholt was stone that extended in all directions from the gate. The bluffs were freshly scraped of moss and grass, leaving only rock under hoof as Lucas and his two companions rode forward. Fresh scars marked the ground. Sir Horne peered down at them as they passed.

"What are these?" she asked.

"Scars struck by iron arrowheads," Lucas said. "Bodkins, probably. They'll be saving the broadtips for us, if this goes poorly."

"They have been practicing their ranges, sir," Torvald said quietly. "In anticipation of our visit."

"Ah," Horne answered as understanding dawned on her, and then a moment later and a little more quietly, "Ah."

"Let us hope their judgment matches their preparation," Martin muttered.

There were no archers to be seen on the walls, but that meant little. A single spotter from the tower could direct flights from the courtyard, as long as the bowmen were trained and the distances known. Lucas could feel the sweat pouring down his back in spite of the early autumn chill. He tried not to flinch when a flock of sparrows leapt from the gatehouse tower. It was all he could do to keep his eyes forward and his reins steady. The horses sensed their rider's tension, speeding up slightly in an effort to close the distance. Lucas kept them at an even trot.

The gate creaked open and three riders came out. Like Duke LaGaere, they were dressed in full regalia, horses caparisoned in the colors of the house of Sir Bourne, lances and shields at the parade ready. Horne and Torvald drew close to Lucas's flanks, their knees nearly touching, with Martin a bit behind. Lucas cleared his throat.

"This is not a charge, sirs. No need to close ranks just yet."

"They know what we're about," Torvald said. "Those three aren't here to talk peace."

"Then it will be a short conversation. One you should leave to me, sir," Lucas said. "I don't want to risk a fight."

Sir Bourne himself wasn't among the three who rode out to meet them. All three had the look of professional men-at-arms, soldiers sworn to their house at birth, accustomed to the blade. Apart from their dark hair and the tattoos that crawled across their brows, these men were indistinguishable from Suhdrin soldiers, with their plate-and-half, heraldry, and saddles.

Bleach their hair and clean their faces, and these three

could grace the court of any southern lord, Lucas thought. The three Tenerrans stopped as he and his companions approached, until the distance between them was close enough for swords.

"The things we fight over are so little," Lucas muttered.

"So little?" the lead Tenerran spat. "Would you call the pillage of the Fen 'so little'? Would you call the rape of our land and the murder of our lord so *little*?"

"My apologies," Lucas said quickly. "I was just musing on our differences, and our likenesses. There is more that binds us together than separates us. Especially in faith."

"We put our faith in the church, and see what that got us?" the man answered. "A Suhdrin army ranging our homelands, and the hold of our lord toppled by Suhdrin treachery. Have you finally decided to come south and deal with our little nuisance of a castle?"

"Peace, peace," Lucas said. "The army of the south has splintered, and their will to fight has broken."

"Don't let LaGaere hear you say that," Sir Horne muttered with a glance over her shoulder.

"No matter," the Tenerran said. "Suhdrin bandits roam the countryside, and banners of the south remain at the Fen Gate. Now you come to Reaveholt in force, no doubt to secure the path for your inevitable and cowardly retreat."

"Does this look like a column of war to you?" Lucas asked, the exasperation plain in his voice. "We carry the dead and dying, along with those who have seen through Sacombre's deception and given up the fight. We have no grudge with you, and would not seek one."

"If it was Sacombre's lie that started this war, why does a priest of the inquisition lead this force?" the man asked.

"Of all the things that binds us together, north and south, it is the celestial faith that is strongest. Have you renounced your loyalty to Cinder, as well as Strife?" Lucas asked. The Tenerran seemed startled by this, but before he could answer, the frair plowed forward. "If the charges against Sacombre are true, and he committed heresy in provoking this war, who is better equipped to negotiate the peace than the inquisition? The same goes for Colm Adair. Would you rather all Tener bear the weight of his sin? Or do you trust the inquisition to shrive right from wrong, and guilt from innocence?"

"The stories about the baron are—" the man began. Lucas interrupted at the top of his lungs.

"*I have stood in the witches' hallow*," he shouted, "and witnessed the pagan rites to which Colm Adair was loyal. I have *faced* the demon summoned by Tomas Sacombre, and hunted the heretics that the high inquisitor corrupted with his lies. *My brother priests!*" He drew himself up. "You do not tell me about the *stories*, sir, I have faced the pagan, and the heretic, and the monster—and Cinder as my judge, I will see them brought to justice if it's with my last breath!"

This silenced the Tenerrans. The men fidgeted on their horses, looking from the walls to the column of Suhdrin refugees.

"You hunt Tomas Sacombre?" the leader said eventually. "Because I swear by sun and summer that he has not passed this way."

"No," Lucas said with a grim smile. "He has not. Yet."

7

IAN'S FOOT LEFT the branch of the nightmare tree. The mists swirled around his face, the forest disappearing behind him as though he was flying straight up into a cloudy sky. He breached the wall of clouds and spiraled into an expanse of blinking stars.

The strange man appeared before him, hunched forward on a promontory of rock that cut into the fog like the prow of a ship. A wide spit of land lurked just beneath the cloudbank, a dark form—*forms?*—masked by the gloom. Ian hung there like a leaf caught in the wind. The man, his bright eyes hazed in shadow, twitched upright. This time Ian's gaze remained steady on them.

"You have not yet found your way home? I thought your tame dawn would be escort enough." He waved a palsied hand at Ian's hovering form, dropping him from the sky. The ground slapped into Ian's feet as he fell. "You cannot stay here much longer. Either of you."

"We'd be happy to leave, Father Night," Ian said. The gheist shivered at the words, a slow smile that cracked the skin of his lips.

"Father Night," he chuckled. "Such an easy title, and so quiet. Call me by other names, son of hounds. I am the child of death. The little winter. Every day's reminder of the end of life itself."

"My father always says the night is nothing more than the home of lies and dishonest men. A place for treachery, for banditry, for behavior unworthy of honorable men. Darkness must be suffered, if we are to appreciate the light."

"Your father says this?" the gheist asked, straightening his back, revealing unexpected height. His gaunt frame rose high above Ian. "Your father will die. Let's weigh the value of his words when they come from the grave."

"You shouldn't be so haughty," Ian said, drawing himself up. "Gods end as well, just like the night, and winter."

"You have a twisted view of the world, child," the gheist answered. "There is no end to the night. Not even dawn can break us. The rising sun is only the promise of another nightfall. A child is born for no reason other than to die." The gheist waved a twisted, dismissive hand in Ian's direction and started to turn away. "I have no time for this."

"Gods die," Ian insisted. "At the hands of mortal men, and women, and children." He reached out, palms up, smiling. "At my hands."

The gheist paused, glancing over his shoulder with a sneer.

"A tiny threat, from a tiny man," the gheist said. "Leave me."

"That is not how this works," Ian snapped. "We are not free to come and go. You've seen to that, with your nightmares and your maze of trees. Elsa would cut her way free if she could, and she is not a woman accustomed to being rescued. We cannot leave you. No." Ian shook his head, drawing his fists even with his waist. "You must leave us."

"Oh? And how will this be accomplished?" The gheist turned, and lurched closer. "How will you expel me from my own realm, Ian of Hounds? You have no bloodwrought blade. You know nothing of the rites of my theos." Closer, the gheist's face grew calm. His smile faded, and the cracked ruin of his lips formed a jagged line. "There is nothing you can do to me, child."

"Does your brother know you are stealing from him?" Ian asked. The gheist paused and became very still.

"My brother?"

"Now you forget? You are the shadow of death, that darkest of gods, and yet you try to claim what is rightfully his."

"I know not what you are talking about," the gheist said too quickly, backing away, then turning. "Return to your companion," he said over his shoulder. "Take what comfort you can in her light before it snuffs out."

"I will," Ian said. "Once we are free." He looked around the spit of land on which they stood, and pointed to the shadows that lurked just beneath the fog. "Did you think I wouldn't see these? Do you think the god of death won't miss them?"

"Be gone!" the gheist snapped. The rolling sea of fog swelled up to Ian's knees, the chill of it leaking through his breeches, hiding the shadows in its murk. "I take only what comes to me. I have been gentle on you so far. The realm of dream has sharper horrors than this!"

"Death counts its cost," Ian returned, gathering the mist closer. The memory of Fianna came to him, the power she exerted to carry her fellow druids on wings of fog, back when they were traveling the Fen. "No man escapes it, no woman, no child. Not even these few."

"You have the witch's touch to you, child. I did not sense it at first, but now... what are you trying to do now?"

"Just clearing the air a bit," Ian said. He pushed outward with his heart, snagging the blanket of fog like a net and throwing it away from him. The murk disappeared with a breath, leaving only rough stone underfoot.

There were bodies all around, their wasted limbs as tangled as driftwood after the flood has receded. They wore Thyber black, the crescent and hand worked into their shields and the pommels of their broken swords. Their skin was stretched thin and gray, but none of them had any obvious wounds.

"Death will count his debt, and find these souls missing," Ian said. "And then what will you do?"

"That is none of your business!" the gheist replied. "My brother has slipped in his duties! And these few lingered in my realm, and so I thought... I hoped..." The strange man rubbed willow-thin hands together. "There should be more to my home than passing guests. I deserve more than that! He is younger, after all, younger and greedier and so damned full of himself."

"Keeping these souls is not your domain, Night, and if you will not bow to the old god, you must submit to another," Ian said. He bent to the nearest corpse, rolling its head on the stone. "I am no priest, but I know Cinder's rites as well as anyone."

"No, you can't!" the gheist cried out. "You don't understand what you're doing!" Before it could interrupt, however, Ian sketched the icon of the crescent moon on the man's forehead, muttering the prayers of severing that would free the dead to return to the quiet. He wasn't sure he was doing it right, but he had seen the ritual often enough in his days at war.

For extra measure, he added in a little of the prayers spoken by Cahl whenever one of the druids died. Ian was just finishing when the gheist's bony hand gripped his shoulder and shoved him aside.

"If he hears that call, you'll ruin everything!" it whispered harshly. "I've worked too hard..." But it was too late.

The dead man changed, and the world with him.

A thin web of dark ink crept from the traditional tattoos on the body's face. It bled down his cheeks, limning his teeth in shadow and oil. The gheist flinched back, as though the body was on fire. The nearby waves of fog grew sharp, grays bleaching white, shadows diving into absolute blackness. Inky tendrils coiled from the body like flames of black light. The body became a pyre, the flames spreading to the other corpses that were scattered around the outcropping of rock. Their burning linens curled into the air. The metal of their armor pinged and cracked, leather buckles boiling away, chain melting into silver beads.

Only their flesh didn't burn, and as the flames consumed them, a voice could be heard in the sky.

"What is this?" the sky asked. "Who has opened this door into night? Why am I needed here?"

"Eldoreath!" the gheist shouted, throwing its arms wide in supplication. "I bring to you these humble dead, who passed through my realm, and now are delivered unto yours! May they pass into your care with..."

"Silence," the voice said. The dark bonfires grew and roared and then disappeared, and the bodies with them, but the heavy presence remained. "Did you think to deceive me, brother?"

"No, no! It was..." the gheist looked nervously around, then threw his arm in Ian's direction. "It was this mortal! He tried to hide in my realm, but I found him, and flushed him from the shadows! These men are his responsibility!"

"There is no courage in night, is there?" Ian said, standing. "It's as my father said. Do you wish you'd let us go?" he asked the gheist.

"These mortals, binding when they should worship, hiding when they should rule!" The sky grew closer, the stars blotted out, followed by a sudden storm of lightning and then ash. "Are you one of Sacombre's pet shamans? Or do you follow a different... No..." The voice in the sky trailed off, then boomed back to life. "NO! You are of Malcolm's blood! This is perfect!"

"As I knew it would be, brother!" the gheist howled. "That is why I trapped him here! It was only a matter of time before I brought him to you. And there is another, tangled in the forests of night. Shall I fetch her, as well?"

"There is no need." The sky rolled, and then the storm battered them. Lightning lashed the stone, carving runes in cinder and scar. "I will take what is mine." The presence of death washed over the stone. Ian flinched away, covering his face with his arm. Chips of stone cut his skin. The ground shifted under his feet. He looked down to see that the rock was as insubstantial as melting ice. It shivered and split.

Another darkness entered the sky, darker than night, older than fear.

"This was a mistake," Ian muttered through gritted teeth. "Elsa!" he cried at the top of his lungs. "There's some... I think this is the kind of problem a vow knight might be able to fix!"

There was a tremendous *crack*, and Ian lay face-up. As he struggled to his feet, he saw the night gheist torn apart like a rag doll. Then a twisting form of ink-black muscles and smiling claws began to materialize in the storm.

"Your father stood against me, young Blakley," it said. "I will take his insolence out of your skin. Yes, that will be very satisfying. Very."

"*Definitely* a mistake," Ian said. He turned and ran down the collapsing spit of stone. Lightning chased him, cracking stone and burning the air in his lungs. When he reached the end, Ian jumped once again.

There was nothing graceful, this time, nothing dreamlike. He fell, twisting, screaming, clawing at empty space as gravity plucked him out of the air and threw him down. He fell like a stone until the forest appeared like dark cracks in the sheet of fog below. Only a breath to think about it, and then Ian was crashing through the trees, dry branches shattering against him, the pain knocking sense from his head and air from his body.

He crashed into a thick copse of trees, shattering them, then lay there, unmoving, unthinking, without breath or thought. Above him, rain began to fall from the churning sky, thick, heavy drops of pitch that sizzled when they spattered against his face. He stared up at the sky and waited.

Elsa's face eclipsed the view, her ash-scarred face smiling grimly.

"My hero," she said, kicking Ian in the side to roll him over, watching carefully until he took a deep, jagged breath. "Not dead?"

"Not yet," he said. He lay in the center of her cage. The life was gone from the tree, the limbs lying about in a ruin of bark and cinder. Elsa had taken her frustrations out on her captor. "Soon, I think," he continued, "but not yet."

"Good. What's coming?" Elsa asked. She looked up at the pitch-raining sky, twisting her sword around in her grip.

"Servants of night? Demons of nightmare?"

"Nothing so small," Ian answered. "The god of death." He rolled onto his heels, steadying himself, trying to find his balance.

"The god of... death," Elsa repeated. "So we should run?"

"That would seem wise," Ian answered. He stood, weaving back and forth on his feet like a drunkard. "Though I'm not sure where we run to, or how."

The forest shivered again, the trees around them quivering like a wind chime. The ground shifted precariously as the world righted itself, aligning again with the natural order of tree trunks and limbs, the ground below, the sky above. Ian and Elsa lurched against the cage's remaining walls, which crumbled quickly under their weight.

They steadied themselves for a minute, then started running.

The storm blew through the forest behind them, crushing trees and undergrowth, tearing the earth apart. Cracks formed in the ground—shifting plates of stone jutting into the air that quickly crumbled under the force of the tempest. Shards of broken rock turned the air into a swarm of stinging grit. Ian stumbled as he ran, faster and faster, bouncing off the ground when it shifted, dodging rubble, Elsa bounding at his side until they ran out of ground and could run no farther.

Then they fell.

And the world fell with them.

8

SHE EXPECTED THE light. Gwen's memories were wrapped in light, in the vibrant heat of spring as the season's first hunt took her to the forests of her youth, in the warm sun of summer, in the tenderly waning fire of autumn as stores were laid in for the long, bitter winter.

What shocked her was the pain.

It felt as if her veins had been replaced with sharp steel, quenched in her blood like a vow knight's blade, then ripped from her body. She tried to lift her hand, but if felt as though her arm was snarled in a bramble of thorns. She opened her eyes to see the wounds and figure a way out of the bramble.

Her arm lay bare on a bed of cut moss. Other than a few scrapes and a mottled bracelet of bruising, she was unharmed. Gwen tried to lift her arm again, and the pain of brambles returned.

"The wounds are deep, and not of the body," a man said from behind her. Gwen started to turn around, but agony pushed her back to the ground. Several heartbeats passed before her vision cleared. The man was leaning over her, a blank expression on his face. "Don't move suddenly. Or at all."

"Yeah, I..." She gasped, winced at the pain, then continued on. "I have learned that lesson."

"You are the huntress. Gwen Adair," the man said. It wasn't a question, but it really wasn't a statement, either. It was as if he was trying to get his head around the idea. "You have stolen the autumn god from us."

"Goddess," Gwen corrected. The man shrugged.

"Pretending the gods are as simple as man or a woman is a foolish path. We wrap them in our language because we need to call them something." He took Gwen's chin between his fingers and tilted her head, as though examining her throat. "Use the words that matter to you. They don't care."

"Who are you?" she asked. "Where am I?"

"I am a man who is constantly disappointed in the struggles of Tenerran lords and ladies, and constantly dependent on their help. You were at the witches' hallow when Fomharra awoke?" He released Gwen's head, settling back on his heels to stare at her. Now that the initial pain had passed, Gwen saw that she was nestled in a bower of trees, the layer of moss resting on a bed of stacked peat. The smoke from a smoldering fire tangled with the branches, filtering the sun into golden beams. The man leaned forward and waved his hand in front of her face.

"You were there?"

"Fomharra?" Gwen asked.

"The autumn god," the man answered. "The harvester."

"Yes, that is the name. It feels familiar." She adjusted herself on the bed of moss and nodded. "I was there," Gwen answered. Each word cost her dearly, yet she had the impression this man had many more questions, and no patience for her discomfort. "I did it. Woke her."

He was silent for a moment. Shadows moved outside the bower. Gwen could see a face peering in between the oak branches, eyes the color of water staring at her from a face of leaves. Finally, the man spoke again.

"I would not believe that if I had not seen you at the Fen Gate," he said. "And here, in this condition. With these wounds." He passed a hand over her body, not touching her, but brushing her skin with a wave of heat. "You have worn a god, and lived. It is unexpected, and unfortunate."

"I'm pretty happy about it," Gwen said crossly.

"For now," he said, then he stood. "You may live long enough to regret surviving."

"Wait—who are you? You said you were at the Fen Gate?"

"My name is Cahl. Do you know of Ian Blakley?"

A memory of battle, of a tower being torn stone from stone, and a boy arguing with her, trying to get her to stop destroying her home. Beyond that, the image of Ian from years long gone, before things had changed. Before she had changed. Not that long ago, really, but it seemed as though ages had passed.

"Since we were children," she said.

"You are still children," he said impatiently, then shook his head. "I was ranging along the Tallow with my cadre. One of our witches found him, nearly dead, and insisted on bringing him with us." Cahl rubbed his hands together, a strange nervousness that didn't sit well with his calm way of speaking. "Trails later, we entered the Fen Gate during the battle. The witch stayed with him, and was captured."

"You escaped?"

"I know when to run, but I will not forget the hound's betrayal."

"Yet still you insist on protecting this one," a voice said from outside the bower. The man who had been watching, his face tattooed with a mask of leaves, stepped into the little shelter. "When will you learn to stop trusting these pretenders?"

"House Adair suffered greatly in their service to Fomharra. The huntress is the last of that blood, and I would not betray it."

The last of my blood. The last of my family... Pain shot through her again, and she nearly lost consciousness.

"She is not one of us, Cahl," the other man snapped. "She does not know us, or our ways, or our paths. She knows nothing of the pagan ways."

"She knew the wardens," Cahl answered.

"The wardens are dead! As we will be, if we lead her down this path."

"It is not our way to sacrifice without need, Aedan."

"I am not speaking of sacrifice," the man answered. He loomed over Gwen, the dark ink of his face and light eyes a startling contrast. "I am speaking of justice. She swore to protect the autumn god, and yet he is lost to us. The stories I have heard tell of her leading an inquisitor to the hallow, as well as a vow knight."

"They are only stories," Cahl said.

"True stories," Gwen answered grimly. "It was best."

"Best?" Aedan asked, raising his brows. "Best for whom? Surely not the god. Surely not Tener, nor the witches who died defending the hallow."

"You don't know," Gwen insisted. The pain threatened to overwhelm her again, but anger kept her talking. "Frair Lucas was dying, and he wanted to help. Without him, the Fen god... Fomharra... would be in the hands of the church, and Sacombre would still be at the head of a Suhdrin army ravaging Tenerran soil."

"I have witnessed the cost of celestial help, child," Aedan hissed. "I have lost enough to the church. I will lose no more."

"Peace, shaman," Cahl whispered. "This is no time for accusations. The conclave will have its answers, in time."

"Yes, we will," Aedan said menacingly. "Our answers, and our revenge." Still seething, he turned and pushed his way out of the shelter. Cahl watched him leave, then sighed and knelt beside Gwen.

"I can not save you from him, should the conclave decide on sacrifice," he said. His voice was gentle. "But know that I mean to hear your story, and make sure the elders hear it, as well."

"What did he mean about not knowing anything of the pagan ways?" Gwen asked. "My blood has been raised in pagan rites, since I was a child. Since my father's father was born."

My father, she thought. *Dead.*

"No," Cahl said. "Not truly. Your family was sealed away from the true path, kept from knowing too much, given just enough power without knowing anything that might damage us, should you decide to turn."

"What?" Gwen forced herself up despite the stabbing agony, squinting in anger. "We would never turn. We would never betray you!"

"And gods bless you for it—but that was a chance the conclave would not take." Cahl raised his hands, his voice soothing. "Peace, child. This decision is generations old. Your greatfathers knew the pact they were signing. They knew the price, and the debt."

"The price was our lives, if the church found out," Gwen said. "A price we paid. And the debt was to the god in the Fen. To Fomharra."

"And now your family is dead," Cahl said. "The church

knows of your heresy, and the Fen god is lost to us."

"You don't need to remind me..."

"Lost, because of your actions. Dead, because of decisions you made, Gwendolyn of the tribe of iron, and so you have paid the price." Cahl straightened, grimacing. "We have all paid the debt."

"I did what I thought was best," Gwen muttered.

"Yes. We all do." Cahl stood and backed to the edge of the shelter. "But sometimes we are wrong. Rest for now. We have tarried too long in this place. The conclave has been called, and we must travel in the morning."

"The conclave?"

"A meeting of the tribes, their elders," Cahl said. "To hear your story, and judge its worth. We have strange paths to walk between now and then. There are many who would not have those secrets revealed to you, even now."

Then he left, and Gwen settled back into pain and healing and regret.

Walking was pure misery. She had always been fit, as much at home in the forest as in the castle. Now her weapons had been taken, fire jolted through her veins with every step, and the bottoms of her feet prickled through her ruined boots. Whenever she stumbled, Cahl would appear at Gwen's elbow to drag her up and urge her on, only to disappear moments later. The other shaman, Aedan, was as constant as a shadow, lurking just behind her, disappearing when she turned her attention his way. The other pagans ignored her to the point of cruelty.

She walked alone. At least it gave her time to think.

Gwen wasn't sure what she had expected, how she'd

thought the pagans would treat her once she freed the Fen god. Fomharra. How had her family lost that particular knowledge—the name of the god they were hiding, or the fact that the old gods even *had* names. When hunting, Gwen always thought of the gheists in more generic terms, like the waterfen spirit, or the gallows gheist, or the little god along the bluffs.

They must all have names, she realized. She wondered if Cahl knew them. She would ask, the next time he appeared.

Cahl claimed that her family had been cut off from the rest of the pagan faith, in an attempt to protect the faithful in case the inquisition learned the truth of Adair's heresy. That startled her. Other than the few covens of shaman, who was left to save? She had been taught that their family was among the few faithful houses that remained. Had that been a lie?

A silent line of pagan outriders slipped between the tree trunks off to her left, spears loose in their hands, cloaks dancing through the air like a flock of mottled birds. She watched sidelong as they disappeared into the deeper forest.

There were dozens in line behind her, and dozens more riding in the horse-drawn van. Small groups had been joining their path throughout the morning, coming in fives and tens. Sometimes it was just a knot of shamans in the company of their witch, other times it was the witches alone. For every face that wore the holy ink, a dozen lesser servants ghosted through the forests, simple worshippers answering to the call of the old gods.

How many are in this caravan? she wondered. *How many more await us at this conclave?*

"There are more of us than you think," Aedan said, appearing suddenly at her side. She jumped, and suffered for it. "Among the trees. Beyond the shadows. Is that a surprise to you? Our numbers?"

"Surprised to see so many," Gwen answered, "when so few came to my family's aid." The shaman unsettled her, but she wasn't going to let him get under her skin. "Or does defending Tenerran land mean so little to you?"

"We are free people," Aedan said. "Your title means nothing to me, nor your border. The true faith has suffered at Tenerran hands, as much as we have suffered from the actions of the Suhdrin."

"At least you could have saved the wardens of the witches' hallow," Gwen said. "They died to protect Fomharra."

"As was their duty," Aedan said. "It is your duty, as well, and yet you live, and the Harvester is lost to us. Celestial blood fouls the hallow."

"I am tired of making excuses to you!" Gwen snapped. She stopped walking, waiting until the shaman paused and turned to look at her with hard eyes. "You are not my judge, nor my lord. We have guarded the hallow for generations, while you hid among your precious trees and sulked about the crusades. My only sin is action, and I will not be condemned by those who refused to act when it was needed!"

Aedan stood and stared at her for a long time. Then he stepped closer, his bulk looming over her, the darkness of his face like a cold fire pit.

"Three children have I lost, and two wives," Aedan said. "It was a priest that took them from me, in Cinder's name and with Strife's fire. When the priests came for them, scrying their souls against the song of ancient gods, what did House Adair do? Where were the spears of the Fen Gate, or Houndhallow, or Farwatch?" There was anger in his voice, but also a weight of loss that even Gwen found staggering.

"Those priests found warmth at Tenerran hearths, and were born of Tenerran blood," he continued. "So if there's judgment to be handed out, or vengeance to be sought, it will not be mine." He gathered up his cloak and turned away. "The gods will judge you. The gods will weigh you. And the gods will take their vengeance."

Gwen was about to answer when a low horn sounded from the trees. A change went through the caravan, caution traded for excitement. The outriders poured onto the path, and from the front of the van Cahl scampered up a gnarled trunk to respond to the horn with his own deep-throated howl. Yipping replies came back through the trees. Aedan looked Gwen up and down with distaste in his eyes.

"I should kill you here," he said. "Before you contaminate the hallow."

"I think Cahl would have something to say about that," Gwen said cautiously. Her hand brushed her belt, where her weapons should have been. "And the conclave, as well."

"The conclave!" Aedan said. "So like a Suhdrin lord, depending on the council of lesser souls. No, child, I will not kill you, but know that you don't belong here. That you will never belong with us."

"And where are we?" Gwen asked. "This place where I do not belong?"

"Someplace truly holy," Aedan said. "Holier than your blood should foul."

"I've walked the witches' hallow, and worn a god," Gwen answered. "It's not your right to tell me where I may or may not walk."

"I will leave it to the gods," Aedan replied sharply, then lurched closer, his smile cold. "May they judge you true."

9

THE AIR IN the stables was thick with incense, the smoke hanging in the narrow space like pulled molasses. A collection of young priests stood solemnly around, busy with the mundane tasks of making the place livable. An older man stood next to one of the stalls, twisting his large hands together nervously. Inside the stall, the hay had been burned away and the stone floor beneath scoured clean.

There were five priests, but only one who mattered. The inquisitor. He was tall and thick, a tree of a man with iron-gray hair shot through with silver and a neat beard that almost covered the scar that ran from the apple of his throat to his temple. He wore the robes of his office over a suit of fine chain, and stood with his palms resting on the hilts of two feyiron long swords.

Malcolm recognized him immediately.

"That's the Orphanshield," he whispered to Sir Doone. "Heartsbridge is taking this seriously." The other four priests were barely of age to take the vows. The man was known as the Orphanshield for his habit of gathering the unfortunate—those who had been cast off—into his doma, seeing to their health and education. From these children, the frair selected the brightest to enter the priesthood. They served as his attendants in the doma and his companions on the road. Of the four he had brought to the Fen Gate, two were of Cinder, and two were dedicated to Strife.

"In my experience, rogue gods tend to summon the attention of the inquisition," Doone answered. "He has already started taking a toll."

Curiously, Malcolm looked around.

"What became of the horses?" he asked. Sir Doone shook her head sadly.

"Dead," she answered. "The inquisitor did it himself. The Adair beasts, anyway. Ours are still stabled outside."

"So it might have been a mistake, you're saying, housing him in the stables," Malcolm said. "Whose idea was that?"

"There's nowhere else to put him. At least here, the air already smells of shit."

Malcolm stifled a snort, which drew the attention of the inquisitor. The man turned and loomed closer, his hands extended.

"Houndhallow," he said, his voice deep. "I am Frair Felix Gilliam, sent by the inquisition to bring Cinder's judgment to this place. Winter's blessing be upon you."

"Frair Gilliam," Malcolm said, shaking the inquisitor's hand. The grip was strong. "I know your name, though I am surprised to find you outside Heartsbridge's holy walls. I thought your days on the road were at an end."

"I walk whatever path Cinder requires of me," Gilliam said, "and this is a serious business. There is deep corruption here, Houndhallow. I am sorry about the horses."

"They weren't my horses, and I don't think Adair will have much use for them anymore," Malcolm said. "Though if you find the need to spill any other blood, please let me know first."

"Of course," Gilliam said. "Unfortunately, the girl was dead before we got here. Her father may live, though."

"What girl?" Malcolm asked.

Gilliam grimaced, then drew something from his robes. It was a bit of metal, black with char, as though it had been lying in flames. The inquisitor held it up. It was a blade, wickedly barbed and carved in pagan runes. The handle had burned away, leaving only the tang.

"There was a child hidden here, along with her father. When the…" Gilliam made a broad gesture, taking in the castle, the sky, the gods themselves. "When whatever it was that happened during your battle came through here, it changed them. They were tucked away in some kind of heathen pocket, a glamour of some sort. Pagan trickery, but it burst. Like a pipe trying to carry too much water."

"That sounds horrific," Malcolm said.

"Yes. I feel bad for the child."

"And the father?" Malcolm asked.

"The father made his own mistakes. There is no room in my heart for sympathy, not for such a man. That he lives is mercy enough. But I did not summon you to discuss the man," Gilliam said, turning to the stall.

"You did not summon me at all," Malcolm said sharply, but the inquisitor ignored him.

"What we found here is cause for worry," Gilliam continued. "This was the work of a powerful witch. I thought at first that Adair's crime was one of knowledge. The secret of a hidden god, while terrible, does not carry power with it. There are those in Heartsbridge who believe the pagans who remain are nothing more than peasants singing in the forests. That only the memory of the gheists has sustained them."

"The feral gods are not threat enough?"

"They are predictable. Manageable. It was thought that the ability to bend them to a human will was lost. We hunt the pagans because their worship sustains the gheists, but few believe that they could actually *control* their gods."

"Few in Heartsbridge," Malcolm corrected. "It's common knowledge in the north."

"Well, in the north, there can be no accounting for the superstitions of..." Gilliam paused, glancing uncomfortably at Malcolm before continuing. "As you know, the knowledge of Tener is not held in high regard in Heartsbridge."

"Why would it be? We're savages, right?"

"That isn't what I meant," the frair said. "There are many things that, as you say, are common knowledge in Tener yet are clearly false."

"Perhaps the celestriarch can ask the high inquisitor about superstition. In particular, the bending of a god's will to your heart," Malcolm said grimly. "Sacombre found that one more than true."

"Dangerously so," Gilliam said. "But it is not my place to judge him. My point, Houndhallow, is that there was a powerful witch here. Perhaps it was one of Adair's blood—the wife or the daughter. Perhaps the baron himself." He waved the charred blade in his hand, then tossed it on the ground, where it struck a spark. "Most likely the child's mother. In which case we must find her."

"If she lives, wouldn't she have fled?"

"Whoever she may be, the witch is still here, or someone just as powerful. There is still a corruption within these walls, Houndhallow," Gilliam said. "When I came through the gate, I could taste it in the air. Your men can sense it. The guards I passed were harried. They are tense, nervous, on edge. The pagan taint of this place haunts them."

"They are on edge because not a month ago, two gods ripped open the sky over our heads, and now the remnants of a Suhdrin army camp outside our gate," Malcolm said.

"There is more to this than the fear of violence," Gilliam said with great certainty. He turned back to Malcolm, resting his wide hands on the hilts and looming close. "They fear for their souls," he growled. "They fear the night."

Malcolm sighed. *They fear the church, you fool. It was your high inquisitor who brought this war.* Yet there was no use trying to explain. The blessed of Cinder saw only what they wished to see.

"Our journey was too long, " Gilliam said, "and we were delayed by those Suhdrin fools. We will start searching the grounds immediately. In his reports, Frair Lucas mentioned chambers that lie beneath the castle."

"Yes. Hidden beyond the crypts."

"We will begin there. I want a pair of guards assigned to each of my acolytes, good men and women of Suhdrin birth, and..."

"You may not have noticed, Inquisitor, but there are few Suhdrin blades within the walls of this castle." Malcolm did little to hide his anger. "Do you not trust my Tenerran faithful?"

"Forgive me, Houndhallow, but I can't be sure of them," Gilliam answered. "They may have been corrupted by Adair's heresy."

"Tomas Sacombre is Suhdrin born."

Gilliam shrugged.

"I am not going to argue this with you, Houndhallow," he said. "I will not risk the blood of my children on the faith of

Tener. We have been deceived once. You trusted Colm Adair, and look where that has gotten you." Gilliam brushed past him. "This is a godsdamned mess, this business. I'm charged with making it right, and I shall. With your help, or with the help of those Suhdrin blades you seem to hold in such high contempt.

"Catrin!" he snapped. One of the priests of Strife, a young girl with silk-white hair and frail features, looked up nervously. "Send a messenger to Duke Marchand, have him provide us with a dozen men-at-arms, and a knight if he can spare one."

"Redgarden has men in this castle," Malcolm said crossly. "Castian can spare your dozen. There's no need to seek aid in Halverdt's host."

"Lord Halverdt is dead, Houndhallow, and frankly, I have had enough of the spat that cost him his life!" Frair Gilliam rounded on Malcolm, pointing angrily. "I will have guards from the Suhdrin camp, and from your host as well. You will learn to stand together with the church, or we will know why you stand against us."

Malcolm clenched his jaw and ground his fist against his thigh, but he kept his mouth shut. Once his initial rage had passed, the duke of Houndhallow bowed.

"As you wish, Frair Gilliam," he said. "I will select my best men for your service. But know this—if Marchand's men spill an ounce of blood..."

"Put your threats away, Houndhallow. I am done listening to them."

Malcolm collected himself, then turned and left the stables. Sir Doone was waiting in the yard.

"We are going to have more visitors," he said. "The inquisitor wants Marchand's men helping guard his precious acolytes."

"Well, that's a joy," Doone answered.

"Indeed," Malcolm answered. "Today has been a source of endless happiness."

MaeHerron gladly volunteered a dozen of his own men to share duty with the Suhdrin, and another dozen to watch their backs. Wherever the priests went, a long string of tense swordsmen followed close behind, their attention split between their wards and one another.

Once everything was arranged to the inquisitor's satisfaction, Malcolm personally led him to the under-chambers of the Fen Gate. The crypts had already been scoured, the stone floors as free of dust as the day they had been formed. Gilliam noted this.

"This is the cleanest crypt I have ever been in," he said. "Adair must have frequented these halls."

"It's clean because we cleaned it," Malcolm said. "There were a half-dozen bodies between here and the kitchens, all butchered. We're pretty sure that was the high inquisitor's work. The manners of their death seemed like his handiwork."

"His handiwork?"

"Sacombre acquired a taste for drama," Malcolm said. "He took to tearing his victims limb from limb. He took Colm Adair apart like a jigsaw puzzle."

"Gods be good, that must have made it difficult to bury the baron."

"Not at all," Malcolm answered. "The body was gone when we went looking for it. His and the rest of the family, as well. Assuming they truly died, as Sacombre claimed."

"A bloody business," Gilliam muttered.

"Precisely. Which is why these crypts have been scoured—

but those that lie beyond are another matter," Malcolm said. "You'll see."

They came to the stairs leading down. The smell of death drifted up, as sharp and bloody as a slaughterhouse. The inquisitor struck flint to his lantern, then led the way down. The children stayed behind.

It was a long descent, made worse by the increasing stink and an uncertain feeling in the air, a horror that clung to Malcolm's skin like cobwebs. The inquisitor slowed, raising his lantern, examining the walls, and muttering to himself.

He's delaying, Malcolm thought. *I wonder if the old man has gotten soft in Heartsbridge.*

The first tangible sign of trouble was the blood. It was spattered against the stones, a pattern of handprints that crawled from stair to ceiling to wall as though they flew through the air. At the edge of the lantern's light, the room opened up. Gilliam paused again, peering at the prints.

"Leaves," he said. "I thought at first it was hands, but no." He beckoned Malcolm closer. "Though it looks devilishly like a hand. Some kind of ritual marking, I think. Nothing to do with the attack."

"Unless the hand itself was made of leaves," Malcolm offered. The inquisitor shrugged, then turned to the open chamber. The room was narrow and high, the ceiling lost in shadow. Niches striped the walls, each holding a small collection of tools that twinkled in the light. An altar nestled against the far side. There was blood and a body and shadows that seemed to move on their own.

"The evil is sharp in the air. We must shrive this place, before it can be uprooted." Gilliam rested his lantern on the altar and produced a small satchel from his robes. He began sprinkling the contents around the room. The air immediately filled with the overwhelming stink of pine and roses and heat. Puffs of smoke curled up wherever the poultice landed.

Malcolm examined the body.

"This must be the stable girl's mother," he said. The cold stone had preserved the horror of her death, despite the time that had passed. There might have been some magic to it, as well. "She has no ink."

"The pagans sometimes deceive us with their guise," Gilliam said. "The savage markings of the old ways speak too truly of the heretic's heart. It is no wonder that she is unmarked."

Malcolm rubbed the tattoos on his cheeks. "I will see that she is buried," he said.

"The body must be burned. Here. Corruption of spirit might remain in her flesh. We daren't risk infecting the castle. Once I have sanctified these walls we will fill in the chamber and seal the stairs. That is the only way to be sure of ending the danger."

"I can't imagine she will rest easy, sealed forever beneath the stones of the Fen Gate."

"A witching wife has not earned the peace of the quiet house," Gilliam said. "She made her choices."

"Frair Lucas was of a more merciful mind—" Malcolm started.

"And by the reports I've read," Gilliam said, "Frair Lucas could have prevented all of this, if he'd been of a stricter disposition. He had young Gwen Adair in his hands, even followed her to the witches' hallow, only to let her slip from his fingers. He was merciful, but winter is not a season of mercy, Houndhallow, and I am here on winter's business."

Malcolm sighed, but relented. He watched while the

priest spread the dust around the chamber, muttering prayers and invocations. When he was finished, Gilliam plucked up the lantern and motioned to the stairs.

"Bring my children," he said. "And the oil."

"Should they see this?" Malcolm asked.

"I will not shield them from horror, Blakley. The world is horror." The priest gave the scene a long, considering look, lingering over the emblems of pagan faith and the butchered remains of the witch. "They must know what they stand against."

Malcolm stood at the foot of the stairs. There wasn't room in the tiny chamber for the guards, so they stood in a tense group in the crypts above, fingering their blades and exchanging cold stares.

Frair Gilliam stood at the center of the chamber, his hands crossed over his darkwood staff, head bowed in prayer. The children splashed oil on the body and into the niches, soaking the pagan instruments. The oil seeped into the dried blood on the floor and walls, making the room look like a fresh slaughterhouse.

When they were done, the young priests filed past Malcolm and up the stairs. Their eyes were stone, their faces still and calm. Malcolm wondered at the things these children must have seen to be so unmoved by the horrors of the room. When they were gone, Gilliam came to stand beside Malcolm.

"We bury a great darkness here, Houndhallow," he said. "This castle will always be haunted in some way," the inquisitor said. "Whoever ascends to the Sedgewind throne must always be on their guard. Perhaps here more than most, but we will see the faithful of Cinder and Strife protected. This I do swear."

"I'm sure you do," Malcolm replied bitterly.

"Stand back, Houndhallow. The fire will be fierce."

"I have burned my share of bodies, priest," Malcolm answered. "Give this woman what peace you can."

Frair Gilliam drew a piece of tinder from his robe and touched it to the lantern, then tossed it onto the body, which went up like a torch. Then the rest of the room caught. It wasn't just the oil that burned, no, but the blood that lined the walls flared like hay, and beneath the blood was something more—runes written in the stone, hidden by the gore and now briefly exposed.

Strange symbols in fire twisted up the walls like a fuse, burning out quickly to leave ghost images floating in the darkness. They rushed up to the ceiling, only to snuff out.

Smoke billowed up, black and inky, and then Malcolm and the priest were choking on it, tendrils of dark smoke roiling with cinders coiling around their heads. They fled, the air stinging their eyes and stealing their breath, until Malcolm thought they might die in the darkness.

A voice followed them, sharp and strange, the words foreign to their ears.

The stairs twisted up and up, longer than Malcolm remembered, and then suddenly they were in the crypts and everyone was standing around staring at them. A pillar of smoke rushed out of the passageway behind them, flattening against the ceiling like a prowling snake, its scales made of embers and cinders and ash.

"What in hell happened down there?" Malcolm gasped.

"Nothing holy," Gilliam answered, weeping ash. "Nothing sane."

"The flames live!" one of the young priests gasped. The

tendril of smoke squirmed down the corridor, seeking escape from the death that lay in the chambers below.

"Quickly!" the inquisitor shouted, running after it. "It must be some shred of the witch's soul, seeking solace. We mustn't let it escape!" In the distance, a woman screamed, the sound muffled by stone and distance. But even then, Malcolm knew his wife's voice, screaming in pain. He waited until the inquisitor and his attendant priests were out of sight, and their Suhdrin guards with them. He turned to Sir Doone, who stood nervously by.

"We have to move her," Malcolm said. "Quickly."

They took another route, longer but hidden from most of the castle's staff, praying they got to Sorcha before the inquisition.

Praying and running.

10

THE THREE SOLDIERS who escorted them into the Reaveholt answered only to the name Duncan. Apparently they were brothers, and so inseparable as to not require their own names.

They demanded that LaGaere and his company surrender their swords, and when the duke refused it appeared as if they would come to blows. Only Lucas's promise of peace won them passage without disarmament.

The design of the Reaveholt was pragmatically pessimistic. The walls were so high and the terrain so difficult that it would be almost impossible to capture without treachery. Even so, the castle was separated into three sections, any one of which could stand defense against the other two. Thus all three would need to fall for the attackers to cross over the bridge without being assaulted.

The Tenerran defenders withdrew to their strongholds, then threw the gates wide open, letting Lucas and his caravan enter the central courtyard. The iron wagon's wheels grated on the stony ground. Walls riddled with arrow slots stared down at them like a stony jury.

Sir Bourne waited at the center of the courtyard, his back to the bridge-side gate. Completely alone, he was a wide man, short red hair bustling over his brow, dark eyes sunk deeply into his cheeks. His hand was slung over the bit of an axe whose blade was etched in the holy runes of summer along one edge, and those of winter on the other.

"If you try to take me, my men have orders to kill everyone in the yard," he said as Lucas approached. "I have no heart for sacrifice, but I would rather die than fall into the inquisition's hands."

"I expect nothing less than bloody-minded fatalism from you, good sir," Lucas answered. The Suhdrin guards who stood on both sides of the iron wagon stared grimly up at the walls, knuckles tight on their shields. Frair Lucas signaled them forward, until the wagon pulled up next to Sir Bourne. "Do you want to see them both, or just the high inquisitor?"

"Both? Who else are you taking to Heartsbridge?"

"A witch by the name of Fianna. She's no one important, but that doesn't keep her safe from trial."

"Is the inquisition in the business of giving trials to common pagans these days?" Bourne said. "Most witches receive nothing more than the sharp end of a spear, usually while they're trying to run away. There must be something important about her."

"It's difficult to explain. She played a role in the battle, and may have saved the life of Duke Blakley's son, Ian," Lucas said. "It's hard to say how the boy would have reacted if we had just, you know..."

"Run her through?" Bourne asked with a wide smile. "I have no interest in your pet witch, frair. Let me see Sacombre, then be on your way."

"If you try anything, Bourne..." Lucas said.

"Keep your threats. Cinder will get his justice." The

knight waved him away, and the guards pulled the bar of the iron door free, then formed a lane between the wagon and Sir Bourne. The door creaked open and, after a few quiet moments, a pale, dirty face peered out.

"Celestriarch," Sacombre called out from the wagon's dark interior. His voice was thin and cracked. "You have changed much in the past few months."

"This is Sir Bourne of the Reaveholt, Tomas," Frair Lucas said. "We must pass his gate, and the toll is a meeting with you."

"Tomas. Tomas," Sacombre muttered angrily. "Awfully informal, frair. I am still the high inquisitor, until Holy LaBrieure says different. I am more than coin to buy you passage."

"Not today, you're not, Tomas. Today you are our coin. So behave. Try to not give him any good reason to murder you."

"I have more than reason enough," Bourne said. "All of Tener has reason enough." The knight shifted on his seat, spinning the massive axe in his palm. "Come out in the light, priest. Let's have a look at you."

Sacombre stepped gingerly from the wagon, blinking rapidly in the glare of the sun. His robes were torn to rags, still bloodied by the strange death god to which the priest once bound his soul, and his hair hung in greasy ropes down his head. Yet even in his ruin, Sacombre bore an air of smug condescension.

"Does this please you, sir?" Sacombre asked. "Am I sufficiently humbled?" Bourne watched him closely, not answering, his dark eyes giving nothing. The former high inquisitor took another few steps into the courtyard. He looked around the walls that glared down at them. "Am I to beg forgiveness? Declare my innocence? What of you, LaGaere? You were anxious enough to bring your sword to my banner. Are you going to judge me, now?"

"This is humiliating," LaGaere hissed to Frair Lucas. "He is still a man of the church, even if he's fallen from grace. The high inquisitor should not be forced to dance for every half-bit Tenerran knight we pass along the road!"

"Peace, Warhome."

"It is not appropriate—"

"Peace!" Lucas snapped. "We are escorting this man to Heartsbridge to be questioned, and judged, and then executed. It will be done with grace and justice, but it will also be humiliating."

LaGaere sighed, staring daggers at Lucas, but said nothing more. Lucas turned back to the proceedings. Sacombre watched them both very closely, the slightest smile on his lips. He nodded to Lucas, then turned to Sir Bourne.

"So, Sir Bourne of the Reaveholt, what do you want of me?" Sacombre asked sharply. "Or is my humiliation payment enough?"

"How did you know about Colm Adair?" the knight answered.

"Oh! Oh, my. Yes. A very interesting question," Sacombre said. Gaining strength, he clasped his hands behind his back and strolled forward as though he were in a garden. "Do you ask to know what you might have missed? To assuage your conscience, to prove to yourself that you couldn't have known your master was harboring such awful secrets?" He wove from guard to guard, as though inspecting them for battle. When he was nearly to Sir Bourne, he paused and smiled up at the enormous man.

"Or are you worried that your own heresy has also been revealed, and want to know what secrets I will spill once I am under the inquisition's screw?"

Sir Bourne clenched his jaw, his face growing a dangerous shade brighter, his eyes glinting darker, his hand tight on the bitted head of the axe. When he spoke, however, Bourne's voice was low and calm.

"My house has stood by Adair for generations," he said. "Since long before the crusades, and the church, and the celestial calendar. Since before time was counted. My loyalty to the baron was only surpassed by my faith to Cinder, and to Strife." Bourne stood, leaning against the axe as though it was a walking stick.

"Colm Adair was blood father to my firstborn, and Gwen Adair took my son on his first gheist hunt. When they dedicated the new doma at Fenton, I helped carry the altar from the quarry at Hollyhaute." Bourne strolled casually down the row of Suhdrin guards toward Sacombre. The guards twitched away from him, fists tightening on spears, eyes shifting nervously to their sergeant. "So when this man—this brother to me, whom I have followed in battle, whose hospitality I have taken—when he stands accused of heresy, I take note. It concerns me."

"As it should, Sir Bourne," Sacombre said. The high inquisitor stood unbent before the giant man, his thin frame as still as stone. "Colm Adair deceived a great many of his fellow lords of Tener."

"Perhaps," the great knight said, pausing and hefting his axe in both hands, turning it over like a spit. "Though the baron will never get his trial. Unlike you, and this fortunate witch. So tell me. How did you know? *What* did you know?"

"This is tiring," Sacombre said. "Frair Lucas, I do not wish to perform for this bully. Put me back in my cage."

"No," Bourne hissed. "I am not done with you."

"And what will you do if I refuse to answer?" Sacombre drawled. "You have it in your hands to kill me. To kill us all, in fact." The high inquisitor threw an arm wide to the waiting archers. "Are you that foolish? To slaughter the wounded, along with the priest who is trying to bring me to justice?"

"It is justice I want, but not for you. We have all heard the stories of Colm Adair's heresy," Bourne said, "but he is dead, and by your hand. If the sentence has already been served, at least you can do him the honor of making your case against him. To me."

"And why should I?" Sacombre asked. "As you said, Colm Adair is dead. I killed him." Sacombre shrugged and walked a casual circle around Sir Bourne, gesturing as he talked. "I killed his wife and child, as well. A lovely boy, such a waste. I don't think he knew why he was dying. The mother did, of course. You could see it in her eyes, the weight of the lie and the loss it was causing. Poor woman."

"You had no *right*..."

"Oh, but I did," Sacombre said, pausing in front of the big knight. "That is my *only* right, as high inquisitor. To doubt the faith of my subjects, and render judgment as I see fit. My doubt was more than proven in the case of Colm Adair."

"Hypocrite. Murderer!" Bourne spat. "You sit in judgment of Tenerrans, with the blood of children on your hands, yet you are the one who has committed heresy! You are no less guilty than Colm Adair, and no less deserving of death!"

"That remains to be seen, of course," Sacombre replied. "It is given to me to judge as I must, and to use whatever means I see fit." He nodded to Frair Lucas, smiling narrowly. "Which is why the good frair here is taking me to

Heartsbridge. That I might be found innocent, and returned to my place as high inquisitor."

"That's not—" Lucas started, but Sacombre rolled over him.

"That is the difference between us, sir," the ragged man persisted. "What you call heresy is nothing more than reasonable faith. What you call murder is simply the burden given me by my god." Sacombre's frail calm began to crack, his face growing flustered with every word. Spit dangled from his lips as his voice grew louder, until he shouted the giant down. "Cinder is just as harsh to his servants as he is to his enemies, sir, and harsher still to those who defy him! I did what was necessary to protect the church from its enemies, and to bring the heresy of House Adair to light, that it might be purified."

Bourne bristled with anger.

"You vainglorious, self-righteous little prick! You start a false war, deceive Gabriel Halverdt, lead hundreds of men and women to their deaths, and you claim righteousness?" He was shaking, his knuckles white on the haft. The guards who surrounded Sacombre nervously closed ranks. "How am I to know this isn't another of your lies? That it isn't *your* sin that stains the walls of the Fen Gate? How is Colm Adair supposed to receive justice? How are his children... his wife?"

"They did not deserve justice," Sacombre spat. "They deserved to die like dogs, begging for their lives. As they did!"

Bourne roared his fury. The guards were ready, though, and closed on him like a steel noose. With the iron-tipped butt of his axe, Bourne shattered the shield of the first man to reach him, swung the haft into the next man's spear, splintering it, then scythed around him with the weapon's cruel head. The steel whistled through the air, dancing sparks off shields and forcing back the ring of soldiers. A pair of men stepped in front of Sacombre, but Bourne put his boot into their locked shields. They fell, clattering, to the stones.

"Treachery!" LaGaere howled. His promise of peace forgotten, the duke of Warhome drew his blade and rushed to the high inquisitor's defense. His knights charged with him, freeing swords and maces from their belts, spreading out into a loose circle around Sir Bourne. The big Tenerran grinned sharply.

"Do you defend the heretic, Warhome?" Bourne asked. "I will be glad to add your names to my belt, and your sigils to the banner of the dead."

"We came here under a flag of truce—"

"You came here under a flag of deceit!" Bourne spat. "Suhdrin deceit, and Suhdrin lies. You're anxious to find the guilt of Baron Adair, but if even a shade of sin colors the cheeks of your precious high inquisitor, you leap to his defense like a trained dog."

LaGaere didn't answer, but his knights closed the gap between their blades and Bourne's neck. The Tenerran knight set his feet and prepared to defend himself.

"Surrender, Sir Bourne, and your offense will be overlooked," Lucas said quickly. "There is no need for blood to be spilled over this."

"The inquisitor is too quick to forgive," LaGaere said. "I am not."

Bourne leapt then, axe high over his head, screaming his frustration. He shouldered past LaGaere, bowling the duke of Warhome aside as though he was a child, and charged at Tomas Sacombre. For a brief second Sacombre cracked, terror filling his face. The high inquisitor stumbled back, covering his head with arms, crumpling to the ground.

Bourne landed with a booming crash, his axe swung down toward Sacombre's skull.

Tendrils of shadow gripped the steel.

Frost traveled rapidly up the haft, reaching Bourne's fingers. The force of the attack pushed the axe just a little, just enough, to deflect it away from Sacombre's quivering form. The axe head bit into the stones of the courtyard, striking sparks and singing loudly.

When the courtyard was silent, the dark coils withdrew from Bourne's axe and slithered back to Frair Lucas. The inquisitor stood with his arms extended, the effort of his casting evident on his face. The ground around him was frozen solid, and cold fog swirled across his shoulders like wings.

"Enough of this," he said sternly. "Guards, put the high inquisitor back in his cage. Sir Bourne, you have had your interview. Open the gates."

Bourne slowly stood, hefting his axe and grimacing at Sacombre. The guards swirled around the high inquisitor, gathering him and ushering him back to the iron wagon, slamming the door. Duke LaGaere and Sir Horne came to stand beside Frair Lucas. Bourne spat, but nodded in the direction of the gate.

Machines groaned, and the portcullis slowly rose. The caravan started to move. Sir Bourne stood to the side to let them pass. Lucas joined him, along with Horne and LaGaere.

"I was with Gwen Adair, sir," Lucas said quietly. "She confessed to me, and to my companion. It is not a matter of wronged innocence, though too many have died in the prosecution of this heresy."

"I have trouble believing," Bourne rumbled. "Any of this."

"If it's any comfort, I believe that House Adair did what

they did to protect Tener, not to harm it. And I think we, the church, have much to learn from them. Or at least I hope so."

"They are dead, and their hope with them," Bourne answered. Then he turned and marched to a near door in the walls, disappearing from view.

"We should have cut him down," LaGaere hissed. "Trying to strike the high inquisitor like that. It's little wonder the north is choked with pagans and their demon gods."

"That would have gotten us filled with arrows," Lucas said.

"Why didn't they fire?" Horne wondered. She peered up at the rows of arrow slits that looked down on the courtyard. The shapes of archers could be seen beyond them, bows ready, quivers full. "When Bourne attacked, and it looked like we were going to overwhelm him. Why didn't they shoot, to protect their master?"

"Because they honestly believed their master could kill us all," Lucas said. "They didn't think it was necessary. They didn't think he needed protection."

"Idiots," LaGaere muttered, then he joined the caravan. He swung up onto his horse, falling in with the few able-bodied knights in their company.

At Lucas's side, Sir Horne sighed deeply. "He would have gotten us all killed," she said. "It's good that you're here to keep him on a leash."

"If someone's going to get us all killed," Lucas said. "I would rather it be me."

He signaled for his own mount, waiting until the last of the caravan wound its way through the Reaveholt before he took to the saddle and rode out. On the walls behind him, the massive shadow of Sir Bourne watched them leave.

11

THEY STIRRED FROM where they lay on the cold stone. The horses stood nearby, cropping from the grasses that grew in the forest's verge. Elsa's face was scored with a dozen slashes, and her armor and clothes were scratched. Fragments of wicker lay all around them.

"What happened?" she asked, pushing herself into a squatting position, staring down at her hands.

"A little brotherly feud," Ian said. "Night was trying to play the role of death, and big brother figured it out and came calling. He came to collect his due." He stood and went to gather their horses. "The whole realm fell apart. Old gods don't like to give up their territory."

"I don't even begin to understand that," Elsa said. "Death collecting his due? We weren't dead."

"No, we weren't, though we were on our way," Ian said. "There were others. Soldiers of House Thyber. Looks like they got trapped, just like us, and never found their way out." He brought the horses back to Elsa and started to gather the things that they had dropped during the night. His knife, his sword, the scattered remnants of Elsa's armor, cut away in preparation for a fight that never came. He talked while he worked. "I figured out what the old guy was doing. Tricked him into surrendering the bodies. I didn't think Eldoreath would like that. Just didn't think he would be so... violent in his response."

"Eldoreath?" Elsa asked. She finally stood and took her horse's reins. "Where did you get that name?"

"I don't... I'm not sure," Ian allowed. "Maybe the old guy said it. Maybe it's something I remember from the legends. I don't know."

"The names of the gheists, the old names... those were purged," Elsa said. "Not even the inquisition kept a record that I know of. Gods have names. Gods deserve worship, but gheists—unnamed, unknown, mad and feral... gheists we hunt."

"I thought we were hunting Gwendolyn Adair," Ian muttered. Elsa didn't answer, but she didn't disagree. She plucked a folded cloth from her armor and laid it on the ground. It was spotted with blood. Ian had seen her with it before, whenever their way was unsure or their pursuit close. He assumed it was some sort of token. After a few moments of frustrated prayer, the vow knight refolded the cloth and returned it to her armor, near her heart. Her face was slick with sweat, and she looked slightly nauseous.

"What is that?" he asked.

"A trick. One that is failing me," Elsa answered. "When Gwen was first in our company, Frair Lucas bound her blood. In case she tried to escape. I've been using it to find her trail."

"And she just happens to be going to the hallow?"

"She was, but the binding is failing, either because the hallow has hidden her, or perhaps she has died. Or something in between." Elsa pressed her hand against her breast, where the token was hidden. "No. She's not dead, but something has happened."

"Then we'd better hurry," Ian said. "The sort of questions I want to ask the huntress, the dead will not answer."

"Speed is out of the question," she said, rubbing her mount's flank. "We will have to walk the horses today, and pray that we are not pursued again. Not until we reach the hallow."

"Do we have far to go?" Ian asked.

"The trail isn't as clear as it was. Not as clear as it should be. We must be close, but last time I was here it was with the huntress. She had to lead us by the hand that last day, because of the wards. Now that the hallow has been unlocked and the Fen Gate overthrown, I hope those wards are banished."

"What if they're not?"

"Then you and I are going to spend some time wandering in circles," Elsa said. She finished loading her armor onto the horse. "First, we need to cross this river."

"The land descends to the north. You mentioned a river that bordered the hallow. Might this be it?" Ian asked.

"Perhaps. We won't know until we try to cross it."

"Because you'll recognize the land beyond?"

"Because the river will try to kill us," Elsa said. She took her horse's reins and turned north. "Come on. I'm not anxious to spend another night among those trees."

The river at the bottom of the ravine was, in fact, the Glimmerglen, but when they reached its banks, Ian and Elsa discovered that it had lost the strength it needed to kill. Though not the will to try. The currents shifted unnaturally around Elsa's boots, sucking at the metal and crawling up her leg in cold, murky coils, but she was able to cross. As they approached the far bank, Ian lagged behind.

"What are you waiting for?" Elsa asked.

"There's something in the trees."

Elsa turned to see that he was right. Deer, wicker thin and dressed in stone, grazed nervously at the forest's edge. Elsa drew her blade, but the creatures spooked and disappeared with hardly a sound.

"This place has changed," Elsa said. "There is less anger here."

"Gwen carries its rage now," Ian said. He took the horses by the reins and led them across the water. "Whatever may have become of her?"

"That's what we're here to discover, isn't it?" Elsa said. She kept her sword drawn, but lowered the tip to the ground. The blade was cracked, a lightning stroke of dark metal that ran along the runnel, thin forks notching the edge. "Let the horses graze here," she continued. "If it's safe enough for those creatures, it's safe enough for our mounts."

"It's getting close to night. Do we want to set up camp before we go wandering through the hallow? Gods know what we might meet."

"Whatever is waiting for us inside, it's no safer in light than it is in darkness," Elsa said. "We might as well get this over with."

"So anxious to die, Sir LaFey?"

Elsa merely snorted, then led the way into the hallow. The trees were larger than she remembered, their bark older and more gnarled. It was as if the witches' hallow had aged generations in the space of weeks, or perhaps its age had been artificially restrained in the presence of the Fen god, and had now caught up with its true antiquity.

A regal autumn had settled in, and seemed unwilling to fade away. The canopy was alive with the million jeweled colors of the season, and the air smelled like plowed earth.

"The leaves are strange," Ian noted. He reached up to a low branch and plucked at a stem, pulling it down. The leaves on it glittered translucently, like stained glass, their colors shifting and liquid. When he released the branch, it chimed with crystalline song.

"Everything is strange," Elsa said. "It's a strange place."

Ian smiled at his companion's manner. Their trip out of the Fen Gate had been awkward at first. They were here for different reasons, after all, reasons that might set them at odds. Ian wanted to find Gwen in order to learn more about her family's heresy, to find out if perhaps abandoning the old ways of Tener had been a mistake.

In his days with the witch Fianna, Ian had seen things he didn't understand, including a manifestation of his family's totem spirit. He hoped that Gwen would have the answers that he sought, even if they led to heresy.

Sir LaFey hunted Gwen in order to kill the god of death that the huntress had ensnared. Perhaps Elsa also hoped to deal with the autumn god the huntress freed from the witches' hallow. What she would do to Gwen, however, remained a mystery.

They moved deeper into the hallow. There was something wrong with the trees, he thought, even those crowned in all of autumn's glory. Veins of ash crept up their trunks, and several had fallen to the corruption, tumbling to the ground to melt into the loamy undergrowth. Elsa moved carefully, the damaged blade of her sword at the guard, Ian trailing behind.

"What was this place like?" he asked. "Before."

"I will never know," Elsa answered. "I came to the hallow in crisis. The wardens were already dead, and their bound servants were fighting off Frair Allaister and his cadre. Gwen seemed to indicate that we changed this place just by being there, Lucas and I. So what it was like before shall remain a mystery."

"And the huntress?"

"You knew her, didn't you?" Elsa asked. "She was about your age, and of noble Tenerran blood. Surely you met in your youth."

"Only in passing. She wasn't bound to the common path, even for a child of Tener," Ian said. "My sister found her a bit wild, and Nessie has never met a storm she didn't like. But I never knew she was a heretic."

"No. I suppose not. None of us did, though Frair Lucas suspected it." Elsa paused and glanced back at Ian. "Why these questions?"

"If your binding is right, she's already here. I'm just curious what sort of person we'll find."

"You saw her at the Fen Gate. What she was capable of doing," Elsa said, casting her gaze at the trees, the sky, the setting sun. "Gwen's no longer here. Or if she is, she is greatly changed. Greatly diminished."

Ian pointed down the trail. "Was that here, when last you visited?" Elsa's attention snapped to the forest ahead of them. There was a clearing, and beyond it a hill. The clearing was ringed in cairns, and bright flowers wafted slowly in the breeze.

"The wardens have been returned to their graves," Elsa whispered. "I thought the river washed this place away."

"Someone must have put it back together."

"Yes." Elsa crept forward. "But who?"

The clearing was alive with color. The ground was carpeted in flowers of every type and season, from lilies to sunflowers to spiny mums. The cairns that ringed the clearing, where the wardens of the hallow were buried, crawled with vines and moss, their stones swallowed whole by lush greenery. The air was light and warm. There was another monument at the center of the clearing, its stones wrapped in shadow.

"Yes," she said. "This has changed. The river spirit destroyed all of this when it killed Frair Allaister. Someone came and rebuilt these. I wonder if the bodies are still here, as well." Elsa tarried at the edge of the circle, pausing as she faced the center. "And that," she said, pointing to the shadowed form. "That was not here."

The monument was made of stone, though of a lighter hue than the cairns. A pillar rose from the ground, and against the pillar rested a sword. It was draped in braided leather cords, each hung with an icon of the pagan faith, representing dozens of different spirits and lesser gods. Elsa went to the pillar.

It was her sword.

She held up the mundane blade that she had brought from the Fen Gate, its steel pitted and scarred from channeling the vast power of Lady Strife, the leather wrapping of the hilt burned where Elsa's fingers had wrapped around it. With a shrug, she tossed the weapon aside. When it landed, the cracks that had formed in its blade flashed once, then shattered. The fragments of the sword bled ash, the steel turning black before crumbling into nothing.

Elsa drew the bloodwrought sword from the pillar. The corded icons clattered like sleet against the steel, slithering against her forearm as she raised the weapon in front of her. Elsa stared with wonder.

"We were expected," she whispered.

"Or hoped for," Ian said. "What are the icons?"

"Dead gods," Elsa answered. She flicked the blade, an expert motion that gathered the cords along the blade. The weight of the icons pulled the cords against the sharp edge. With a breath, Elsa flared the invocations that lined the blade, drawing Strife's power into the weapon, a gentle glow that bled from the runes that ran the weapon's length.

The cords broke, the icons clattered to the ground.

"Dead by my hand," she said. "Dead beneath this blade."

"Surprising the pagans didn't try to destroy it, if it's killed so many of their gheists," Ian said.

"Yes," Elsa answered, her voice quiet, almost reverent. "Surprising." A moment passed, and then she sheathed the blade. When she looked back at Ian, there was something different about her face. Something lighter, as though the weariness of the journey had been lifted from her bones.

She smiled. "Whatever we seek, it awaits us above," she said, pointing to the hill that rose from the clearing's edge. Ian went to stand beside her, gazing up at the summit. The hill was broken, and darkness poured out. The grass at the summit's peak was blasted into tar, and raw stones lined a massive crack in the earth.

"The place of young Gwen's birth, and perhaps her death," Elsa said. "Come on. Someone left this sword for a reason, and I mean to understand it."

The vow knight marched up the hill. Ian took one last look around the clearing, at its cairns and the wild, improbable flowers, like a nobleman's garden that had been dumped into the forest and forgotten.

As he started after Elsa, his foot dragged through the discarded icons that had ringed her blade. One clung to his boot, and he bent to remove it. The cord was still intact. He raised it to the dying light of the sun.

It was a hound, forged in iron, teeth bared, jaws slavering.

Ian looked from the icon to the retreating form of the vow knight. Then he tucked the hound into his belt and raced after her, his heart thudding in his chest.

12

THE PATH CURVED steadily upward. They were near the edge of the Fen, the limestone bluffs and swampy lowlands giving way to gentle foothills that rolled into the distance. From the ridgeline, they could see the far mountains of Hartsgard, Manson Dougal's holding now that his father was dead.

Gwen had no idea where they were, exactly. The girl who thought she had walked the whole Fen had never stood on these hills.

"This place is warded," she said. "It must be. Otherwise I would have been here in my hunting."

"Or perhaps you're not as thorough as you believe," Aedan answered. "We have tricks enough for the likes of you, without having to stoop to magic."

"Bullshit. Anyone else, maybe, but I was born to the Fen. My family's blood runs through the waters, our dead are buried in its stone. I know the Fen, and it knows me."

"Well," Aedan said, "perhaps not these stones, and perhaps not this water."

The ridgeline folded into a valley, the dirt trail they had been following slowly changing. Cut-stone steps led them down, the way marked with shrines of balanced rocks and tiny braziers of clay and marble. There were ribbons among the trees, mingling with autumn foliage and streaming in the breeze. Two sounds reached Gwen's ears. Bells hanging from the trees and singing the wind's song, and the distant thunder of a river.

Her pain had faded to the point that it was bearable. Each step reminded her, however, of the gheist that had been ripped from her body. It lurked constantly in the background. She fought through it.

The trail became crowded. Gwen could see a similar road on the other side of the valley, its stone surface full of people in various garb. Some wore the green and black of her company, the familiar gear of druids on the hunt, but others wore bright reds and startling yellows, jewelry of silver and stone that flashed in the sun. It looked like a plume of autumn leaves flowing along the mountain.

Both trails twined to the valley's head. Blue and silver glittered from between the trees, flashes of light that caught Gwen off guard. As she allowed herself to be swept along with the crowd, Aedan slipped away into the forest. Gwen looked around for Cahl, but there were no familiar faces close by. She thought briefly of making a run for it, stopping between the trees while the river of humanity continued on.

Still she continued, and all thought of escape fled when they reached the valley's head. Jagged stone framed the deep blue waters of a pool, and a waterfall cascaded down the cliff face and into the valley below. The waterfall traveled the height of the valley, a long, thin veil of sparkling white foam that stretched like cascading diamonds between the trees. Mist clung to the foot of the fall, and the grinding thunder of its descent carried up the valley walls.

A bridge crossed the river far below. The crowds were working their slow way down the trails, to stand briefly on the bridge before crossing to the other side. The tumult drowned out all other sound, but as they descended the valley, Gwen could see the druids pausing on the bridge to face the waterfall, sometimes with hands outstretched, other times with heads bowed. Several children dashed across, hands over their heads, while frustrated parents tried to hold them back.

The first, cold flecks of mist touched Gwen's face.

Then she saw the gheist. It nestled at the foot of the waterfall, the veil of mist and foam gathered around its mass like a cloak. Its body was the color of granite shot through with white marble, its mouth a massive cave of small teeth, each as bright and sharp as crystal. The god stirred sluggishly, its vast, empty eyes watching the bridge with disinterest.

Gwen stumbled to a halt. The crowd flowed around her. She took a nervous step backwards, then another. An iron hard hand closed around her arm.

"You have to go through," Cahl whispered into her ear. "Our paths are not your paths. We do not travel from place to place, but from god to god, and this is the god of our journey. So you must go through."

"I don't understand," Gwen said. "Roads go places. We're going to someplace." She pulled free from his grip. "What does this gheist have to do with us?"

"Why are you afraid?" Cahl said. "Gwendolyn Adair, proud heretic and twice-damned huntress of the very gods she's meant to worship, and you balk at the presence of a divinity in its place of worship?"

"How do you know it isn't mad?" She looked down at its gaping mouth, at the rings of teeth flexing slightly in the mist.

"You're putting children in front of it. What if it demands a sacrifice? Who here will keep it from taking what it wants?"

"You are brave only when there is a need for fear," Cahl said. "There is nothing here to fear. There is no danger in this place." He prodded her down the mountain. "Go. See the god… and be seen. Try to understand."

Gwen stared at the shaman for several long moments, then joined the crowd of pagans down the hill. They slowed as they approached the bridge. From this new position she was able to get a better look at the proceedings, and saw that some kind of priesthood attended the gheist. Several people in red and yellow stood at the foot of the bridge, speaking briefly with each person before they crossed.

Aedan, tall and stiff and deadly serious, crossed a short distance ahead of Gwen. He made his way to the center, bowed briefly to the god at the waterfall's base, then hurried to the other end of the bridge.

And then it was Gwen's turn. A priestess took Gwen by the shoulders, looking into her eyes and muttering something in a tongue Gwen had never heard. The woman was crying, though her eyes weren't red and she didn't seem unhappy. She was about to push Gwen onto the bridge when she paused and looked at her again.

"I was not expecting someone like you," she said quietly. Gwen wasn't even sure how she could hear the woman. The priestess pulled Gwen off the steps, holding tight to her shoulders as she looked her up and down. "Troubled whispers have floated in the mist for weeks, but this is not what I was expecting."

"Makes two of us," Gwen muttered.

"Are you prepared? Has your shaman instructed you?"

"I'm not..." Gwen grimaced and looked over her shoulder. Cahl was up the trail, staring at her back. When she turned to the priestess again she could see Aedan on the opposite bank, a hooked knife in hand. She sighed. "You don't know who I am?"

"Not at all, which is why I'm worried," the priestess answered. "A girl your age should have passed through this gate a half-dozen times, at least. And your clothes, your manner... you are Suhdrin born?"

"We are standing on my father's land!"

"Oh! Oh, I see now," the priestess said. She leaned forward quickly, gripping Gwen's face in both hands and tilting it like a bowl to the sky. She pressed her thumbs into Gwen's eyes, pressing and pressing until Gwen struggled to be free. "Tears, child. I need the salt of your blood," the priestess whispered. Just as quickly as she had struck, the priestess released Gwen, smearing the wet of the huntress's eyes down her cheeks. "There. That is all the blessing I can manage. Pass, and be known."

The priestess stepped aside, motioning to the bridge.

On the other side, Aedan grew very tense.

"Go on, child," Cahl shouted from behind her. "The river waits."

Gwen took a tentative step onto the bridge. A fresh blast of mist washed over her, wetting her clothes and hanging like dew on her lashes. The chill took her breath, filling her lungs with clean, damp air, dismissing what pain remained. Slowly she walked out to the center of the bridge, keeping her eyes down and her shoulders hunched. Finally, at the middle, on a worn bit of cobble, Gwen stopped, and turned, and faced the waiting god.

This close, the gheist was massive. The veins of silver and white turned out to be miniature rivers cutting through the flesh of the god's body, tumbling over shoulders and chest in waterfalls as delicate as lace. The stone of its skin was vaguely translucent, as though its body was made of hard-packed ice, old and gray with age. Deep veins of crystal blue pulsed beneath the surface. The gheist gave off an air of weight, of time, of inevitability. The wide bowl of its mouth, ring upon ring of flaked teeth as delicate as grass, huffed and flexed in the mist. Its eyes were open wounds in the rock, scarred and blackened.

Gwen took a deep lungful of the gheist's breath. It turned her blood to steel, her skin to stone. The smeared, cold-salt tears that ran down her cheeks burned like hot lead. The gheist, disinterested and sluggish, took notice of her blood. It flexed forward ever so slightly. Its body broke through the waterfall's veil, spray arcing over the stone, dashing rainbow light through the valley.

"Lost child," its breath said to her breath. "Wandering child. Wounded. Bright." The mist hung in the air, frozen in space, dancing slowly over the river. "Coming home. Walking home, alone. Welcome."

"I'm not alone," Gwen stuttered through the chill. "I'm not..." And then she thought of her father, her mother, the soft face of her brother, broken and battered and dead. Then she was crying, on her knees, breaking inside. "...alone."

"Peace between us, child," the god's breath said. "Peace and..."

Something twisted inside Gwen's chest. Hot blood filled her mouth, the taste of iron and the summer sun. She felt the attention of another divinity, stretching out across the horizon, touching the sun and then arcing down to earth, to rest in the steel gauntleted hand of a woman.

"Elsa?" Gwen whispered. The pain returned to grip her. Pain and bright light. Her eyes flashed the heat of the sun, boiling away her tears and flaring spears of molten light that burned off the mist. A cry went up from the gathered crowds. Aedan's voice rose above the crowd.

"Child of Strife!" he yelled.

The gheist roared and surged forward, gathering the mist like a cloak and throwing it, blasting her with a wave of cold water. The fire in her eyes snuffed out, and the pain with it. Gwen stood, stumbling back, holding out her hands. The sound of the god's movement was like a mountain being torn out at the root.

The valley shuddered, and a chorus of screams drifted down from the paths. The cascade of water threw a wall of wind in front of it, whipping trees and knocking the pagan faithful from their feet. Those closest to the river scampered away, trying to escape the tumult, but the shaking ground kept them down.

The path began to crumble.

"Child of summer! Exile! Corruption!" the gheist howled, its voice echoing down the valley, ringing off the stone bluffs and quivering the trees like a squall line. Its mouth peeled open even wider, eclipsing the bridge, which collapsed like a puzzle, and was carried downstream by a wall of water. The current lapped up onto the shore, picking up those along the bank and smashing them into the bluffs. Gwen had only a moment to witness this before the wave reached her.

She slipped from the broken bridge, was picked up and thrown like a leaf. Gwen screamed and the river's water filled her mouth. It dragged her down, the broken stones falling and battering her flesh, bruising her, spinning her around like a top. She felt the gheist's crystal-sharp teeth against her skin. They ground her down, pushing her to the river's bed, pressing the air from her lungs, squeezing the sense from her head. Numbness leaked into her hands, her arms, her feet, stealing into her chest like a poison.

Her family waited for her in the darkness. Her family and the silent dead.

Cahl's face was horizon wide and as bright as the sun. The constellation of Aedan's scowl hung over his shoulder. Gwen shifted against a bed of river stones and sighed.

"I am tired of this," she said. Her voice was sticky with mucus, her throat wet and thick and tired. "Nearly dying at the hands of your tame gods, then waking up to your foul visage." She tried to stir, and the fire in her blood blossomed through her flesh. She gasped, then forced herself into a sitting position. "Waking up in pain. This is a load of shit."

"What happened?" Cahl asked.

"I don't know. Ask the waterfall," Gwen answered. She turned to look at Aedan. "Did you do that? Order it to kill me or something?"

"The god does not answer to my call," the dark-faced shaman answered. "Something shifted in your blood. Something divine."

"She has worn a god," Cahl said. "It is no surprise that her soul is unsettled."

"No," Aedan hissed. "This was another. A binding of the blood priests. Do you doubt her heresy now?"

"What does he mean, a binding?" Gwen asked.

"As it was with Fomharra and your spirit, so can it be between your spirit and something else," Cahl said. He settled back on his haunches, looking at her thoughtfully. "It's the way the vow knights of Strife bind themselves to their blades, and sometimes their armor. It is a very old rite, from before the church's arrival in Tenumbra."

"She knows what it is, Cahl," Aedan said. "She has bound herself to them. Probably before she led those priests to the hallow, as a bargain for her life." The shaman leaned down into her face. His breath smelled like loam and rotting leaf. "What was the deal, huntress? Did you swear allegiance to their calendar, with the promise of leading them to our hidden places with your blood?"

"Yes, of course," Gwen said, grimacing through the pain. "It was my plan to kill half the Suhdrin army, uncover the high inquisitor as a heretic, and then get dragged through the forest by a crowd of unwashed farmers."

"Do not joke at treachery, child," Cahl muttered. "They will quarter you for mirth just as quickly."

"I am *not* in league with the church," Gwen said. "I am not loyal to Heartsbridge, nor bound to…" She paused, struck by a thought. "By blood. They did."

"They did what?" Cahl asked.

"They took my blood. Frair Lucas, when he and Elsa freed me from Frair Allaister on our way to the witches' hallow. I had forgotten, because… well. Because so much else was happening."

"By her word," Aedan said. "She is bound to them!"

"Yet not by her will," Cahl answered. "That is hardly grounds for conviction."

"Something must be done about it," the other shaman

said. "We cannot lead them to the conclave, simply because you are soft on the girl." He gestured to the river that murmured peacefully nearby. The roar was distant. "This place has already been corrupted. The waterfall will have to be sanctified, assuming this vow knight doesn't come and slay the god before then. We can't afford to risk any more holy sites—not until her blood is pure!"

"The binding of Fomharra would have disrupted the blood magic," Cahl said. "It is possible she has shaken free of their hounds."

"They are still scrying her! You saw what happened. I sensed the binding, if not its source." Aedan stood, and suddenly a wicked knife, bright and barbed, filled his hands. "You have lost Fianna. You have lost the child of hounds, and stood witness to the discovery of Fomharra and the hallow by the celestials. I will not stand by and let you surrender this opportunity, as well."

"And I will not stand by and let you murder this girl, not while she might still be of use to us." Cahl remained squatting, and though he didn't draw steel or shift his stance, there was a violent tension in his shoulders. "That is all there is, Aedan. Put away your foolishness."

"I will not..."

"You will," Cahl said calmly. "The girl is going with us to the conclave."

Aedan stood there, bristling and angry. Finally he leaned down and drew his blade silently across Gwen's shoulder. The skin parted and blood cascaded down her flesh like a waterfall. Cahl shifted slightly, ready to strike, but Aedan stood up and backed away. He held the blade in front of him.

"They are following her blood. I will lead them to it," he said.

As Gwen watched, the crimson lace of her blood squirmed against the knife's edge. Like rain soaking into dry earth, the blood sank into the runnel, tinting the steel. The blade took on a rusty tint, darker along the edge that had cut into Gwen.

"Very well," Cahl said, "but the conclave will not wait for your arrival."

"My voice will be heard," Aedan promised. He glanced down at Gwen with a sneer, then slid the blade into his belt. "Once I am done cleaning up this child's folly."

13

THE CASTLE WAS in an uproar. The aftermath of the inquisitor's shriving filled the corridors with unholy smoke, and the stones of the Fen Gate shook underfoot.

Malcolm ran past a window on his way to the ruined chambers of the tower. A storm brewed beyond the shutters, a gray sky looming oppressively overhead. Horns shouted from the Suhdrin encampment, and panic was in the air.

"We need faithful hearts," Malcolm snapped. "Men and women we can trust with our souls, if not our lives."

"Any sworn to the hound will be faithful to you, my lord," Sir Doone answered. "Even to death."

"I need more than that," Malcolm said. "They must be willing to lie to an inquisitor, and the weight of that extends beyond the grave." They turned a corner, dropping into a brisk walk until they were sure the way was clear and returned to a run. "Gods help me, I never thought I would ask that of my people."

"These are strange times," Doone said. At the next corridor she turned left while Malcolm continued ahead to his wife's hidden chamber. The guard on duty was dressed as a drunken soldier, napping in the crook of a broken pillar. The man dropped his act when Malcolm came into view.

"Sir Doone will arrive shortly," Malcolm said. "Go to your quarters and pack a bag. Enough for three weeks in the woods, and no less."

"My lord, I'm to stay here to guard..."

"Go!" Malcolm snapped. The man stumbled away, the stink of whiskey thick in his wake, and Malcolm wondered how much of his disguise was an act after all. Once he was alone in the corridor, he slipped inside.

His wife was as he had left her, the strange light lurking beneath her skin and the submerged grace of her hair twisting slowly in the dimly lit chamber. Malcolm went down on one knee and took her cold, dead hand.

"It is time, my love," he said. Sorcha's eyes slowly turned to him, unfocused and wet. "We must go."

"To my son?"

"No, north, to Houndhallow. It is no longer safe here. The inquisitor has sensed your presence. The time has come to flee."

"Home," she said, then turned back to the empty wall. "I haven't the strength."

"Well, we haven't got a choice," Malcolm said. He stood and went to her trunk, which lay half-open in the corner of the room. He started taking out cloaks, robes, and a brace of knives. "You must dress warmly. The woods will be cold this time of year, especially at night. I won't save you from war, wounds, and the inquisition just to lose you to fever."

"I do not feel it," Sorcha whispered. "The wind, or the winter."

Malcolm stood uncomfortably in the silence left by the lady's voice, her willow-thin words drifting between the stones like a dream barely forgotten.

"Be that as it may," he said finally, "I will have Sir Doone pack extra blankets, and enough wood to blaze a trail from here to Farwatch."

A knock hammered the door. Malcolm froze, then drew his feyiron blade and stood beside the door.

"Who is it?" he whispered.

"It is the MaeHerron boy," Sorcha said. "Don't be so silly."

Malcolm pulled the door open before MaeHerron answered. Grant stood in the doorway, axe in hand, mouth opened. His eyes flickered between Malcolm and Sorcha.

"Houndhallow," he said finally. "I saw Sir Doone running about like a scalded cat. I figured to find you here."

"How did you know about this place?" Malcolm asked.

"Your wife's condition is a poorly kept secret," MaeHerron answered. He stepped into the room, his eyes locked on Sorcha's strange form. "What do you intend to do?"

"Sneak her out. I won't let her fall into the inquisition's hands, not while the Orphanshield has his blood up." Malcolm ducked into the hall to see that the coast was clear, then shut the door and pulled young MaeHerron close. "Once this trouble with Colm Adair has blown over, I will go to someone I trust. The high elector, or maybe Frair Lucas. Until then, we must keep this secret."

"It doesn't look good," MaeHerron said nervously. "You understand that? Keeping secrets from the inquisition, especially now."

"Yes, yes, I know, but sometimes what is best is not necessarily what is most truthful," Malcolm said. "I won't lose my wife. Not after what she did for me. I can't just surrender her to Heartsbridge. Surely you understand that?"

MaeHerron looked nervously from Sorcha to Malcolm

and back. "What will you do?" he whispered.

"Take her back to Houndhallow. Go over the wall, so honest men don't have to lie, and dishonest men won't take advantage. Plus it lets us avoid the Suhdrin camp." Malcolm returned to packing his wife's clothes, shoving everything into a satchel and throwing it over his shoulder. "I'm sending a few men, along with Sir Doone. Not enough for their absence to be noticed."

The room was silent for several minutes while Malcolm worked.

Finally, MaeHerron broke the silence.

"What can I do?" he asked.

"I won't ask anything of you, Grant. With your father dead, you're now lord of the Feltower, and beholden to Cinderfell." Malcolm stood in front of the man, his eyes dire. "All I ask is your silence, and your faith. I'm doing the right thing, for Tener, for the church, and for my wife."

"For the church?"

"I won't let them take my wife. And if they come for her..."

"You'll fight," MaeHerron finished, "and all Tener with you. I understand."

"Good. Now..."

There was another knock at the door, this one quieter. "For a secret chamber, we receive a lot of visitors," Sorcha said wistfully.

"Who is it?" Malcolm demanded.

"It's Doone," came the answer. Malcolm opened the door. Sir Doone stood outside, alone.

"The men?" Malcolm asked.

"Waiting by the wall," she said. She was carrying two

heavy trail bags, and enough spears to hunt a forest of deer. "Only eight. They were the only ones Baird would trust to lie to an inquisitor, if it comes to that. Some of them already were guarding this chamber, so we shouldn't stick around here for long."

"There were at least a dozen guarding this chamber at various times," Malcolm said, his brow wrinkling in a frown. "Were they not all trustworthy?"

"Not all of them knew what they were guarding," Doone explained. "Sir Baird thought it best to limit this escort to those who will not balk at your wife's appearance." Doone glanced briefly at Sorcha before she blushed. Then she saw Grant MaeHerron, and froze.

"What is he doing here?"

"It's alright," Malcolm said. "He has sworn his silence."

"My silence, aye, but I would rather not be seen in her ladyship's company," MaeHerron said. "So if you'll excuse me..." The big man shouldered his way past and retreated down the hall. Doone watched him leave.

"Who will he tell?" she mused.

"Let's not wait around to find out," Malcolm said. "Take these things to the wall. I will meet you there."

"Shouldn't we travel together?" Doone asked.

"MaeHerron came here because he saw you running around like a maniac. We can't risk going together. Make your way quickly to the wall. Be seen, and let them see you alone. If anyone asks, you are preparing supplies for a hunting expedition. I will take another route, past the ruins."

"The inquisitor is making his way through the keep, my lord. It's only a matter of time before he finds this place. If you were to go to him, you might be able to delay..."

"I have failed my wife once already," Malcolm said sternly. "I will stay at her side until she is out of danger."

"Which of us is in danger, really?" Sorcha whispered. Her voice carried through the air like an arrow's flight, narrow and sharp. "Who will need to be protected, in the end?"

"All of us, if we don't get moving," Malcolm said. "Doone, I will meet you on the wall."

Sir Doone nodded and disappeared into the corridor. Malcolm took his wife by the hand and led her out. As her arm slipped free of the cloak, the light in the room grew brighter. Her fey blood glittered like streams of quicksilver beneath her skin. Sorcha noticed her husband's look, and smiled.

"Do I disconcert you, husband?" she asked brightly. "Is my manner no longer pleasing to you?"

"You will always please me, love. It is the displeasure of the church I fear."

"What of it?" Sorcha asked. "Why should we fear them?"

"There's reason enough, I promise," Malcolm answered. He took the edge of Sorcha's cloak and tucked it over her arm, then pulled the garment's hood tight over her face. The unworldly light diminished to a bare glimmer. "There now. Let's be on our way."

With the guards now gathered at the wall to accompany his wife on her flight, the corridors were eerily quiet. In the dim light of the corridor, her glow was indistinguishable from the flickering illumination of the torches. Malcolm led Sorcha through the ruined hallways of the Fen Gate, careful to avoid wandering patrols.

"Who would have thought to find Malcolm Blakley sneaking through the halls of a broken castle, hiding from the inquisition?" Sorcha said.

"This is temporary, my love," he replied, his voice low. "The church has its own problems to sort through right now, and until this business with Sacombre and Adair is settled, I will not risk handing you over to an inquisition eager to spill Tenerran blood—no matter that we have been faithful. In time, in a few months, or a year, I will approach the high elector about your condition. Or the celestriarch."

Malcolm paused at the end of a long hallway. The courtyard beyond was empty, but voices could be heard somewhere further along. He lowered his voice as he peered around, trying to judge if the way was clear.

"Someone we can trust. Someone I can trust."

They crept across the courtyard. The ruined husk of the keep was visible, its shattered top dark against the lightening sky. Sorcha paused to stare at it. Malcolm dragged at her arm.

"We have no time, love. The priests are searching the castle."

"They are closer than that," she answered.

"Closer? What do you..."

A woman dressed in white and gold entered the courtyard, her head turned up to the broken tower. She was small, perhaps even a child still, though she wore the robes of a sworn priest of Strife. The gold circlet of her order glimmered at her forehead, even though there wasn't enough light in the courtyard to reflect. The priest carried a bundle of books over one shoulder, and was humming tunelessly to herself.

She reached the center of the tiny courtyard before she noticed Malcolm and Sorcha. When she saw them she stopped, smiled, and swung the books around to set them at her feet.

"Do you know the way to that tower?" she asked, nodding at the ruin that loomed above them. "I thought it was this way, but all I've found are empty halls. Last time I was here there was a path through the doma, but obviously the doma is destroyed, so I... oh."

She was a child, Malcolm realized. A talkative child with bright eyes and too many damned questions, and she was staring at Sorcha and her strange, glowing skin. Malcolm remembered seeing her in Frair Gilliam's company. Catrin, that was her name. His hand was already on his sword.

"You have come the wrong way," he said sharply.

"I'm sorry, I didn't..." Catrin took a step back, tugging on the heavy leather strap of her bundle of books. "Frair Gilliam is all in a tangle about these gheists, and when he gets like that he doesn't want me around at all, so he sent me back to the stables. But I just wanted to see what remained of Grieg's rooms." She looked from Sorcha to Malcolm, and back. "We were friends, you know. He used to come down to my father's doma on the high days, whenever his family came to Heartsbridge."

"You knew the Adairs?"

"Yes, of course. I mean, I was as surprised as anyone to learn of their heresy. I still can't believe it." She bent and pulled a book from her stack. "This was Grieg's. A book of rhymes. I was going to give it back to him. Now, I guess..." She shrugged. "I guess it will have to go with the rest of his things. To be buried or burned, as the inquisitor decides."

Malcolm grimaced and slid his sword back into its scabbard.

"How old are you? Young for a priest, I think."

"Fourteen. Oh, you're the Duke of Houndhallow!" Catrin said with a start. "Beg pardon, my lord. I didn't recognize you. And duchess." She bowed to the pair of them, though her eyes lingered over Sorcha. Malcolm stepped between them.

"Go back the way you came. The keep is closed for now, though I'm sure an escort can be arranged. Find a bed. I'm sure you're exhausted."

"Yes, my lord," the girl said, bowing again. She hoisted her bundle, tucking away the small book of rhymes, then returned the way she had come. Malcolm waited until the sound of her footsteps was nothing more than an echo. Then he took his wife's hand and continued to the wall.

Sir Doone was waiting, along with the promised men. A block and tackle hung over the wall, with a basket suspended from it, dangling precariously in the void. Doone looked nervous. The morning sun was just peeking over the trees.

"Did you lose your way?" she asked as Malcolm and Sorcha emerged from the stairwell.

"Near enough," Malcolm said. He glanced at the assembled men, and recognized them all, good men from good families. He wondered what the inquisition would do to those families if they found out about this little expedition. Malcolm shook the thought from his mind. Sir Doone fussed with Sorcha's cloak, binding it tighter around her to keep it from getting tangled in the ropes. "Where are the supplies?"

"Already down. The near patrol has just passed, and will be back again in ten minutes. We have to get her ladyship away before then," Sir Doone said.

"My husband almost killed a child," Sorcha said with a smile.

The gathered men, who had been busying themselves with the pulley, froze. Malcolm shook his head.

"A priestess. One of the children this damned inquisitor brought with him." Malcolm twisted his hand over the hilt of his sword and grimaced. "The moment passed."

"Gods be blessed," Sir Doone muttered. She finished with Sorcha's cloak and led her to the basket. "Down you go, my lady. There are men waiting for you below."

"A moment," Malcolm said. He went to Sorcha's side and bent so that he was staring into those clear, watery eyes. "I will come to you, my love. Soon. I will not abandon you to the night."

"As you abandoned our son?" she asked, and then she folded herself into the basket. Malcolm hesitated on the wall's edge, shook his head, and gave his men the signal to let her down.

The basket descended slowly to the ground. Malcolm waited until the faint glow from his wife's unnatural spirit disappeared among the shadows of the trees before he turned back to Sir Doone.

"You will stay with her?"

"Yes, my lord. Until you are able to meet us and escort us north."

"Very good. I will send word when I can. Get the rest of these men over the wall as quickly as possible." He walked briskly to the stairs. "I must intercept Frair Gilliam, and pray the child has said nothing of my wife."

"And if she has?" Sir Doone asked. The creaking sound of the pulley echoed in the background, mingling with the songbirds of the early morning.

"Then she will have to be dealt with," Malcolm said. "One way or another."

14

FIANNA KNELT WITH her forehead pressed against the wall of her cell, listening to the soft jangle of chain as the high inquisitor shifted in his sleep on the other side of the wagon. She was praying. But in her heart, she was waiting for him to wake up and resume his questions. He had been asleep ever since his short interview at the Reaveholt, several days earlier.

Voices reached her from outside the cell. Her side of the wagon had no window, the only opening the narrow slot through which her captors shoved food. Very little light came through that. Being cut off from the sky was painful to her, a very real searing that leaked from her bones and into her blood. She could feel the rivers as they passed, the water calling out to her. There were rivers in Heartsbridge, she knew, but Fianna didn't think they would be as accepting of her prayers.

The wagon started forward with a jerk. The wheels creaked beneath Fianna's knees. A chorus of panicked voices started up, and a distinct sound reached her ears, of knights riding fast in heavy plate. In the other cell of the wagon the high inquisitor startled awake with a grunt.

"A short night," he muttered. Sacombre's voice had gotten rough in their weeks on the road, its soft purr replaced by a groan that stretched into his bones. Fianna turned, resting her back against the wall, and fixed her eyes on the priest's shadow.

"Something's wrong," she said.

"Fundamentally," Sacombre agreed. "Chains do not suit me. And the food is desperately lacking."

"Can you see anything out the window?"

"It is late. I can see the approaching nightfall," Sacombre said. He was still lying down, his scrawny head buried in the straw of his bed. Fianna didn't get a bed, or straw, or even a rag to clean herself. She gritted her teeth.

"I thought the trouble was past us," she said. "You said that once we were clear of the Reaveholt, it would be smooth travel."

"And so I thought," Sacombre said. "Perhaps Frair Lucas is simply eager to get me home to Heartsbridge. Very anxious to see my guts spilled. Silly, when he could just do it himself, and save all of us the trouble."

"He means to put you in front of a judge."

"Every priest of Cinder is a judge… and tribune and justice. I could read my own sentence, if the fool would just let me." The high inquisitor eased his way into a sitting position, rubbing his eyes with the hem of his robes. He still wore the formal vestments of his position, though Lucas had torn the iron seals from the hem, and stolen his icons of office. "Shall I judge you as well, witch? Are you ready to confess your heresy, and accept the true shadow of Cinder?"

"Stop being a mule and look outside, will you? Something's going on."

Sacombre sighed, then slowly stood and went to the tiny slot of his window. The wagon was traveling at a steady pace, so he had to brace himself against the wall as they swayed back and forth.

"Roads and trees and darkness," he said. "Nothing to unsettle my sleep. But there's my old friend, Lucas. Frair!"

Hoofbeats hammered closer, and a face appeared in the window. Even Fianna could see the worry in the old man's eyes.

"What do you want, Sacombre?"

"I have not had my sleep for the evening, and yet we travel. Are you trying to kill our horses?" Sacombre asked. "What's the rush?"

"Have you lost the gift of dreams, Tomas? Can you not feel them? There's a Suhdrin army to our south, marching toward Greenhall." Lucas pulled closer to the wagon. "I would rather reach those gates before them, if I can."

"Do you think Greenhall will welcome us?" Sacombre asked. "I did kill her father, after all."

"Her father, whose body we carry with us. I have sworn to return the duke to his hall," Lucas said. "Hopefully that will buy us some shelter. I can only hope they don't try to lynch you while we're here."

"This is how your people thank you, Sacombre," Fianna said. "You would have found a better reception if we had ridden north."

"It doesn't matter which direction we go," Sacombre said over his shoulder, then fixed Lucas again with his gaze, leaning closer to the window. "Cinder's justice will find us. I have faith in his shadow."

Lucas grimaced. "We will speak more of this, Sacombre," he said, then he disappeared. The horn sounded again, distant and shrill. Sacombre laughed and slid down the wall to sit cross-legged with his back against the bars.

"What did your words mean?" Fianna asked. "He didn't like them at all."

"Oh, nothing," he replied. "There are always shadows, witch. Wherever there is light, there is darkness. There's no running from it, just as there is no running from the night. Cinder's justice will find us both, Fianna."

She stood, passed her hand between the bars, and circled her fingers around Sacombre's neck. The high inquisitor's pulse beat beneath her fingertips. The old man raised his head, actually leaning *into* her grip. What would it take to strangle him? Would he fight? Would she?

"We have a deal," Fianna said. "You promised me a war." She released his throat.

"I promised you nothing," he said. "I only showed you a path, the landmarks that might get us to that path, and a destination. A *possible* destination."

"War between Tener and Suhdra, with the church leading the charge," she said. "Enough that the northern lords would throw off the shackle of Heartsbridge and return to the pagan ways. Those were your words—and Adair's heresy should have given you that. So where is my war?"

"Where is your faith?" Sacombre sneered. Fianna leapt at him, clanging into the iron bars. The high inquisitor backed away.

"Not with the likes of you!" she yelled. "I should never have trusted you. I should never have told you of Adair's secret, nor showed your pet pagan how to bind the gods to your flesh. Allaister was a poor servant."

"Well, trust me you did—and while Allaister had his faults, he had his strengths, as well. Sufficient to flush the harvester from his grave. I thank you for entrusting us with those secrets, but the time for secrets has passed." Sacombre sat again on his bed, his eyes dark pits, smoldering in the shadows. "When we are to Heartsbridge, you will tell your story. They will put you in the witness's box, and they will compel the truth from you."

"And what will that gain you, other than a quick execution?" Fianna asked. Her palms were bleeding from the rough iron of the cage, but she clenched her fists, digging fingernails into the wounds. Pain would make her strong. Pain would see her through this trial. "They will learn fully of your heresy, idiot."

"They will, if they ask the right questions," he acknowledged, "but if they ask *other* questions, they will learn something else." Sacombre lay back on the straw. "The court of Heartsbridge will hear one name from you, over and over. One name, and the efforts you made to corrupt him."

"My hound," Fianna muttered.

"Yes. Ian Blakley, son of the hero Malcolm, run off to find Gwendolyn Adair. And then we will see who they call heretic, and who they call prophet. So you see." Sacombre sighed deeply, settling deeper into the bed. "It all depends on which questions they ask first. And I know the men asking the questions.

"Good night, witch. Sleep well."

Fianna pushed back from the bars, curling up on the filthy floor of the wagon. The wheel creaked beneath her. There was a river in the distance, but it was silent, jealous of its secrets, wary of the pagan heart.

15

THE HILL THAT led to the earth's wound was slick with black blood. The grass that lay matted against it was brittle and gray. Even the stones that lay like scattered dice, thrown there as if by an explosion, seemed somehow fragile in their bulk. The sky above whipped past, turning dark. The first stars appeared on the horizon, opposite Strife's descending glory.

"This is not the place we left," Elsa said quietly. "It is changed."

"Whatever power was held here, surely it influenced the hallow greatly. Its departure—" Ian started. Elsa cut him off with a rapid shake of her head.

"No," she said sharply. "There was much strange about this place before Gwen broke the gheist free of its bonds, but if anything, that departure should have returned the hallow to its natural state. It should have returned it to the Fen."

"The Fen is a foul place," Ian said. He kicked a stone and watched it crumble into pebbles. "But it is not like this."

"So something has happened—something more than I was expecting." Elsa adjusted her grip on the sword and crept forward. "Stay on your guard."

"Right. My guard," Ian muttered. "Against some

unspoken danger, of which I have neither knowledge or hope."

"You have hope in me," Elsa responded with a smile. "Just stay close, and yell if you see something horrific."

"How horrific, exactly? Because we're walking through a field of dark blood and ash, and I think..."

"Shut up," Elsa said casually. Ian nodded and followed the vow knight as closely as propriety would allow.

They found a pit at the top of the hill, its edges dark with the vile blood, and smoke rose in gentle curls from the stones that remained. The cloud that hung overhead was alive with swirling forms, claws and teeth and twisted faces that leered in the day's dying light. The hair on Ian's neck stood on end, and a gentle hum started up in the bloodwrought tip of his hunting spear.

"It was less... evil... when you were here?" he asked demurely.

"The autumn god that waited here was the harbinger of winter, the first servant of the god of death." Elsa paused, staring up at the scything pillar of greenish smoke that hung above the chasm. "But it wore brighter clothes," she said. "It was a different kind of horror."

"I think I would prefer its cheer," Ian answered.

"At least this spirit is honest," Elsa said. "Though I don't think it's a gheist at all. Merely the scent of one, burned into the air until the everam itself holds the stink of it."

"Not a gheist?" he said hopefully. "So there's nothing to fear?"

"There's always something to fear," Elsa said cautiously. She edged her way to the lip of the chasm, looking down cautiously. "Falling into that, for example."

Ian moved to her side and looked down. The bottom of

the pit was swallowed in darkness.

"Is it deep?" he asked.

To answer, Elsa drew a tinder from her belt and ran it like a whetstone down the length of her blade. The runes of the holy weapon sparked, drawing fire from the air and setting the tinder ablaze. The vow knight tossed the burning brand into the pit. It disappeared into an unnatural darkness, a void that knew no depth.

"Ah," Ian said, backing away.

"Gwen was here. She must have returned after the battle."

"With the death god in tow," Ian said. "But why?"

"Perhaps to seek the help of the wardens, though they were dead," she replied. "Or in the hope that the sanctified ground might have some effect on the gheist. Or maybe she intended to release the god as far from hearth and home as she could manage, that the wards might protect it from the church's interference." Elsa peered around at the ruin of the hill and the close-pressed nightmare of the cloud. "Whatever she meant to do, it seems as if she failed."

"So she's dead?" Ian asked.

"No, I can still feel her bond, though it is weak. Something is shielding her from me. I can…" Elsa paused, closing her eyes and moving her lips in silent prayer. The cloud swirled away from her, like fog scattered by a stiff wind. She breathed in deeply, held it, and then opened her eyes. "No, there's nothing. She lives, but that's all I can say."

"Perhaps if we return to the Fen Gate and summon an inquisitor, he would have better luck at tracking the girl."

"I will not bring the inquisition into this," Elsa said sharply. She turned and marched down the hill, leaving Ian alone with the angry sky. "The faithful of Cinder have done their part, Sacombre more than most. I will finish the doom that they have written."

He hurried after her. "Why do you care?" he asked. "Frair Lucas rides even now to Heartsbridge to deliver the high inquisitor to trial. Sacombre is in chains. Cinder's judgment will be rendered."

"Their judgment means little—and besides, what judgment is there to be found in the cold court of winter? They will gather in stone rooms, and make speeches. Frair Lucas is a good man, a better servant of the gray lord than any I've known, but that is the problem. He alone do I trust, and he will not be alone in Heartsbridge."

"Then why didn't you go with him?" Ian asked. "To make sure judgment was rendered? He may need you." They were at the bottom of the hill already, Elsa tromping through the wild garden at its foot. The sun had set, and the darkness between the trees already was impenetrable.

"There is no place for my kind in that ritual," Elsa said, her words clipped close together. Ian was surprised to find this depth of anger in the vow knight. Her temper always had been quick to rise, but it was just as quick to disappear—as sharp and brief as lightning on the horizon. This was different. Deeper.

"The judgment of Cinder was born to twist, to find fault where there is only folly, and innocence where there is guile," she continued. "The fate of the high inquisitor should be clear enough. Any blade could have dealt it."

"Then why didn't you?"

The vow knight came to an abrupt stop near the pillar that had held her sword. Her armor flickered with a ghostly flame that sprang from the metal. Ian stomped to a halt, nearly running into her.

He was unable to prevent himself from probing further. "You were there. Sacombre was in no condition to fight. You could have ended it right there. Any of us could have."

"Any of us," Elsa said without turning. Her voice was raw. "So why didn't *you*?"

Before Ian could answer, however, the vow knight stormed away, disappearing among the trees, her light like a brand quenched in water.

"Well, enough of that line of questioning." Ian looked around the strange garden. "I'll have to find a place to sleep. Somewhere else." Light danced among the petals. The flowers swayed quietly to an unheard song, brushing up against his legs like plump cats. "Somewhere else." Cautiously moving out of the garden again, Ian settled into the crook of the most normal looking tree he could find, resting his head against dry leaves and listening to the buzz of insects and the splashing current of the river.

He woke screaming several times. Of Sir Elsa he saw no sign. Not even among his nightmares.

When he woke, the vow knight was standing over him, blade drawn. He blinked the sleep from his eyes. His back was killing him.

"Sir LaFey," he muttered, though his throat was choked with the grit of dry leaves. "I have—"

"Why didn't you?" she asked. "End it?"

"I don't think—"

"Why didn't you put your blade into him, Ian Blakley? Hero of the Allfire gheist at Greenhall, brave son of the Reaverbane, champion at the gate, future lord of Houndhallow. What stayed your hand?" Elsa loomed closer, the tip of her sword hovering at Ian's throat. "Your father I understand. He fears the wrath of Heartsbridge, simpers for the approval of men who hate him for his blood and his ink. But not you. You don't seem the simpering type. So. Why?"

Ian stared up. Her eyes were rimmed in red, her cheeks scalded in trails that ran down her neck, blood lining her teeth. The air smelled like burning metal.

"Because it was not my place to judge him," he said eventually. "Nor could any other. We must leave it to the church."

"Because you've committed your share of heresy—is that it?" Elsa said. "Because for all that you bend your knee in the doma, you know the call of older gods. You won't be able to put the blade to Gwen Adair, for the same reason. Do you even think her guilty, Blakley? Does her sacrilege mean anything to you?"

"Do you think her guilty?" Ian asked. "If I have my story straight, you were here with her. You were in the chamber when she summoned the gheist, and did nothing to prevent it. You could have—"

"That is not the matter at hand!" Elsa shouted. Her voice rattled the leaves above, and the earth below. "Why did you follow me here? What mission has brought you to the witches' hallow, Ian Blakley? Ian of the tribe of hounds! I know of the hallow that rests beneath your castle walls, the iron hound, its head black with soot from blood sacrifice! Does a witch attend it, as well? Do you seek to return the house of Adair to its rightful place among the tribes? What treachery can I expect from you?"

Ian raised his hands and slowly stood, his back scraping against the bark of the tree. Elsa's blade followed him, unwavering.

"I am here for Gwen, not the hallow. You know my faith."

"I knew hers, as well."

"I would know her heart," he said. "What led her family to this corruption. What they hoped to accomplish by hiding their god from the church. What the church hoped to do by destroying it. Her father is dead, and her mother, and all of their blood. She is the last Adair, perhaps the last in a long line of heretics, going back to the crusades. And yet I prayed with her at festivals, I knelt beside her in my family's doma, when they would visit. She was faithful."

"She had a strange way of showing it," Elsa said. "Worshipping at the foot of a hidden god. Harboring a witch inside her walls. Holding common cause with the wardens of the hallow. Doesn't that sound like a heretic to you?"

"How many of the feral gods did she slay? And when she turned her blade against mortal man, it was in defense of her blood. Surely you can't believe that Volent was justified in killing those peasants at Tallownere? That Halverdt's war was good and right and holy? And yet it was the church that led it. Does *that* sound like a heretic?"

"I knew her," Elsa replied. "I heard her confession. She was careful, but she was fallen." The knight stepped closer, the heat from her blood washing over Ian's face. "Gwen Adair was one of them. A pagan."

"Yet when it came down to it, you were the one she looked to for help. You and the frair were the ones she guided to this very hallow. She may have been a heretic, but to whom? Do you think the wardens would have wanted that? I have known pagans, Elsa, and the only thing they trust less than an inquisitor is a knight of the vow."

"She didn't have a choice," Elsa growled.

"Did she *ever* have a choice?" Ian asked, holding out one hand, placing it gently against the blade that was inching toward his throat.

"What are you saying?"

"Just this. Gwendolyn Adair was born into her heresy, she was raised to it. Her father led her to the hallow, and her blood commanded it. Yet when everything else failed her, it is the church she depended on. You, and Frair Lucas. She depended on you."

"For all the good it did her."

"May aye, may nay, but she held both things in her heart. The hallow and the doma. The celestial and the pagan. And while she lives, and before the cold courts of winter have had their way with her, I would know that heart. Know what it cost her to bear that burden, even from birth."

Elsa stood, quivering. The blade warmed beneath Ian's fingers, hot enough that he had to draw his hand away, blinking as the dry heat stole the water from his eyes. He was just about to flinch away when Elsa stepped back, and the storm of her anger passed.

"We cannot stay here," she said uneasily. "There are demons in the shadows."

"Have you found her trail?" Ian asked, as though nothing had just passed between them, as though her sword had not been inches from his throat.

"No. I can still feel the bond, but the blood has been corrupted. Maybe something happened to her when the god took her. Something in the flesh. Or perhaps she is dying, and the echoes carry through the bond. Frankly, I don't know. I have never tried to use the blood bond to track a god-touched heart. No one has."

"Then what do we do?"

"We will have to find another way to track her." Elsa sheathed her blade and turned away. Ian saw that their horses waited among the trees, already packed and brushed and fed. "Now that the wards are gone, it will be easy to find our way out of the Fen. North, I think. I remember there being a castle just beyond the borders."

"Elsa?"

The vow knight paused for a heartbeat, then swung herself into the saddle. She flicked the reins, and started toward the river. Ian raised his voice.

"Elsa! You've heard my reasons. Why are *you* here? What brings you to the hallow, and Gwendolyn's trail?"

"I could have stopped her," she called back. "I should have stopped her."

"And what then would have become of Sacombre's gheist?" Ian shouted at her retreating back. "Who would have stopped that demon?"

"Gods know," she answered, and then she was too far away to be heard.

They followed the river along the hallow's edge, a short journey that turned east and then north before joining another stream that marked the far border of the sacred grove. From there they struck north, finding the way easier than expected, as the Fen faded behind them.

Leaving the silent trees of the hallow behind, Ian and Elsa failed to notice a figure watching them from the cleft peak of a rock. It crouched among the shadows, a hood pulled tight across a face broken and red with blood. A body lay at its feet. When the pair disappeared over a hill, it bent to the body, cradling the limp head in its palms.

"You were meant to tell them, yes?" it asked, with a voice as rough as broken spears. "You were left behind to show the way. Abandoned. Alone." Lovingly, the figure passed its hand over the dead boy's face, closing his eyes. "Sleep restfully, child. Have no fear."

The figure stood, blinking into the bright sun, tracing the path the vow knight and her companion had followed.

"I will be your messenger, yes? The messenger for the dead."

16

THEY WRAPPED HER in elk-hide hung with bone runes and anointed in blood, and then lifted her into a splint. Every step of the trail brought pain. The faces of the caravan were dark and grim as they traveled beside her.

She struggled to stay awake, and when she slept her dreams were haunted by crushing water and sharp sun, and the anger of the shaman.

Days passed. Weeks. Gwen reached the point where she was able to walk, but Cahl prevented her. She was as much a prisoner as a patient to the team of pagans who carried her litter between their shoulders. By the time they reached the grove where the conclave was to take place, Gwen was sore and tired and restless.

The grove was a shallow bowl dotted with smooth boulders scattered throughout, each inscribed with old runes as soft and eroded as if they were written in sand. The gathering had an air of nervous expectation. By the time Cahl and his companions arrived, the meeting had already started. The shamans and their witches were waiting in a semi-circle a dozen bodies deep, the far ranks disappearing into the trees of the grove like stalking wolves.

Cahl lifted Gwen from the litter and set her down on

a stone plinth. The elk-hide clung tight to her shoulders, pinning her arms against her ribs and restricting her breath. The audience shifted silently among the trees. A handful of pagans sat closer to her, each heavily tattooed and wearing symbols of the pagan faith. Cahl had warned her that many of the elders would be there. It was their word that would decide her fate. She kept a close eye on them as Cahl addressed the crowd.

"We all know why we are here. Fomharra's release resonated through every henge in Tenumbra. Not in ten generations has the god of autumn risen, and now that he has..."

"She," Gwen muttered.

Cahl glanced back at her, grimacing before he turned back to the crowd. "Now that Fomharra once again roams the land, we must decide what to do. The balance was maintained by our circles. By the church, and Suhdra, and the loyalty of the lords of Tener. Now that balance has been broken."

"Bloody form of loyalty," a voice called from the audience. A murmur went through the grove. Cahl raised his hands.

"There is blood on both sides of this fight. We must put that behind us."

"A debt unsettled must be repaid," one of the elders said. She was a woman, dressed in the warm furs of the northern crags. The tattoos that scrolled across her cheeks looked like a brace of elk horn.

"There is too much debt to be paid," another elder muttered. "Blood upon blood. Generations of it, more than even the dead can remember."

"Perhaps you are concerned with the payment of the dead, Judoc," the woman said, "but I have buried sons under

Suhdrin stones." She turned to Cahl. "Am I to forgive those debts as well?"

"Do not speak to me of Suhdrin stones, Cassandra," a second woman said. Gwen was startled to notice that she was dressed in southern clothes, and had no ink on her face. Her amber hair was neatly braided and she sat with her legs crossed, her hands folded delicately on her knee. "You have old forests to hide in, and friendly villages among which to live. Even the lords of Tener turn a blind eye to your rites."

"Why are you even here?" Cassandra asked sharply. "How are we to trust a face without the ink, and a heart that sleeps beneath a Suhdrin roof, and lives with a Suhdrin husband?"

"Noel heard the autumn god's call, and she came," Cahl said. "We have no right to judge her faith." He looked at the southern woman. "Not yet."

"Not ever," Noel answered. "Mine is the only blood that remained behind when the tribes fled north. We are the ones who stayed on the coast of our ancient blood when cowards—"

"Cowards?" Judoc said. He stood, and his necklace of tiny skulls clattered loudly against his chest. "Our ancestors fought every step of the way, and when we were pushed back, it was at the cost of many Suhdrin dead. How did the tribe of the sun keep their place on the Burning Coast? It was by cutting their braids and striking the ink from their skin!" The man's voice boomed angrily over the grove, but Noel watched him placidly.

"If we are to discover who taught the shaman's art to the high inquisitor, why do we not start with your people, Suhdrin bitch?" he continued. "Who is more likely to bow to the church, than the fools who already bend the knee at their altar?"

"And who has more to gain from Adair's fall? Which tribe has agitated for war with Suhdra more than yours, Judoc?" Noel asked. She stood, unfolding like a flower in bloom, her hands caressing the air. "How long have we had to listen to you complain about Suhdrin influence in Tenerran courts? As if the actions of this baron or that earl had any impact on us. Colm Adair was loyal to the old ways, Judoc. Did you begrudge his family their Suhdrin charms?"

"Such things have no place in the north," Judoc said. He loomed over the slender witch, his furs and necklace of tiny skulls rough beside Noel's silk. "Suhdrin food. Suhdrin titles. Suhdrin prayers at night and Suhdrin priests by day! Mark my words—"

"Mark *my* words, Judoc of the tribe of bones," Noel interrupted. "Suhdrin or Tenerran, it is possible to be faithful without wearing furs and grubbing around in the forests. You care more for your braids and your persecution than you do for your gods. Besides"—The lady stepped close to the towering shaman, nearly overshadowed by his bulk and his anger, then grabbed his necklace of skulls and held it out for all to see.—"The heretic Sacombre is said to have bound Eldoreath, the forbidden god of death. Who would be most able to guide him in that binding, Judoc? Who among the tribes has that knowledge, if not you?"

"I will not endure being accused of treason by a southern coward," Judoc growled. Turmoil spread through the watching crowd, those of the tribe of bones muttering angrily while others begged calm or threatened violence of their own. An inky cloud began filtering down from Judoc's shoulders. "If we are to compare our loyalty to the gods," he added, "I will happily introduce you to my faith!"

"Accusations and threats," Noel said lightly. She stepped away from the seething cloud of dark energy that was whipping around the shaman's bulky form. "Let me show you the strength of a true god of Suhdra!"

In a flash her silken robes turned to flame and heat. A corkscrew of fire twisted through the grove, buffeting the conclave and driving the shadows from the trees. Noel rose, and hung in the air on a spear of fire. Her eyes flashed copper bright, and curls of flame cut through her cheeks, mimicking the pagan tattoos of the conclave, but with ember instead of ink.

"Witness the endless power of the sun, Judoc of bones!" Her voice became the raw, crashing howl of the conflagration, wind-whipped and hungry. "Witness, and know fear!"

"I live among the dead, woman. What do I have to fear from you?" Judoc said. He stepped forward, drawing his hands together, grinding fist into palm. The sound that emanated from them was like the grinding of gravestones. Darkness spread across the ground, a mist of ink and twisting shadows that squirmed with strange shapes. A ridge of bones emerged from the mist, burrowing its way toward Noel and her pillar of flame. Skeletal hands rippled along the surface, dragging the monstrosity forward, digging into the earth, grasping for the witch.

"Anything can burn, elder. Even fear," Noel countered. She flashed her hands forward. A spinning wheel of cinders rolled off her fingertips and into the grasping bones. At the flames' touch the bones blackened and cracked, splintering apart as they traveled, until only a shuffling mound of flakes remained.

Judoc hissed, reeling the bones back, lifting them up into a quivering column of fragmented ivory.

Cahl took a step forward, but Aedan held him back,

lacing strong fingers around the shaman's arm. Noel struck again, this time lashing down with a pillar of flame that flickered with amber light. The pillar of broken bones collapsed like dust, but when the fragments cleared, Judoc was nowhere to be seen. A rut in the earth quickly filled up, leaving only smooth earth behind.

"What trickery is this, elder?" Noel called out. She lowered herself to the ground, the grass beneath her feet turning to cinder. She turned slowly, staring into the crowd, a coruscating disc of spinning flame in each hand. "Do you run from the light?"

Judoc's hand erupted from the ground beneath her, grasping her ankle and dragging her down. The earth yawned open like a giant mouth. Shades of the dead drifted out of the freshly opened grave, their faces twisted in rage. Noel shrieked and filled the air with flame, indiscriminate, torching trees and setting the clothes of those closest on fire.

"There has been enough dying." A quiet voice came from the edge of the grove. A man stepped into the clearing, travel pack on his shoulders, which were bent with fatigue. He leaned heavily on a walking staff. "And enough threats. *Silence*, all of you."

He produced a stone from around his neck, suspended from a leather strap, perfectly square and held in a circle of iron. The man held it out in front of him and, with a muttered invocation, let it drop to the ground.

The stone struck the earth with the sound of an iron gong. The ground seemed to bend toward it. Gwen felt herself pulled forward, as though the world had wrapped itself around that single point. A great rush of wind burst out of the trees, howling toward the man and his strange stone.

The cloud of the dead that surrounded Judoc drained into the stone, as did the cloak of fire that Noel wore. The open grave vomited out the elder of bones, sending the two druids spinning. Noel screamed as she tumbled across the ground, fluttering banners of flame snapping from her skin. The rest of the conclave reacted as well, erupting in gasps of distress and pain as various spirits and bound gods were snatched from them. Something stirred in Gwen—a void that yearned to join the emptiness that swelled around the stone.

And then there was utter silence.

The world rushed in again, the sounds of the forest and the muffled distress from the crowd. The old man stooped and picked up the stone, settling it once again around his neck. Noel and Judoc looked up at him as he passed, anger and tears in their eyes. He ignored them, and walked directly to Gwen.

"This is the girl?" he asked. She looked up at him. His face was incredibly tired, the flesh hanging from his skull like a loose mask. Her eyes locked on the stone. It looked ordinary enough.

"Yes," Cahl answered. He seemed to have recovered from whatever had just happened, though his face was pale. "Gwendolyn Adair, of the tribe of iron."

"There is no tribe of iron," the man said. "Just as there is no tribe of the void. My station is not handed from blood to blood. It is earned. And so I have no tribe. One person does not make a tribe." He bent closer to her, looking almost lovingly into her eyes. "That makes us the same, in a way. Last of our people, or the first."

"Who are you?" Gwen asked.

"Folam," he said, patting the stone at his neck. "My name is my station. This is a pretty mess you've put us in."

"I didn't mean—"

"No one ever means anything," Folam said, then straightened his back. "Cahl, I expected more of Fianna's shaman. I come to join a conclave of elders, and instead I find you all spitting and cursing and summoning gods."

"Fianna always led our henge, voidfather. I am not suited to the task."

"I know the ways of my daughter, Cahl. Still. I expected more." He turned to face the conclave, many of whom looked back with fear in their eyes. "There will be no more discussions tonight. Say your rites, and sleep, and in the morning we will discuss what must be done."

"An army of Suhdrin heretics waits in the wilds of the Fen," one of the shaman yelled from the crowd. "Our path should be clear enough."

"Clear paths are the most treacherous," Folam said as a murmur began to spread. "Quiet, everyone. Enough. We will talk in the morning." As the crowd dispersed, he glanced back at Gwen. She was starting to get up, and he shook his head. "Not you. You and I will talk tonight. I need to know what happened, and why. I need to know the sort of men who hold my daughter."

The old man sat in the tiny bower, hastily constructed by several of the druids, listening to Gwen tell her story. Cahl sat with them. When she was done he bent even lower over the stone that was around his neck, until his shoulders nearly reached his knees. Folam was quiet for a long time.

"What do you know of this frair?" he asked, eventually. "Lucas, you say his name is. Tell me of him."

"I know only what I have told you. That he believed the

purge of the gheist was a mistake. That Suhdra is paying for that mistake, in famine and in war. The spirits of the south are out of balance."

"Sounds like heresy," Folam said with a grin. "And he is the one escorting my daughter south?"

"He is," Cahl answered. "Along with the high inquisitor. Inside the Fen Gate, there are still those sympathetic to us. They reported that Frair Lucas left with the prisoners, and a portion of the Suhdrin army."

"A portion, but not all?"

"No," Cahl said. "Mostly the sick, in body and spirit. More than enough remain to take the castle, should they choose to do so. Enough to march farther north, perhaps to Houndhallow." The shaman hesitated. "Are we to interfere?"

"Let the lords have their war," Folam answered. "Let them trade stone houses and titles and churn their fields into blood. We have other concerns." After a long moment he stood, pulling himself up with his staff. "Now, if you will excuse me. I have traveled weeks to be here, and I suspect weeks more lie ahead of us. I must rest."

"What will we tell the conclave in the morning?" Cahl asked.

"The conclave will have its meeting. They will argue, and they will fight. Then I will tell them what must be done, and they will do it." Folam brushed the limbs of the bower aside with the staff and stepped into the night.

Cahl and Gwen sat in silence for a few minutes. Finally, Gwen spoke.

"I thought there was no king in the north?" she asked.

"We answer to no king. Only our gods."

"Then who is he, to assume command?"

"Folam is bound to the empty god, an elder among elders. We ignore him at our peril."

"And this empty god gives him the right to rule?"

Cahl shrugged uncomfortably. Gwen had noticed that he talked differently when she wasn't around, more brusquely. More directly. With her it was either condescension or silence. When it became clear he wasn't going to elaborate, she pressed onward.

"You don't trust me, do you?" she asked.

"I don't know you. None of us do."

"That's ridiculous. My family regularly prayed with our village witch, we followed every rite of the gods, and were in constant contact with the wardens of the witches' hallow. Surely that has gained us some trust?"

"All of those people are dead, Gwen," Cahl said, shaking his head. "Better that some lived, even if it was only to speak ill of you."

"You can't think we were responsible for that? My family died—"

"By your own word, you led priests of the celestial church to the hallow. We have only your story to know what happened there, and only the disastrous results of the battle of the Fen Gate by which to judge your wisdom." Cahl stood. "We are far from trusting you, baroness."

"I'm no baroness! I am Gwen Adair, of the tribe of iron!"

"As Folam said, there cannot be a tribe of one. The god of the waterfall did not accept you. Tried to kill you, even if that was because of this blood bond, as Aedan claims. You don't belong among us, and the other Tenerran lords will never trust you again." He stepped out of the bower, pausing just long enough to say, "Best you make your peace with that, and with the gods."

17

GREENHALL WAS MUCH changed. The remnants of the tournament ground lingered around the curtain wall, the wreckage of tents and vendor-halls trampled in the mud, the bleachers from the stadium left to go to rot. Banners hung like gallows from the walls of the castle.

The sky threatened snow as it had for days, and the air felt heavy. More than four months had passed since Malcolm Blakley and the other Tenerrans had fled the Allfire celebration, and the people of Greenhall hadn't taken the time to clear out the wreckage.

"Now that's a sad sight," Sir Torvald said. "Only takes a bit of effort to maintain the honor of your walls."

"They've had many things on their mind, I expect," Lucas said, "and will have a great many more in the days to come."

Their caravan was strung out along the godsroad. Lucas and his small troop of noble guests had reached the verge of Verdton in the early hours of the morning, having marched through the night. The one wagon they had brought with them—the iron wagon containing Tomas Sacombre—lay tucked among the trees, in the hope that it would remain hidden from the watchers on the castle walls.

The reason for their hurried flight bristled along the southern road, stretching to the horizon. A Suhdrin army, banners of the great houses flying above rank after rank of spears, marched north toward Greenhall. Lucas had spotted their dreams in the brief moments before he fell asleep, and ordered his column to fly south as quickly as they could. He wanted to reach Greenhall before the Suhdrins, to treat with Halverdt's heir before the lords of the Suhdra bent her ear.

"Why the hurry, my frair?" Sir Horne asked. She was anxious to be included in the advance party, even leaving her armor behind in order to keep pace. She sat now beside Sir Torvald, with LaGaere and young Martin Roard behind her. "What's the point of arriving here before the army?"

"He wants to shape young Sophie's heart before the Suhdrins convince her to lend her strength to their army," LaGaere said. The duke of Warhome spat over his shoulder. "Present her father's body as a warning against war, or some such bullshit."

"You're not far wrong, Warhome," Lucas said. "I would rather the young duchess hear the true story from people who were there, rather than the rumors from those who were not."

"I was there, just as much as you," LaGaere said.

"Yes, and I'm sure you'll have something to say," Lucas said. "Sir Roard, do you know the duchess? You're of an age."

"Sophie has kept to herself," Martin answered. "Or rather, her father has kept her to the sanctuary. I don't know the girl you'll meet beneath that banner."

"Then we'll all learn together, I suppose." Lucas looked back at the caravan as it began catching up to his advance party. A black iron hearse separated itself from the rest of the train, and trundled toward the castle.

A party was descending from the castle, flying the acorn of Halverdt slashed in black. "Bringing a young girl her dead father," Lucas said. "Not the best way to make an introduction."

"No, I suppose not," Martin said. "She's like Gwen in that. Her family dead, and the church to blame."

"Let's not walk down that line of thought, sir," Lucas said. He turned to the droopy Sir Torvald, who looked more uncomfortable and less happy with every word. "Gather the honor guard, Sir Torvald. We will show the duke the respect he earned, if not the love he craved." Torvald bowed and returned to the caravan, speaking to his pages.

Many of the knights who had fought under Halverdt's banner were already gathered. Lucas watched as half a dozen of them pushed their way past the onlookers to stand solemnly beside the hearse. Duke LaGaere was joined by his marshal Sir Daviau and a trio of knights of House Fabron, themselves escorting the body of their dead lord home to be buried. So many had died at the Fen Gate, or fled into the forests on the long road home.

Lucas rode to the head of the group, with Martin Roard on one side and Sir Horne on the other. The frair was dressed in the formal robes of his station, stiff from months in his saddlebags. He adjusted the stole around his neck, the iron icons of Cinder jangling from the hem as he laid it flat against his chest. The men watched him solemnly, and with a little distrust. It was known that Lucas had stood beside Malcolm Blakley at the siege, but he was the only priest in the train, and gods forbid the body be handed over without a representative of the celestial church on hand.

"Very well," he said. "Let us see Gabriel Halverdt to his home."

"And may peace find him in the grave," Martin said.

The hearse creaked as it rumbled down the road. The iron points of the candleholders were empty, leaving the wagon disturbingly bare. The silk burial shroud and dried flowers looked like a crown made of wicked barbs. Lucas and his companions took a place beside the coffin, Stefan LaGaere on the other side, with the rest of the knights following. They followed the muddy road until it began to rise toward the castle.

The party from Halverdt waited for them there.

The girl who came to greet them was dressed in a mendicant's robe over plate-and-half, surrounded by a dozen guards of her father's house. Her house, now. Her guards. And a girl no longer.

Frair Lucas dipped his head as he approached.

"Lady Sophie," the frair said. Her soldiers were spread across the road. Sophie was a severe looking child, with dark hair that was pulled back into the chain mail of her cowl, and eyes as green as moss. Her mien was hardly surprising, considering her years spent among the acolytes of Strife. The girl ignored Lucas, staring at her father's coffin.

"I offer my condolences on your father's death," he continued, "and greet you in the names of just Cinder and loving Strife."

Sophie was silent for a moment, finally tearing her eyes away from the black barbs of the hearse to look directly at Lucas. There were no tears in her eyes, though some emotion roiled in their depths. It was not the grief Lucas had expected.

"I will accept your condolences, but it is not your place to offer the bright lady's greeting, inquisitor," Sophie Halverdt answered. "Her light has no home in your heart."

Anger, then, Lucas thought. *Well enough. I would*

be angry, too, if my father had suffered the lies of Tomas Sacombre, and died as a result.

"There is more to my faith than my title," Lucas said, "but I will not argue the point. I have spent much of my life in the company of Strife's faithful. Years in the field, doing the church's work, with a vow knight at my side."

"And where is your vow knight now, frair?"

"There is unfinished business in the north. She remained behind."

"Such is always the way," Sophie answered sharply. "Knights of the vow finishing the business of the inquisition, and frairs of Cinder telling their stories. Is that why you are here? To tell me the story of my father's death?"

"I come only to carry your father's remains and to honor his passing," Lucas answered. "Whatever our differences, he was a man of the church, and deserves the respect of its priests."

"I have my own priests, inquisitor. Return to Cinderfell, and to your god of dying and silence."

"My lady shouldn't speak to a priest of the church in this way," LaGaere said.

"It's no matter, Warhome," Lucas said. "The girl has a right to her anger. It was a priest of Cinder who deceived her father, after all." He waved LaGaere off, then nodded to Sophie. "The high inquisitor will pay for his crimes, my lady. We escort him to Heartsbridge, to face his judgment."

"Sacombre is with you?" she asked. Her face remained carefully neutral, betrayed only by the curiosity in her voice.

"In chains," LaGaere answered, though there was a hint of dismay to his words. "Caged with a witch."

"Cinder's judgment sees no difference between pagans and heretics," Lucas said, though he knew that to be untrue.

"With your leave, Lady Sophie, we will escort your father's body to the doma."

"Of course, though only this honor guard may join you," Sophie said. For the first time she looked the party over. "Warhome and the prince of Stormwatch may join us at our table. The rest will have to make do in the barracks."

"Thank you, my lady," Lucas said. "We have much to discuss. You may have noticed the army to our south. I was hoping to speak with you about their intent."

"You can ask them directly. Their commander rode ahead of the column, and awaits us inside." Sophie gave Lucas a knowing grin, then turned back to the castle. "I'm sure you have much to talk about."

The walls may have been left to ruin, but inside Greenhall was a different place. The roads were strewn with garlands, and fresh banners celebrating the sun hung from every window of the narrow streets and alleyways that branched off the main thoroughfare. Every corner sported a bonfire, and the guards that roamed the village wore crowns of flower and vine.

"If I didn't know the calendar, I would think they were preparing to celebrate the Allfire," Martin said. A chorus of women passed by, their feet and shoulders bare, singing the evensong prelude. He turned to watch them pass. "Aren't they cold?"

"Strife warms the body as well as the heart," Lucas said. "Though she won't protect them much if these clouds break. This is all very odd," he mused.

The approach to the castle had been scrubbed cleaner than any street Lucas had ever seen, though the buildings that lined the street showed signs of fire damage. The gates themselves were twined with ivy and hung in cloth of gold and crimson, stitched with the icons of Strife.

"Lady Sophie certainly brought her faith with her," LaGaere said.

"One faith, at least," Lucas answered. "I haven't seen a sign of Cinder."

"It was the High Inquisitor of Cinder that brought her father low. Be glad she stays true to the church at all." LaGaere stripped off his riding gloves and tucked them into his belt. "Can you blame her for raising up Strife, and slighting Cinder's dull cowl?"

"Not yet," Lucas said. "Not truthfully."

They were escorted into the courtyard. The stables were bustling with activity, as were the barracks and doma. The doors to the doma were thrown open, and waves of heat rippled into the cold evening air. The evensong filled the stone chamber. Lucas paused to listen.

"The springtide," he said quietly. "They're singing in the summer."

"This way, my frair," one of their escorts said, motioning to the great hall. Lucas allowed himself to be drawn inside, along with Stefan LaGaere and Martin. The rest of the procession, bearing the body of the fallen duke, continued into the doma.

The hearth at the end of the hall was ablaze with a fire so hot that at first Lucas winced away from it. The flames burned clean and nearly smokeless, constantly attended by a pair of maids. The girls were drenched in sweat. A table ran the length of the room. Much of it was empty, with only the head closest to the hearth set with linens and ware. The guards motioned toward that end of the table.

"Are we going to be given the opportunity to refresh ourselves?" LaGaere asked. "We have been in the saddle for weeks, and have not seen a proper washroom since the war began."

"Her ladyship will be with you shortly," a guard said. Then he and his companions went to stand at attention by the door.

"Well, this is madness," LaGaere muttered. He began stripping off his armor and the heavy wool of his doublet. "We're as likely to broil as be fed in this place."

"There will be food," Lady Sophie said. She swept in from one of the chambers that bracketed the hearth. She still wore her armor, though her mendicant's robe had been traded for a light frock of cream silk. Her brow beaded with sweat as soon as she entered. "And wine, and whatever else you require. I am not rude, my lords. Merely cautious."

"Your father was a cautious man, as well," LaGaere said. "Cautious to a fault."

"His fault was in his faith," Sophie answered, "not his caution."

"I always held Gabriel's faith as his greatest virtue, my lady," Martin said. "Our families disagreed on many things, but he was always faithful to the church. There should be no shame in that."

"I misspoke," Sophie said quickly, looking Martin over slowly before she motioned to the seats. "Let us eat, and be at our ease."

Servants brought in food and wine, then left the party alone. The vast expanse of the great hall echoed with the clatter of goblets and plates as the knights tucked into the first real meal they had seen in months.

"When will your other guests be joining us?" Lucas asked.

"Soon enough," she answered. "Has the rest of your party performed their duties?"

"Your father rests in the sanctuary," Lucas said. "I sent Sir Horne back to the caravan, carrying orders to make camp."

"Don't get too comfortable, frair," Sophie said. "You won't be with us long."

An awkward silence followed, filled only by the crackle of the hearth.

"A fine spread, my lady," LaGaere said finally, raising his glass. "Quite a change from your previous arrangement, I'm sure."

"You recall the meals of the cold halls of Cinderfell, sir. Even the humblest shrine of the bright lady knows how to enjoy a good meal."

"Tell us of your time among the faithful of Strife, my lady," Martin said. "Your father sent you away quite young, didn't he?"

"I was a child," she said.

You still are, Lucas thought, but kept to himself.

Sophie grinned into her cup of wine as she continued. "He wanted to protect me from the north. His court was no place for ladies, he always said."

"With your mother gone and no brothers, it's hardly a wonder Gabriel wanted you elsewhere," Martin said, "but he could have warded you with another court of Suhdra. You would have been welcome in Stormwatch."

"I'm sure you would have been more than happy to welcome me into your home, Sir Roard," Sophie said with a smile. "However, I think he wanted more for me than a wardship and a courtly marriage. He could have sent me to the Lightfort, I suppose. I'm eternally grateful that he didn't. The convent life was better for me."

"You certainly dress the part of a knight," LaGaere said, nodding to Sophie's armor. "Have you trained in the gentleblade?"

"I have trained in the sword and the spear, though I hope to never use them," she answered. "Most of my time was spent in prayer." Her face calmed, her eyes becoming unfocused as she stumbled onto a memory. "I was at prayer when they brought me the news of my father's death." She sat quietly for a moment, the table awkwardly silent. The moment passed, and Sophie forced a smile. "At least the food was good."

"Sir LaFey complained endlessly about our meals on the trail," Lucas said. "Doubtless she missed her days in the Lightfort."

"I'm not so sure," LaGaere answered around a cut of ham. "The sworn of the vow are a hard lot."

"They are faithful to their calling," Sophie answered. "I'm sure you can attest to that, Frair Lucas."

"I have never known a purer heart than Sir LaFey," Lucas said. "Though she could be dreadfully stubborn on occasion."

"A lesson the inquisition could learn, perhaps," Sophie said. "Stubborn in faith, to both gods and men."

"We all mourn the betrayal of Tomas Sacombre, and the deaths to which it led," Lucas replied. "Your father's chief among them."

"Let's not hold Adair blameless in this story," LaGaere said. "Without Lord Halverdt's sacrifice, we might never have learned of the Fen Gate's secret heresy."

"Without Sacombre's heresy, we might have been able to

prosecute the baron properly in a court of law," Lucas said, "rather than a trial by war."

"Tener would never have allowed that," LaGaere snorted. "Even that tame bastard Blakley stood in Adair's defense. It took the full strength of the south to bring the hound to heel."

"The full strength?" Sophie smirked. "There wasn't time to draw the full strength of the south, thank the gods. If that had occurred, we may have had a true war, rather than the murderous squabble that passed through the Fen Gate."

"I stood beneath the walls of the Fen Gate, and drowned friends and enemies in the waters of White Lake, my lady," LaGaere said sternly. "That was war enough."

"We all drew blood," Martin said. "All of us."

"Aye," LaGaere answered. "Some of us from both sides."

"When it became clear that Sacombre had deceived us, all of us..." Martin started. LaGaere waved him aside.

"Sacombre's crime was no worse than Adair's," he said. "You would know enough about the turncoat's excuses, Roard."

"And what do you mean by that?" Martin asked. The young man gripped his wine glass tightly in one hand, his other drifting dangerously close to his knife.

"When the banner of Warhome rides, it rides true," LaGaere said quietly. "We do not switch loyalties in the middle of a fight."

"And now who is being stubborn?" Sophie asked, sipping at her wine.

"Gentlemen! My lady! Peace." A voice called from the door to the great hall. The party turned to watch Helenne Bassion, Duchess of Galleydeep, walk into the room. She wore a formal dress, without blade or plate, though the complicated necklace that spilled down her breast could have turned a blade as well as it drew the eye. A young girl followed close behind, drawing back her chair to let the lady sit at the opposite end of the table from Sophie Halverdt. A flock of servants swept down to bring food and wine to the new arrival.

"Let's not fight before dinner, shall we?" the duchess said.

"Galleydeep," LaGaere said stiffly. "Are you in charge of the army looming to our south?"

"The wide and varied banners of the south rallied to my side, as soon as I heard of the tragedy at White Lake," Bassion said.

"Men of Galleydeep fought bravely at that battle, and on to the Fen Gate, as well," LaGaere said. "Why do you call it a tragedy?"

"War fought quickly is war wasted," she answered. "Yes, there was a contingent of Bassion troops in Halverdt's doomed column, led by the great and greatly missed Sir Eduard Leon. I am told he died gallantly at the hands of your dear friend, didn't he, Martin?"

"Ian Blakley slew him, yes," Martin answered. "In open challenge, and with honest blade."

"Such foolish words. 'With honest blade.' Those men were sent as a concession to my brother. Anxious as he was to show his support to Greenhall, Vincent chose to remain at home." Bassion speared a slice of roasted apple with a long, thin knife and brought it to her lips. "They were good men, wasted. This whole enterprise has been a game of who can lose the most, and most pointlessly."

"Then why do you march at an army's head, my lady?" Lucas asked.

"To see that their loss is not in vain, frair. These questions of guilt, of whose wrong was greater, they do not interest me." The duchess ate her apple, tapping the knife thoughtfully against her chin. "I leave the judgment of Cinder to the wisdom of Cinder, and seek only to ensure such needless battles are not fought again."

"My father fought to bring the peace," Martin said. "As did Malcolm Blakley, and Castian Jaerdin. Will you join your forces to theirs, and stand united with the church?"

"We shall have to see," Bassion answered. "We shall simply have to see. More wine?"

18

THE ORPHANSHIELD STALKED the halls of the castle like a man possessed. A week had passed since the shriving of the hidden chamber. That had left the inquisitor paranoid, convincing him that another witch remained in the Fen Gate, and still he walked the corridors at night, sword in one hand, torch in the other. He did not sleep, for fear of letting the demon in through his dreams.

Malcolm wasn't sleeping much either, but for different reasons. With his wife hidden beyond the castle walls, every waking moment was filled with the fear that some wandering patrol of overzealous Suhdrin knight might stumble upon her secret camp. He lay awake at night, waiting for the horns to sound, or for iron boots to kick in his door.

The guards assigned to protect the inquisitor were a mixed lot. There were Suhdrins from the camp outside, included at Gilliam's insistence, alongside Tenerrans who still mourned their dead comrades. Both groups were wound tight, and each blamed the other for the war, so when young John Halfpenny made a joke about dead Suhdrin wives and the maggots that were raping them, the Suhdrin scout who was walking behind him took exception.

Before anyone knew better John Halfpenny was lying

on the floor of the doma with his belly the wrong way out, gasping his last few breaths. He was one of Rudaine's men—a dwindling group determined to protect their own. The Suhdrin guards who were present for Halfpenny's murder got to choose between throwing down their arms or receiving the blade.

The first man to resist was cut down, and the rest surrendered. Then they were marched down to the crypts and locked away.

The man who had resisted was one of Lorien Roard's, supposedly allied to the Tenerrans but none too interested in giving up his sword. The group locked away in the crypts belonged to both Roard and Marchand, and their absence left the inquisitor's contingent unguarded.

Thus, while Malcolm and Roard argued at the tops of their lungs in the tumbled down throne room of the Fen Gate, one of the priests disappeared—and this drew the attention of the inquisitor. He summoned Malcolm, Lorien, and the marshal in charge of Rudaine's contingent, Franklin Gast.

They found Frair Gilliam in the stables. The inquisitor had built a chair from the wreckage of the altar from the doma, splintered stone icons lashed together into something that looked like a mad god's throne.

The room was lined with torches and the remaining priests, all looking young and weak and frightened, busied themselves in the flickering light. When Malcolm walked in, he quickly took stock of the children, to see which of them was missing. The girl who had seen his wife was in the corner, her head bent in prayer.

Of course it wasn't her, Malcolm thought bitterly. *I couldn't be that lucky.*

"Houndhallow," the inquisitor growled. "What is this business? Why have you lost one of my charges?"

"As I predicted and warned, my frair, the men were on edge and their tempers got the better of them," Malcolm said. "It will be made right at once, and then I'll personally lead the search for your priest."

"Made right?" Lorien said. "How will you make it right? My man is dead, and for what? Because your goons can't tell the difference between an ally and an enemy?"

"Fairness, my lord, it's easier to know the difference between Suhdra and Tener," Gast answered. The grizzled old sergeant rubbed his nose. "Easier still to stick a man when he's told to put down his sword and he don't, especially when there's already innocent blood on the ground."

"I will not sit here and listen to petty squabbling," Gilliam said. "Nor will I hear excuses. You all fall under the authority of the gods and the church. We face the greatest heresy to touch these lands since the crusades, and *this* is the service you render to Cinder!" The inquisitor stood, his eyes burning. "Sometimes I question your loyalty, Houndhallow. Your loyalty and your faith!"

"There is no need to question either, my frair," Malcolm said, steeling himself against the need to glance in the direction of the young priestess. "But there are real problems—dangerous problems—that need to be addressed."

"The one thing you will address is the fate of my child!" Gilliam bellowed. "I am consumed, *consumed* with the care of this castle and the repudiation of its gheists. Meanwhile your men are too busy knifing one another in the back to do your duty. That cannot, *will* not continue. You will release the prisoners from the crypts. *Immediately*."

"Lads aren't going to like that," Gast muttered.

"The lads don't have to like shit," Gilliam said. "Not unless I tell them to, and then they'll beg for it." The inquisitor swept down on the sergeant, his thick hands closing around the man's collar, his grip like a vise. "If another drop of Suhdrin blood is spilled in these walls, it will be your scalp mopping it up. Do you understand?"

"Aye, aye," Gast said quickly. "No need to get violent about it."

"There is *every* need to get violent about this, and since none of you can keep your knives in your sheaths, we will have to go one step more. I wanted this to be a joint effort, but that is clearly not going to work. I want every Suhdrin body out of this castle by noon tomorrow."

"About damned time," Malcolm said. "It was a mistake to bring southern blades into the castle to serve as your guards, my frair."

Gilliam turned to him, his face grim. The inquisitor marched slowly to Malcolm's face. He pointed at Lorien Roard.

"Every.

"Suhdrin.

"Body.

"Every Roard, every Galleux, every Jaerdin! All of them! Out!" The inquisitor drew himself up to his full height, resting his hands on the pommels of his blades. "We will cleanse the Fen Gate together, Malcolm. You and I. Alone, if we must."

"But... but..." Lorien stumbled over his words. "We held the castle gates during the battle. Castian Jaerdin has stood with the Blakleys since Halverdt first marched north. Our loyalty—"

"*What of it?*" Gilliam demanded. "What of your loyalty? What of your honor? What does any of that matter to me, when you keep killing each other in my doma?"

"They won't be greeted with open arms outside these walls," Malcolm said. "Not yet, anyway."

"That stopped being my problem the minute you all decided that your blood was more important than your faith," Gilliam said. He turned to Lorien. "You have served as you saw true, and Cinder alone must judge that, but it's time for you to move on. Pack your trunks, gather your banners, and be out that gate by noon tomorrow. Make sure Castian Jaerdin goes with you."

"Frair, without the men of Stormwatch and Redgarden, I'm not sure we can hold this castle," Malcolm said. "We certainly can't properly protect you and your charges."

"Surely it couldn't get any worse," Gilliam said. "And if you can't protect these walls, perhaps you'll simply need to sue for peace. I'm sure Duke Marchand will be accommodating." He returned to his chair of broken stone, dismissing them with a wave of his hand.

"Go."

Shocked, Lorien looked from Gast to Malcolm. Then before Malcolm could say anything, the duke of Stormwatch rushed out, his face as red as fire.

Gast shrugged. "He'll have his own problems getting home," he said. "I don't envy him."

"Nor will he envy you, if you fail to find my child," Gilliam boomed from his chair. "Now get out. I must pray for patience, and the calm of winter."

Without another word, Malcolm left the man there, stewing in an anger that wasn't very becoming of a priest of

Cinder. As he left, Malcolm glanced back to find that the girl was staring at him, her hands knotted in prayer.

Malcolm called for MaeHerron and Manson Dougal, earl of Hartsgard. Gast he sent back to the crypts to see that the Suhdrins were released and safely escorted out the gate. No sooner had the order been given and the Tenerran nobles arrived than Castian Jaerdin burst into the meeting.

"Where am I supposed to go, Malcolm?"

"Redgarden, I assume. You do still have a castle there."

"You know what I mean," Jaerdin said. "I took a tremendous risk standing with you. The other dukes in the Circle of Lords have cut my trade routes. Wheat rots in my silos, and my tolls go uncollected. If not for the support of the church, I would have bowed out of this insanity months ago! And that support is thinly given. Now that the inquisitor has kicked us out of the north, it's likely to dry up."

"You can always join the siege camp," Malcolm said bitterly. "No doubt they'd be pleased to have an insider's advice on our defenses."

"Advice?" Jaerdin stood stiffly by the door, his eyes wide. "Do you think I'd betray you, Malcolm? Have not enough of my men died in your service? Have I not risked enough to prove my loyalty?"

"The inquisitor doesn't seem to think so," Malcolm said. "There is nothing to do, Castian. Go home. Your neighbors will forget your transgressions, more quickly than they'll forget my ink. It is the Suhdrin way, after all."

"The Suhdrin way," Jaerdin said bitterly. "Indeed. Perhaps it is Tener who needs to bend their stubborn necks, forget the sins of their neighbors, and move on down the road." The duke of Redgarden looked slowly around the room. A great fatigue settled on the man's shoulders. "Very well, my lords, may the gods grant you light to warm your hearts and cold to steel them, in equal measure. Good day."

He strode from the room, and the door closed soundly behind him, leaving the three Tenerran lords alone. Manson Dougal cleared his throat and went to the jug of wine in the corner, pouring a healthy mug.

"Well," Dougal said, "he has a good question. What is he to do? What are we *all* going to do?"

"What do you mean?" MaeHerron asked. "What's the choice? My da died holding this castle. I'll like as not join him."

"Let's not abandon all glimmering hope, gentlemen," Malcolm said. "We each have healthy contingents, if some reduced, and Rudaine's bannermen will stay true to us, as long as Gast can keep them in order. The loss of Jaerdin and Roard will weigh heavy, yes, but it's not devastating. Colm Adair had fewer men than this to man this castle, after all."

MaeHerron snorted. "The hell, you say. He had fewer men, but a great deal more walls. There are more gaps and tunnels in this ruin than a rabbit's warren. Half our men are sleeping in the open courtyard, and the rest don't sleep at all, for fear their rooms will collapse on them while they dream. And as for dreams..."

"Aye, dreams," Dougal said. "Nothing good has come from dreams." He offered Malcolm a mug of wine.

"As for dreams," MaeHerron repeated. "Those that do sleep are haunted by the ghosts of this place, Houndhallow. There's something in the stones. There's something soaked into the mud of the Fen, and it's nothing holy."

Malcolm cleared his throat, waving off the mug, then sat

down beside the hearth. His eyes were heavy with sleep, and the bruises and aches of battle still lingered in his flesh. He felt like a man beaten nearly to death.

"I know the troubles," Malcolm said. "I've felt them myself, as have my men. I'm no fool, Hartsgard. This will be a rough task."

"And what *is* this task?" Dougal asked. "What are we even doing here?"

"Doing? We're protecting Tener," MaeHerron said. "That's a Suhdrin army beyond the walls. We stand on tribal land, land that has been part of the north since before the church."

"Halverdt's lands were tribal lands, once," Dougal said. "As were Malygris, and Roard, and Heartsbridge itself. This whole island was Tenerran." The earl leaned against the hearth, frowning into his mug as though the wine had turned to vinegar. "But whose land is this now? Adair? Blakley? Sir Bourne still holds the Reaveholt. Perhaps he means to hoist his own sigil over the walls of the Fen Gate. But it's not my land."

"What are you saying?" Malcolm asked.

"I came to the Fen to protect a brother wronged. I marched beside Sorcha Blakley, to save her husband from Greenhall, and then to fight at his side on the shores of the White Lake. And then, among the dead and dying, I found myself here, in this castle, protecting the honor of Colm Adair. That's when I found my trust misplaced, and my own honor in question." He tossed the last of his wine in the fire, which hissed, then placed the mug on the mantle and folded his hands into his belt. "So I ask, what are we doing here? Who are we protecting, and why?"

"Did your father ask these questions at the battle of Highope, when he and I stood together to defend those walls against the Reavers?" Malcolm asked. "Those Suhdrin walls? Did he ask who we were protecting? Or did he fight against their twisted iron gods, and spill the blood of their bondsworn?"

"My father is dead, and most of those who stood at your side are with him," Dougal answered. "This is not Highope, and those aren't Reavers at our gate. As for twisted gods, you will find plenty enough of those beneath our feet, and in the night." A shadow passed over his features. "I will not die to defend a pagan's honor, Houndhallow. I will not die for this place. Let the Suhdrins have it. They can sleep restlessly beneath its shadows, and lose their souls to its madness."

Manson Dougal left. The door shut behind him, and the room was silent for a long time.

"That's the way it will be," MaeHerron said. "Even if we stand, and we fight, someone will betray us. It won't be a Suhdrin blade that ends us here." He turned to Malcolm and grimaced. "It will be some Tenerran son, longing for home, missing his ma, just as scared of Adair's ghost as he is of the Suhdrin charge. Or some daughter of Farwatch, or the Feltower, or Houndhallow, listening to the inquisitor's accusations and deciding her soul is better tucked in the faith of the church, rather than her lord's heart. It won't take more than one." He stood and set his mug on the table, shaking his head. "To open a door. To poison a well. To whisper a secret, and let the gates fly open. Only one."

"Aye," Malcolm said, staring at young Grant MaeHerron, counting the secrets that could be told, and the wells that could be poisoned. "Only one."

19

THE WEATHER TURNED the moment they stepped out of the Fen, as though winter waited in ambush. The road was narrow and straight, overhung with whip-elms that had long since shed their leaves. A light dusting of snow whitened the branches and lined the grass along the verge. The sky threatened more, and the air was bitterly cold.

The going was slow, and their spirits were failing.

Elsa huddled under a cloak of wool and fur, her breath huffing out from the hood in clouds. Ian rode beside her, purposefully neglecting his cloak and the weather.

"I don't understand how you're cold," he said. "I can feel the heat of your skin from here. Hells, the snow is melting in your wake."

"The fire never feels the flame," she muttered, her voice muffled under layers of cloth. "It's not the weather that chills me, though. I owe my discomfort to the calendar as much as to the snow. Strife's power is in decline. We are on the verge of Cinder's age."

"Of course," Ian said with a twisted smile. "You're not cold. You're just really, really holy."

"Shut up." Elsa paused for a minute, then cast her hood back and fixed Ian with a steely gaze. "Your lips are blue."

"I'm fine," Ian said quickly, suppressing a shiver as a gust of wind howled down the road. "Winter has hardly started. Your thin Suhdrin blood has betrayed you."

"I've spent more winters in the north than you, boy, and not one of them huddled by the blazing hearth of a duke's great hall. Speak to me of winter when you have spent a month trekking along the coast from Fogdeep to the Lesser Shieldisles, chasing a gheist." She shifted under her cloak, adjusting her sword against the saddle. "The ocean waves froze in mid-crash, and the mist of our breath froze in our lungs."

"Well, part of Tenerran wisdom means knowing to not go out in such weather," Ian said.

"Then perhaps part of Suhdrin wisdom means living in a place where the weather isn't complete shit half the year," Elsa answered. She folded the cloak back over her head, giving Ian the opportunity to settle his cloak more tightly across his chest. The wind was picking up.

"I will admit, though, that even for Tener, this is a little early for..." Ian started.

His words trailed off as a dark wind crossed the road ahead of them, a slice of night dressed in ice. It churned between the trees for a long moment, the growl of its passing echoing through her bones. Elsa threw back her cloak and flared Strife's blessings. A stream of melted snow ran down her horse and onto the damp ground. Ian winced at the sudden change, then drew his own blade.

In a breath, the darkness disappeared into the forest. Trees rattled in its wake, knocking snow to the ground in buckets.

"A little early for gheists," Ian finished.

"No," Elsa answered. "Not a gheist." She was still, blade in one outstretched hand, her other cupped to the sky. "But certainly a manifestation."

"A manifestation of what?" Ian asked.

"This storm, perhaps. It seems harsh for autumn, doesn't it? And Gwen was riding the autumn gheist while holding the death god." Elsa scanned the tree line. "Perhaps they have infected one another."

"A blizzard made of death," Ian muttered. Unconsciously, he drew his cloak tight, shivering. "Yes, that sounds like the kind of thing that happens to us."

"You are going to have to get used to dangerous jobs, if you mean to ride with me, Ian Blakley," Elsa answered. "Stay here. Watch the horses."

"Watch the horses against what? The weather?" Ian looked around nervously. "What am I supposed to do if the wind attacks?"

"Kill it," she replied. "Or wait for me to get back. A boy like you shouldn't need lessons in foolish heroism." Elsa slid from her saddle, laid her cloak across it, and walked forward, arms wide, leaving a trail of muddy ice in her wake. Ian sighed and gathered her horse's reins.

"I'm not that young," he said quietly.

The vow knight paused where they had seen the apparition. The corona of fire that flickered from her sword snapped in the wind, the flame guttering loudly. Elsa knelt to examine the ground, then turned to look at the forest where the spirit had departed.

"It feels like an echo," she said. "The memory of a lesser god. Perhaps a gheist *has* manifested."

"Could it have been Gwen?"

"If this is an echo of Gwen's power, then I fear for her soul, and our safety." She stood, holding a squirming fragment of dark energy in her hand. "Though if she is still holding the death god, there is no telling what may have become of her." She tossed the fragment into the air, striking it with her burning blade and watching it dissipate with a shriek. Turning, she walked back toward her horse. "I believe we are on the right path—and even if this has nothing to do with the huntress, any gheist powerful enough to cause a ripple of that sort must be dealt with. Quickly."

"Well," Ian said, looking past Elsa and down the road. "You should collect your cloak before you freeze to death."

"I'm feeling much better, thank you," Elsa answered. "A little action was all these old bones needed to feel alive."

"No, I mean..." He nodded down the road.

In the near distance, a wall of churning white was rushing at them, ground to sky. The trees quivered as the squall line passed through them, snow and ice and cutting sleet roaring through the air as the storm rumbled forward. Lightning flickered in the clouds as the blizzard swallowed the horizon.

"Gods. Damn," Elsa muttered. She ran to her cloak, throwing it over her shoulders before hoisting herself back into the saddle. Ian hunched down, drawing his cloak tight, gripping it shut with both hands.

The storm hit them with a roar. The wind nearly snatched the cloak from his fingers. Frost laced its way through his patchy beard, sliding chill spears into his blood. The horses shied away from the wind, murmuring their displeasure.

"Aren't you going to say something about your Tenerran spirit, Houndson?" Elsa shouted over the gale. "Make a joke about what a refreshing breeze this is, or some such shit?" Ian didn't reply, fighting to keep the cloak around his shoulders, the buckle stubbornly refusing to shut, the fur-lined hood snapping back and forth like a banner. The vow knight drew close, her bulk shielding the boy just enough to let him close the toggle and secure the cloak around him.

"This is more than winter usually offers," he said.

"Yes. A good deal more. We must find shelter." Elsa's voice was barely a whisper in the storm. "Do you know where we are? What village may be close, or what lord?"

"There's a scrabble of barons and earls on this side of the Fen, before we reach the border of Duke MaeHart. It is impossible to learn their disposition, or their roads."

"Impossible, or was it merely too boring for you to manage?" Elsa shouted. Already their cloaks were rimed in frost, and the horses had small piles of snow on their noses. The vow knight squinted into the storm. "No matter. Roads don't happen naturally. Where there is a road, there is a town, and a road so straight and lean must go somewhere safe. Or at least warm."

"We could be days from the nearest town!" Ian yelled back. "We should shelter here. Find a lean among the trees, and pray to the gods for mercy."

"This is winter," Elsa said. "Cinder's season. The gray lord is not known for mercy. Come on."

The pair drove their horses forward, the wind cutting the warmth from their bones and the light from their hearts. Among the clouds, thunder rumbled like a death knell, sounding a dirge for summer.

From atop a storm-wracked elm, its branches groaning under the gale, Aedan sat perched and comfortable. He wrapped a bandage around his hand, staunching the blood. The wound was deep, necessary for a storm of this fury.

He held up the cobweb-patterned blade. It pulsed with the magic of Gwen's blood, yearning for the bond that waited on the road below.

The hunt was on. The quarry was flushed. The forest would have its toll.

There was nothing left of the world. The burning, churning void of the blizzard was everything, everywhere, cutting through the feeble wool of their cloaks. Ian felt nothing, not even pain.

He rode at Elsa's side like a shadow, emptied of his will and his hope. And still they pressed on. Pressed until Elsa's horse drifted to a halt, its knobbled legs shaking with cold and fatigue. Ian pulled up and glanced over. The knight didn't move, hunched over in the saddle, the hood of her cloak tipped down until it was touching the horse's frozen mane.

"Hey!" Ian yelled, but the storm stole his voice. He nudged his horse closer and tried again. "Hey! We have to keep on! If the horse is spent, we'll walk, but… hey, are you in there somewhere?"

He put a gloved hand on Elsa's shoulder and shook. The vow knight leaned away from him, farther and slower, until she fell in a heap from the saddle. Ian yelped and jumped down, falling to his knees as his numb legs betrayed him, crawling to the pile of frost-lined fur that was Sir Elsa LaFey.

When he turned her on her back, Elsa's hood flopped back. Her face was pale, eyes wide, and the scars that danced across her cheeks were angry and blue. The usual radiance of her eyes, copper-bright and sparkling, had frosted over. There was more to her condition than just cold, Ian knew. He shook her again.

"Elsa! Elsa, wake up! You damned stubborn fool, you don't get to die here! This is not a death worthy of a knight of the vow, is it?" He looked around the road. The storm had swallowed the surrounding forest, leaving nothing but a swirling white void all around. There was no shelter from the gale. "We have to keep going, Elsa. We have to keep moving."

The vow knight didn't move. Ian looped one of Elsa's arms over his shoulder and tried to lift her, but between her armor and muscular bulk, he wasn't able to budge her. Exhausted, he collapsed to the ground beside her, gasping for air.

"This is not... how I thought... I would die," he yelled at the storm. "This is not... the fate... I was promised..."

"Promised? Who said anything about promises?" The voice was deep and rumbly, something Ian could only hear with his bones. He raised his head. A dark mass slid out of the storm.

The hound.

It trotted easily through the snow, quickstep paws the size of dinner plates crunching through crust, its fur tangled with icicles, a beard of crystal breath dangling from its jaws. It jogged between Ian and Elsa, the smell of its breath sharp in the frozen void of the storm. One eye watched Ian as it passed.

"You have died once, Ian of hounds. When were you promised only the one death, or the one birth? You are given what you take. You are gifted with what you wrestle from the gods. That is our way." The words hummed through Ian's skull like the reverberations of a bell, his teeth chiming each sound, his eyes watering with the silent tumult.

"They are coming for you, Ian. The anger and the void." The hound glanced over its shoulder, one pale eye staring at the fallen prince. "They are coming."

And then the beast padded by, and disappeared into the storm. The snow and the wind swallowed him, leaving only tracks in the ice. Slowly those began to fill in, and in moments all trace of the gheist was gone.

Ian rolled over onto his knees, leaning over Elsa's still face. She hadn't moved, hadn't seen the totem spirit, nor heard his words. Ian sighed.

"You'll skin me for this, but..." Ian tugged his glove free and tilted Elsa's head, then slapped her across the cheek with all the force he could muster. A tear leaked from her frost-rimed eye, but she didn't move. Ian gritted his teeth and hauled back to slap her again.

"You're either brave or an idiot," Elsa said softly. She blinked several times, shuffling a skin of ice from her lashes. "Thinking you could strike me a second time."

"I'm not sure even the first was wise," he said, "but I can't get you onto the horse without a little help."

"This isn't a bed? We aren't beside a hearth?" she asked. "I feel warm enough. Let's stay here."

"No, no, that's called freezing to death. I think even a knight of the vow is subject to that. Only a little farther, I promise. Then you can rest."

"If you insist," Elsa said. She threw an arm over Ian's shoulder. When she hauled herself up, the force of it nearly crushed him into the ground. Together they reached Ian's horse. "This isn't my horse. Much too ugly for my horse."

"Your horse has given up, and I can see why, hauling around a lunk like you. Animal cruelty. Up you go," Ian said, grunting as he pushed Elsa into the saddle. After a moment of tottering back and forth, the vow knight settled into the seat, limp hands grasping the pommel. Ian clung to her waist, unsure that he was steady enough to walk on his own.

"Ian?" Elsa asked from the saddle.

"Yes?"

"There was something here," she said. "Wasn't there?"

Ian didn't answer. The storm moaned steadily around them, snow and frost gathering on his arms, melting whenever it touched Elsa's skin. The vow knight snorted.

"Ian? You can stop hugging me, now."

He pulled his arms awkwardly away from her waist, realizing suddenly that his face had been resting on her thigh. He looked up to see she was smiling bitterly. He gathered the reins of both horses, unwilling to mount Elsa's beast for fear of killing it on the spot, then started trudging down the road.

The prints were gone, but he was sure he could just see the shape of a hound in the storm ahead of them, like an afterimage of black fur floating in the snowy void.

His feet were numb, and his knees. The cold traveled slowly up his legs. He marched on, alone in the storm, following the ghost of a forgotten god.

Night came and went, the dawn little more than a brighter gale of biting wind and sleet that knifed through Ian's cloak. Hours more passed before he saw a shadow in the distance, and hours more than that before the shadow became a tower of stone, and a wall, and a gate.

20

THE MORNING WAS subdued. The crowd that had muttered and argued and threatened the previous evening now sat in stunned silence. Folam, the voidfather, sat beside Gwen, attended by the elders of the tribes. Cahl stood off to the side, hands clenched at his waist, hood pulled tight to his eyes.

The voidfather held an orange in his hand, which he peeled with slow precision, dropping pieces of skin at his feet like flower petals.

"So," Folam said after several moments of perfect silence. He glanced up at the elders. "What is happening to us?"

The elders looked among themselves, Judoc and Noel avoiding one another's eyes, the other tribesmen more curious than nervous. It was Morcant, elder of the tribe of tides, who spoke first. He stood, tall and thin, his cloak crusted with salt.

"The world is changing around us, Folam. We are here to discuss those changes, and what must be done about them."

"The world is always changing, Morcant," Folam said. "Every sunrise brings a new trouble, every birth and death and rebirth another opportunity. Such changes are the natural order of the world. The order that is the will of the gods. The order that we are sworn to uphold. But these days are different. These days, that order itself is changing, and that is not natural."

"We maintain the order as well as we can, voidfather," Morcant said. "If the natural order is upset, that is the fault of the celestial church. They hunt the gods. They disrupt the order. Only the Suhdrins can answer for that."

"We have one among us," Judoc muttered. "Perhaps she would like to speak for her southern kin?"

"It is easy to blame the Suhdrins for our troubles, elder bones, but there are domas in every village in Tener, as well. It is easier for us to maintain the rites in the north, but a mistake to think of the lords of Tener as our friends." Folam fixed Judoc with a gaze that would burn stone. "Simply because we share braids and ink. They wrap themselves in ancient clothes, but not ancient faith. Betrayal is betrayal."

"We can't go looking for enemies everywhere, elder," Morcant said.

"Nor can we assume friendship at every Tenerran hearth," Folam answered. "Nor among every tribe. We have become lazy. We have become weak."

"Weak? The church culls our faithful like wheat at the harvest," Judoc snapped. "The damned inquisition pulls down our henges and puts our witches on trial, or slaughters them in their beds. Your own daughter is being dragged to Heartsbridge in chains, and—"

"I know the fate of my daughter," Folam said. He stood, throwing aside the remnants of his orange, and began yelling, his jowls shaking. "She knew the risk when she left her henge to answer the call from the Fen hallow. A call that the rest of you *ignored*."

"The inquisition was massing at the border," Morcant

protested. "An army of priests was marching on the Fen Gate. Only a fool..."

"Enough!" Cahl snapped. "Enough of this bickering. The voidfather is right. Something is happening to us. Something is tearing us apart."

"Yes," Folam said. The old man settled back, calming his features. "Yes. We have defended the order on this island since the Spirit Wars, long before the Suhdrin landed here, with their domas and their priests and their iron. The crusades could not disrupt us. The betrayal of the Tenerran tribes, their conversion to the celestial church, and their assumption of Suhdrin titles could not ruin that balance. We have held true throughout the generations."

"And we will hold true for generations more," Morcant said.

"Will we?" Folam asked. "When I arrived yesterday, two of you were manifesting your gods and threatening violence. Don't we have enemies enough without that sort of foolishness?"

"Voidfather, it's clear that the celestial church has corrupted someone of our faith," Judoc said. He stood and pointed at Noel, who sat demurely at the edge of the elder's council. "The high inquisitor bound a god, summoning it in the battle of the Fen Gate to try to kill Malcolm Blakley. And who is more likely to have succumbed to the church's seduction—"

"Better to ask who would be better equipped to summon the god of death," Noel countered with a tight smile.

"I have heard these arguments," Folam said, "but there is more to this than the binding of Eldoreath, as disturbing as that is. Eldoreath is an aspect of death whose worship was forbidden, long before Suhdra was founded on our shores. Even the tribe of bones speaks his name with fear."

He shifted on his seat, and uncomfortably adjusted the stone around his neck. "We must ask how such knowledge came to the inquisitor—but there is more. Another god, forbidden of old, and yet walking the earth once again."

"Elder? What god is this?" Morcant asked.

"You have heard the words of this girl, but you have not listened to them," Folam said, turning to Gwen. "Tell us, child. You were pursued to the Fen hallow, by a priest of the inquisition?"

"And in the company of two other priests!" Judoc said. Folam glared him into silence and then gestured for Gwen to speak.

"Yes," she said. "The largest gheist... god... I've ever seen. Until the autumn god, at least."

"Tell us of this other god. By your tale, it led these priests to the hallow, despite the efforts of the wardens."

"The wardens died defending the hallow," Gwen answered. "They tried to keep it away, but it was relentless. It took all our effort, and nearly our lives, to kill it. And even that wasn't enough. Frair Allaister still found his way to the hallow."

"A relentless god, possessing the bodies of the dead. Hunting its prey, and so powerful that even the combined energies of the wardens of the Fen hallow could not deflect it." Folam slowly turned to the crowd, facing each elder, each tribe, one at a time. "A similar god attacked Greenhall at the height of summer, at the peak of the church's power. Does anyone know the name of this god?"

"No such spirit answers the rites of my tribe," Judoc answered. "He is not of the realm of death."

"Nor of tides," Morcant said. "Nor of any tribe that I can name."

"We do not know it in Suhdra," Noel said. "Do any of you?"

There was a long silence in the grove. The gathered tribesmen muttered among themselves. Folam waited patiently.

"You will not name it," he said finally. "Because its theos has passed from our knowledge."

"But how is that..." Morcant started, then paused as knowledge dawned. "One of the forbidden?"

"Yes. Like Eldoreath, and forgotten by all but a few." At the sound of the name, a shiver passed through the gathering. Folam raised his arms, palms up. "As elder of the tribe of voids, it has passed to me to hold all these names, even those who have been exiled from the world. So you may make your accusations, Judoc, you may make your assumptions, Noel, but they are empty. The hunter god does not belong to any of us. And yet the church holds it."

"How was it summoned?" Noel asked. "Where did they get this knowledge?"

"That is the question that remains. A group of rebels, little more than angry farmers, raided the doma at Gardengerry. That is where it began."

"How can farmers summon a god?" Judoc asked.

"One of them was more than they seemed," Folam answered. "This priest, Frair Allaister, led them in peasant's guise. How he accomplished his task, I cannot say. From there it went to Greenhall, and then on into the Fen. If what this girl tells us is true," he said, gesturing to Gwen. "It took the combined might of the wardens and two priests of the church to turn it aside."

"A battle that cost the wardens their lives," Cahl said.

"Yes," Folam agreed. "But with the wardens dead and

the shrine in the Fen Gate compromised, Allaister and his priests were still able to reach the hallow."

"How then did the autumn god rise? We have heard stories and accusations, but no truths," Morcant said. "Surely this girl couldn't..."

"This girl has a name," Gwen said. "And a station, and will be addressed appropriately!"

"The little princess is used to her Suhdrin manners, and her Suhdrin title," Judoc said.

"You will not give me a place in this conclave, nor listen to what I say other than to denounce me as a traitor," she answered. "So I will take my place, whether you approve or not."

"Peace, peace," Folam said gently. "The matter of Gwen's connection with Fomharra isn't important, not right now. What *is* important is how the church knew about him, how they found him, and how they have bound not one but two of the ancient gods to their will."

Gwen and Judoc continued glaring at each other, but when no one else spoke, Folam continued.

"And not just any gods. Forbidden gods. Sacombre bound the god of death, Eldoreath, condemned and hidden from even the tribe of death. Eldoreath was drawn from his shrine, weakened, and buried in the far north. How the high inquisitor found him and bound him is a great mystery. One whose answer, I suspect, stands somewhere in our midst."

"The name of this god is barely known to my tribe, and then only by reputation and fear," Judoc said. "An aspect of death bent by winter, corrupting its henge and driving its shamans mad. Its final prison was a secret, even to the tribe of bones."

"And what of this other god, bound by Frair Allaister

in Gardengerry?" Noel asked. "The hunter. No record of it stands, even in my most ancient tomes."

"Nothing more is known. Only that it rose from Gardengerry, a place all wise Tenerrans avoid. The villagers claim the walls are cursed." Folam spread his hands. "I suspect that's simply a memory of the god hidden within, and a proscription against its worship."

"Are there others? Forbidden gods the tribes have forgotten?" Noel asked. "If the inquisition has discovered these two, they may have stumbled upon some ancient text that details the remaining spirits."

"My thoughts exactly," Folam said. "So that is the question for this conclave. If we can determine where Sacombre's broken priests will strike next, we can perhaps stop them. Or at least slow them down."

"And why would we do that?" Morcant asked. "Let the celestials kill each other. Let the south rise up and fight. Tener will crush them on the stones of winter, and wash our fields in their blood."

"A red wish from the elder of tides," Noel chuckled. "Shouldn't that be the business of our friend Judoc?"

"We do not rush to death's embrace," Judoc answered. "Nor do we wish that realm on any, friend or foe. As to the question, we know of none other than Eldoreath."

"There are stories of deeper gods, out among the Broken Isles," Morcant said. "Shadows that move beyond the reach of mortal souls, far beneath the waves."

"If they are out of reach, they are no concern of ours," Folam said.

"So much of our history was lost in the crusades," Cahl said bitterly. "Here we stand, the eldest of our creeds, comparing folk tales in search of some forgotten truth."

"Forgotten truths are often the most powerful," Judoc said. "What of the harrowight?"

"The inquisition would have no need of binding that demon," Morcant answered. "If what the girl says is true, the harrowight still roams the land, eating souls and wearing them like a cloak, no matter how many times we banish it."

"But every god is an unfolding of some greater god," Judoc said. "Hiruk-Who-Waits is an aspect of the devouring rain, who is in turn an aspect of Maghuk, mother of storms."

"Yes," Folam said. "What of it?"

"What if the harrowight is an aspect of some other god? One we don't know, or have forgotten."

The conclave was quiet for a while. It was Judoc who broken the silence.

"If the harrowight is an aspect of anything, it is death, and we already know the fate of Eldoreath."

"We don't, actually," Judoc said, just loudly enough for Gwen and the elders to hear him. "The bitch let him go."

"I am well finished with your bullshit," Gwen said. "My family has borne the burden of our heresy for generations, while you hid in the woods and fucked trees. If you think for one second that that makes you holier than me, or wiser, I swear to the gods old and new that I'll cut the holiness right out of you."

"Gods forbid that I have to live in a castle while pretending to pray to the old gods," Judoc said. "What a tragedy that must have been! What a trial! Surely, you are blessed of the spirits." Murmurs of agreement spread through the room.

"Enough, the both of you," Folam snapped. "I will not have this conclave split open by a Suhdrin whelp!" The murmurs died down, and he continued. "There is the vernal spirit," he said. "Or what remains of him."

"The vernal..." Gwen began, then she fell silent. The others continued on, forgetting all about her.

"His shrine was destroyed, and his body broken," Cahl said. "Surely the church couldn't raise him, much less bind him?"

"They went after autumn," Noel said. "Perhaps they know of both, and know that spring would be harder to bend to their will. But having failed at the witches' hallow..."

"Autumn's twin remains?" Gwen asked, pushing into the conversation. "My family was told that the god of the Fen was the last of the great spirits hidden during the crusades. If Spring is still alive, we should protect it at all costs."

"The vernal god went mad, long before Suhdra waged war against us. Gave birth to a season of storms that threatened to tear the earth apart. Spring is still the most unsettled of the seasons," Cahl said. "Though in this case, it was the followers who drove their god insane, and not the other way around."

"The tribe of flowers was... enthusiastic in their worship," Folam said delicately. "They tried to conquer winter, and summer as well. They wanted to end the rites of death."

"And what's wrong with that?" Gwen asked.

"Imbalance," Folam answered. "Ultimately, the vernal spirit's core aspect had to be fragmented, his shrine profaned, and his lesser spirits bound."

"And his tribe?"

"They realized their mistake, and fought to keep their god from fulfilling its mission. It cost them their lives, and their place in the afterlife, as well," Judoc said.

"Their souls rest in the emptiness," Folam said, his

fingers brushing the stone around his neck.

"Very well. So that is our plan," Noel said. "We go to the profaned shrine of the vernal god. Hopefully before the inquisition finds it."

"And what of the vow knight who follows this one?" Judoc asked, gesturing to Gwen. "Will we lead the church to this shrine as well?"

"We could leave her behind," Morcant said. "Give her to Cahl and send them south."

"I won't be left behind..." Gwen started.

"We can't risk compromising this shrine, as well," Judoc said. "You have proven trouble enough."

"I agree," Noel said. "Send them away, or kill her and be done with it."

Cahl stepped between Gwen and the elders, his eyes glittering angrily.

"You would oppose the will of the conclave?" Noel asked. "Has this child touched your heart, Cahl of stones?"

Folam stood, grimacing at the assembly.

"That is not the will of the conclave," he said.

"We haven't voted," Noel said. "Who are you to say—"

"That is *not* the will of the conclave," Folam repeated. "She comes with us. It is necessary."

The conclave sat quietly, no one objecting, no one agreeing. Folam nodded.

"It is necessary," he repeated.

21

THE MEAL ENDED quite suddenly.

Duchess Helenne Bassion drank wine and mostly pretended she wasn't in command of an army camped just down the road. LaGaere and his flustered attendant made sortie after conversational sortie against the duchess, trying to determine what her plans were, whether she was going to take the fight to Tener or simply secure the border.

Again and again they tried. Did she mean to cross the Tallow at White Lake or lay siege to the Reaveholt? What sort of ranks did she have with her, and were they equipped with the tools necessary to build the trebuchets, towers, and rams that would be necessary.

Bassion dodged all of these questions with ease, giving only enough information to maintain the upper hand. She had an army. It was marching north. That was all they needed to know.

Lucas watched this exchange nervously. Warhome's departure from the Fen Gate had been bitter, and the loss of friends and honor stung the man. It wasn't the frair's job to keep the peace in the north, but the more he saw of LaGaere's enthusiasm for the Suhdrin army, the less he trusted it.

"Surely the Reaveholt cannot be left standing," LaGaere

said. "Not just conquered, nor merely occupied. It must be uprooted from the earth like a weed!" He held his cup out for more wine, never looking away from the Lady as he drained it. "The border has festered long enough. The infection needs to be purged, before it can spread."

"You speak of infections and uprootings, but what is the infection?" Bassion countered. "Is it the Reaveholt? Or is it the scant collection of men you have left behind at the Fen Gate, irritating the host and gathering pus around them?" She turned ever so slightly toward Sophie. "It was Halverdt's lie that created this wound. It will take Halverdt's blood to correct it."

"My blood, you mean," Sophie responded. "Am I to be sacrificed, to forge a peace with Tener?"

"Your family has given enough," Bassion said. "It is time to see your debt settled. This is a dangerous situation, Sophie, and I—"

"Greenhall," Sophie said. Bassion and LaGaere paused their argument, peering at the young girl. Sophie continued. "I am Greenhall, now, Duchess of my father's throne and heir to this title. You will address me as such."

"You are remarkably young to be sitting a duchess's seat," Bassion said carefully. "Not impossibly so, of course, but you may want to consider the options that are available to you." The woman smiled delicately, jewelry glinting, wine extended like a blessing. "A soft bride, encumbered by a throne not of her choosing. And if Adair's territories become available, there is a case to be made for folding it into your demesne. A tempting package."

"Package?" Sophie asked. "You would offer me up as a gift, to whichever prince is most in need of a bride? Is that why you're here, Roard?" she demanded, staring daggers at the young heir. Martin choked on his lamb, hurriedly clearing his throat. "I will not be a piece in your game of marriages, Bassion."

"You may address me as Galleydeep," Lady Bassion answered. "If you're going to play at nobility, child, and hope to claim a title for yourself, learn to respect those who have come before. I hoped to keep this friendly." She pressed a napkin against her lips, folding it small before laying it in her lap. "But perhaps that was a mistake.

"All I am saying, Sophie Halverdt, is that you have a lot of options laid before you. Consider them all before you go charging into destruction. It's advice that your father could have used."

Sophie stood. She wasn't a tall girl, and even on her feet she barely looked down on LaGaere beside her, or Lady Bassion across the table.

"I hope it won't offend your sensibilities," she said curtly, "if I attend to my father now. He has rested in the doma long enough. There are prayers to be said, and the blessings of the gods to seek." She threw her napkin down on her plate, glaring at Helenne Bassion. "That is a lesson *you* could use, my lady."

She stormed out, leaving the servants to awkwardly clear the dishes while the remaining guests watched. Helenne snorted angrily.

"A child," she said. "A child is running the most powerful Suhdrin throne in the north. No wonder the place is overrun with savages."

"Cut their hair and wash the ink from their skin, and you would never know the difference," Lucas said quietly, remembering the guards who had greeted them at the

Reaveholt. Bassion turned her glittering eyes toward him.

"Oh, I think I would—my nose still works, after all," she said, then she laughed lightly and finished her wine. "What of you, Frair Lucas? What do you hope to achieve here? Justice? A reasonable war? Aren't those the sorts of things Cinder demands?"

"Winter is a harsh season, my lady, and Cinder a harsh god." Lucas stood slowly, unbending tired bones, wincing when pain shot up his legs. "He gives disease, and war, and death, to every living soul. Then he gives us the judgment to overcome those things."

"And what is your judgment?" LaGaere asked. "What should young Sophie do?"

"My judgment rests on Tomas Sacombre, and the heresy he committed to start this war. Its ending is none of my business. Not yet, at least."

He left them there, talking and arguing about what should or could be done with a dead man's house, and with his daughter, and with the war they had created around them.

Frair Lucas felt remarkably like the prisoner he was supposed to be escorting. While Greenhall celebrated a spring that was still a winter away, and young Sophie observed the funereal rites of her betrayed father, Lucas and his small band were confined to the keep, separated from the city proper by a sturdy wall and hundreds of suspicious eyes. They received regular updates from their column, camped outside the city walls, but were otherwise cut off from the world.

As night began to fall and their third day in captivity ended, Lucas watched as the moon rose, witnessing it from a parapet of the keep. Sir Horne found him there. The knight was dressed in fine chain and silk, not quite battle-ready, but far from unprepared.

"Frair," Horne said as she ascended the stairs, as quiet as a breeze. "I trust the night finds you well?"

"Well enough," Lucas said. "Though I would like to be on my way. Ever since our disastrous dinner, Lady Bassion won't see me to arrange an escort south, and Sophie refuses to give audience, either. I don't know how I'm supposed to negotiate passage if I'm not allowed to talk to anyone."

"Those two have been spending a good amount of time together, so I'm told. Arguing, mostly." Horne laughed, leaning against the parapet stone. Her dark hair was tightly knotted to her head, with strands of dark gems twisted into the braids. When she wasn't kitted for war, the knight might easily pass for a lady of the court. "Sophie may have rejected her father's love of the inquisition, but she has more than inherited his paranoia."

"Not a bad lesson for a girl joining the Circle of Lords, if that truly is her intent. She will earn more with caution than with trust."

Horne didn't answer, only nodded and looked down at the valley below. The army of Galleydeep nestled among the trees to their south like a meadow of golden gems, their campfires twinkling between leaves and along the road. They watched it in silence for a long time.

"When you get to Heartsbridge, will they accept you as a hero, or as a traitor?" Horne asked. She shifted on the wall, turning to face Lucas, resting on her elbow. Lucas shrugged.

"The inquisition? I'm not sure. Tomas Sacombre was popular in the south, especially among those priests who saw the north as little more than a problem to be solved. They won't like seeing him brought low."

"And you? Were you popular in the south?"

"I never stayed long enough to let them form an opinion," Lucas said with a smile. "I was born on the road, raised on the road, belonged on the road. One day I will die on the road."

"Most men hope to die in their beds, of old age or with their lover. Perhaps both," Horne said. "While they live, they talk of dying in glory or for honor, but in their hearts they hope for the easy exit."

"Few of us get that," Lucas said. "Especially in my profession."

"Death by god, that is your usual fate," Horne said. "An unpleasant way to go."

"The gheists are rarely gentle."

"Where is your vow knight? I have seen none of Strife's faithful in our company."

"She hunts," Lucas said. He stooped lower in his shoulders, his chest nearly to the rough stone of the parapet. The weight of Elsa's absence pushed him down, but only when he thought about it. "As she is sworn to do."

"My mother thought to make a vow knight of me," Horne said wistfully, only the slightest trace of bitterness in her voice. It surprised him. "It turned out that I wasn't cut out for that sort of light."

"It is not an easy path," Lucas said, his eyes clouding as he thought of the pain on Elsa's face every time she manifested Strife's gifts—the blood that seared through her veins. "I would not..."

He paused. There was movement in the darkness far below. Without thought he twisted naether through his eyes and drew the night close, spanning the distance. A column of men creeping through the woods. Their armor was blackened. Lucas was only able to see them because of his bond with Cinder and the clear night air.

"Frair?" Horne asked. She put a gentle hand on his shoulder. "Are you well?"

Lucas shook his head, snapping out of the naether vision.

"Galleydeep is moving to surround our camp," he said. Sir Horne straightened, confusion on her face. "Wake LaGaere and Roard. Tell them we're riding out of this place, and cutting down anyone who tries to stop us."

"But, we can't..."

"Go!" Lucas roared. He gathered his robes around him, drawing a silvered blade from his belt and touching it to his forehead as he knelt. "We need to get Sacombre out of there. Now!"

And then he loosened his soul, and let his spirit flee out into the night.

Torvald sat facing the fire, listening to the men complain. With Frair Lucas ensconced in the castle and an army looming to their south, there was a lot of tension in the camp, finding its way out in arguments and fistfights. He knew he would never be a great warrior, or a famous general, or a legendary duke, but Torvald liked to think he ran a tight camp.

So he liked to walk among the campfires, pausing at each one long enough to calm the spirits of those hunched around, listen to a story or two about the battles at White Lake and the Fen, or if the wounds were too recent, older stories of home and lovers and the like. Then he would go to the next fire, and the next, all through the night.

"It's time I continue on my rounds," Torvald said as he

rose to move to the next group of men. This had been his first stop of the night, the moon having only just risen. He wished the frair was around to say the prayers and soothe the fears. The men trusted the frair.

As he approached another campfire, Torvald looked around, smiling through his massive moustache. "Good hunting, tonight?"

"Bassion's outriders have flushed the countryside," one of the men growled. "All the farms are picked, the forests bare, and the women fled to their castles. We'll be eating jerky and tickling our own stones until Heartsbridge."

"Clarence will tickle your stones, Yohn," a second soldier laughed. "Or Maudette. Hands like hers, though, you may end up a eunuch."

"At least we don't—" Yohn stopped midsentence, staring at the fire. Then he dropped his mug of thin wine and lurched backward.

At the heart of the fire, a shadow grew. It curled outward, snuffing flame and turning coal to ice. Ribbons of darkness grew upwards in a spinning braid of black light. The ribbons wove themselves into a man, laced with embers from the fire, his features flickering in the dim light of the dying blaze. Flames spun out from the pit like a flock of sparrows startled by the storm. The other men seated around the fire shoved away from the pit, scrabbling on hands and butts, falling over backward in their terror.

Sir Torvald said a prayer and drew his blade.

"In Cinder's name, I defy you!" he shouted, or tried to shout through quivering lips and moustache. The gheist stepped forward. Behind him, the fire swelled back to life, framing the shadowy figure in amber light.

"Be sensible, Torvald," the shadow hissed. "It is your frair."

"Lucas?" Torvald asked. "What... how..."

"Silence," Lucas said. He looked around the fire. "All of you, keep silent. I am still in the castle, but I need you to act, and quickly."

Torvald collected himself as the men stood, shuffling awkwardly before they knelt. Lucas's shadowform waved them off.

"No time for that," he said. "Bassion's army is moving against us. I think they're coming for the high inquisitor."

"Let 'em have the creepy bastard," Yohn muttered, then he was silenced when Lucas glared at him.

"The man is right, my frair," Torvald said. "You won't find many souls in this camp willing to die for Sacombre. If the duchess is coming to take him, I say let her have him."

"It's not for Bassion to see Sacombre to justice, nor is it for you to surrender that duty. I am not asking you to die in his defense." Lucas grew, the ribbons of his shadowform coming loose, drawing the man in broader strokes. "Here is what you must do. And quickly. Time is fleeting."

Lucas gasped to life, spitting the naether essence from his lungs as his spirit returned to his body, then dragged himself to his feet. Still alone on the wall. He tottered down the stairs, making his way back to the chambers Sophie had set out for them.

A hand grabbed his shoulder from the shadows. He was reaching for the naether, to drive a spear of ice through his attacker, when Sir Horne's face loomed out of the darkness. She hissed him into silence.

"They have guards looking for us. Whatever is happening, Sophie is part of it."

"What of Roard and LaGaere?"

"Waiting behind the stables. The rest of our party will be more difficult to disentangle," Horne said. "LaGaere's men are bunking in the barracks, and can not be reached without rousing the guard."

"Then we will leave them behind. I don't think their lives are at risk," Lucas said. "At least, not yet." Together the pair snuck down to the stables, where they found LaGaere sitting on his horse impatiently. He was fully armed and armored, as though he had slept in his gear. Two of his knights stood nearby, preparing their saddles. Both were clearly accustomed to a squire's assistance.

"Where is Roard?" Lucas asked.

"Saying good-bye to the sweet stable girl," LaGaere said. "We wouldn't have horses if not for that boy's charm."

"Good of him to think ahead with his affections," Horne said wryly. "If he was thinking ahead at all."

"You're besmirching me, I assume," Martin said, leading his horse into the alley. He tossed a bag over his saddle, then mounted smoothly. "What are we doing, my frair? This doesn't seem as if you have secured our safe passage..."

"Well, we *are* going to pass through that gate," Lucas answered as he settled into his saddle. Horne settled into hers. "Gods know if it will be done safely."

The six riders stamped around the stables and toward the main gate. A cluster of guards, talking nervously near the sally gate, peeled free from the wall and spread out, cutting off Lucas's escape. There were more spears along the catwalk than usual, and archers watched from the parapets.

"We are expected," Horne said quietly.

"We are," Lucas agreed. He raised his voice, addressing

the guards. "I demand to speak to Lady Sophie! Go fetch your master!"

"You will have to wait," came the response, from a woman. "The young duchess is otherwise involved." The speaker stepped out of the guardhouse. Lady Bassion was attended by a trio of knights, her dining room finery traded for simpler garb. She gestured to the walls, and the archers bristled to attention.

"What have you done with her, Galleydeep?" Lucas asked.

"I have made a deal. Her loyalty, and my support in the Circle, when she claims her father's throne."

"She would not have negotiated for what she could rightly claim by blood," LaGaere said. "What else have you given her?"

"Sacombre's blood," Lucas muttered before she could answer. "That's it, isn't it, Galleydeep? You hold us here while she avenges her father's death?"

Bassion didn't answer, merely inclined her head.

"He is under my protection, Galleydeep!" Lucas cried. "You have no right to judge him, much less offer out his execution as a favor to an angry child!"

"The high inquisitor will not meet his end this way," LaGaere agreed. He drew his sword, followed seconds later by his two knights. Roard and Horne looked nervously to Frair Lucas before unsheathing their own steel. The duke of Warhome continued. "This is not a worthy death for that man."

"I am only doing Cinder's business, Warhome," Bassion said. "Let's not be fools. Sacombre was only going to Heartsbridge to die. Death there, death here." She shrugged elaborately. "He will still be dead—whereas if you try to cross this gate, you will precede him."

"Cinder's business is not yours to attend, duchess!" Lucas said stiffly. He started forward at a slow trot, gathering the heavy shadows of the courtyard around his shoulders. "Winter does not hold court in the Circle of Lords, nor does the god of judges attend to the will of a petty duchess!"

His form swelled, the torches that lined the yard flickering away from him, the shadows gathered at his shoulders and twisted into his cloak, billowing into a larger and larger storm cloud of black lightning. Lucas proceeded toward the gate. Tendrils of shadow dragged behind him, dancing closer to the increasingly nervous guards.

"In the name of Cinder, you will stand aside! By the writ of the celestial church, by the vows you have sworn and the prayers you have offered to the twin gods of heaven, you will stand aside! You have threatened us with death, Lady Bassion, but I threaten you with death unending, a death unquiet and eternal!"

The Lady Bassion was unbowed, but her men were broken by Lucas's display. The gate began to creak open. She whirled around.

"Stand your guard, fools! He's nothing but show and shiver!" She grabbed a sword from her attendant guard and waved it at the gates. "Stand your ground!"

"Let's not test the inquisitor's power, my lady," Sir Horne said. She appeared beside Lady Bassion, and struck the duchess on the temple with the pommel of her dagger. The woman flopped to the stones like a fish. "Open the gates!" Horne yelled.

The gates opened, and Lucas rode through, followed by LaGaere and his knights. Martin waited for Horne before rushing through himself.

Horne hurried up to Lucas's side.

"You're an angry little storm front, my frair," she joked as they clambered down the wide road into Verdton. The windows on either side of the road filled with startled faces. Horne looked over at Lucas. Her eyes went wide.

"Frair Lucas?"

The frair hung onto his reins with white knuckled fists, his face pale, his eyes fluttering shut. When Horne reached for him, the priest nearly fell from his saddle.

"I may have over... extended." He swallowed loudly, grimacing. "Overextended myself."

"Warhome!" Horne hissed. "Get back here! We need to stop somewhere!"

"No," Lucas said. "No, we must continue. Torvald has moved Sacombre out of the camp, hopefully before Sophie got there." The frair pulled himself upright, staring grimly ahead. "We will meet them along the river, but only if we hurry."

The knights exchanged worried looks, then closed ranks around the priest and rode hard for the city walls.

2
MAD GODS

22

MARCEL SAT OVERLOOKING the tumbled down ruin of the keep. The stables were alive with light that glimmered off the clouds of incense smoke wafting from inside. The prayers of his brother and sister priests mingled with the light. They would notice he was missing, but Marcel didn't care. Something had to be done. Something apparently only he was willing to do.

The sound of steel and the smell of blood was still sharp in his mind. Marcel could hear the horrible, wet cough of Sir Xander as the man sank to his knees, a Tenerran blade in his gut. And that foul-mouthed savage, Halfpenny, the one who had been calling them all names and fingering his blade, curled up and dying in the corner. Then the arrest of men who had only been protecting themselves.

The trip north had come with fear, fear that only grew worse with each step. Frair Gilliam warned them to say their prayers at night, lest the gheist take them, and their blessings in the morning, lest the pagan witches steal the light from their eyes. But it was the men who were supposed to be guarding them that terrified Marcel. The Blakleys, and the Adairs, and the Rudaines, with their rough clothes and crude manners, their false faith and pagan hearts. Gilliam preached patience and the love of Strife, but Marcel was sworn to Cinder, and the time for judgment had come.

He wrapped his cloak tightly around his shoulders and eased his way to the base of the curtain wall. This section of the defenses suffered worse then most during the gheist's attack, and the stone barrier lay in ruins. The Tenerran occupiers had set up a thicket of wooden palisades to compensate, but there were gaps in the defenses. Gaps Marcel started looking for the day he arrived at the Fen Gate, just in case he and his fellow priests needed to get out in a hurry.

Or in case someone else needed to come inside without being seen.

It wasn't a wide path, no more than a shoulder's width between looming boulders, but enough for a man to pass. A trick of the light, and it had missed the attention of the defenders, the entrance blinded by a boulder that looked massive but had splintered into a thin sliver that screened the way.

The first few steps were difficult to manage, with rubble threatening to turn an ankle, but once he was past Marcel was able to walk easily through to the outside. Minutes later he was in the thick woods that surrounded the northern side of the castle. In Suhdra, this brush would have been cleared to protect the approach. Apparently the Adairs couldn't be bothered, or perhaps they trusted the spirits of the forest to guard them.

Muttering prayers of protection, Marcel trudged in the direction he hoped was east, toward the godsroad. The way was difficult, choked with ironwood and rotten leaves, and clouds hid Cinder's guiding light. He didn't dare light a torch, but after a while his eyes adapted somewhat to the gloom. The wind that whispered through the trees sounded like a song, sinister and dark. Marcel was sure he saw faces in the bark of passing trees, and eyes blinking from the shelter of low hanging boughs.

A fretful hour passed before he stumbled onto the smooth stones of the road. He was farther north than he hoped. He would have to hurry if he meant to be home before dawn. Frair Gilliam might forgive his absence at the evening prayer, but if Marcel wasn't back in the stable for the dawnsong, alarms would be raised.

He was so tired, so wrung out from his trip through the haunted forest, and so relieved to be safely on the sanctified stones of the godsroad, that he didn't notice the shadows peel away from the forest. They loped behind him for several minutes before a boot struck stone and drew his attention.

Marcel whirled around, drawing a thin knife from his belt.

"I'm not carrying money," he hissed. The shadows paused. There were two of them, large men carrying swords. Probably armored, though it was difficult to tell in the shadows. "I'm a man of the gods. The true gods!"

"True gods, eh?" the nearest shadow said. A woman's voice, to Marcel's surprise. "And which would those be?"

"Cinder is watching you!" Marcel said. "He will judge your actions, and see justice done to your souls."

"Stow it, man of the gods," the woman said. She sheathed her blade and signaled to the forest. Another dozen shadows appeared. One of them unhooded a lantern, flooding the road in light. The shadows resolved into soldiers. They looked rough, like they'd been sleeping on the ground. The woman's eyes were creased with worry. She looked Marcel up and down.

"You must be part of the lot come to save the Fen Gate."

"Are you with the Suhdrin camp?" he asked anxiously.

"Matters in the castle have gotten out of hand. One of my guards was killed trying to defend himself from those savages, and the rest have been put in chains! The inquisitor's life is at risk."

"One of your guards? Savages?" The big man somehow drew himself up taller, his shoulders stiffening. "What do you mean by that?"

"The Tenerrans, of course!" Marcel snapped. "Come with me. There's a secret way into the castle, unknown to the guards and beneath the sentinel's eye. A small force could make their way inside and secure the gates, I'm sure of it. Quickly, before my absence is noted!"

"Oh," the woman said, shaking her head. "The mistakes we make in our youth."

"Good thing is, we usually only make them once," the big man said. He loomed closer, the light from the lantern splashing across his face. Tattoos ringed his eyes, as crude and profane as a pagan's prayer. Marcel drew a sharp breath and stumbled away, only to fall into the arms of another member of their company.

"You're pagans!" he hissed.

"No, lad, we are not," the woman said. "I am Sir Caris Doone of Maebrook, sworn to Houndhallow, as well as to the celestriarch and all the frairs of Heartsbridge. But I take a sour view of you trying to lead a Suhdrin force into the castle I'm meant to be protecting."

"Please, don't kill me! You can't kill a priest of Cinder. There will be repercussions..."

"Gods, stop your burbling. I won't kill a priest, not without better reason than this," Doone said. "Now let's try again on what you were planning, and why."

"Does it matter?" a voice asked from the woods. The trees were lined with silver in that direction, as though a false dawn had broken among their boughs. The cadre of soldiers looked around nervously.

"My lady, it would be best..." Doone started.

"Do not tell me what is best," the voice answered. A woman emerged from the forest. She was wrong. Her hair twisted sinuously in the air, her skin shone like dulled pewter, and her eyes looked at Marcel with a piteous, almost unearthly glare. "This man threatens my husband."

"Lady... Lady Blakley?" Marcel stuttered. He had never met the duchess of Houndhallow, but the woman wore the colors of the hound, and fit descriptions that he had heard. Other than the glowing skin, of course. "What has happened to you?"

"I have lost my trepidation," Sorcha Blakley answered. She raised a hand in Marcel's direction. "And you have lost my patience."

"My lady, no!" Doone yelled, but it was too late.

The ground beneath Marcel's feet grew muddy. He tried to take a step back, but his foot broke through the muck, revealing a hidden spring that welled up. Marcel stared down in horror as the water crawled up his leg, cold as steel. The weight of it started crushing his chest.

He looked up at Sorcha. "In the name of Cinder and the holy inquisition, I cast you out, demon of old, god of the broken—"

"Hush," Sorcha whispered. The water gheist enveloped Marcel's head like a cowl, icy strands of living water filling his mouth and pressing hard against his eyes. The pressure in his skull grew and grew and grew, until it became impossible.

* * *

The column of swirling, steely water clouded into red. The boy's face pressed against the surface of the gheist, mouth hung raggedly open, eyes wide with terror. His skull was misshapen.

Sorcha's guards stood in horror at the spectacle. Sir Doone approached the lady, a hand at her throat.

"My lady… Sorcha. You should not have done that," she whispered.

"Shouldn't I? The inquisition seeks to conspire with the Suhdrin army. This man wanted to lead soldiers into my husband's castle, surely not for a festival." Sorcha slowly lowered her outstretched arm, watching as the priest's body settled to the ground, its broken parts arranging themselves awkwardly into the mud. "Sacombre defied us, tricked us, tried to undo us with his lies. Why should I be merciful to one of his followers?"

"This man… this boy," Doone said, prodding the broken child with her toe. "He was a fool, and perhaps a dangerous one, but he didn't deserve to die. Not like this."

"No one deserves to die like that," the big man whispered. Sorcha shot him an angry look, then shook her head.

"My husband has abandoned me to the forest. The inquisition would hang me in my current state, and my son has left me to chase after some girl. And now you, the very souls meant to guard me, you doubt me when I act only to defend myself." Sorcha backed away from them. "Are you keeping me here for them? Are you holding me just long enough for the inquisition to find me?"

"My lady, I will protect you with the last of my blood," Doone said. "You must believe my loyalty. To you, and to your husband."

"Must I?" Sorcha asked, tilting her head. "Very well,

but there has been enough hiding. Malcolm thinks me ill, or mad, or both. I will show him otherwise. I will show him my love, if not my mercy." She stalked off, leaving the cadre to stand around nervously.

They looked to Sir Doone.

"Let's get this cleaned up," she said, nodding to the dead priest. The mud was quickly drying around his body, the blood and water staining his clothes like rust.

"Leave the priest," Sorcha called over her shoulder. "Let them see what is waiting for them. Let them know I am coming."

Doone looked around at her men, then shrugged. Together they walked into the forest, disappearing among the trees like smoke in the wind.

Moments after they were gone, a lone figure appeared. She came from the direction of the castle, following the same halting path that Marcel had taken. The woman, wrapped in tight black leathers and armed with a huntsman's sword, paused when she saw the priest's body.

She went to it, prayed over it, drew patterns in the dirt and on his flesh with her own blood. Then she disappeared the way she had come.

When the sun rose, certain shadows lingered on the corpse, gathering in its eyes, and around its heart.

23

"THIS IS WHERE they're meant to be," Lucas said. They waited in a copse of trees that overlooked a narrow cart trail. The first light of dawn crept through the sky, tinting the horizon gold. Lucas turned to the other riders. "We have to go back."

"You better have a pretty good explanation of why we ran," LaGaere said. He and his cadre of knights lurked at the edge of the copse, separated from Sir Horne and young Martin Roard. "Especially after your little display, my frair."

"We had to get out," Lucas said. "Bassion would have let us sit in that courtyard until Sophie returned with Sacombre's body on a spit."

"Sophie Halverdt already fears the power of the inquisition," Martin said. "When she hears—"

"Yes, yes," Lucas snapped. "I'm becoming used to being unpopular." He peered around in all directions. "Where is that fool Torvald?"

"Perhaps he didn't get out in time," Sir Horne said. "Or perhaps his loyalty is more to Suhdra, rather than a grumpy old man who threatens him with nightmares."

Lucas grunted but didn't answer. The others in the group shifted uncomfortably, waiting and watching the sun slowly rise. Finally LaGaere cleared his throat.

"We must do something," the lord of Warhome said. "Bassion will have sent out patrols, and alerted Lady Sophie to our escape. If Sacombre is not already in her hands, he soon will be. I'd rather not stand here while the high inquisitor is murdered by an angry child."

"Murdered? To whom are you loyal, Warhome?" Martin asked. "You realize we're taking the man to Heartsbridge for execution, don't you?"

"We are taking him to the celestriarch to be judged," LaGaere answered. "He may still be innocent."

"If that's the case, it may be best to leave him with Sophie," Martin said.

"We already know where your loyalty lies, Roard," LaGaere said. "Blakley probably has you with us just to put a knife in the high inquisitor's back, if it looks like he might escape what you consider 'justice.'"

"Quiet," Sir Horne said. "There's a rider." The others quieted, instinctively hunching down in their saddles. She pointed. "There, among the grasses."

Deep in the thick grasses that lined the track, the stalks rustling off his armor, rode Sir Torvald. The man looked all around, traveling slowly, one hand on his blade. The sound grew louder as he approached.

"The fool thinks he's sneaking along," LaGaere said. "No wonder it's taken so long for him to arrive, traveling at that rate."

"Where's the damned wagon?" Lucas muttered. "Where's Sacombre?"

"Only one way to know," Horne said. She rode out of the copse, waving to catch Torvald's attention. The rest followed, and they all rode down together to the cart path.

"Sir Torvald," Lucas said. "Where have you been?"

"My frair," Torvald said. "Lady Halverdt was on us faster than we thought. She was securing our perimeter before we were able to get the full team rigged."

"Then she has the high inquisitor?" Horne asked.

"No, we rode with half a team, and even then only narrowly escaped, because some of Halverdt's men got into it with our guards."

"Was there bloodshed?" LaGaere asked. "Gods help me, if that bitch killed some of my men over this foolishness—"

"Silence," Lucas snapped, and something dark growled through his voice. The frair was losing patience. "Torvald, where is the high inquisitor?"

"In the wagon, my frair."

"And the wagon is...?"

"This way, my frair." Torvald turned back to the cart path. "Right this way."

The creek had overflowed its banks, swollen thanks to the late summer storms and the unnaturally cold ground. Even so, the ford was easy enough for horses and most carts, but in their haste to flee Halverdt's encirclement, they hadn't been able to hook up the wagon's full team.

The sides of Sacombre's wheeled prison were lined in steel and heavy oak. The horses strained against their bridles, but the wagon only dug deeper into the loose scree of the creek bed. Icy cold water lapped up against the wagon's side.

"That's a confounding mess," Martin said. He and Sir Horne waited by the bank, while LaGaere and his men surrounded the wagon and watched the surrounding trees nervously. Frair Lucas rode out to examine the wagon. "Can you do something for it, Lucas?"

"This is beyond prayer," Lucas said. He slid off his horse and bent to examine the wheels, then made a curious sound. "The axles are splinters, Torvald."

"Explains why the wheels aren't turning," Horne muttered.

"How can that be?" LaGaere asked. "The current isn't that strong, nor the horses that hardy."

"How, indeed?" Lucas muttered. He reached beneath the wagon, coming out with a handful of slick, soft wood. "That's some poor luck."

"Trouble, Lucas?" Sacombre called from inside the wagon. His eyes appeared in the narrow slot. "We're getting a bit of an unnecessary bath in here."

"You fouled the wheels, Sacombre."

"Why would I do that? We're running from young Sophie Halverdt, aren't we? I can't imagine she has my best health in mind."

"Either way, they're ruined," Lucas said. He tossed the rotten wood into the creek, watching the current carry it away. "So we have two choices. We can stay here and wait for Sophie to catch up with us, which will not be particularly healthy for you, or me, or really any of us."

"I am not in favor of this," Sacombre said sweetly. "What is the other solution?"

Lucas sighed long and hard, rubbing his hand over his face. He walked back to the bank, signaling to Sir Horne, Martin, and LaGaere.

"Cut the horses free," he said. "We're going to need them."

"For what?" LaGaere asked.

"We will abandon the wagon. There are no saddles for

the draught horses, so Sacombre and the witch will have to ride bareback, at least until we can find a better alternative. And then..."

"You mean to free the prisoners?" LaGaere asked. "Has the season gotten to you, priest? Has Lady Strife gifted you with madness at last?"

"They will not be free. Both are shackled in bloodwrought iron," Lucas said. "I will lead Sacombre myself. You may guard the witch, if that makes you feel better." He motioned to the guards on the bank. "Get your men moving, Warhome. Halverdt's scouts will find us soon enough."

LaGaere didn't answer, but gestured angrily to his men. Lucas sloshed out of the creek, then took some supplies from his saddlebag, moved to the shadow of a nearby tree, and started preparing for some kind of ritual. Martin and Sir Horne went to watch.

"Is this wise?" Martin asked. "We're going to a lot of trouble to escape Suhdrin justice."

"What Lady Halverdt has in mind is not justice," Lucas said. He was laying out runes of pitted iron, arranging them and whispering a prayer over each. The air grew colder.

"What are you doing?" Sir Horne asked nervously.

"A contingency, in case Sacombre isn't as helpless as I've claimed."

"But the bloodwrought manacles..."

"Yes, yes. Very effective, but not perfect. And intended mostly to work on pagans. I don't really know how well they protect against the workings of an inquisitor." Lucas glanced over at the wagon. "If there's anything of Cinder left in that man." LaGaere's men had got Sacombre out of the wagon and were leading him toward the shore. The high inquisitor looked around with bemusement, his pale face creased with a smile.

"You could have warned us about this," Martin said. "If Sacombre still had access to his powers, we should have been prepared."

"Prepared for what? How do you prepare for a man who could hunt your nightmares and pluck your soul like an overripe fruit? What would you do each night, knowing that Tomas might be waiting in your dreams?" Lucas looked up. His eyes were tired. "How do you guard against that?"

"This isn't putting me at my ease, frair," Sir Horne said quietly.

"It's not your burden to carry, sir," Lucas said, returning to his runes. "It is mine."

"Still," Horne said. "I would prefer—"

She was interrupted by a scream. Horne and Martin both drew blades, whirling in the direction of the sound. It came from Fianna. The witch, her robes filthy from weeks in the cage, face darkened with runes and eyes wide with terror, was being dragged to the nearest tree by LaGaere's men. The duke of Warhome watched with casual interest.

"What are you doing?" Martin barked.

"There's no reason to drag this bitch all the way to Heartsbridge," LaGaere said. "We will do what Houndhallow lacked the nerve to carry out."

"He's quite right, you know," Sacombre said. "The woman has been nothing but a bore on the journey so far."

"You don't have the authority to do this," Martin said.

"Why in hells do you care?" LaGaere asked. "If you came across her on the road, are you telling me you wouldn't cut her down? Do you have sympathy for witches now?" The duke turned to face Martin, a corner of his mouth twitching up. "You abandoned your Suhdrin brothers at the Fen Gate. Have you gone completely over to the pagan side, princeling? I'll just as happily hang you for treason. There's room enough on that branch for you both."

"There will be none of that," Sir Horne said, stepping between Martin and the duke. "The sins of that battle weigh heavily on all involved."

"Do they?" LaGaere said. "My soul is light enough." He turned back to his men. They had a rope around Fianna's neck, tossing the other end over a low branch. "Do your duty, gentlemen."

"They will not," Lucas said, finally standing. The men froze, looking from their lord to the inquisitor. LaGaere clucked his tongue.

"This *is* disappointing, Frair Lucas. If it's how the inquisition handles confessed witches, it's no wonder the north has fallen into rot and ruin."

"Lucas was always one for mercy," Sacombre said. "A pity it doesn't extend to his own kind."

"You'll both have your day in court," Lucas said. "Now cut her free."

"You're fooling yourself, Lucas," Sacombre said. "I *will* have my day—before the gods, before the lords of the Circle, and the celestriarch himself. They will understand why I did what I have done, and once I am free, it will be your day to be judged." Then he nodded toward Fianna. "This one they will throw into the cells to be forgotten. If she's lucky."

LaGaere laughed, short and sharp. He walked to his horse, clapping Lucas on the shoulder.

"She's yours to watch," he said. "Gods help you if she gets free."

Once LaGaere was past, Lucas collapsed a little on himself. Martin moved to his side, in case the inquisitor fell.

"I will watch her, my frair," Martin said. "Day and night."

"Gods bless you, lad. I don't think I could have kept an eye on them both." Lucas gathered his robes and walked to where Sacombre was waiting. "Wipe that smile off your face, Tomas. This isn't going to end well for you, no matter what you believe."

"It won't end well for anyone, I'm afraid," Sacombre responded. "But we'll see. We will see." Lucas led him to one of the horses, then limped slowly to his own mount.

"Best get moving," Sir Horne said. "LaGaere is already heading down the road."

Martin shook himself out of his reverie, then went to gather up Fianna. It took a while to get her on the horse and sorted out. The witch paid him no mind at all, but stared daggers at Sacombre's back the entire time. By the time they were on the road, the others were well ahead, and Martin had to hurry to catch up.

As he left the creek behind, his eyes caught the circle of runes that Lucas had been preparing. They were gone. Only ash remained, burned down into the ground like hot coals, the dirt and stone and leaves that surrounded them burned away.

They snaked down the cart path until the sun was heavy in the sky, then cut into the forest. The sounds of their pursuit were all around them.

"They must have found the wagon," LaGaere said. He rode just behind Lucas, who in turn was just behind Sacombre. The high inquisitor was bound hand and foot, with a chain running from his belt to Lucas's saddle.

"By now, yes," Lucas answered. He craned his neck to look ahead. Sir Horne rode at the front. The rest of the party, with the witch in their midst, trailed close behind the knight. "All the more reason to keep moving, and keep quiet."

"They know where to look. They know we aren't slowed by the wagon. There are hundreds of them, and Sophie Halverdt will not stop until Sacombre is dead."

"In that case," Lucas said lightly, "it will save us the trouble of the journey south.

"Why are you doing this?" LaGaere asked. "You want him dead as much as the girl does. Why risk your life and reputation?"

"There is little risk to my reputation," Lucas said, "but as for Sacombre..." He shrugged, though there was no uncertainty to it. "Sophie Halverdt wants him dead. I want him tried, and sentenced, and executed. Mob rule belongs to Strife, and the anger of summer. Cinder demands a more civilized approach."

"He will still be dead," Sir Horne said over her shoulder.

"That I will," Sacombre said. "Soon enough."

"*Not* soon enough, perhaps," Lucas said. "But soon."

They rode in silence for a long time, twisting between trees and over ridgelines, skirting each clearing they came to and hurrying across roads that could not be avoided. Near the middle of the line, Martin Roard rode beside the witch, Fianna. She rode stiffly, each bounce and waver nearly knocking her from the horse's back, her balance made worse by the lack of a saddle. As they crossed a ridgeline, her horse danced sideways, and it was only Martin's quick hands that kept her from the ground.

"Have you never ridden a horse before?" he asked, once she was secure.

"Never had the need," she said. Her face was all sharp planes and tattooed skin, her eyes much older than the rest of her. She smiled weakly and shrugged. "We walk everywhere."

"Must take forever to get from place to place," Martin said.

"Where would I go? My henge, my heart, and my gods. They are all the same place, so why would I need to go someplace far away?"

"Ian said you traveled a distance with him, and that you were already far from home," Martin said. "So there must have been a need."

"Yes," she said sadly, nodding. "A great need. Great enough that the gods gave me the necessary roads, when I asked." She seemed wistful. "Perhaps not great enough, though."

"Well, it must be better than the wagon," Martin said.

"Anything is better than being trapped in that cave," she said. "With that man."

They were quiet for a while, Martin still riding at her side. The chains that bound her clattered softly together whenever Fianna shifted. The iron of her shackles was dark and pitted, and runes circled her wrists. The skin beneath was raw.

"Do those truly work?" Martin asked. "The inquisition's iron?"

"Would I be here if they didn't?" she asked.

"Do they hurt?"

"They take from me the only thing I care about," she said. "They put a wall between me and the gods. I can still feel them, bumping through the nights, breathing through the rivers, but they are not there for me." Fianna turned old eyes at him and shrugged. "Yes. They hurt."

"If we knew we could trust you..."

"You cannot. Ian's father made that clear enough," she said.

"Ian said you saved his life, and his mother's, as well."

"Are you a friend of Ian of the tribe of Hounds, that you care about his life?" Fianna asked.

"Since we were children." Martin nodded. "We have supped together, chased women together, and fought side by side." He turned toward the forest, remembering better days. "Our fathers nearly died together during the Reaver War."

"And that is how friendship is forged in Suhdra, I suppose," she said. "Yet still you march north with the heretic's host. Why is that?"

"Against the heretic, you mean?" Martin asked.

Fianna chuckled. "Ian Blakley is your friend, yet you march against him. Tomas Sacombre is your inquisitor, yet he wears these same chains. It is no wonder the gods have forsaken you."

"I would rather be forsaken by your gods than judged by mine," Martin said.

Fianna's gaze got distant, her eyes unfocused and glassy. She heaved a sigh that carried the weight of ages, as much regret as anger. She nodded at Martin.

"You may end up with both."

24

THE MAJESTY OF Greenhall spread out before them, bright red and gold standards fluttering from the battlements. Like a gaudy bracelet the walled city circled the tight fist of the castle keep, bright roofs of blue and green and slate sparkling like jewels amid the rough stone.

Songs rose from the castle's doma, mingling with lesser choirs from the city. They sang the praise of summer, and the air seemed to sing with them, preserving warmth that had fled the rest of Tenumbra. An army was drawn up along the road, tight columns marching slowly away from the castle, taking the route north, to Tener.

"You have got to be shitting me," Gwen said. They stood on a rise overlooking the city, their numbers hidden by the forest and the witches' magic. Cahl shifted uncomfortably at her side.

"All cities are old cities. All holy places are holy, even to us," he said. "Greenhall was once the home of the henge of flowers, and before that the earthly seat of the god of spring." Cahl knelt, pressing his hand against the raw stone beneath his feet. A faint shimmering outlined his fingers as the shaman communed with the stone. Gwen could feel the power of the casting tugging at some unhinged part of her soul, as if she could fall into the earth at the shaman's touch. Cahl breathed in deeply, then broke the connection with the stone.

"It is still there. Buried."

"Then we must move quickly," Folam said. "If Sacombre's allies have access to the vernal god, there's no telling the sort of damage they could wreak."

"If it's pagans we fear, isn't Greenhall the last place they would venture?" Gwen asked. "Other than Heartsbridge, I don't think any hearth is less friendly or more treacherous to the people of the ink."

"Sacombre's agents dress as priests and carry Suhdrin titles," Folam said. "They would be welcomed there."

"Priests of Cinder," Gwen said. She pointed at the banners fluttering from the walls. "But those are the icons of Strife. And since it was the high inquisitor of Cinder who killed her father and led her house to war, I don't think Sophie is going to be close friends with the faithful."

"That's not a chance we can take," Folam said. He stood, gesturing impatiently to Cahl and the other shamans clustered on the hilltop. "There has been enough talk. Preparations must be made."

"But wait," Gwen said, still not convinced. "If Sacombre knew of this broken god, why did he go to so much trouble to uncover the witches' hallow in the Fen? Why did he stir Suhdra to war, just to summon one god, when he had another lying under the castle of his ally?"

"While it is clear Sacombre had allies among the faithful," Folam said, "they may have not known about the vernal god. But if they did, they would also know of the difficulty in raising him, much less controlling him. Remember the history. This god was broken, nearly destroyed. The god hidden in the Fen was laid to rest. Docile by comparison."

Gwen thought for a moment. She stood slowly, frowning down at Greenhall's massive gates, and the ruined tournament ground that lay fallow at its feet.

"Goddess," she said. "Fomharra is a goddess. Now"—She turned to Folam.—"How do you intend to get us inside without getting us hanged?"

They waited and watched, counting the hours until the army disappeared from view, huddling at the bottom of the rise, hidden among the trees, discussing plans and arguing about the various ways they might die in the morning.

"That army is marching to the Fen Gate," Gwen said. "We should at least warn the Blakleys they are coming."

"The troubles between Tener and Suhdra are not our troubles," Folam said. The voidfather was becoming more and more irritated each time Gwen spoke. The other pagans bowed to his will with ease, but Gwen always had questions. "With luck, this will have drained Greenhall of its guards."

"There were no banners of Halverdt among the ranks of those who departed," Gwen said. "The initial campaign north would have thinned the garrison here, but not depleted it entirely. I counted Bassion, Galleux, Maldieu... the southern lords who wouldn't have had the time or interest to get involved in Sacombre's campaign."

"They've taken an interest now," Cahl said.

"Aye, and for their own reasons, I'm sure," Gwen settled back against a log, her legs sprawled out in front of her. At least for now her pain had subsided, but she would never be able to perfect the looming crouch the shamans used, balancing precariously on the balls of their feet, cloaks gathered around their shoulders like crow's wings. It looked impressive, but was terribly uncomfortable.

"Lady Bassion has never raised a blade in her life," she continued, "but I'm sure I saw her sigil in the van. If she has come all this way, you can be sure it's not to avenge some half-mad northern duke. She has another motive."

"We are not going to get involved in their war," Judoc said. The elder of the tribe of bones had looked increasingly uncomfortable ever since they set foot in Suhdrin land. "Let the celestials kill one another."

"More skulls for the gray palace, elder bones?" Noel asked. "Sharpening tensions between Tener and Suhdra isn't going to calm the spirits of either land."

"You're just arguing because it's me," Judoc said. "You want nothing to do with it, either."

Noel didn't answer, but settled into a resentful silence.

"Enough. That has nothing to do with why we are here," Folam said. "Our business lies in Greenhall, at the henge of flowers."

"Fine," Gwen said, "but there's no way we're getting inside the castle. Besides, if there really is a henge of flowers hidden somewhere in there, how did Halverdt never notice? There must have been hundreds of priests that have served that house over the generations. Surely one of them would have sensed something."

"It is their vigilance that has kept the henge hidden," Folam said. "The fragments of the vernal god are buried deep, shattered by his followers in the wars of madness, long ago. After the crusades Halverdt claimed this throne from the tribe of flowers, and wards were put in place by the celestial priests, to sanctify the ground. That drove the fragments deeper."

"That clears the way, then," Gwen replied. "All we have are the castle walls, a city of zealous celestials, a duchess still mourning her father's death, and whatever priests and vow knights remain inside. Hardly a problem at all."

"The castle walls will not trouble us, because the henge is not inside the keep," Folam said. "The vernal god's shrine is in the city, its original purpose forgotten. We need only reach it unseen."

Gwen looked slowly around the circle. Inked faces stared back at her, their hair tangles of braids, tied with the icons of a forbidden faith. All of them dressed in camouflaged cloaks and leather.

"No problem," she said.

"Yes, well..." Folam said with a shrug. "Our party will be small. I will be a part of it, as only I hold the knowledge necessary to secure the god."

"I will go, as well," Cahl said. "Cities are places of stone. Wind, earth, and water will be cut off, but stone will remain."

"Yes," Folam agreed. "You will be able to sense the god's embrace. Very good, and we will need someone familiar with this particular city. Gwen?"

"We can't trust her," Judoc said quickly. "Aedan claimed it, and I've seen nothing to prove him wrong. She led celestial priests to the Fen god's hallow. Who's to say she won't betray you as soon as she's inside?"

"She knows the city, and she doesn't have the ink," Folam said. "We have placed our faith in her family for generations. We must do so again."

"Someone has to watch her," Judoc insisted. "Someone we can trust."

"I'll do it," Noel said. "My tribe has spent generations passing as faithful Suhdrins. No one here will know the difference."

"Very well, it is settled, then," Folam said, heading off any further dissension. "Cahl and I will go in disguise, to mask our faces, while Gwen and Noel lead us. The rest of you wait here, and pray to the gods for our success."

"You're forgetting something," Gwen said. She motioned to her face. "I'm wanted throughout the north. The daughter of House Adair is well known in these parts. I step foot inside that city, I'll be dead before nightfall."

"The daughter of House Adair, yes," Folam said. "The girl with the distinctive red and black hair.

"We can manage that."

Her curls came away under Cahl's knife, the scalp beneath as pale as an egg. The bindings across her chest hurt, but when they were done, Gwen looked nothing like a lady, much less one from the Tenerran court.

She shrugged into a pair of linen breeches and a shirt with a narrow collar and a hood that covered her freshly shorn skull. She felt naked without knife, spears, or leather, but at least they let her keep her boots.

"They're a bit nicer than a peasant could possess," Noel said thoughtfully, "but you've worn the hell out of them. Should be fine." She stepped back to inspect the results.

"No one is going to mistake that for the Lady Gwendolyn Adair," Judoc said confidently.

"You'd have achieved the same effect by washing away the dirt and putting me in a silk dress," Gwen said. "Though I imagine those are in short supply around here."

"Stop complaining. You make a handsome lad," Folam said. "The rest of you, get someplace safe. It won't do to have a random patrol stumble on your camp and alert the guards. We're going to have enough trouble with this."

"What about the two of you?" Noel asked, gazing at Cahl and Folam. "We can't march you in looking like that."

"Our clothes don't matter—it's our faces that will give us away," Folam responded. "By the grace of the gods, there's a war going on. The streets will be full of the injured and infirm." He produced a length of bandage and began to wrap his head. "Cahl and I will be blind, so it's up to the two of you to guide us."

"Very well," Noel said, then she helped Folam with his bindings. She nodded to Gwen. "See to Cahl. He's not going to bite."

Despite Noel's promise, Cahl looked ready to chew her face off as she approached. His whole body was tense as Gwen slowly wrapped his head, keeping the bandages loose enough for breathing but tight enough to stay fixed. When she was done, he stood uncertainly, his hands outstretched.

"My spears," he said, motioning.

"No weapons, Cahl," Folam said. The blinded voidfather looked much more comfortable, sitting with his legs crossed, hands folded on one knee. "We are supplicants and beggars, not warriors."

"How am I supposed to find the stone path if I'm blind?" Cahl asked.

"With your heart, and with Gwen's hands. Now, ladies," Folam said, holding out his arms to be helped up. "If you please?"

Reluctantly, the four of them wound their way down the hill, joining the road when there was no traffic, and well out of sight of the gates. They weren't alone for long. Armed patrols passed, each one raising the hair on Gwen's neck as they passed. A quick wagon of produce rattled by, the driver clutching a rusty axe and refusing to slow down. As they approached the gates, the road became crowded with refugees from the north, nervous farmers from east and west, and hopeful merchants, mercenaries, and priests from the south. Traffic slowed to a grind. Many passersby gave the four nervous looks, some with sympathy, others fear.

"What is happening?" Folam asked quietly.

"We are nearly to the gates, father," Noel said cheerfully. "Surely the Lady Halverdt will have sympathy for one of her faithful soldiers, injured in war."

"Lady Sophie has little enough sympathy for anyone," the farmer walking next to them said. He led a donkey piled high with jugs of cheap wine. "Whatever joy that woman has, she's plunged into anger and revelry. It's good business, though."

"If you're in the right business," Gwen muttered.

"Young lad like you should be able to find good work as a guard," the farmer said. "Pretty mouth like that, maybe better work in a back room."

Cahl, blind and hulking, turned toward the man.

"Do not speak to my son like that," he said. The farmer backed away, pushing through the crowd with the weight of his donkey.

"He's gone, Cahl. You can stop threatening the empty air," Noel said. A space formed around them as the other journeyers gave them a wide berth. "We're calling a bit too much attention to ourselves with that kind of thing."

"Enough talking," Gwen said. She looked up at the gates. The sigil of House Halverdt hung from the battlements on giant flags, too heavy to be stirred by the wind. In addition to the tri-acorn of her family, Sophie had added a tongue of bright flame, the icon of Lady Strife.

"Lady Halverdt seems to have found the gods," Noel said quietly.

"One god, at least," Gwen murmured back. They passed beneath the shadow of the gate and entered into the city. An oppressive heat settled on them, stoked by golden braziers at every corner and torches on every wall. Despite the heat, Gwen couldn't help but shiver. "Lady Strife, holy of anger, and vengeance, and war."

"And madness," Folam whispered back. "Do not forget madness."

"Aye," Gwen said. "Madness."

25

IAN LEANED AGAINST the gate of the small keep, hammering it with his fist and screaming at the top of his lungs. The wind stole his voice, and the hard wood swallowed the pounding.

The wall was hardly twice the height of a man. On a better day Ian could have scaled it, but his hands were numb and bloody. These were not better days. Finally he gave up and collapsed to the road. Their only remaining horse whickered softly against his cheek.

"Oh, *now* you care," Ian mumbled. "Couldn't be bothered to kick in this door, could ya? Be a great help."

The horse snorted and swung its head to the side, cropping stubbornly on a pile of snow at the edge of the road. Ian laughed.

"That's what I thought. Lazy bastard."

"Lazy who?" a voice said from above. Ian startled up, scrambling to a sitting position and trying to back away from the horse before he realized the voice had come from the top of the wall. He twisted around to squint into the driving snow. A man peered down at him from the side of the gate.

"Were you talking to your horse?"

"We've been through a lot together," Ian answered. He got to his feet unsteadily, not bothering to brush off the crust of snow that had gathered on his furs. “My companion and I were traveling the Fen when we were caught in this storm. We seek shelter, and probably medicine for my companion.”

“Your… horse?” the man asked.

“No, the vow knight,” Ian said, turning angrily and pointing to the saddle. The saddle was empty. Confused, Ian looked back down the road. Elsa lay in a heap just ten feet away, the snow already piling up over her head. “She’s fallen… we must get her.”

He began walking toward Elsa’s drift-smoothed form, but about halfway there realized that he was in no condition to be walking, much less lifting someone else off the ground. He weaved drunkenly through the snow, falling to his knees next to her still form. He cleared the snow from her face, then started tugging on her shoulder.

“You’re going to have to get up, Elsa, because I can’t do that for you, and this lot doesn’t seem very helpful.” With some effort he was able to get her arm across his shoulder, but when he tried to stand he ended up only rolling her over and tumbling headfirst to the ground. He lay there until he heard the gate open.

Shadows loomed over him.

“Good of you to come out. Now if you could just…”

The blow took him across the back of the neck. There was stinging pain, then nothing but darkness.

He woke in stone and fire. The walls flickered red and black, and a haze of smoke stung Ian’s eyes when he sat up. He tried to breath, but the stink of frairwood choked him, burning his throat and filling his lungs with sacred incense. A fit of coughing racked his body, leaving him gasping for breath through his tears.

"You'll get used to it," Elsa said. Ian blinked several times, wiping his eyes clear until he was able to see the vow knight lounging on a bed on the other side of this narrow room. At the foot of their beds was a hearth, overflowing with burning wood and hot coals that spilled out onto the stone floor. Little of the smoke made it to the chimney, leading to the thick air.

"They've made a mess of that," Ian said, his voice coming rough from his throat. His head throbbed, either from the smoke or the blow he had suffered. More likely both. He felt under his hair, probing gingerly around the knot, his fingers coming away with flakes of dried blood. "Mess of this, too. Are we held prisoner?"

"Nothing so exciting. The master of this house seems the nervous type. Frairwood in all the hearths, and guards about as friendly as broken glass. But at least it's warm, and they've fed us well."

"Speak for yourself," Ian grumbled. "How long have I been out?"

"Hard to say. I'm not even sure how long we've been here. A priest came in and saw to your wound, but I think all he did was mop up the gore and then drug you to sleep." Elsa stretched her back, her joints popping. She was dressed in a loose cotton shift that was dotted with blood. It was the first time Ian had seen her out of her armor. "A day, perhaps."

"And the storm?" Ian asked. Elsa nodded to the window, which was lashed closed, the shutters creaking. "So whatever is causing that hasn't yet left."

"Or it has followed us here," she replied. "Can you walk?"

Ian struggled to his feet. His legs were as stiff as driftwood, and his knees groaned the whole way up. Elsa chuckled.

"You were closer to dead than I thought, young Blakley—you won't be doing much walking, not right away. Doesn't matter, really. I don't think we're going anywhere. The storm still rages, and the master of the house is curious. About us, and our business in the Fen."

"Who is this master? One word from my father and he'll let us go, if he knows what's good for him. Do they even know who it is they're holding?" Ian tottered carefully to the edge of the bed, supporting himself on the post. "Do they understand the consequences of delaying us on our mission?"

"That's the curious thing," Elsa said. "I'm not sure who rules here." She made no effort to rise, and looked comfortable enough. "The guards wear no tabards, and name no lord. There are no crests on the walls, nor among the tapestries. Twice I have left this room, but I've seen no banner or charge to name the lord of this house."

"It's not so unusual," Ian said. "Not every house has the money to carve their name into every stone."

"That's not the case here. Look at the hearth, if you will," Elsa said, pointing. "Some very nice scrollwork in the stone mantle, and good andirons, fancy enough for a lord's fireplace. Yet they are suspiciously unadorned."

"Not just unadorned," Ian said, limping painfully to the hearth, where he ran a hand over the mantle. At the corners the stone was broken and raw. "Disfigured."

"As though they were hiding a name," Elsa said. "So."

"So," Ian said. "Who is our host, that he will not meet us, and holds us so confined?"

"We will know soon enough," Elsa said casually. "They have taken my weapons, and my armor. Now that you are awake and moving, however, they will discover the futility of their precautions. When next they come to feed us, I will either secure us an audience or a glorious escape."

"There's no other way?" Ian asked.

"Of course there is," Elsa answered. "We could die—also gloriously."

A short time later the guards came with their food. Elsa stood and demanded to see the master of the house. The guards looked from her to Ian, bowed, and escorted them into the hallway.

The vow knight almost seemed disappointed.

"The place seems a bit drab, but I see what you mean," Ian whispered, his head on a swivel as they walked. "No heraldry, no sigils. Nothing. Any lord could rule here."

"Or none," Elsa said quietly. "Winter is a good time for treachery."

"That's a cheerful thought. Hello, my Lord Nobody, I am Ian Blakley of Houndhallow. I see that you've murdered the previous lord, do you mind if I skulk out in the dead of night? Oh, and may I have my armor and weapons back, and maybe some supplies so I don't freeze to death in this blizzard? No?"

"If it comes to that," Elsa said, "we will not ask permission."

"You talk awfully tough for a lady who is one singed cotton shift away from being naked," Ian offered cheerfully as they walked through a grand hall. The tables had all been pushed together, and the hearth lay cold and empty. The dais at the end of the room was missing a throne, though the attendant chairs and long table were still present. The guards sped their way through this empty space, hurrying Ian and Elsa along.

"Not many feasts, it seems," Ian said.

He and Elsa followed their escorts through a kitchen, the maids bustling through the work of making the next meal. The air was filled with comfortingly normal smells—of bacon, of beans and wood smoke and spilled vinegar. As they passed through, Ian snatched a silver goblet from a shelf and held it up for Elsa to see.

"Here," he said, pointing at the face of the goblet. There was a shield etched in the metal. It was a fist gripping a pair of antlers, with stars nestled between the points of the horns. "Halfic. An old house, and loyal to the church."

"*Very* loyal," she agreed. "If some tragedy has befallen them, it would not sit well with the church." Ian returned the goblet and they hurried on.

"Neither would it sit well with my father," he said. "That might explain the rude reception, if they've recognized me."

"Then why leave us alive at all?" Elsa asked.

The next room was close and narrow, a library crowded with books. A separate hearth stood at each end, both burning bright and clean, and a window capped the far wall. Heavy curtains were drawn tight, but still the howling storm sent gusts rippling through. There was a sharp chill in the air, despite the fires. The guards swept aside as they entered, enabling Ian and Elsa to face the lord of the manor.

The man sat in a heavy chair between the fires, his elbows on a table that was too large for the space. The chair was actually the throne from the great hall, dragged here for some reason. The table was covered in open books and unbound codices, shuffled one atop the other until the whole space looked like an accident. His fingers were stained with ink and blood.

Ian struggled to recognize their host, and failed. He and Elsa stood still for a long moment, entirely ignored by the man at the table.

"My lord," the guard said from the doorway. "Our guests have awoken."

"Took bloody long enough," the man said. He looked up distractedly. "See that they have... oh. Oh, they're here. Aren't they?"

"Yes, we are," Ian said. He sketched a courtly bow, stepping forward. "Allow me to introduce myself. I am Ian Blakley, son of Malcolm, heir to the throne of Houndhallow and champion of..."

"I bloody know who you are. Only reason I let you in at all." The man stood, blinking rapidly. "Shouldn't do that, you know. Show up at a man's gate without a proper introduction, demanding to be let in. This is winter! The gates were closed!"

"We had little choice," Ian said. "The blizzard took us unawares. If we hadn't stumbled across your castle, my companion and I would be dead."

"Hm," the man answered. "Hm. Well, gods will it. What brought you to that road, Ian of Houndhallow? Did your father send you, to beg my help in his fool war against Halverdt? I've already sent my answer. Halfic swords stay home! Halfic spears guard these walls. I won't waste my precious blood."

"Lord Halfic," Ian said. "It *is* you, isn't it?"

"Yes? Of course? Who did you think I was?"

"Beg forgiveness," Ian paused, struggling to remember the name of Halfic's backwoods holding. Harthal, that was it. "Beg forgiveness, Harthal. Sir Elsa and I were unsure of the state of this castle. We saw no sign of your sigil, and the hearth in our room was damaged."

"Hm," the man grunted. "Winter is a treacherous season. That is what you thought? That I'd been thrown over, and so you came to sound out the new lord of Harthal? So bloody like you hounds, lapping at whichever hand is sweetest!"

"I am not here on my father's business, though if I were I would expect better treatment than this!" Ian approached the table, planted his fists among the books and leaned in close to the lord's face. "Know you nothing of the events of the Fen Gate?"

"I know of Colm Adair's heresy," Halfic said. "I know that your father continues to raise arms against the inquisition's chosen banner, and I know the god of judges has brought his hand down against Tener for the sins of these two men!" Halfic stood to his full height, and Ian realized the man was easily twice his size, broad and tall and heavy with muscle. "Now his son has come crawling to my door. To beg for spears, or mercy, or simply my approval—I do not know or care. You are here on my mercy, and if you cause trouble I will throw you out of Harthal without a second's thought. Storm or no storm. Do I make myself clear?"

"My lord," Ian began to protest. Elsa grabbed his arm.

"Very clear, Lord Halfic," she said, "and may I thank you, on behalf of the church and all its priests, for your faithful service. These are trying times for all of Tenumbra. Good men like you are the hope of all people."

Halfic seemed taken aback by this, but he nodded slowly, looking from Ian to Elsa. He seemed to weigh the vow knight before speaking.

"When the son of a heretic and a vow knight arrive at your door, you must either suspect the heretic of deception, or the knight of heresy," he said. "But I see you are neither a fool nor a heretic. Return to your chambers." He flipped closed the book he had been reading and turned to the door. When Ian didn't move, Halfic took him by the shoulders and guided him forward, waiting until Elsa followed. At the door he stopped and made a show of thinking very carefully.

"I will see that your weapons and armor are returned to you, vow knight. My mother belonged to the vow. It would honor me greatly if you would say words at her tomb."

"The honor would be mine," Elsa answered. The man nodded deeply.

"Very well. Pardon my manner, please. I am very busy. The storm has caught us unprepared, and there is much I must do before true winter falls." He glanced at Ian, wincing slightly. "And forgive my words, Ian Blakley. Your father is a good man, if easily deceived by his faith in others. I was afraid you were coming to chastise me for not joining his idiotic... for not adding my strength to his effort."

"I tried to tell you..."

Halfic waved him to silence. "We can discuss it later. I truly am busy. Go, rest. Your things will be with you soon enough." He turned and tramped back to his desk. Ian gave Elsa a questioning look, but the vow knight shook her head and led him back into the kitchen. The guards followed at a proper distance.

"What was that about?" Ian asked with a hint of irritation. "One word from you and he turns into the bashful host."

"I think he was startled by our arrival," Elsa said. "The guards had not warned him, though doubtless there were standing orders to escort us to him, should you wake. He speaks truly. The lord of Harthal is a busy man."

"As you say, but it seems very strange to me."

"Stranger than you think." Elsa dipped her head, lowering her voice to barely a whisper. "He changed his tune merely to get rid of us—or at least get rid of me. He didn't want me to see his books."

"Books?" Ian asked.

"The ones you were too offended to look at, but I saw my fill." She straightened her back as they entered the vast emptiness of the great hall. The guards marched behind them, their iron shoes echoing loudly. Elsa glanced at Ian. "Let us pray our weapons reach us soon."

"Why?" Ian asked.

"Because Lord Halfic is trying to summon a gheist. Or banish one. Or both."

26

THE HORSES SMELLED it first, getting nervous, sidestepping into the verge whenever their riders loosened the reins. At the base of a familiar hill, Frair Lucas's borrowed mount refused to go even a step further.

"What's their problem?" LaGaere asked angrily. Lucas gave him a sidelong look.

"I think I know," he said. "Have your men guard the horses. We'll have a look on foot."

"What about the high inquisitor?" Martin asked.

"He should come with us," Lucas said. "He should see this."

Lucas, Sacombre, LaGaere, Sir Horne, and Martin Roard all dismounted, leaving their horses and the witch with LaGaere's men. The hill wasn't very high, but by the summit, Sacombre was breathing heavily.

"Out of breath, Tomas?" Lucas asked cheerfully.

"I am an old man, frair, not accustomed to being paraded through the forests like a prize buck."

"You will rest soon enough," Lucas said. The high inquisitor chuckled.

When they crested the hill, LaGaere and Roard inhaled sharply. Sir Horne was silent, but something curious danced in her eyes.

"This is where it all began," Lucas said. "Long enough ago to be forgotten, though not even a season has passed."

The town that spread out below them was a ruin. Those few thatch roofs unclaimed by fire had fallen to neglect, the bare ribs of their staves poking out. The walls were laced with ivy, the front gate hanging jagged like an open wound. A flock of songbirds danced up from the shattered skull of the doma at the village center. They swept low over ash-grimed buildings before disappearing into the encroaching forest.

Other than the bird song, the city was buried in silence.

"Gardengerry," Lucas said. "See what you have wrought, Tomas."

"There are always sacrifices," Sacombre said. "Soldiers assigned to hold a doomed gate. Flanks that can not be rescued."

"Children, still on the teat," Lucas said. "Mothers and wives and grandfathers, waking up for the last time, to hear a forgotten god tearing their front door from its hinges." Lucas turned to face the high inquisitor. "Priests, celestes, congregants, sworn to the gods, serving no sentence but their faith. Murdered in their doma at your command!"

"Frair Allaister's actions were his own," Sacombre said sharply. "I set him a path. How he traveled that path was his choice, and his to atone."

"Give a mad dog a hand to bite, and don't be surprised if he takes the whole arm," Lucas said.

"You had these people murdered?" Sir Horne asked quietly. "Celestial souls, sacrificed to your plan?"

"Not all of them," LaGaere said. "We gathered many refugees from Gardengerry on the path north. Some were willing to fight the Tenerrans who had murdered their neighbors. Others simply sought shelter. The rebels killed dozens, and the gheist they summoned murdered hundreds, but most of the residents fled."

"In fear of the inquisition," Lucas said bitterly.

"Then why haven't they returned?" Martin asked. "The walls still stand. The well is probably still salvageable, if a priest could be found to bless the font."

"Would *you* return?" Horne asked. "To the place your family died? And not just that, to walls haunted by demons. Imagine the horror of learning that the place you held holy for generations was cursed of the old gods. How could you sleep easily in such a place?"

"Gods pray that we can," Lucas said. "We're staying here tonight."

"Are you mad?" LaGaere asked. "Who knows what lurks between those walls?"

"As Roard said, the well is still clean, and the walls still stand. It will be shelter enough. Whatever haunted this place has gone north." Lucas tugged at Sacombre's bonds. "I was there when it died." He turned began to descend, back the way they had come.

LaGaere followed angrily, leaving Martin and Sir Horne to stare down at the ruin. The knight turned slowly, taking in the entire vista of untended walls and broken roofs.

"Is the whole north like this?" Horne asked. "Forgotten demons lurking under the floorboards of our holy places? Whole villages wiped clean from the land? Murderous gods and farmers sowing war and reaping death?"

"It was a southern priest who raised these demons," Martin said. "Let's not forget that."

"We can't lay it all at Sacombre's feet, nor Halverdt's," Horne said. She turned away from Gardengerry, gathering

Martin behind her. Behind them, the birds returned to the town, to settle on empty roofs and empty streets.

The courtyard was eerily quiet. This shouldn't have surprised Martin, but the overgrown common and the gaping mouths of empty homes still unsettled him.

They walked their reluctant horses to the common, then hobbled Sacombre and the witch, shackling them to the disheveled remains of the iron stocks. LaGaere set his men the task of assembling a picket, then he and Frair Lucas huddled quietly in the shadow of the broken doma.

"Stay here," Sir Horne said to Martin. "I'm going to search the city."

"You shouldn't go alone," Martin said.

"I'll be fine. Frair Lucas says the ruins are safe from gheists, and there's no mortal threat that I fear," she said. "See to the horses. LaGaere's men are too busy preparing for an invasion, and the frair has his hands full with the duke."

"But..."

"But nothing. I'll just be looking for food. We lost most of our supplies in the flight from Greenhall, and we've a long way to go to Heartsbridge. Lucas doesn't like to think about it, but now that we're in Suhdra the gheists will be the least of our problems. Bassion's army will have emptied the farms south of here. The harvest has already been scarce enough these past few years. There will be no warm welcome for us between here and the Celestial Dome." She nodded toward their prisoners. "Especially with that pair in tow. We'll have to keep a low profile. Hunt what we can. Scavenge the rest."

"I can help," Martin said.

"By staying here, and ensuring the horses are fit to ride

tomorrow," Horne said. She gave Martin's head a rub, which left the heir of Stormwatch blushing and furious. "Have patience, little Stormwatch. There will be glory enough later."

He refused to watch Horne march away, glancing nervously at LaGaere's men to see if they had observed the exchange. Horne was right, of course. Without spare mounts to switch out, the horses were in a sorry state. The business of seeing them brushed and fed took the rest of the afternoon, and by the time evening fell and the dinner fire was crackling, Martin was exhausted.

Horne returned some hours after she had left, her hands empty, and she ignored him. The ruins must have already been picked clean, either by bandits or the residents before they fled.

Later that night, they ate in silence around the fire. What little food they had was hardly satisfying. Only Sacombre seemed to not mind the poor quality of their meal. LaGaere watched him with narrow eyes.

"This doesn't bother you?" he asked finally, taking the high inquisitor by surprise. Sacombre looked up as if startled by a predator.

"Bother me?" he said. "No, not at all. I've certainly eaten worse. Mostly in temples." He smiled. "The faithful of Cinder aren't known for their culinary skills."

"Not the food, damn you," LaGaere said. "This place. These walls, standing idle in the forest. A whole town left to rot!"

"It's little concern of mine. As Frair Lucas said, most of the victims were murdered by Tenerran farmers, looking to atone for some imagined slight, I'm sure. Who were in turn killed themselves, by the very gheists they worshiped." Sacombre shrugged. "At least they served a greater purpose."

"Greater purpose?" Martin asked. "What greater purpose? To provide the excuse for war between Suhdra and Tener?"

"That honor would fall to the citizens of Tallownere, I believe," Sacombre said. "Slaughtered by foul Sir Volent, only to be rescued by their heroine, kind Lady Gwen Adair. I really had nothing to do with that."

"Like hell. You knew what Halverdt would do if provoked."

"Perhaps, but my eyes were elsewhere, on a higher goal." Sacombre held his palms up, turning his eyes to the rising moon. "Cinder gifted me with certain knowledge, and the wisdom to use it."

"Make what excuses you like," Martin said, "but the fate of Gardengerry is on your soul. It was your servant who unleashed this demon."

"If the harvest is bitter, who do you blame?" Sacombre asked, leaning toward Martin. "The man who harvests, or the man who plants?" His chains scraped against the dirt, leaving ruts in the ground. "Or do you blame the seed itself?"

"So poetic, Tomas," Frair Lucas said. "Who will you blame when you're on the stand? Are you the reaper, or the sower, or the seed?"

"Or am I the harvest itself, my friend? Am I simply what comes of bitter soil?"

Lucas huffed, but didn't answer.

LaGaere watched Sacombre with a thoughtful look on his face. Only Sir Horne seemed uninterested in their talk. Which was why, when her head came up sharply and she turned toward their surroundings, Martin noticed.

"A sound," she said suddenly. "Somewhere in the night."

"The night is full of sounds," Sacombre said. "You are

on Suhdrin soil now, good sir. You needn't—"

"She's right," Martin said. He stood, dropping his bowl of soggy biscuit to the ground. "I hear it, too." The rest of the party went quiet. Out among the buildings, something moved. Something large.

"I thought you said that whatever haunted this place had passed out of it, Frair Lucas," LaGaere said.

"That doesn't prevent something else from taking up residence," Horne said. "While I was searching the ruins, there was no food—not even a discarded apple left rotting in the street. I thought little of it at the time, but..."

"But if something else is eating everything, that would explain why there is nothing left," LaGaere said. "There's more to the night than gheists. Could be a bear, or a pack of wolves."

The sound grew, and a rattling crash echoed through the empty streets. It ended with a crack. The stones of the courtyard shook.

"Big bears in this part of Suhdra," Horne muttered.

"There's no reason for a gheist to stalk a place that's been claimed by another," Lucas said. "Even with the hunter-god gone, the wards the pagans put in place should prevent—"

He was interrupted by another crack. Some distance away, one of the few intact slate roofs burst open like an egg. A sinuous form arced out of the building like a water snake breaching the surface. Long and thin, with short, clawed feet and a mouth opened wide, showing rows of teeth. A beard flowed from its jaw, and its body was covered in bright scales, each a different color, though the flesh beneath was as dark as shadow.

The serpent dove into another house, the impact sending up sparks and setting fire to the piled thatch that remained, its long body slithering through the air for several seconds before it disappeared.

The rattling sound returned.

It was all around them.

"Enough conjecture," Lucas said. He grabbed his staff, jabbing one of LaGaere's men to life. "Gather the horses! Grab what you can and leave whatever you can't carry. We'll make for the hill."

"What's to say it won't follow us?" he asked as the others began to stir.

"My prayers, and yours as well, if you're wise," Lucas snapped. He prodded the men again, and then they were up and running, weapons to hand, staring wildly at the surrounding courtyard.

"Lucas, my friend," Sacombre said, raising his shackled hands and nodding to the chain that held him captive to the rust-pitted stocks. "Surely you won't leave us behind."

Swearing, Lucas fumbled through his robes for the keys. The rattling sound grew louder. Then the serpent broke free of the stones of the courtyard and vaulted over the doma, its belly brushing the shattered dome, striking sparks from the marble. Martin could see long, wispy tendrils on the creature's face and down its sides, and its scales looked like saucers of hammered light.

The serpent itself appeared to be made of shadow, and it was wearing its scales like a shirt of mail, each individual link linked to the next. The scales made a thunderous noise as the creature passed by, clattering together and against the stones. It turned a languid eye in Martin's direction, an iris of shapes like twisted antlers hanging suspended in the dark fluid.

"To hell with this," Lucas spat. He drew his staff above

his head, whispered an incantation, then struck Sacombre's chains. The icons on the manacles flared brightly, then the cuffs snapped open. After a second's hesitation, he did the same to the witch's bonds. Lucas snatched Sacombre to his feet and drew him close, hissing. "One misstep, and Cinder's judgment will not wait for you, Tomas. I will burn you down myself."

"If we both survive this, yes," Sacombre said. The ground began to shake, grinding loudly as the cobblestones began popping up, first across the open courtyard, then closer and closer as the serpent burrowed below, faster than seemed possible.

They ran. The man sent to fetch the horses cut them loose, swinging onto the last one before leading the charge out the front gate. LaGaere bellowed at him, but the panicked mounts were gone before anyone else got a chance to mount.

Sir Horne tarried, letting Martin grab Fianna as he tumbled down the road. The three of them watched the serpent approach, but the gheist seemed drawn to the high inquisitor. Frair Lucas erected a hasty barrier of shadow, which seemed to turn the gheist aside for a brief moment, giving them the opportunity to flee.

Sacombre and the witch were still hobbled, and their progress was greatly slowed, dragged behind Frair Lucas and Martin Roard respectively. By the time they reached the exit to the courtyard, LaGaere was already at the gate. The duke of Warhome grabbed his remaining men, giving orders. Two of them rushed off, and the rest formed a nervous shieldwall across the gate.

"We will hold," LaGaere shouted. "Get into the woods! Those fool horses disappeared among the trees!"

"We are safer… upon… the godsroad," Lucas gasped as he stumbled past, Sacombre in hand.

"We are safer on horseback," LaGaere countered. "Now go!"

Lucas didn't question. He ran into the woods, towing Sacombre behind him. Horne and Martin followed. LaGaere and his men formed a skirmish line across the gate, half of them in full armor, the rest nearly naked but wielding their blades. The gheist slithered toward them.

"Steady!" LaGaere said. "We protect the high inquisitor. The will of Cinder will protect us!"

The gheist flickered its tail, crushing a house that stood beside the gate, sending stones and splintered wood across the road. Those unfortunate enough to wear only cloth and faith were struck down, screaming as broken rock cut through their flesh. The others went to their knees as the force of the impact stunned them.

LaGaere was the first to recover. He shook loose scree from his shoulders and rushed forward, swinging downward with his sword. The blade glanced off the shimmering plates of the gheist's body, ringing like a struck bell. The creature turned to face him, opening its mouth wide and hissing.

"On your feet, fools!" LaGaere ordered. The handful of men who still lived stood slowly. The gheist's attention focused entirely on LaGaere, and none of them seemed interested in drawing its gaze their way.

LaGaere spat. "I am cursed with cowards," he muttered. "I pray you serve better when it's mortal flesh you face."

With a shriek, the gheist launched itself again, plowing forward with its snout. LaGaere spun to the side, striking at its eye as the creature passed, barely missing the mark. He struck the hard earth with a grunt.

Seeing their lord thrown to the ground roused the

knights, and they ran forward. The strong plates of the gheist's flesh turned aside their blades, but the men wielding maces shattered scales and drew blood. The gheist howled and rippled his body, knocking them aside with a thick coil.

"This is worthless," LaGaere said, coming again to his feet. "Gods pray the others have gotten away. Move the injured, if there's any hope of life, and leave the rest. Save your lives." He backed away, grimacing at the twisting body of the feral god. "We will fight another day, if we must."

The men didn't need a second order. They hauled their injured companions to the tree line, drawing moans and shrieks of pain. Once they were clear, LaGaere followed.

The gheist ignored them now. It passed the gate and coiled up like a rattlesnake in the center of the road, its dazzling scales glinting with internal light, its beard of shadow tendrils tasting the air.

Then it dove into the ground. A brilliant glow came up from the cobbles like sunlight seen through heavy clouds, brighter in the cracks between stones. Martin tugged the witch close, then ducked behind a tree. Horne hesitated, then came back to kneel beside them.

"It is hunting for us. Or one of us, at least," Martin whispered. The gheist swam down the road, its light flickering off the canopy of trees like lightning. "What do you think..."

"Hush," Horne said. The creature paused, then dove into the forest, breaching the ground in an arc of sharp scales of sunrise light for half a breath before disappearing among the trees. They watched it go.

"I think we need to find those horses," Sir Horne said. "And our inquisitor." She glanced at Fianna, grimacing. "Keep a close hand on that one. This is likely her doing."

"The gods do not come when I call," Fianna protested, but Horne was already up and running. The witch looked to Martin, then nodded to her hobbled legs. "You will have to trust me not to flee. There's no way we can escape so hampered."

"I prefer to take my chances with the gheist," Martin said. He hauled her up, and the two of them followed Sir Horne into the whispering night.

27

THE SUHDRIN FORCES camped outside the Fen Gate had built a barricade across the road. It was nothing more than a picket with shields strapped to the wicker, and behind it a tower of barrels. Suhdrin eyes peeked out from behind the barricade on occasion. Behind them, the southern camp held the crossroads and fields, setting up in the ruins of Fenton. From inside the Fen Gate, Saph and Dunce watched.

"How long will they stay, you think?" Saph asked. The other guards ignored him. The boy wasn't comfortable in the silence. He shrugged narrow shoulders to ease the discomfort caused by his mail shirt, and asked again, "When you think these buggers'll leave?"

"When they're tired of us kicking their asses," Dunce mumbled. "Or they get tired of kicking ours. Either way." The big man sniffed loudly, drawing enough mucus into his lungs to drown a horse. "Not soon enough."

"Yeah, but..." Saph said. He edged closer to Dunce. "But don't you think the winter'll break them? All that soft southern skin? All that silk? Nae good for winter, yeah, you think?"

"I think you need to shut up, Saphon," Mallie said. "Shut up and keep your eyes on that soft southern skin, before they put some of that soft southern steel in our bellies, all while you're running your mouth."

"Ain't nothing happening," Saph said. "Ain't nothing ever happening..." His eyes had trailed to beyond the barricade, into the camp that surrounded the crossroads. There was a commotion along the northeastern road. A thicket of spears had grown up from the tents, and shouting could be heard, even at this distance.

"There's something," Saph said quietly, but it drew all of their attention. As the guards watched, the spear wall buckled, even though there didn't seem to be any attackers. A square of sharp steel, pointing inward, surrounded a figure that was entering the camp. Quickly the scene disappeared behind the intervening barricades, but a rising chorus of shouts and whispers could be heard.

Saph turned to Mallie. "Should we do something about that?" he asked.

"Not yet. Don't want to disturb Sarge if it's nothing more than nervous Suhdrins. Couldn't really see what it is they were panicking over, could you?"

"Nah. One guy, maybe in black, maybe just covered in shit," Dunce said. "You think maybe those southerners ain't seen shit before?"

"Course they have, Duncie," Mal said. "They gotta eat something." The three laughed half-heartedly, a mirth that dried up as the chorus of shouts reached the barricades.

"Yeah," Mallie said nervously. His narrow eyes danced across the barricade. There was movement along the makeshift wall. "Yeah, this is starting to matter to us. Saph, you get the Sarge. Tell him... well, I'm not sure. Tell him to come down here fast-ish."

"He's going to want more than that," Saph complained.

"Gods pray it's nothing," Mal said. "Just..."

He stopped talking as the barrels at the center of the Suhdrin barricade opposite them started to shift. The old wood of the staves ground together, and then the first barrel collapsed, bursting inward like a soap bubble. Another popped, and another, and then the whole structure collapsed like a house of cards. The shielded barricade twisted once then tore apart.

A child stepped into the gap. He wore the savaged robes of a priest of Cinder, but his skin was rumpled and pale. The boy's hair hung like a thatch over his face, and his clothes were grimed with the forest floor. Strands of dark energy drifted from his eyes, his hands, from the folds of his clothing, arcing slowly into the ground like soft lightning. He looked up at the broken doors of the Fen Gate and opened his mouth. His teeth glittered like diamonds in a pool of oil.

"I have come to speak judgment against Malcolm Blakley," the child said in a voice that was a whisper, each person hearing it as though the speaker's lips brushed the soft flesh of their ears. "Bring him to me."

The guards huddled behind their makeshift gate, staring at the dead child.

Above them, the gheist horn sounded.

A bristling square of pikemen clustered just inside the gate of the castle. Repairs on the portcullis had continued steadily for most of the week, and while the gate was defensible, it was hardly secure. This led to the constant vigilance of those inside the walls.

As soon as the gheist horn sounded every able-bodied man, woman, and child rushed to the walls or took a place in the courtyard where the hedge of iron-tipped pikes wavered like heavy wheat in a breeze.

"Get these fools into shelter," Malcolm ordered as soon as he saw the disorganized mess. "I won't risk women and children in pitched battle. If this is some ruse of the Suhdrins, we'll face it with trained steel. And get those fools down off the walls!"

"My lord, if the Suhdrin forces take advantage of the chaos and attack, we'll be defenseless," Baird said. "At least leave the sentries at their posts."

"Fine, but any soul not wearing the Blakley colors is to be hidden away. I'll risk my own, but that's it," Malcolm said. *Plus,* he thought, *if this is something to do with Sorcha, and she tries to return to the castle, at least my people will recognize her. Anyone else is likely to shoot her on sight—especially with the gheist horn in their ears.*

"Where are those damned priests?" he demanded.

"They have returned to their stable, my lord," Baird said. The pair of them stood at the foot of the keep, looking out over the seething chaos of a castle gripped by fear. "The horn has taken them by surprise."

"All of us, it seems," Malcolm said. He had been at breakfast when the horn sounded. He could see the priests moving around inside the stables, their shadows darting back and forth. "It would be a damned help to have an inquisitor up here, calming the people's fears."

"The Orphanshield isn't much for comfort," Baird said. "I swear to gods I've seen more calm in a rout!" He turned to a gaggle of messengers standing nearby, relaying Malcolm's orders and threatening the youngest with a good walloping if he didn't stop crying. Malcolm watched quietly. Sir Baird had stepped into Sir Dugan's role as master of the guard after the man had been killed in Greenhall, but he lacked Dugan's touch with the servants. When the red-faced knight turned back to his lord, Malcolm took him by the elbow and drew him close.

"This castle has just survived an attack by the two greatest gheists in memory. You cannot blame them for a few tears or a little panic. Not even the priests were prepared for this. Gods know I'm not, either."

"Yes, my lord," Sir Baird said, looking ashamed. "Just seems like this is the time for calm heads. Panicking is a good way to get killed."

"The world is full of good ways to get killed, Baird. Let's not stand here and list them all."

Baird dipped his head, then rushed off to see to the evacuation of the courtyard. Malcolm sighed and turned his attention to the walls. There was a great deal of rushing about, but no one seemed to have spotted a gheist. He headed to the Hunter's Tower, where the horn was housed to see what had caused the alarm. Soldiers milling about in the courtyard pressed back to let him pass.

The Hunter's Tower had survived the gheist's attack unharmed, its narrow height now the tallest structure in the Fen Gate. The lower levels, which once housed the barracks for the castle's guards, were now stuffed to the rafters with the various peers of the Tenerran nobility and their attendants. This area was bustling with activity, with knights strapping on armor, pages searching frantically for bloodwrought blades among the luggage, and at least one duke of Tener in a state of undress. Malcolm ran past them all.

The platform that held the gheist horn had seen some changes since House Adair fell. The tiny space now held a rough lean-to and fire pit, along with several travel cases salvaged from the Tenerran army's baggage train. One of Rudaine's displaced knights, a lanky man by the name of Sir Havar, had claimed the roof for himself, only to be crowded into the corner by the constant changing of guard necessary to man the gheist horn.

Sir Havar sat miserably in the shelter of his lean-to, muttering to himself and struggling to secure his breastplate. A round woman in the red-and-black of House Adair—most likely the guard currently on watch—stood nervously next to the horn, working the bellows with her foot. Her clothes were in disarray and her face was as red as a beet.

Watching them all was the child priestess of Strife, making both the knight and the guard highly uncomfortable in her presence. As soon as Malcolm emerged from the stairwell, Sir Havar jumped to his feet, upsetting the precarious lean-to.

"My lord!" Havar yelped. "You must do something about this... this child! This impudent child!"

"That child is sworn to Strife, sir," Malcolm responded, "and therefore carries the full authority of the celestial church, despite her age."

"Yes, yes, but she can not simply burst in here and demand that the horn be sounded! It is the duty of the guard, as well as..."

"Enough," Malcolm snapped. He turned to the priestess, and recalled her name as Catrin DeBray. The girl was standing calmly at the center of the platform, staring toward the front gate, with her arms folded across her chest. "Is this true? Have you sounded the horn without a sighting?"

"There is a sighting," Catrin said. "It just hasn't been reported yet. Your men are panicking, Houndhallow." She was infuriatingly placid, even condescending.

"Because you have panicked them!" he said. Malcolm tried to step into the girl's gaze, but she shifted to the side, her eyes stubbornly focused on the gate. "Look around, child. The forests are quiet. And my guards..."

"My lord!" a voice shouted from the courtyard, thin against the babbling voices of the castle's host. Malcolm grimaced and went to the tower's edge. "There is someone at the gate! We think it's the missing priest!"

"Very well," Malcolm returned. "I will meet him in a moment. See that the inquisitor is notified."

"My lord, he is... changed," the messenger called back. Malcolm shot a look at the priestess, and when he looked back down into the courtyard, the messenger was gone. A surge of soldiers in the black-and-white of House Blakley rushed the gate, spears and shields in hand.

"Well, there you have it," Malcolm said, turning back to the young girl. "Your brother-priest is found, and is manifesting some aspect of Cinder, and it has frightened my guards."

"No," she said. "He is not the same. Marcel is gone." The girl closed her eyes and reached out her hands. A soft corona of summer light graced her shoulders, settling on her face like snow. "He is gone, and yet returned. He comes for you."

"Well, then I must meet him," Malcolm said. "Before anyone gets hurt in this panic."

"No, he is..." she paused, Strife's light shivering on her face. Her eyes opened, startled. "He has passed beyond the veil of death," she said. "He waits for you there."

In the silence that followed, Malcolm could hear screaming, distant and soft. Frowning, he peered in the direction of the gate.

The ground shook.

The shadows grew.

Something rose from the road just in front of the Fen Gate, a twisting shadow rising on wings of tangled starlight. Startled screams came from the Suhdrin camp.

"He came," the girl whispered, "and you will answer."

28

GREENHALL WRAPPED AROUND them like a smothering blanket. After weeks in the wild, surrounded only by the forest and the silent presence of the druids, Gwen found the city's bustle deafening.

A carpet of children and geese and hungry dogs swarmed underfoot. Buildings reached to the sky on either side of the street, leaning closer together the higher they got, stringing ropes of laundry between them, until the cobbles lay in squalid shadow despite the sun. The streets were thick with filth flung from the windows above or dropped by the endless stream of passersby. The air stank of stale sweat and fresh shit, yet none of the citizens seemed to notice.

If Gwen thought it overwhelming, the druids found it abhorrent. Cahl kept gagging beneath his bindings, while Folam breathed deeply and evenly, as though in meditation. Only Noel, raised in the cities of the south, seemed comfortable on Greenhall's streets.

"Gods, do they just shit where they walk?" Cahl asked, then he fell into a spasm of coughing and gagging that nearly undid his disguise. They were forced to stop until he collected himself.

"We aren't lucky enough to have rivers everywhere we go," Noel said. "It's better after a rain, or in the winter."

"In Fenton, we have groups whose job it is to wash away the filth," Gwen said. "They must have a similar operation here."

"On the nicer streets, perhaps," Noel said.

"These are apparently not the nicer streets," Folam said quietly.

"They are not," Gwen agreed, "and the less time we spend on them, the better, I think."

"Yes," Folam said. "Cahl, can you sense the shrine?"

The shaman slowed, turning his bandaged face up to the sky. The crowds pushed around them, swearing at the blockage, bumping into Gwen and Noel, shooting nasty looks as they passed. Cahl shook his head.

"There's too much here. I need..." He turned his head, blind, his hands reaching out for nothing. "I need quiet, and raw stone."

Gwen looked down between her feet at the swirl of refuse and stagnant water. She grimaced.

"There's little of either here," she said. "Let's keep moving." They walked on for a while in silence, each woman leading a shaman by the hand. Most of the passersby gave them little notice, though a growing crowd of children followed at a distance, whispering among themselves.

"Is it always like this?" Noel asked, quite suddenly.

"Crowded? Yes, Greenhall is always packed. Though it's probably worse now, with the war. Anyone isolated and scared of the pagan night will seek the blessed safety of Halverdt's walls—any who aren't marching to war, that is," Gwen said. "Though I've seen enough able-bodied men."

"Not that," Noel said. She motioned to the banners that hung from the buildings. Each one was red and yellow, Strife's holy flame stitched across the face. Some were much nicer, while others looked to have been made quite recently, and in great haste. The braziers that burned at every corner were laced with frairwood or lesser incense, and contributed to the stench in the air.

"As you said," Gwen said, "Sophie seems to have found her faith, if only for the goddess of summer."

"Yes. Strange that she keeps the sigil of summer up, even though we are at the threshold of winter," Noel said.

"Celestials and their calendars," Cahl muttered. "The spirits move the weather, not the cycle of days."

"And yet winter is always winter," Noel countered, "and summer always summer. It's as though the young duchess seems determined to hold on to the light a little longer than she should."

"It feels desperate," Gwen said. "It feels mad."

"I find it comforting," Noel said quietly, and Gwen was reminded of the cloak of flames that had wrapped the witch when she faced off against Judoc.

"There is less traffic this way," Gwen said suddenly. All the talk of celestials and calendars was making her nervous. They couldn't afford to attract attention. So she led them down a different street, though truly it didn't seem any quieter than the one they had been on. Nevertheless, Noel followed.

In fact, each turn they took brought them to a narrower, louder street, more crowded and less clean than the last. Gwen was getting antsy. Cahl was getting sick. Finally, they stopped beside an old well situated in a tight courtyard with barely enough room to walk around the watering hole's ancient walls. Strangely, there was less traffic here. Noel led Folam to the well's edge, guiding his hand to the stones.

The old man smelled the air, puffing out the bandages

around his face, leaning down into the well's gaping mouth. He coughed, drawing back quickly.

"The water is fouled," Folam said around a mouth full of bile.

"Small wonder there are fewer people," Noel said. She pulled Cahl out of the corner of the courtyard, where the shaman had been hugging the wall nervously. "The water may be foul, but the stones are true. Tell us what you sense, shaman."

Grimacing, Cahl knelt, shifting his bandages so he could see. He ran calloused fingers over the stone of the well, tracing the wall until his fingers reached raw earth.

"This is good," he said. "An ancient vein. The children of flowers drank from these waters and knelt at this font."

"And now it lies fouled by this open sore of a city," Folam rumbled, showing uncharacteristic anger. "This insult should be answered."

"We've no time to right every wrong we will find within these walls," Gwen said. "Let's locate the shrine and be gone."

"It is... deeper. The sun does not touch it, nor the wind." Cahl stood, rubbing his hands together to brush them clean. "There is no hint of frairwood tangled in its breath."

"That's helpful," Folam muttered. "No sun, no wind, and none of this damned incense. The shrine must be buried deeper than I thought. Perhaps too deep."

"There is a section of collapsed homes in the north end of the city," Gwen said. "Halverdt's Curse, it's called. When the first Lord Greenhall claimed this land he built a palace in true Suhdrin style. Marble arches, iron trellises, the works. They say it collapsed under the weight of its own pretension."

"More likely destroyed by the disrupted spirits of Tenerran dead," Cahl said as he readjusted his bandages to once again cover his face. "Especially if it was built over the vernal shrine."

"I agree," Folam said. "Take us to this place."

"Going to be hard to find," Gwen said. "They built over it after the collapse."

"Get me close," Cahl said gruffly. "I will find a way."

With their disguises secure, Noel and Gwen led the two shamans out of the quiet courtyard and back into the busy crush of the streets. As they were leaving, Gwen glanced back.

There was a child perched on an archway overlooking the well. He was dressed in rags, but carried a length of wood across his back, like a paladin's sword. As soon as he saw Gwen looking at him, he swung into a narrow window, disappearing from view. The child's wooden blade clattered against the window's shutters as he leapt. Gwen paused, straining to listen, watching the window.

"What did you see?" Noel asked.

"Gods, woman, nothing!" Cahl answered. "Have you forgotten that I'm blind?"

Gwen shook her head. "Let's get out of here," she said. "Before it becomes something."

Where they ventured next made the main boulevards of Greenhall pristine by comparison. Not even the braziers of frairwood could mask the scent of rotting filth. Many of those braziers had been robbed, the smoldering wood snatched by nimble hands, to be burned in one of the hovels that lined the narrow road.

The road itself was splintered and uneven, the cobblestones jutting in every direction, often buried under generations of accumulated grime. A sluggish stream ran down the center of the road.

The banners that hung in this part of town were stained, and the people who watched from open doors or alleyways were thin and desperate, or too drunk to care. There was no shortage of children, but the usual cloud of animals that haunted the rest of the city was missing.

"We mustn't spend long here," Noel said. The Suhdrin witch's clothes were more suited to a merchant than a pauper, and while Gwen and the two shamans fit in nicely with their forest-stained rags, Noel was attracting unwelcome attention.

"It's getting easier," Cahl said. He walked with outstretched hands, brushing the rare stone lintels and chimneys as he walked. Most of the buildings were clapboard and piled trash, but there was enough of the essential element for the shaman to find his way. "Shouldn't be long now."

"Very good," Folam said. "Very good, indeed."

"There's sun and wind enough," Noel said, grimacing at the sky. "Even if we're close, we're going to have to go down at some point."

"The Curse is little more than an open sewer," Gwen said. "There will be gates enough. We just have to find them."

"I can lead you to the Curse, if that's what you're looking for," a voice said from their side. Gwen and Noel turned to see a boy, the one who had been watching them at the well, sitting and swinging his legs from a ledge that overlooked the road.

"And what will that cost us?" Gwen asked.

"Our coin, I imagine," Noel said. "And probably our throats slit in a back alley."

"That's the price if you wander around here much longer," the boy said. "A merchant girl, her skinny brother, and two blind farmers?" He waved a hand down the street.

"Continue on, if you must. I'll say a prayer at your burial. If anyone finds the bodies."

Noel snorted derisively. "You make a hard sale, little one, but I think we can handle ourselves against a bunch of bread-starved beggars, if you please."

"Not in the Curse, you won't," the boy said. "Folks like you step into those shadows, and it's your life for the quiet house, and nothing less." He dropped down from his ledge, bandage-wrapped feet slapping lightly against stones as he crossed in front of them, barring the way. "Sir Horold will lead you to safety, though. You can pray on that!"

"Sir Horold, eh?" Gwen asked. The boy's rags were cut to look like a knight's tabard, and the smear of stains on his chest might be mistaken for a flame. "And what is your price, Sir Horold?"

"For a lady such as this?" the child asked, bowing to Noel. "It is my honor."

"Well, your honor will earn you half a crown, if you get us there and back safely," Noel said. "No tricks."

"My honor forbids it," Horold said. The child bowed again, an awkward, gangly motion that revealed the scabs along his legs. "Follow me."

"He thinks himself a knight," Gwen whispered to Cahl as they set off.

"A vow knight," the child piped in. "I have dedicated myself to Lady Strife, and the glories of summer." He winked sideways at Noel. "The season of love, my lady."

"Gods preserve," Cahl muttered.

True to his honor, Horold led them to an entrance to the Curse. On the way there they passed several more obvious paths down, from storm grates to a gaping archway hung with chains and leading into darkness. Their guide took them through several abandoned buildings before pulling back a trapdoor. A ladder dropped out of sight, followed by the sound of splashing water.

"Most ways are guarded by unsavory characters, my lady," Horold said. "Black marketeers, slavers, possibly even servants of the pagan gheists. But not this path. This way is as safe and true as Strife's embrace."

"Of course it is," Noel said. "And what waits for us beyond? Your band of earnest little knights, ready to take our possessions?"

"You harm my honor," Horold said, "but I will allow it. After all, trust is built on action, yes? I have led you here, as I swore I would, and I will guard your passage through these depths, as is only befitting a knight of my station."

"You should quit playing this foolish game, boy," Gwen said angrily. "It will get you killed. Or worse."

"Game? This is no game," Horold said. He stood away from the trapdoor's edge and drew his wooden sword. "When Lady Sophie took her throne, she swore to raise a true army of the goddess, one that will cleanse the corruption from this land. I took my pledge that day, to work with each dawn and each dusk, that I might be worthy of the bright lady, and one day take the winter vow."

Gwen and Noel exchanged dark glances, but it was Folam who spoke.

"Such a bright child," he said. "You have surely done the bright lady's will in bringing us here, but now we can find our own way."

"So you say," the boy answered, and he turned his

attention again to Noel. "Why are you seeking the Curse, anyway? A lady such as yourself is better served in sunlight, is she not?"

"I am no lady," she hissed, "and you are no knight." She slid onto the ladder and wormed her way into the darkness. There was a splash a moment later. "We will need light," she called up.

"Your blind friends won't know the difference," Horold said. "But for the ladies, I will bring Strife's light into the darkness."

He scampered out of the room, leaving the pagans alone in the dimness.

"We should go, before he returns," Gwen said.

"I would rather keep him close," Folam said. "He is harmless enough, but now that we are this far, I do not want to risk the child talking. Especially not one so earnest in his faith."

"And when we find the shrine?" Gwen asked. "What then?"

Folam turned bandaged eyes to her, his old lips parting in an understanding and patient smile.

"He is a child," the voidfather said. "What do you think I am?"

"I agree with Gwen," Cahl said. "We don't need him any longer. I can feel the shrine in my bones. We are close."

"Maybe I should stay behind with him," Gwen said. "Keep him distracted while you find the vernal god's shrine. Then once you've done whatever it is you need to accomplish, we can be safely on our way. All of us."

"No, no," Folam said, shaking his head. "That will not do. We're not leaving anyone behind."

"I don't like it," Gwen said. "I don't like any of this."

At that moment the boy returned. He was carrying a brand

from one of the braziers in the street outside, its end wrapped in the linen from his feet. He held it up like a benediction.

"The bright lady has provided us light, just as she will provide us safety in the darkness," Horold said. "Come, let us bring the light into the darkness." He rushed past Gwen and Cahl, disappearing into the Curse. With a sigh, Gwen motioned to the ladder.

"Try to remember you're supposed to be blind," she said. The two pagans felt their way slowly down into the tunnel. Gwen followed a moment later, closing the trapdoor behind her.

29

IAN AND ELSA were given better rooms, though just as isolated. The tower where they were held had burned at some point in the recent past, and the stone was charred. The wooden floors were newly hewn and still smelled of sawdust and pitch. However, they each were given a room, with a common area between, all with windows. The shutters hammered day and night with the force of the storm outside.

"There is much of this I don't understand," Ian said, sitting in the common area and preparing to eat. The servants brought them their meals. They had yet to see the other occupants of the castle, though two days had passed since their strange audience with Lord Halfic. "To begin, why should we give a damn? We'll be on our way as soon as this storm passes, unless you think Lady Gwen is hidden somewhere within the confines of Harthal."

"No," Elsa said. She was back in her armor, clearly more comfortable wearing steel and blade. "You may be right. This may have nothing to do with us, but I'm getting restless."

The shutters clattered loudly as a strong gust struck them. Cold air leaked through the slats, stirring the flames in the hearth and giving Ian goosebumps. He laughed.

"The storm is hungry for us, sir," he said. "Perhaps we

should just leave. Give the god of winter what he wants." He tore off a hunk of bread and dipped it in a miserable stew. "A fair fight, and our frozen bones."

"No, I want to get a look around the castle. It seems strange that we've seen so few people, especially in this weather. It's not as if they could simply be beyond the walls, hunting or some such."

"The kitchens were busy enough," Ian said. "There must be people here, even if the great hall lies fallow. We're just being kept away."

"What do you know of our host?" Elsa asked.

"Halfic? He keeps to himself, always has. Protects his lands and pays his vassal gold," Ian said, then he shrugged. "I've had no hint of pagan heresy from him. But I knew nothing of Gwen's faith, either."

"It might explain why he didn't lend spears to Adair's defense," Elsa mused. "If he didn't want to draw attention to himself. Yet if Halfic were a pagan, you would think he would want to protect his fellow heretic. If only to protect himself."

"If he's trying to summon a gheist, though..." Ian started.

"Or cast one out," Elsa said. "Let's not assume anything. And I haven't been able to sense anything unholy on the castle grounds. Inquisitors are better for that. Gods I wish Frair Lucas were here."

"Right, or cast one out. If he's trying to do either of those things, the presence of a vow knight in his castle could change things for him," Ian said. "So why not speak with us. Why keep us isolated?"

"Something has happened here. Something strange." Elsa finished her meal with the efficiency of a wildfire and stood. She walked to the window. A light glimmer of frost framed the shutters. She ran a finger along it, the ice melting at her touch. "This isn't natural. None of it."

"Might the storm have something to do with the gheist?" Ian asked. He tossed the crust of his bread into the thin stew and pushed it away. "You said that the death god had come this way. Perhaps Halfic is trying to banish its presence. Or hide it."

"If he was hiding a pagan god, the man wouldn't even have opened the door to us, or he would have killed us while we slept. No one would have suspected. Everyone would simply assume we were lost in the Fen." Elsa grimaced at the howling wind. "And if he's trying to banish it, why not ask for help? Why leave us sitting here, as much prisoners as guests?"

"Well, we're never going to get any kind of answer in this room," Ian said, "and those guards follow us everywhere else." He leaned back, rubbing his eyes in frustration. "There must be another way."

"Yes," Elsa said, staring meaningfully at the shutters. "There must."

"Ready?" she asked.

"No," Ian snapped. She looked back at him with frustration, checking the rope around his waist, tied to the bed frame and further secured to the andirons of the hearth. The fire had been out for nearly an hour, to give the anchor time to cool, and the room was turning cold.

"You're ready," Elsa snapped back. She turned to the shutters.

"No! I'm not! I'm really..."

Elsa slipped the bar from the shutters and stepped back. The wood panels boomed open and the storm howled into the room. Driving snow swirled over the bed, rattling the

door and stealing the breath from Ian's lungs. He drop
the rope in his hand, stumbling away from the gale, gasp
for air in the ice. He nearly fell against the bed, but E
tugged twice on the rope, jerking him upright. Then
barreled out the window, disappearing over the ledge a
into the churning white wall of the blizzard.

Ian followed. The tug of the rope pulled him to t
window's edge, nearly dragging him into the air. At the la
second he grabbed the frame, leaning out over the voi
Tears froze against his cheeks. The gale tried to pluck hi
from the tower, and forced him to grip the window tightly
the winds swirled around him.

Elsa was crawling crablike upward across the tiles o
the stable roof, her head down, the rope snaking betwee
them. Ian took a tentative step out onto the roof, clingin
to the window while he scrabbled for purchase with hi
feet. Elsa reached the end of her rope, paused, then tugge
him forward. He lost his grip, fell heavily onto the roof
and started to slide.

Ian screamed, but the storm stole the sound. Ice and
snow gathered under his sliding feet. He scrabbled at the roof
with his rapidly numbing fingers, trying to find a handhold,
starting to panic as the edge got closer and closer. The rope
that stretched between them swept a wide arc of snow off the
roof, triggering an avalanche that rumbled.

Elsa watched him slide, grimacing as she braced herself.
Finally the piled snow beneath Ian's feet accumulated enough
that he slowed, and then stopped. Balancing on the icy slope
he found one handhold, then another, then edged his way a
little up the roof. She waited until he was moving surely, then
continued her climb.

In fits and starts, they made their way to the end of the stables, where Elsa swung off the roof on the block and tackle of the hay elevator, dropping into the loft. Ian watched from the edge of the roof. A few moments passed before Elsa stuck her head out.

"I can't do that," Ian said. He looked from the elevator to the loft, then down to the ground twenty feet below. "No, I can't do that."

"Well, you can't stay there," Elsa said.

"I can lift you back up when you're done," Ian said.

"You'll freeze to death," she said. "Just jump. It'll be fine." As if to emphasize her words, a strong gust of wind struck him. Ian sunk lower against the surface.

"I'll just stay here," he said.

"Have it your way," Elsa said. Then she gathered the rope in her hand, braced herself, and gave it a tremendous pull. The force of it jerked Ian off the roof and into the open air. He didn't have time to scream before the rope around his waist went tight. Behind him, the length that led to the distant window of their room snapped taut, squeezing the air from his belly. He dangled over the ground, spinning slowly, staring at Elsa's frustrated face.

Reaching precariously outward, she grabbed him, swung him into the loft, then cut the rope at his waist and tied it to a post.

"Enough screwing around," she said. "Come on."

Ian was still recovering his breath as she led them down into the stables. Nearly all of the stalls were full, the horses whickering peacefully despite the cold. Elsa marched down the center until she found their lone surviving horse. She took the time to check its feed and blanket, rubbing the

beast's nose before continuing on.

Harthal was a small holding, with a narrow wall designed to repel bandits, and few buildings. It had no siegeworks. The tower where Ian and Elsa were being kept was tucked into one corner of the castle, bordered by the stables on one side. They were across the courtyard from the great hall, and there was only one other building within the walls, a low-slung doma that looked as old and worn as the cliffs that surrounded Houndhallow.

Ian and Elsa huddled in the shelter of the stalls for a minute, warming numb fingers and—in Ian's case—recovering his pride. When his bones had stopped rattling, he turned to Elsa.

"What's the plan?" he asked. "There aren't a lot of buildings to search, and yet there are enough horses here to mount a company. These rooms must be full."

"Yes. Strange. Especially considering the fact that we know the great hall is abandoned." Elsa crept to the stable door and looked around.

"Well, they have to be somewhere," Ian said. "We just need to find them."

"A poignant observation," Elsa answered. "I'm glad to have you along on this journey, so you may bless me with your wisdom. Now shut up and get moving."

"Gods," Ian muttered. "Who lit *your* candle?"

"Sitting in bed does not agree with me," Elsa said. "Being carried into a castle by a mulish boy because I was too weak to walk does not agree with me." She turned and glared at Ian, and all the humor in her tone vanished. "And being kept in the shadow of mystery does not agree with me, either. Now, let us burn the darkness from this place."

With that, Elsa marched into the storm, straight for the doma.

"For once I'd like to walk away first," Ian muttered, then he hurried after the vow knight before the storm swallowed her.

The doma was brilliantly lit, the calendar windows limned in golden light, and a heavily packed trail led from the front door to the great hall. Elsa struggled through the deep drifts until she reached the trail. Fortunately, this meant that Ian could follow in her wake without much trouble.

Fragments of hymns reached them, snatched from the howling gale in tiny pieces, like sparks from a bonfire. When they reached the door, Elsa kicked it in as she drew her sword.

The song stopped. Someone screamed and began crying.

The vow knight stood in the doorway, the storm swirling around her. The pews were crowded with people, some of them in armor, others in rags, all of them staring at Elsa with fear in their eyes. Swords rattled out of scabbards. Children, gathered along the wall, scrambled to get away from the door. They caught Elsa's eye.

They were maimed. Not wounded, not sick, but physically changed in cruel and horrific ways. Boneless legs trailed torsos dragged along by arms as pale and slick as a fish's belly. Mouths gaped where faces should have been. Wooden bones sprouted branches through flesh, leaves visible just beneath the surface, veins pulsing in chalky bark, hair of grass and root and soil.

The room became very silent. Ian heaved his shoulder against the door, shutting it against the blizzard. Snow melted off of the pair to drop in puddles on the cobble floor. Every candle in the doma was lit, and splinters of frairwood burned in a dozen braziers. The adults, some of them bearing lesser growths, more looking perfectly normal, started moving toward them. Those with swords held them at guard, though their hands trembled.

"Hold!" the frair shouted from the front of the room. "Stay your blades! You must not spill the blood of a priest, *any* priest." He pushed his way past the closing circle of angry parents. "Not even this priest. Not here."

Elsa took her eyes off the villagers to glance at the frair. He was past the bloom of youth, but not yet fallen into the frailty of age. Wiry limbs told of a life given to hard labor, and his hands were calloused and lined with dirt. Many priests of Strife served their goddess this way, saying the rites of summer and tilling the fields beside their congregation. The man reached out.

"Stay your vengeance, sir," he said. "They are children, after all."

"What is happening here?" Elsa said. Ian drew his sword and stood beside her. The malformed children cowered behind the pews, peeking out to stare at the pair of them with eyes made of stone and wood and fire. "What happened to them?"

"We should not have hidden this," Lord Halfic said. The earl stood up from among the pews, his hands folded penitently at his waist. "We should not have hidden our stain, but now that you have seen it, know that we will not let you destroy those we love." He raised his hands, and the frair stepped away from Elsa. "We cannot let you do that."

The guards, farmers, servants and fools edged closer. All of them were armed, all watched Elsa through angry, tear-stained eyes. They were terrified, and yet determined.

Ian and Elsa backed up. Heat blossomed through the air as Elsa drew Strife's power through her runes. The vow knight pushed Ian toward the door.

"I will not kill the innocent," she said. "But if any one defies me, they will share the pagan's fate."

"We are all innocent, and all guilty," Halfic said, "but we have seen how the church deals with the gheists. None of us wants to die by your blade, but we will not let you take our children. Not like this."

"Blood doesn't have to spill," Elsa said. "Let me help. Perhaps I can burn the corruption—"

"The north has had enough of the church's fire," the frair said. He slipped behind the wall of advancing men, his eyes sad. "Not in the doma, my lord. I beg you, don't stain the floor of this holy place with holy blood."

"Take them outside," Halfic called over the heads of his men. "See that no one misses them."

The wave of men rushed forward. Elsa knocked the first one down, striking with the flat of her blade, searing flesh and singeing hair. Another followed, and another, each scrambling to get close to the vow knight. Ian jumped forward, but was knocked flat by a big farmer with a wooden mallet. The tide of flesh passed him by. Elsa was overwhelmed, unwilling to kill, unable to keep her attackers at bay. They carried her into the storm.

Ian lay on the floor, staring up at the ceiling mosaic and trying to force air into his lungs. The frair stood over him, looking down mournfully.

"And you, my lord Blakley? What shall we do with you?" the frair asked.

Ian raised an arm to defend himself, but the frair struck him with the silver-tipped butt of the communion staff. Darkness took him, fringed with the sound of Elsa's shouting, and the roar of the blizzard's fury.

30

THE LIGHT FROM Horold's brand was inconsistent. Embers fell from it whenever the child brushed against a wall, falling with a loud hiss into the muck underfoot. The corridor was too narrow for more than one of them abreast, so Noel followed Horold, with Gwen just behind. The two shamans made a show of blind-man follow, but as soon as they were hidden in the shadows, both loosened their bindings just enough to be able to see.

Through the flickering shadows and flooded corridors, they slipped, crawled, slithered and fell. The floors of the Curse were never straight. Other than Horold, none of them could stand upright, and Cahl was often bent double as he shuffled forward.

"Shit!" Noel hissed as she bumped into a broken column. She sat heavily on her ass, staring unhappily at her ruined clothes for a handful of heartbeats before sighing heavily. "This is a miserable place."

"It is, my lady," Horold said. The child turned and tugged Noel to her feet, so enthusiastically that he nearly dragged her back into the same column. "The worst of all possible places. What glorious quest has brought you here?"

"We have... we're looking for something. A shrine," she said. "A very old one."

"What does this shrine look like? I might be able to help."

"No," Cahl said from the back, his rumbling voice carrying far in the narrow stone corridor. "You will not have seen it. It was hidden, long ago."

"Then how are we to find it?" Horold asked. "Do you have a map? But no, you couldn't have a map, or it would have led you to the entrance. And I had to do that, didn't I?"

"Yes, Horold," Gwen said. "You've been very helpful to us, but perhaps you had better go home now. There's little more that you can do for us."

"Nonsense," Horold chirped before Folam could protest. "I've taken you this far, and I will see you to the end. Now, how are we going to find this ancient shrine of yours?"

In the shadows, Cahl and Folam turned toward each other, their heads bent low in mumbled conversation. When they straightened up, Cahl hid his eyes from the light with his hood.

"We are close. Perhaps no more than thirty yards," he said.

"Is this the right path?" Gwen asked.

"It has to be," Horold said. "There are no other clear passages in this direction."

"Then we have no choice but to push forward," Noel said, "and no further need for a guide, sir. You may go."

Horold looked from Noel to Gwen and back, then shrugged. "We only have the one light. I couldn't possibly find my way back in the dark, and there's no way you can go forward without it."

"That is... fine. Fine, lead the way, but stay close to me," Noel said. She turned Horold around by the shoulders, stealing a glance back at Gwen once the boy was looking forward. "Gods know what dangers lie ahead."

"No fear, my lady," Horold said. "I can keep us both safe."

They crawled forward, the way getting narrower and narrower, until all four of them were on their hands and knees, slipping through generations of rainwater and moss and rat shit. Horold dropped his torch several times, until only the barest illumination leaked from the embers.

"It is becoming difficult," Cahl whispered, though they could all hear him in the close confines. "Everything is bright."

"You have an odd idea of bright, my lord," Horold said. "In fact..."

He stumbled into silence. The light from the brand failed to reach the walls, and the close ceiling vaulted away from them. A soft glow broke out above them, as dull and gray as pewter.

"Well," Horold said. "Here's something." He stood, holding his hand out to help Noel to her feet. "I've seen this before. Part of the old palace's doma."

The four of them spread out, stretching bruised limbs and blinking in the dull light. A half-dozen archways led off from this room, their mouths shrouded in darkness. Cracks lined the ceiling, revealing flakes of colored plaster and smooth stone. The floor was a scree of chipped marble and vegetation. Cahl felt his way around the perimeter of the room. Ghosts of light echoed from his fingertips as he plucked at the stone's essence, causing Horold to watch curiously. Noel went to the center of the room and looked up.

"Another well, it looks like," she said. "Though this one has been boarded up. Do you know where this comes out?"

"There are a dozen blocked wells in the old city," Horold said, tearing his eyes away from Cahl. The opening above them was covered with close fitting boards. Thin sunlight crept between the joins. "I can't hear anything from up there. No merchants, no traffic... perhaps we're outside the walls?"

"Or inside the castle," Folam whispered. "Wouldn't that be a feat?"

"Is this it?" Gwen asked. "Is this our place?"

"No, but it is close," Cahl said. He paused in his fingertip search, stepping back. "I need more light."

Horold's torch was nearly out, casting only bare light against the wall. He drew another from his belt, lit it from the dying embers of the first, and tossed the dead torch to the ground. New light blossomed through the room.

Gwen drew a sharp breath. "Gods bless," she said.

The dim light of the torch revealed a mosaic of great age. Many tiles were broken or missing, but still the faint image of a sun and field could be seen. There were figures in the sun, possibly women, dressed in flowing robes and dancing through the rays of light that radiated down. The field itself progressed from winter's desolation through early spring, and into the riot of summer. Flames flickered at the borders of the mosaic, consuming the field.

"The Lady Strife, blessing the earth with her light," Horold said with awe in his voice. "I never noticed it before."

"It is not for every eye," Folam said. The voidfather stood at the center of the chamber. He lowered the hood of his cloak and started to unwrap his bindings. "Just as this place is not for every soul."

"Voidfather, wait," Noel said. "This isn't necessary."

"You know otherwise," Folam said. He took the length of bandage that had been covering his face, tucked it into his belt, and looked at the child. "I am sorry, boy." Horold looked mutely at the older man, confusion dashing across his face.

"What are you... what is this? You're Tenerran?"

"I am much more than that, child," Folam said. He raised a hand to Horold, beckoning. "I am the blood of the empty tribe, bearer of the hollow rite. Not even death can fill me."

"Horold, run!" Noel barked. She pushed the boy toward the nearest exit, an ivy-hung archway that stirred with a cold wind. Horold moved as if in a dream, his eyes still on Folam's outstretched hand. "Run!"

"Empty your lungs," Folam intoned. His voice scraped across the stone walls of the room. A web of thin light drew up from Horold's skin, the dancing highlights of natural illumination growing sharp until they flared away from his body like spider webs caught in a breeze. The twisting skeins of energy crossed the room, gathering in Folam's hand. "Empty," he groaned.

Horold fell to his knees. A sound came from his bones, grinding and fast, as the boy's essence fled his body. Folam drew a deep breath, and the web of light grew stronger.

Noel screamed.

"He's only a child, Folam! He's nothing but a boy!"

"Boys become men," Folam said. In the midst of the ritual, his voice tangled with the keening of Horold's death, both sounds echoing through the buried chamber. The voidfather raised his other hand and pulled harder against Horold's soul. "Men become soldiers, and soldiers end in death, for us, and for them."

Noel threw herself at Folam, but Gwen grabbed her before she reached him. They twisted together, arms locking, hands grappling. Noel's skin grew hot.

"This is what sacrifice looks like, pagan," Gwen whispered. "People die. Usually the wrong people."

"He has a family, Adair! What if he was your brother?"

"Then he would already be dead," Gwen said. "Let it go."

Noel collapsed to her knees, Gwen on top of her. She stayed there, panting, tears rolling freely down her cheeks. Horold slumped to the floor. His skin was withering like dried fruit. One side of his youthful face was puckered, and his blond hair turned white as snow.

"Do not mourn this child, Noel. He is already pledged to the enemy. If he did not die now, he would have raised his sword against us as an adult," Folam said. "Better he pass now into silence, than..."

There was a dull thud. Folam collapsed to the ground. Instantly the whisper-thin strands of light snapped like molasses, reeling back into Horold's skin. The boy took a startled breath. He folded against the wall, lying there, breathing shallowly.

Cahl loomed over the unconscious form of the voidfather. He held a sap in one hand. Its head was speckled with Folam's blood.

"Better that he live, and follow his faith, and grow in his understanding of the world," the shaman rumbled. "If his path leads him to war, and then to death at our hand, the gods will it. But I will not see a child murdered."

Noel twisted free of Gwen's stunned grip and ran to the child. She bent low over him, murmuring quietly. Flames flickered around her knees, washing over Horold's wrinkled skin.

"I thought the voidfather's will was absolute," Gwen said. Cahl shrugged.

"Perhaps not," Cahl said. "Perhaps even he can be wrong."

"So what now?" Gwen said. "What will you do when the old man wakes up?"

"Apologize," Cahl said.

Noel carried Horold down one of the corridors that branched off the domed room. The boy was delirious, whispering words that made no sense, shivering despite the heat. She laid him at the base of a stairwell that circled up toward the light. The sounds of voices and footfalls echoed down the steps.

"Someone will find him here," she said, her voice strained. "Or he will recover enough to make his own way out."

"This is a mistake," Gwen said. "What tale will he tell?"

"We'll be long gone before he wakes up," Noel said, "and by then it won't matter."

"It will matter. Lady Sophie will not like stories about pagans lurking beneath her city. We are creating problems for our Tenerran brothers."

"They are not our problems," Noel said. "Not today."

The two of them went back to the chamber. Folam was sitting in the corner, glaring at Cahl and nursing his head. The big shaman ignored the voidfather's attention, busying himself with the mosaic. Noel went to a knee at Folam's side.

"I can ease the pain, voidfather. If you wish."

"It is nothing," Folam said.

"The boy is safe. He won't talk, not today."

Folam grunted and stood, brushing past Noel. Gwen bristled as the voidfather approached, ready to defend Cahl if the man struck, but Folam went to stand beside the shaman, staring at the mosaic.

"A relic of the old faith," he said, "though not old

enough to belong to the tribe of flowers."

"No. Celestial hands crafted this, though perhaps they didn't understand what they were forming. There is enough here of Lady Strife to pass the inquisition's attention, but it contains the vernal god's markings, as well." Cahl ran a finger over the depiction of a field, tracing lines among the missing tiles. "The petal cloak. The broken staff, freshly grown, and his host of saplings. It's all here." Gwen looked where Cahl pointed, but could see nothing of what he was saying. All she saw were flowers and trees, and the burning rays of the sun.

"It's a warning to pagan eyes," Folam agreed. "That Strife's madness has infected this ground."

"Or that the vernal god has been broken, and should not be allowed to wander," Cahl said.

"So this is it?" Gwen asked. "This is the shrine?"

"No," Cahl said, shaking his head. "That is beyond this wall. Farther down."

"Then what are we supposed to do? Are we close enough to perform your ritual, voidfather? Do we need to search these other corridors, in case there's another path down?" Noel asked.

"That will not be necessary," Folam said. He bent his head to Cahl. "Draw us down, elder."

Cahl nodded sharply. He stepped away from the wall, pulling the bindings from his head, using the linens to wrap his hands. Folam backed away from the mosaic. He drew Noel and Gwen to his side. As Cahl knelt at the center of the chamber, Folam began to weave a circle binding around the trio.

"I will forgive your rebellion, Noel, if you will forgive my outrage," he whispered. Noel flinched away, but nodded once.

"We do what is best. All of us," she said.

"There must be silence," Cahl said. "If I'm to do this without waking the city."

"I am familiar with silence," Folam said. He finished his binding. A wall of emptiness rose up from the ground, blurring the air, pressing hard vacuum against their faces. All sound died. Gwen's skin tingled numbly, and her eyes began to water.

Cahl glanced at them and nodded. In absolute silence, he ran his hands across the stone floor. Lines of blue light trailed from his palms, leaving patterns in the stone like piled sand. The scree melted beneath Cahl's fingers, running together as veins of soft light shot through it, slowly accumulating into a crescent of thick stone.

He bent close to the earth, his forehead resting on the formed rock. He whispered words of power into the crescent, each breath fogging the lightning-bright glow that seemed to come from within the earth. Pressing his palms against the stone, Cahl pushed out.

The earth moved. The stone rose in a wave that crashed against the mosaic, breaking over the tiles. A pale illumination traveled up the images, until a frozen stroke of lightning appeared in the middle of the wall. With wrenching grace, the dome split, raining flakes of plaster down on Cahl, dusting his hair white. The wall opened, the sound swallowed by Folam's aura of void space.

Like birds flushing from the bush, a spray of flower petals arced into the room. They hung suspended in the air, their edges slowly turning into ember and then ash, until they drifted down to join the broken plaster on the floor.

With a snap, Folam dropped his vacuum, and the world of sound and air rushed back in. Cahl turned to look at the voidfather. He gestured to the opening.

"The shrine of flowers," he said. Now that the air had returned to the room, Gwen could smell damp and thunderstorms, and the heady musk of spring. Folam stepped past her, to step tentatively into the entrance to the shrine. Gwen started to follow, then saw that Cahl wasn't moving. She knelt beside him. The shaman's face was sheened with sweat, and his eyes were pressed shut.

"Are you alright?" she asked.

"I will be fine," he said. He stood with a grunt, weaving on his feet until he found his balance. Gwen took his arm to steady him. His skin was pale and clammy to the touch. "He asks much of me, sometimes."

"Yes," Gwen said. She looked over at the voidfather as he disappeared into the shrine. "He asks much of us all."

31

MALCOLM STOOD AT the base of the Hunter's Tower. A cloud of squires bustled around him, fitting the plate-and-half that he traditionally wore in battle. The square below was chaos. Half of the people were trying to flee, half were forming up into battle lines, ready for when the gate fell. And it was going to fall.

"Be quick about it," Malcolm snapped. The squire at his feet stumbled back, grimacing as he lost his grip on the sabaton, sending it clattering to the ground. The man snatched it up and started once again to attach it to Malcolm's boot. "My men need me at their front. And I'm not sure what bloody good this will do against a gheist."

"Mortal hope lies in immortal strength," the Orphanshield said as he approached. The inquisitor trailed his pack of lesser priests, all of them burdened with various implements of the faith. "Stay behind, Houndhallow. This is the church's business."

"I should say so," Malcolm said. "Do you want to explain to me how one of your children succumbed to Sacombre's corruption?"

"What do you mean?" Frair Gilliam asked. He looked back on his cadre, brow furrowed. "My priests are faithful celestials, as you can see..."

"What I can see is young Marcel tearing a hole in my wall," Malcolm said, pointing to the front gate. "And those do not look like the blessings of Cinder."

The party turned to stare in the direction Malcolm was pointing. The gate, already damaged and half-hung, buckled under a titanic blow. The men holding the line stumbled back, then surged forward behind spears and shields and courage. This gave a brief view of the road beyond the gate.

Frair Marcel hovered in the air, encased in a rippling aura of dark matter. A halo rotated slowly behind him, sprouting spears of black energy, each one tearing through the earth like a plow. From his hands and feet, scything limbs of shadow grew, their tips blooded by the gate's defenders. Marcel's face was twisted and slack. Too many teeth bristled from his mouth. Too much light came from his eyes.

"This is not the work of the gods," Gilliam whispered.

"Not your gods, at least," Malcolm said. "How am I to trust you to counter this threat, when it springs from your breast, Inquisitor?"

"Marcel is faithful to the church," Gilliam said. "I trained him myself. Raised him by my hand, lifted him from the sewer, guided him in Cinder's path..." the inquisitor turned to Malcolm. His eyes were hollow with shock. "Whatever has happened to the boy, the fault lies in the north. And with me. I... I should never have taken them out of Heartsbridge. I shouldn't have exposed them to this corrupt place. His faith wasn't enough to protect him from the pagans."

"A faith untested is no faith at all," Catrin DeBray said. The child priestess of Strife was standing on the steps of the Hunter's Tower, having followed Malcolm down. She stepped forward. "What has befallen Marcel is not your fault, Frair."

"Perhaps not," Gilliam answered, "but it is my responsibility to put it right. Children, with me. Houndhallow, clear your soldiers from the courtyard. Enough of the innocent have died today."

"If my men fall back, who will protect the gate from the Suhdrin?"

"That is not my problem," Gilliam said. Then the inquisitor raised his staff and started to gather the lingering shadows of night. He strode forward, chanting the holy words of Cinderfell. "Let Winter judge!"

Malcolm sounded the retreat, though already there were few enough of his soldiers in the courtyard. Most had seen the darkness that they faced and fled. Those who remained moved aside at the inquisitor's approach. Marcel, still gripped by whatever power had corrupted him, pushed the castle's gates away with a flick of one talon-tipped finger.

"Your wife will answer for this!" Marcel howled in a half-human voice when he spotted Malcolm. "She will answer for what she did to me! As will you, pagan-king!"

The rest of his rage was drowned out by Gilliam's chant, but the boy had said enough for Malcolm's blood to run cold with fear.

The inquisitor's form twisted into a giant of forged shadow until he towered over the castle walls. The two dark figures, Marcel rippling with corrupted power, Gilliam bound in Cinder's holy darkness, crashed together in the middle of the courtyard. The sound of their battle washed over the walls of the Fen Gate.

A hand gripped Malcolm's elbow. He turned to see Catrin staring at him.

"Your wife," she said. "Where is she?"

"I will not sacrifice her, child," Malcolm said. He drew his feyiron blade. "Not to the sort of justice Cinder would provide."

"Then she cannot stay here," Catrin said. "Where is she?"

"Safe," Malcolm snapped. He was about to say more when Sir Baird ran up to him. The knight was flushed.

"My lord," Baird said, not sparing a look for Catrin or the two demons wrestling at the center of the courtyard. "The Suhdrin are moving."

"Little wonder," Malcolm said. "What are they doing?"

"Forming up to charge the gates. Once the matter of the gheist is settled, I suspect they'll attack."

Malcolm growled, giving Catrin another angry look before turning away.

"Gather the remaining knights at the sally gate," he said. "And fetch my banner. I've had enough of skulking behind broken walls."

Sir Doone kept a careful watch at the top of the ridgeline. Their campsite, nestled into the head of a small hollow, was rapidly being taken apart and packed away. From her post, Doone could see the walls of the Fen Gate, as well as the low haze of campfire smoke that marked the Suhdrin army. If trouble came, it would come from there.

Footsteps scrabbled on the leaf-slick hill below, and Doone drew her blade before seeing Davon's lumpy face peering up at her.

"What do you want, Dav?"

"Lady's not comfortable. She's getting... precious."

"Precious?" Doone asked. "I have never known Sorcha Blakley to be precious."

"No, well," Davon winced as the lady's voice carried up the hill to them. "She has become very particular about how things are done. Quite suddenly."

"Very well, you stay here and maintain the watch." Doone slid down the toppled tree she had been straddling. "I will speak with her."

Sorcha was standing in the middle of the camp, an array of food items, blankets, bedrolls, and cooking utensils spread out around her. As Sir Doone was descending, she saw Sorcha brush past one of the soldiers and start pulling things out of a woman's saddlebag.

The woman, Katra Sion by name, stepped away from her horse and waited until Sorcha had unpacked most of her bags. When Lady Blakley wandered away to another horse, Katra started in on repacking.

"My lady!" Doone called as soon as she was close enough that her shout wouldn't travel to the nearby road. "What the hells do you think you're doing?"

"We don't have time for this," Sorcha said. Her usually placid voice was agitated. "All this packing and carrying. We'll just have to put it all down again, anyway. Just leave it here." She turned, saw that Katra was re-bundling her bedroll, and swooped down on her, grabbing it. "I just took that out, child! Are you always so stubborn?"

"My lady, these are things that we will need," Doone said, easing the bedroll out of Sorcha's hands and passing it back to Katra. "We don't know how long your husband will be delayed at the Fen Gate."

"I am not waiting for my husband to quit the Fen," Sorcha said sharply, "any more than I'm waiting for the Suhdrins to give up on Halverdt's foolish crusade. I am done with waiting."

"Even worse, my lady. Without supplies from the Fen Gate, we'll be weeks on the road to Houndhallow." Sir Doone picked up the camp stove that Sorcha had just pulled from Katra's pack, collecting the spilled pots and utensils. "We can hunt, but none of us wants to eat raw hare, I promise."

"We are not going to Houndhallow," Sorcha said. "Nor Dunneswerry, nor the Reaveholt."

"There are no safe harbors that lie closer, my lady," Doone said. "Not north, at least, and I don't think Suhdra would welcome you."

"I am not looking for safe harbor, Sir Doone," Sorcha said. She yanked the stove out of Doone's grip and tossed it clattering to the side. "I am seeking heavy weather, and the storm that follows."

"What do you mean?" Doone asked. Sorcha was about to answer when a gheist horn echoed down the hollow. Everyone froze.

Everyone except Sorcha.

The lady of Houndhallow glided up the ridge, her stride as smooth and confident as the tide. Doone rushed to keep up, clambering gracelessly through the slick mud that seemed to follow Sorcha wherever she went. Beside the toppled tree that served as their lookout post, the two women stopped and stared down at the castle. The horn was still sounding.

"They have discovered the child," Doone said, "and now they will be hunting for us."

"No, it's not..." Sorcha paused, looking puzzled for a heartbeat. "Another has emerged. We have no time to waste."

"Another what?" Doone asked. Then a pillar of black energy blossomed just outside the Fen Gate's walls. "Ah. Gheist. What are we going to do?"

"Get ourselves to the godsroad?" Sir Davon asked. The big man was still perched in the tree above, peering down at the castle. As he talked, he scrabbled down, haste making the descent precarious. "Hope the inquisition can handle the demon before it decides to roam in our direction. Hope more that it's alone."

"Consider our present company, Dav," Sir Doone said nervously. Sorcha ignored her.

"It is not roaming," Sorcha snapped, "and we will not leave its fate to hope."

"We need to get you to safety, my lady," Doone said. "We can't linger here any longer, and that means my people need to finish packing their kit. Dav, get the horses loaded. Lady Blakley and I will remain here."

"No," Sorcha said. She turned on Doone, glaring. "We are not lingering here. Nor are we carrying all that junk with us. It will slow us down."

"There is nowhere that we can safely get without bedrolls, food supplies, cooking..." Doone started. Sorcha clapped her on the shoulder and spun her around. She pointed at the Fen Gate.

"That is our destination, sir," Sorcha said. "And you will not need to cook anything between now and our arrival. You would not carry a stove into battle, would you? Nor a blanket." She turned to Sir Davon. "See the troops to their horses, and be sure they carry not an ounce of extra weight."

"If we go to the Fen Gate, the inquisitor is sure to see you," Doone said. "I am sworn to protect you, my lady. I am sworn to see you safely to Houndhallow."

"And so you shall," Sorcha answered. "As soon as we have ended this threat to Tener, and driven these fools from our land. No sooner."

Sir Davon stood uncomfortably between the two women, looking from one to the other for direction. Finally, Doone nodded.

"Leave the saddlebags behind. We ride fast and hard, with battle to greet us at journey's end."

The sally court was a tight stone box, meant to serve as a muster point for small units of troops preparing to strike out from the castle's flank. The entrance to the sally was a narrow gate, and outside the approach was hidden among the bluffs and easily defended. Neither was designed for a host of armored knights.

Malcolm and his men were packed in knee to shield, their lances tangling in the close air above. The gheist horn continued its drone. The horses were nervous, surging together and muttering into their bits. The nerves spread to the men, as well. A feral god was churning through the castle behind them, and an army of angry Suhdrin waited beyond the wall. Blakley hitched himself high in his stirrups and looked out over the host.

"This will not be a good fight," he said. The riders quieted, looking up at their lord. He looked at each of them in turn. They were all knights of Houndhallow, born of families that had been true to his house since the time of the tribes. "I think the time of good fights has passed us by. The sort of battles that make poets sing and artists paint belong to history. Our fathers carried those banners. Our mothers rode those charges, and, with us on their knee, told stories of glorious times. More glorious, surely, than this.

"Powers beyond our ken do battle on our hearths," he continued. "They break the walls our families raised, and break the promises our houses have sworn. Gods walk among us, but there is no glory left for mortal blood." Malcolm shifted uncomfortably. His knees were screaming at him for standing in the stirrups so long, and his back groaned under the weight of his battle plate. "But Suhdrin bastards at our gate are trying to take advantage of this. They will let the pagan god destroy our defenses and rout our guards, and then walk in to pick up the pieces like crows. Well, I for one am sick of hiding behind these walls and waiting for them to pounce!"

A rumble of agreement went through the troop, calming their nerves. Malcolm tightened his grip on the lance, then continued, raising his voice.

"I am tired of waiting for the glorious fight! I am tired of praying to Suhdrin gods for protection, and Suhdrin priests for mercy, while Suhdrin spears gather at my door!" His knights answered heartily, their voices echoing off the close walls of the sally court. "I am going to fight! They wait for us to falter, but I am going to show them that Tenerran spirits never fail." More yelling, more spirit in their hearts. "They will meet us with steel, but we will answer them with blood!"

The knights surged forward, nearly knocking Malcolm from his horse in their enthusiasm. He twisted in his saddle, leaning down to the man at the door.

"Open the gate!" he yelled. "Open the gate before they crush each other!"

The man nodded, throwing his weight into the winch that handled the heavy barrier. Gears creaked and thick rope groaned, and the sally port slowly peeled open. The armored column streamed through, raising a cloud of dust and scree as they rattled down the narrow approach, banners unfurling as they cleared the walls. Malcolm waited until most of them were through, then followed.

To his surprise, a rider in white and gold joined him. He looked over at the priestess of strife. She wasn't dressed for battle, and her robes were already grimed with the dust of their hasty exit.

"What are you doing here?" he shouted over the hammer of hooves. "Isn't your place with the inquisitor?"

"My place has never been with the inquisitor," Catrin yelled back. "Strife has given me another path!"

"Go back! You are not fit for battle!"

"There is more to war than fighting, Houndhallow," she answered. "I am where I belong. I am where the gods have placed me."

Malcolm was about to answer, but then the host was riding free of the narrow path that hid the sally port. The forest was cut back, and at one time this clearing was overlooked by the castle's northern tower. But the northern tower had fallen—along with the rest of the Fen Gate during Gwen's supernatural assault—and now no eyes guarded the sally port's exit. The knights milled about in the clearing, waiting for their lord to lead them forward.

"Form a column," Malcolm said. The priestess stuck to his side, which was annoying. If she insisted on riding beside him, Malcolm wouldn't feel right leading from the front, as was good and proper. "Form on Sir Baird. Bannerman, to the front. Spears of Maebrook and Tollee, beside them. The rest fall in behind. We will take to the godsroad, and find the Suhdrin flank before they can gain the castle."

The column formed while Malcolm watched the cloud of spider-thin tendrils of shadow that occasionally arced over the castle walls, telling of the inquisitor's battle inside. He wondered how long he had before the Suhdrins made their push. He wondered if he was leading his men into death.

The first arrow fell at his feet. Another dozen rattled off of armor, more than a few striking flesh and drawing blood, riders falling to the rough ground with a scream and the crash of steel. The priestess was among them. Her white robes blossomed red, and she slumped against her mount, spooking the courser into the forest. Malcolm whirled to face the surrounding tree line.

The Suhdrin were waiting. Their spears stirred between the trees, sunlight shining off hard helms and harder eyes.

"To me!" Malcolm screamed. He put spurs to his mount and charged into the forest. "The Hound! The Hallow!"

32

IT WAS A god of fire and shadow. Lucas caught glimpses of it between the trees, its body arcing over the canopy, clouds of ember drifting in its wake as the dry autumn leaves of the forest caught fire at its touch.

As they ran the frair wove ghosts of naether, trying to put the gheist off their trail. Sometimes it worked. Sometimes his tricks seemed to draw the demon closer.

"We are never going to get away from it on foot," Sacombre said. The high inquisitor had discarded his casual mockery. Fear lined his eyes, and his voice trembled as he ran. "We need those damned horses."

"I would pray for them, if I trusted you enough to close my eyes," Lucas said. He and Sacombre both were running ragged, their age showing in empty lungs and quivering legs. "We never should have left the godsroad."

"Nor stayed the night in a haunted city," Sacombre said. "But the time for mourning our errors has passed, Frair."

"It was safe. I thought it was safe," Lucas said. He stopped at the edge of a clearing, leaning against a withered elm as he tried to catch his breath. The night air hung on his lips in a ragged fog. "The demon was gone from the stone."

"Apparently not," Sacombre said. The high inquisitor

settled against a tree, opposite Frair Lucas, his arms folded over his knees like a fisherman. It had been some time since they had seen the gheist, and their greatest danger now came from old bones and the chill night. Lucas watched the man warily.

"Why haven't you run?" Lucas asked.

"Have you not been watching?" Sacombre said. "We've been running all night."

"From me, I mean. From your shackles. You've made threats enough. I would think you would want to make good on them." Lucas folded a little bit in to himself, letting the fatigue weigh him into the cold ground. "You wouldn't even need a knife."

"Are you so anxious to die," Sacombre asked, "that you remind me of my threats? Do you hope to stir me to violence, so you can do away with the trial and see me dead tonight?"

"If I wanted you dead, I'd have left you in Sophie Halverdt's care. Or shackled to the fountain. It's you the gheist seeks."

"Or you," Sacombre said. "My captor, and the two of us separated from our guards. Did you ever consider that this might be the work of some slighted pagan, seeking to kill the man who revealed Adair's heresy?"

"You still see pagans in every rogue gheist," Lucas said, "and yet you won't admit the wrong in yourself. You're unbelievable, Tomas. Simply..."

The gheist's roar took them both by surprise. It shuddered the trees around them, sending loose leaves to the ground. Sacombre cowered behind his trunk, staring up at the sky. The sound came again. Closer.

"We can't stay here," Lucas said. He pulled himself up to his feet, the bones in his knees snapping and cracking as he stood. "Even in Suhdra, the godsroad is better protection than flight. Come on."

Before Sacombre could stand, the sky to their east flared into brilliant color. Lucas barely had the time to draw the shadows of the forest to his beck before the gheist vaulted over their hiding place. Lucas shifted the light, hiding the two priests of Cinder from the gheist's vision.

The feral god hovered over them, turning in slow circles and figure eights, as though it chased its own tail. Its face was turned toward the earth, the long, thick tendrils of its beard dancing over the trees like wind. Slower and slower it turned, until the snake hung directly above Lucas and his hidden dome of shadow.

Sweating through his vestments, Lucas held his staff in white knuckled hands, the tip planted firmly in the mud between his feet, the iron icon of Cinder pressed against his forehead. He mumbled prayers into the gray lord's ear, weaving just enough of his body into the naetherealm to hide himself without disturbing the natural world enough to draw the gheist's attention. The old gods were creatures of the unnatural processes of Tenumbra, keen to scent the workings of Cinder's priests, just as the inquisition was tuned to the disturbances wrought by a gheist's presence. If he could hide himself well enough, the gheist would go on its way, leaving Lucas alone.

Gods willing. Gods pray.

The gheist bent lower. The trees peeled apart to let it pass. A gentle song traveled through its scales, like a wind chime set to dancing. Light from its coat of plates filled the grove, turning the shadows of the trees into narrow spears, criss-crossing the grass in darkness. Lucas huddled beneath its gaze.

The creature huffed, sending a wall of air through the grass. Its breath smelled like stiff leather and stone. It came closer, bending its head to where Lucas was hiding.

The frair opened his eyes and looked up into the wide grin of the feral god. Its eyes swam with fog and small, bone-like chips that circled the center like whirlpools. The mouth folded open, revealing teeth as clear and thin as icicles.

"Gods bless," Lucas whispered to himself, then let his hand slide from the staff, undoing the bindings that kept him hidden.

From behind Lucas, Sacombre pushed a wall of shadow through the air and into Lucas's staff. The vein of purple light that traveled from the high inquisitor's hand into the ashwood staff traveled as fast as lightning, as hard to see as spider webs on the breeze. It reinforced Lucas's veil of naether, driving the frair further into the naetherealm, extending the deception to the rest of the tiny grove.

The world darkened, and a film sprang up between the priests of Cinder and the gheist. Like a face peering into troubled water, the creature grew murky and indistinct. To Lucas's clouded mind, there was a moment of recognition in the feral god's eyes, something that passed quickly, to be replaced by confusion. The frair knelt there for a heartbeat. The gheist rose back into the sky and continued its hunt, disappearing into the forest. The song of its scales mingled with the shuffling of autumn leaves, and then it was gone.

Sacombre unwound his arcane grip on Lucas's veil. The deception collapsed, starlight returned to the grove. The high inquisitor stood stiffly. His face was pale, his brow bright with sweat. He turned away from Lucas.

The frair stayed in the center of the grove, his hands limp in his lap, his knees sinking into the cold grass. When he looked up, Sacombre was staring into the woods, in the direction the gheist had fled.

"You fear death," Lucas said. "That is why you stay with me. With us."

"Afraid of death?" Sacombre asked. His voice cracked with tension, but he cleared his throat and continued, sounding much stronger. "I have bound death to my soul, Lucas. Or had you forgotten?"

"And what did you learn in those months you were bound to pagan death?" Lucas asked. "Is that why you fear the quiet house? Did you gain a glimpse into what waits beyond this life? Something more than what Cinder promises? Or something less?"

"The pagans live their bestial lives, and they die their bestial deaths. It has nothing to do with me. I am high inquisitor. Faithful of Cinder. Faithful of the celestial church. Besides, if I truly feared death, why would I stay with you? Have you forgotten our destination?"

"No," Lucas said, shaking his head. "And neither have you, but that is a distant death, cold and merciful at Cinder's hand. Months away, if not years. If I turn you loose here, however, in the wilds, there are countless knives willing to cut you down."

"Now, or months from now," Sacombre shrugged, still not looking back. "I would still be dead."

"If it isn't the fear of death that keeps you at my side, it must be something else," Lucas said. He cocked his head. Curiosity had always driven him. "Bestial lives of pagans, and bestial deaths. Do you seek redemption in the eyes of the gray lord? Are you afraid of being named pagan by the celestriarch, and denied the quiet house? Is that it?"

Sacombre sniffed dismissively, but didn't answer. Lucas stood, wobbling on ruined legs, propping himself up with his staff.

"Redemption, then," he said. "That is not Cinder's way, you know. He judges, and harshly. You will not find mercy in his court."

"I do not seek mercy," Sacombre said. "Do you? We are inquisitors, Lucas. Of different station, and different method, but we ply the same waters. You traveled with Gwen Adair, fully aware of her heresy, dealt with pagans, you even defended the witches' hallow from an agent of the inquisition! If our positions were reversed, if it was Halverdt who triumphed at the Fen Gate, and not Blakley, you would be riding south in dark iron chains."

"That is hardly relevant..."

"No?" Sacombre said. "Would you resist? Or would you submit to Cinder's judgment, to justify your name, and free yourself from suspicion? You believe that you did what was right, yes?" He turned and came closer, bending to look close into Lucas's face. "You did what you thought was necessary, and I did no less."

"You bound a pagan god, and drove these nations to war..."

"War, because the inquisition is not enough. And a pagan god, because we use the tools Cinder has given us. The tools we need. The tools that will do the job."

"You're mad," Lucas said.

"No," Sacombre said stiffly. "The world is mad. I am necessary."

Lucas was about to answer when footsteps shuffled through the leaves behind him. He turned to see Stefan

LaGaere, leading his horse and in the company of his men once again.

"Gods bless that you're safe, Warhome," the frair said. "We have to get the prisoner back in his chains and down the godsroad before the gheist returns."

"No," LaGaere answered. "Not chains."

"Do you... are you defying me, duke? I am charged by holy Cinder to see this man taken to Heartsbridge and tried for his crimes. If you think for one minute you'll stop me, you are sorely mistaken."

"Am I? Because unless I miss my guess, you weren't even able to hide from that gheist, much less fight it. You wouldn't be alive without the high inquisitor's intervention. So, no, I don't think we'll be putting him in chains." LaGaere walked casually forward, putting one meaty hand in the middle of Lucas's chest and shoving the old man to the ground. "As for your protection? I'll do without, thank you."

"You don't know what you're doing!" Lucas cried, struggling to get the air back into his lungs. LaGaere led a spare horse to Sacombre and held it steady while the high inquisitor mounted. "You saw what he did at the Fen Gate. The lives he took!"

"People die in war," LaGaere said simply. Then he signaled to his men, swinging onto his own horse. The knights of Warhome flowed around Lucas, hooves hammering the leaves just inches from his hand, leaving him lying on the ground gasping for breath. Sacombre followed them. Before he left, LaGaere paused at the edge of the forest. "We'll take him to Heartsbridge, frair, but I think it's the Circle of Lords that'll judge our friend Sacombre. For what he did to Halverdt, and Adair."

“That is not your place,” Lucas said. He stumbled to his feet. Cold mud slid down his back, miring his robes. “Judgment belongs to the church!”

“The church has done damage enough,” LaGaere said. “The church has my faith, frair, but it doesn’t have my trust.”

33

IAN WOKE AS they dragged him through the snow. Drifts piled up around his shoulders, and his arms screamed in pain as the people of Halfic hauled him by the wrists through the courtyard. He spat bloody snow from his mouth and screamed.

"You can't do this," he said. A farmer wheeled and put a boot in Ian's ribs, causing him to double over. When he lifted his head, he saw two long tracks of bloody sleet carved through the courtyard. The broader track led to a squirming pile of bodies off to the side. The men dragging Ian paused to watch.

At the center of the pile, Elsa's golden armor shone. One of her eyes was swollen shut, and her teeth were bright white against the smeared blood of her gums. Farmers and servants wrapped arms around her waist and grabbed at her limbs, only to be thrown aside to land gracelessly in the snow. The frair stood at the edge of the fray, mincing his hands together and muttering prayers.

The earl was nowhere to be seen.

"Frair!" Ian shouted. The man startled around, staring at Ian with saucer-wide eyes. "Do you think you'll escape judgment, just because no mortal eye will see this crime? Cinder will see you! The gray lord will judge your actions!"

The frair walked over, and bent low to Ian's face. "We

have already been judged, Blakley," he said. "The sentence has been passed. What more can be done to us, that hasn't already been done?"

"Never underestimate the vengeance of winter," Ian spat. "The gods will have their way."

"A strange warning, coming from one such as you," the frair said. He pulled a rag from his sleeve and shoved it into Ian's mouth, forcing it so far down his throat that he started to gag. "An ally of the iron hand should not be making threats."

Ian choked around the stinking rag, saliva and blood clogging his throat. The frair nodded to the men holding his wrists. They resumed their slow, jerky drag through the snow.

His head lolled back, hanging limp against his shoulders as the snow piled up. The pain radiated down through his neck and back, giving sharp jabs with each lurching step. Twice he'd been struck in the head since he arrived at Harthal, twice knocked out, and still he had no idea what was actually going on in this place. If he got out of this alive, Ian swore he was going to start wearing a helmet. All the time. Even to bed. He could learn to sleep in a steel helm.

The men who were dragging him stopped and, after a short conversation, dropped Ian's arms. His shoulders wrenched flat, muscles popping back into place. He rolled onto his side, trying to catch his breath through sleet-frozen nostrils, his lungs burning. They had reached the gates of the keep. The men were arguing about who would open the doors, and who would drag him through.

"He's heavy," the first man said. He was tall and thin, his clothes cut for a man a foot shorter and forty pounds heavier. "You pull him."

"He's a whelp. The bar is heavy, mate. You've never had to open the gate." The second man was average in every way, except his arms nearly reached his knees, and his forearms were as thick as Ian's legs. "You can't even move the gate, I'll wager."

Tall and thin frowned, looking down at Ian as he chewed his lips. "You open the gate, then we both drag him through. Get it done faster."

"One of us needs to be able to close the gate, if something tries to get inside the keep," Forearms said. "Can't let anything else in. Caused enough trouble the first time."

The first man grunted but didn't seem convinced. He stared down at Ian.

"Could get help," he said eventually. They both looked back at the pile of farmers tangled around Sir Elsa. Three or four of the wrestlers skidded away, lying on their backs for several seconds before struggling to their feet and, reluctantly, rejoining the fight.

"Nah," Forearms said. "They're... busy."

"Let me give the gate a try," Tall said. "If I can't get it, fine, I'll do the dragging. But you're stronger. You can get him outside and back quick."

"Fine," Forearms said, shaking his head, "but you'll never get it."

Ian watched with detached interest as the tall man sized up the heavy iron-and-ashwood bar that lay across the gate. He rubbed some warmth into his hands, then bent at the knees and hooked his shoulder under it. He pushed, collapsed, reset his legs and pushed again. His face turned turnip red, his lips peeled back from his teeth, and then suddenly the bar shifted. With a groan, it levered away from its seat. A small avalanche of snow tumbled from its face. The man pushed it to the side, sliding it into the sleeve at the side of the gate.

"There!" he said, panting desperately and smiling. "Told you. Told you I could..."

The gate boomed open, knocking the tall man aside. Forearms stepped back and hesitated, but any question of fighting back disappeared as the barrier swung fully open.

On the road beyond stood a man in black, wrapped in a cloak of blizzard. He hung just above the ground, his toes dragging in the snow as he slid forward. Fists of clenched ice swung at his side, powered by muscles of gale winds and sleet. His face was nearly black with ink.

Ian rolled out of the shaman's way. The man ignored him, digging a trench in the snow with his gheist. At the center of the courtyard the frair fell back, stumbling over himself as he retreated to the doma, where he slammed the door shut.

The crowd still fought Sir Elsa, but those closest to the gate stopped and stood as they became aware of the new threat. As more stepped away from her, Elsa fought her way to her feet, thinking she had finally beaten back her attackers. She stood at their center, whirling back and forth, waiting for the next attack to come.

Then she saw the gheist.

"Gods damn it," she muttered.

Elsa straightened, loosening her shoulders and staring down the shaman and his bound gheist. The citizens of Harthal drifted away from her, afraid to move too quickly, their prey-minds telling them that sudden movement might attract the predator's eye. Elsa held out her hand.

"My sword. Someone give me my sword."

That broke the spell. The farmers and servants and fools

ran, scattering to cover, diving behind snow-covered wagons or running into the stables. A few tried to hide in the doma, beating at the doors before giving up.

"I'm going to have a word with that frair," Elsa said. "I find his service to the celestial church extremely questionable."

"Your wards were doomed to fail, vow knight," the shaman said. "Winter is not your season. You should not have tried to hide within these walls. It has given me time to gather my strength."

"I don't know what the fuck you're talking about," Elsa said. She cast around for her sword, finally spotting it near the door of the doma. Ian was behind the shaman. The boy rolled stiffly to the side, slowly struggling to his knees. No good to her. She started edging toward the blade. "But what you did to those children is entirely unacceptable."

"Children?" the shaman asked. "Do not play games with me, priest. I have come to break the bond with Gwen Adair. You will not use her as bait any longer!"

"Ah, there it is," Elsa said. She backed up further, keeping her attention on the shaman. Her head throbbed from the beating given her by the people of Harthal. "You're one of Adair's pet pagans. I knew I should have killed that girl when I had the chance."

"It would have saved us both a great deal of trouble," the shaman said. He clutched a knife to his chest. The blade was shot through with veins of crimson light. The man flicked the knife in Elsa's direction, and she felt a burning pain in her chest. He had somehow captured her blood bond with Gwen. "But without her," he added, "I wouldn't have been able to find you."

"Something you'll regret doing, I think," Elsa said. She

clasped her hands together, making a circle of her arms and drawing Strife's power into the runes of her armor. She had hesitated to use her powers against the citizens of Harthal, but had no such qualms about a shaman of the old ways. The heat from her invocation began melting a ring of snow around her.

"I have the blood of a dozen vow knights in my blade, woman," the shaman said. "One more isn't going to frighten me. Besides, you seem to have lost your sword, and what is a knight without her precious weapon?"

"Far from helpless, I swear you that," Elsa said.

The shaman swelled, drawing power from the storm that raged all around them. Elsa had a moment to wonder what he meant by the wards that had been hiding the castle, but then the pagan advanced. The weather was turned in his favor, cloaked in winter as he was. It was difficult to tell where his gheist ended and the storm began, and as the man swept toward her, he seemed to collect snow and wind from the swirling grounds of the courtyard.

Small snow-choked tornadoes twisted down from the sky to settle on his shoulders, and sleet rattled the ground as he passed. His fists rose from his sides, clenching knuckles sheened in ice.

Elsa attacked before the shaman could reach her. Even without the sword, her hands burned with summer's fury, and the gheist cloaking the shaman was bound to winter's power. In some ways they countered each other, cold and hot, fire and ice, each the weakness of the other, each strongest in the other's flaws. She slid forward, stepping inside the reach of the bound god, swinging directly at the shaman at the center of the gheist. Gales of wind met her attack, ice forming and melting and forming again as she struck.

The layers of gale force wind parted under Elsa's attack, but she wasn't able to reach the shaman. Instead, her fists bounced harmlessly off the bound gheist. Light flared from her runes. A thin coating of sleet-stained ice crusted her armor, and when she moved to retreat, the ice shattered and spun into the air, filling the courtyard with reflected light. As she fell back, one of the gheist's massive fists clipped her shoulder. She spun, fell, and rolled through the snowdrifts.

"I am not new to this war, knight," the shaman said. He turned ponderously toward where Elsa had fallen. "I will end you, as I have ended so many before."

"Funny, I don't remember a lot of my friends dying of frostbite," Elsa said. She forced herself to her knees, easing gingerly back to her feet, weaving bindings of protection into the air around her. The shaman hovered in front of her, haughty and unafraid.

"I hunt in different forests, and through all seasons," the shaman said. "This is the guise I take today, because it is the power that is available today. Our gods are not like yours, Suhdrin. Jealous in their worship! At war with one another. Petty!"

"No, nothing like your gods," Elsa agreed. "Your gods are mad, like dogs, frothing at the mouth. Waiting to be put down by their masters."

The shaman laughed, but the sound was full of anger. He struck again, heavy fists spinning through the air like tumbling boulders, crashing into walls and barrels and stone on his way to Elsa. She dodged him easily, taking summer's swiftness in hand to dance across the icy courtyard.

Unable to slow his charge, the shaman plunged into the stables, spooking horses and sending a plume of hay into the air to mingle with the blizzard. Slowly he stood and moved to the entrance. The gheist was still wrapped around him, but it was showing signs of strain. As Elsa walked around the stables toward the doma, the shaman appeared to struggle with his god. His face was clenched in concentration, and the bands of screaming gale that made up the gheist's body began spinning loose, like a bolt of cloth unraveling.

"This is the failing of all your gods, pagan," Elsa said. She brushed snow from her shoulders, smiling. "Too feral. Too much like beasts to be tamed, and yet you insist on binding them, putting them to the lash. Then you are surprised when they slip loose and bite the hand."

The shaman didn't answer.

The storm spoke for him. Like a giant hand pressing down from the heavens, the skies unleashed a wind like none Elsa had ever seen. With teeth cut from sleet, it sliced through her Strife-borne defenses and shredded her flesh. Elsa fell to a knee, covering her face with one gauntleted hand, steadying herself with the other.

She heard the horses screaming, followed shortly by the sound of the stable's slate roof coming apart like a child's toy. The world disappeared into a haze of snow and ice. The feeble light of her runic armor flickered out. Everything became freezing cold and howling wind. A darkness rose above her. It was the shaman, and his god of winter's might.

"You are mistaken," the shaman said, and his voice was laced with madness. Elsa squinted up at him. His robes were shredded, and the flesh that showed through was marbled with the same crimson veins that filled his knife. He had plunged the blade into his belly, both fists wrapped around the handle, now slick with his own blood. "The gods do not answer to my lash. I answer to theirs."

The demon hurtled forward, riding the blizzard's wrath into Elsa's waiting arms. He brushed her defenses aside like they were cobwebs. In the tumult of the storm, the screams were lost to the wind.

34

THE FIRST CHARGE was a ragged, headlong rush into the forest. Branches crashed off Malcolm's steel helm, battering his ribs and slowing his mount. He braced himself for immediate impact with the enemy, but once he was among the trees, all he saw were flashes of bright color among the trunks, the scattering of archers and the high, lilting shouts of Suhdrin retreat.

Malcolm whirled around, getting his bearings. Tenerran soldiers rushed past him, plunging deeper into the trees, chasing individual archers and running them down. Screams filtered through the underbrush.

"Stay close! Stay tight!" Malcolm shouted, but his voice fell muffled into the dry autumn canopy. His column quickly became a cloud, dissipating into the woods. Sir Harrow clattered past him.

"Harrow! Rein in! Where are you going, woman?"

"Sirs Dannock and Leigh have made contact near the road. A column of spear with archers in support." Harrow spun her mount around impatiently, anxious to be engaged. Malcolm barked at her.

"Hold! Why would their archers be in advance, if the spear still waits along the road!" he shouted. "Why are they here at all? How did they know?"

"Questions that will not be answered by mincing about the verge, my lord," Harrow answered. "The enemy is before us. We must meet them!"

"It isn't right," Malcolm muttered. Harrow gave him an impatient look, then thundered into the underbrush. Screams filled the air beyond. Malcolm could hear the steady hammer of spears on shields, and hobnailed boots on hard packed stone. "Something about it isn't right."

He pulled his horse to the side, running parallel to the clearing, listening to his troops clash with the Suhdrin line far to his right. The whisper of arrows sang through the air, piercing leaves and thudding into trees. Arrows would do little to his riders in the close canopy of the trees, which would prevent the archers from concentrating their fire. Mail caparisons, plate-and-half, strong shields and steel. It was the column of spear that could undo them. The crash of blades continued in the distance. Malcolm thought he should be with them. He should be at their head—but something wasn't *right*.

Something among the trees.

There was a flicker of light among the trees. Malcolm slowed, then saw a length of rumpled white linen, and blood. The priestess. Malcolm spurred his horse forward, rattling through a grove of thick trees, drawing his sword as he went.

Catrin had fallen from her horse and lay among the ferns. Her mount stood at the edge of the clearing, cropping at the ground, oblivious to its rider's wound. Three horses stood beside it, and three men stood beside the fallen priestess. Suhdrin men-at-arms, with their blades drawn. One knelt, his knife going hesitantly to the child's throat.

"Face me!" Malcolm shouted. The three men looked up in

shock. As he thundered forward, the kneeling soldier dropped his blade, standing and stumbling back, falling over himself as he reached for his sword. The other two ran for their mounts. Malcolm shifted his charge, cutting off the runners, forcing them back to the fallen priestess. There he circled them.

"This is what Suhdra has come to?" he said. "Murdering the holy of Strife while they lie wounded?" The men didn't answer. Two of them looked terrified. The man who had been kneeling, though, had collected himself. He stared at Malcolm with cold hatred. Malcolm pulled closer to him, glaring down from his saddle. "Were you commanded to murder this child? Or did it just seem like a good idea to your mud-filled head?"

"I have learned that Tenerran traitors can dress in holy robes," the man said. "Just as they can dress as nobles."

Malcolm snorted. "This girl is of Orphanshield's company. She is Suhdrin born, and Heartsbridge sworn."

"A gods damned pity, then, if she were to fall while riding with a Tenerran lord," the man said. "A child murdered by her host. A tragedy."

"Ah, so that is your plan," Malcolm replied. "But how did you know we were here? Whose word turned your head. Who summoned your spears to this door?"

"The word of god," the man said. "A voice you no longer hear, pagan."

"No god I know would ask for this girl's blood," Malcolm said. "Yours, however, seems fine with it."

The Suhdrins fell back a little bit, lifting blades. Malcolm edged around them, calculating risk and weighing his position. Three of them, but they were on foot, and wearing only chain to his plate-and-half. Not an easy fight, but one he would have to try if he meant to protect the girl. He moved far enough that he was between the priestess and her would-be attackers. They began to spread out, threatening to encircle him.

He had to strike soon.

A thunder rose in the forest. Malcolm whirled. Just at the edge of his line of sight, barely glimpsed between the thick growth of the forest, a column of armored knights streamed past. They rode in tight formation, battering down trees, their armor smeared in mud and leaves. Their progress was slowed by the forest, but their passage was devastating. The ground was churned into mud and broken roots.

They bore down on Malcolm's knights. From this position, they would fall on the Tenerran flank, trapping them between the column of spear on the road and their own iron-shod hooves.

Malcolm turned back. The three had scattered, running to their mounts and riding off the second he had looked away. His thoughts turned to the priestess, worried that they had finished the deed while he was distracted. But there was no new blood on her robes, and her chest rose and fell slowly. Malcolm hesitated.

Aid the child, or warn his men.

With a grimace he tugged his reins aside and plunged toward the road. He hurried across the ruined forest through which the Suhdrin column had just ridden, pushing through the trees beyond and finally coming onto the godsroad. If he hurried he might be able to follow the road to where his men fought the Suhdrin spears. He might get there before the riders, still fighting their way through close-grown trees and soft mud. He might be able to warn them in time.

The godsroad was in ill repair—far worse than he had expected. The forest around the Fen Gate seethed with feral vitality, and the cobbles of the road were buckled beneath a carpet of vines and gnarled roots. Malcolm charged ahead, ducking beneath overhanging branches and vaulting over trees that had fallen. By the time the sound of fighting closed, Malcolm was sure he was too late.

He was wrong. The Suhdrin force was formed into a shallow arch of spear and shield, the tips bent into the forest, the base anchored in the center of the road. Two small detachments of archers sheltered behind the tips of the arch, and at the center—behind the strongest ranks of the spear wall—a handful of mounted knights watched the battle, waiting their turn.

In the shallow bowl of the arch, still encumbered by the forest and a lack of discipline, the Tenerran knights churned against the spears. They dove in like wolves, striking at the steel tips of the spears, batting them aside like blades of grass in an attempt to contact the shields sheltered beneath. But the Suhdrin troops held their ranks, so that each layer of spears was backed by another, three ranks deep. Those few Tenerran knights foolish or brave enough to fight past the first bristling grove of spears were spitted against the others.

Dead horses and dying men lay in clumps along the godsroad's verge. Not many so far, but without a clear field to build up the charge, the knights of Tener had no chance to overcome their opponents.

"The bloody fools," Malcolm muttered. He drew his feyiron blade, tied his reins to the pommel of his saddle, and settled into his stirrups. He could see Sir Harrow milling along the edge of the spear wall. "Harrow! Riders approach!"

The knight heard her name and looked around, only catching site of Malcolm as the Suhdrin archers also noticed the lord of Houndhallow and wheeled to attack. The archers were dressed as hunters, their tabards of House Marchand fresh and clean over hardened leather. They struggled to form a firing line, each man trying to take the best ground, clearly unfamiliar with unit tactics. Malcolm spurred his horse before they could get set. Harrow and the other knights would have to fend for themselves.

He charged.

A disciplined line of professional archers would not have broken. They would have stood their ground, drawn their bows, and filled Malcolm full of bristling fletches. But these men were peasants, probably poachers drawn from Halverdt's jails, pressed into service. When the Duke Lord of Houndhallow—the Reaverbane, famous for killing a god and bringing the high inquisitor to justice—bent his head, raised his sword, and bore down on them with the full might of legend, these men broke.

A few scattered arrows hissed through the air over Malcolm's head, then the ground cleared in front of him and the flank of the spear wall stood naked before him. One man could do little to move a line, but Malcolm fell on them before the nearest spear could turn, chopping down through skull and mail and steel. The line shivered as the three ranks on that side curled back to present Malcolm with their shields. Spears, too cumbersome to be brought to bear, dropped to the ground and swords were drawn.

Malcolm whirled, spun at them one more time to hammer shields and fend off the short, abortive counterstrikes that followed, and then the clutch of knights at the spear wall's center, held in reserve against a breakout or to exploit the inevitable rout, came thundering down the road toward him. They formed a wedge of sharp steel, aimed at Malcolm's heart.

He turned and ran, put spurs to his horse's flanks, leaning low to the surging crest of its neck, and he fled. The rough cobbles of the godsroad pitched under his mount, slowing him, bringing the pursuing Suhdrins closer. He vaulted the fallen tree, landing with a jolt that crushed his spine and nearly threw him from his saddle. Behind him, the obstacle disrupted the knights' formation, breaking them into a crowd of riders rather than an unbreakable wedge. At least one rider fell behind as his horse refused the jump, forcing the man to go around.

The rest drew closer. Their horses were rested, their riders furious at Malcolm's attack. He was losing ground, and there was nowhere that he could run. Soon he would either have to turn into the woods and make for the sally port, or hope that his pursuers would drop the chase somewhere north of the castle.

There was little hope for either.

A small stream splashed under his mount's hooves. Malcolm blinked in confusion, worried that he had already passed the castle turnoff. He didn't remember a stream, and even though the godsroad had fallen into disrepair, he didn't think there was a spring or creek nearby that could have formed the current. How far had he come?

Starting to slow, he twisted in his saddle, trying to get his bearings. A column of shadow flashed far to his left, arcing over the forest canopy. The inquisitor and the gheist, so he wasn't that far from the Fen Gate. But where had the stream come from. He looked back.

The gentle stream that Malcolm had just crossed began to swell. As he watched it burbled higher, forming a mound of swirling water that lay across the road like a strap. It grew and grew, its current as clear as glass. As the first Suhdrin knight tried to cross it, the surface of the water ruptured into a geyser of foam, crashing into the mount's broad chest, throwing it into the air. The toppled horse's rider crashed forward, pinwheeling down the road like a discarded doll. He came to rest awkwardly on the side of the road, legs splayed and head folded against his chest.

The other riders balked. The wall of water slithered closer, a river that had thrown its banks and wandered the floodplain. Larger and larger it grew, until it filled half the road with a bulbous snake of smooth-faced water, as unreal as the gods themselves.

"Sorcha," Malcolm whispered. "No, love. No!"

He whirled his mount around and raced down the road. The ground where the new river flowed was eroded and damp, as though the cobbles had suffered generations of water, rather than brief moments. The thrown knight was dead, and those who faced the water gheist drew their swords in the hopes of cutting a river.

The gheist smashed into them like a battering ram, breaking steel and bones, scattering the knights across the road. The river reared up like a maddened bull, rising into the air only to come crashing down in a torrent that ground the cobbles into rubble, leaving behind only mud and broken bodies.

As quickly as the gheist had risen, it disappeared. The stream seeped into the earth, a flood of blood-laced water that lapped against the trunks of trees and melted into the grass. Soon there was nothing left, of the knights, of the river, of the godsroad. Malcolm stood alone.

Sorcha emerged from among the trees. She was unchanged, or rather, still as horrifically changed as she had been the last time he saw her. The hem of her robes was damp, water and blood and something darker wicking up from the ground until it nearly reached her knees. Bright veins pulsed beneath her pale skin. Her eyes wept, but her face was still, her brow smooth. She looked around the wreckage of her work, then turned to her husband.

"Malcolm," she said. "I have grown tired of waiting."

35

DAWN BROUGHT AN end to the gheist's hunt. Whatever spirit had inhabited the great snake's body, it disappeared into the rising sun. Martin saw it from a distance, saw it stretch into the clouds and curl into Strife's golden disk, like a cat in a sunbeam. He turned to Fianna.

"Now will you run?" he asked.

The witch was folded against a tree, her head slouched down between her shoulders, hands dangling in the open air. She looked exhausted. She looked dead. Life in the wagon had been hard on her, Martin knew, harder than a month in confinement should have been. The night had been just as difficult. They had followed Sir Horne into the woods when the gheist attacked, but had immediately lost track of the Suhdrin knight, and never saw her again. He and Fianna hid among the trees, praying to different gods for their protection.

Fianna's face was drawn and slack. Dark rings circled her eyes. She smiled joylessly.

"Run?" she asked. "No, I don't think I will run... but I may be able to walk."

Martin held out his hands and pulled her upright. She stood unsteadily, but when Martin reached out, she stepped away as though she had been struck.

"Were they not feeding you?" he asked.

"Food, yes, but there is more than food to my body." She slid farther away, shaking her head. "Don't worry about me. I will recover. The high inquisitor was a difficult companion, that is all."

"Did he hurt you?" Martin asked. "I've been told he's a monster."

"A comfortable word, monster. You name our gods such, and your criminals, but they are more and less than that." She sighed and leaned against a tree. "Monster. No. Sacombre is just a man, like any other."

"Well, I'm not sure about that," Martin said. "I've known many men of the celestial faith, and not a few women. None of them have ever bound a pagan god to their soul. Not in my presence, at least," he added.

"Gwendolyn Adair, of the tribe of iron," Fianna said. "You knew her, didn't you?"

Martin paused. "Not very well, honestly. A girl I saw at tournaments. Nothing more."

"You seem like the sort of man who knows a lot of girls at tournaments, and nothing more," Fianna said. Martin glanced over at her, surprised to see the witch smirking, as well. She gathered the few things she had scavenged before they fled Gardengerry. "Don't worry. Adair was very good at hiding her true faith. It's something we Tenerrans have perfected since the crusades."

"That is what the south fears," Martin said. He had taken little with him during their flight. His sword, and the bedroll he had been lying on when the gheist attacked. Nothing to eat. The witch seemed to have a bag of withered apples, but that wasn't enough to get them to Heartsbridge. "We need to find food."

"Perhaps the others were wise enough to gather supplies before they ran. Or we could sneak back into the city. I'm sure it's safe, now that the gheist is gone."

Martin shuddered and shook his head. "I'm not going back inside those walls, and as for the others, we can search, but I'm not hopeful. Better to make for civilization and hope we meet up. Nearest city is... Doonan, I think."

"Doonan if you're heading toward Pilgrim's Rest. Which we're not," Fianna said. "I assume you won't want to make for Greenhall."

"Not unless you feel like being executed on the spot."

"No, not really," she admitted. "Though little else remains for me in Heartsbridge, I imagine. But if it's south we go, we've little choice but to follow the godsroad to Noosehall."

"Three days by horse," Martin said, "and unless LaGaere and his men come back for us, we're walking. I don't like that distance."

"There's another choice," Fianna said.

"Oh? I suppose you know the north better than I, but I can't think of any domas between here and the Gallowmoors. It's always possible, I suppose, that some knight or merchant founded Suhdrin walls in the wilds, but nothing along the godsroad. After last night, I doubt I'll want to stray from the holy cobbles any time soon."

"Not a doma," Fianna said. She walked with her head stubbornly down. Martin grunted.

"What then?" he asked.

"You know the sort of village I might be familiar with. The kind of holy ground I can lead you to." She glanced up. "Someplace the gheists won't bother us."

"Pagan henges and pagan hearths," Martin spat. "What

are the odds you'll let me leave such a place alive, hm?"

"Ian Blakley walked in such places, and he lives," Fianna said.

"Yes, I have seen what became of young Blakley," Martin said. "Hardly recognized him at the Fen Gate. He was brother to me, once. He barely raised a word to me after the battle, before he ran off in search of your Gwen Adair."

"He spoke of you," Fianna said. "With love, I think. He hasn't changed that much."

"So you say," Martin said. "And yet—"

He was interrupted by a sharp sound to their left. Martin froze, his hand going to his sword. The sound came again. It sounded like someone coughing.

"Gheists don't cough," Fianna hissed.

"No, but brigands might," Martin said. "Stay here. If I call out, run."

The forest here was thick, but he could see hoof prints in the thick loam between trunks. He crept forward, cursing when his chain shirt jangled sharply against the low branches of a speartree. The sound came again, but this time ended in a laugh.

"Come out, Martin Roard," a voice called. "You couldn't sneak up on a deaf man if you were wearing a suit of pillows. Gods pray you have some water."

"Frair Lucas?" Martin answered. He hurried forward, coming to a narrow clearing that was trampled and scorched. The inquisitor was tucked into the shadow of a tree, appearing to have dragged himself through the mud. Martin knelt beside him, checking for wounds.

"I will recover," Lucas said, waving him away. "My body, at least. My pride might take longer."

"What happened here?" Martin asked.

"Treachery, or gods damned honor, or something," Lucas said. "LaGaere is gone. He took the high inquisitor. Decided he's going to try Sacombre at the Circle of Lords, or some such foolishness."

"Well, he always was something of an idiot," Martin said. He gave Lucas what little water he had with him. "The horses? Or Sir Horne? We lost track of her when we fled Gardengerry."

"Gone. We should probably return to Greenhall and face Lady Sophie's wrath. We've nothing left to take to Heartsbridge." Lucas sighed and leaned back against the tree. "I should have seen this coming. A man of LaGaere's stubborn faith would never allow the high inquisitor to be brought to trial."

"A curious thing, celestial faith," Fianna said. She stood at the edge of the clearing. "That this man would take something as true, just because it came from his high inquisitor."

"You're still with us, my lady," Lucas said with wonder. "Did the gheist fail to free you from your bonds, as it intended?"

"That gheist was nothing to do with me," Fianna said. "Not all the gods answer my call."

"Well, whatever your reason is for remaining, I'm glad you're here," Lucas said. He struggled to his feet, rubbing mud from his robes and grimacing. "This is not something I can do alone."

"I will provide what help I can," Fianna said. "I've already suggested a near village where we could find shelter and food. Your companion doesn't seem too interested, though."

"Food and shelter?" Lucas said. "No, those are the least of my concerns. Cinder will provide, somehow."

"Least of your concerns?" Martin said. He sheathed his sword. "We have a bag of apples, and you just drank the last of our water."

"We have food and water in plenty," Lucas said. "With the horses."

"LaGaere has the horses," Martin said.

"And more than that, LaGaere has the high inquisitor. So we can solve all of our problems at once."

"You mean to pursue them? But they… they're already…"

"They have the horses, they're already miles away, and we know little enough about which way they're going," Lucas said. "Yes, yes, I know. What of it."

"Oh, purely physical things. Distance, a lack of food, the fact that even if we find him we'll be outnumbered," Martin said.

"As you say, physical things. The world was made to be overcome, young Roard," Lucas said. "It's not even winter yet. The season of trials has yet to truly start. Come, we have much to do! And all of it to the south."

"South, then," Martin said. He glanced to the witch. "You sure you don't want to run?"

"Not yet," Fianna answered. There was surprising anger in her voice. "Sacombre needs a trial. He needs to face what he's done. To me, at least, and mine."

The roads through the Gallowmoors were as numerous as the veins in a leaf, and the rolling hills limited sight lines and masked the sounds of hoofbeats that might have otherwise given away their path.

"Which road are we to take," Martin asked, despairing. "They could have gone anywhere."

"LaGaere's action was one of opportunity, not plan," Lucas said. "He will not have people waiting for him, and he'll want to avoid Halverdt's patrols—at least until he's farther south."

"So he'll stay off the main roads, but he'll still want to make haste," Martin said. "He's at crossed purposes."

"The fastest route to Heartsbridge isn't to the south," Lucas said.

"Has the world moved since we marched to war?" Martin asked. "Heartsbridge still sits on the Burning Coast, doesn't it?"

"It does," Lucas said, peering at the rolling horizon. "Three weeks by horse, assuming the roads are free of gheists. But a boat could get you there in half that time."

"West, then," Fianna said. "To Felling Bay."

"West," Lucas said with a nod. "On lesser roads."

"This would be easier with horses," Martin said.

"Everything could be easier," Lucas answered. "What is a test worth, if it's easy. Come on. We'll rest atop that hill," he said, pointing. "It should offer a good vantage."

As they reached the top of the third hill, higher than the previous two, there still was no sight of LaGaere and his men. Martin was beginning to wonder if they had gone wrong when Fianna drew in a sharp breath.

"There is water near here," she said.

"That will be a relief," Martin said. "My waterskin is as dry as ground wheat." He squinted as he looked around. "I see nothing."

"Some things don't need to be seen," Fianna said. She knelt in the dirt, brushing grass aside until the hard cracked earth was revealed. "Some things must be drawn out. Like so."

Drawing a deep breath, she squatted beside the patch of earth and tipped her head up to the sky. Something surged through her body, as though her pulse became an aura of light and energy. Frair Lucas stepped back. The earth turned dark. A trickle of water seeped out of the dry cracks, little more than a bead of damp silver. It ran uphill, south and east. Fianna opened her eyes and pointed.

"That way," she said. "A river, and old. I have never known the southern waters, but it is eager to share its name."

"So we will have water," Martin said, "and perhaps fish. That's better than starving to death in the Gallowmoors."

"Water and fish and more," Fianna said. "If your priest has crossed this river's path, the spirit will know of it. We will have his trail again."

"Ah," Frair Lucas said. "Well, maybe we won't need the armies of Heartsbridge after all." He squinted across the moors, in the direction the water was flowing. "Maybe all we need is a witch."

36

THE CORRIDOR BEYOND the mural cut through soft, loamy earth, tangled with the snow-white veins of exposed roots, dripping with condensation. The air smelled like a spring downpour. Flower petals of every color were crushed beneath their feet. Gwen hung back, watching Cahl's slow progress and Noel's ecstatic reverence. Several times Folam stopped to urge her forward.

"Why do you hesitate?" he said. "We have come all this way, come to the heart of our enemy's house, and yet you tarry by the door? What is holding you back?"

"I don't belong here," Gwen said. "Go on without me. I'll guard the chamber, and make sure you're not disturbed. Go on."

"What foolishness is this?" he asked. "If anyone belongs here, it is you. Huntress of the Iron Hand, last of the tribe of Adair. The only girl to touch one of the greater spirits, and she stands trembling at the threshold of another? We are the ones who do not belong in this place."

"I don't know," Gwen said. "I really don't feel as if this place is for me." She wasn't lying. Something emanating from the chamber ahead pressed against her spirit, as though a harsh wind had snagged her skeleton and was trying to pull it free of her body. Folam was watching her closely, as though he could sense her discomfort. "I would rather stay by the mosaic," she added. "In case the child wakes up, or if someone finds him and gets curious."

"And what would you do if that happened?" Folam asked. "Would you kill him? I saw you grab Noel when she tried to stop me, but letting someone else murder a child is very different from pushing the blade in yourself. Could you do that?" Folam took her by the shoulders, holding her away from him, studying her closely. "He is of an age with your brother, isn't he?"

"I would do what was necessary," Gwen said, looking down. "I always have."

There was a long moment of silence between them. Noel and Cahl had continued forward, disappearing around a bend. Their voices disappeared into the muddy walls of the tunnel. Finally, Folam nodded.

"Yes," he said. "Yes, you have, and you must again. Stay with me, Gwen Adair. Stay close. We have to stick together, you and I. Tribes of one. We must stand side by side." The air prickled with the same void energy that Gwen had felt while Folam shielded them from Cahl's earthquake. "You need to guard me against them. In case Cahl tries something again."

Voices echoed up from the tunnel. Cahl at first, and then Noel. Calling out in rapture.

"They seem to have found our broken god," Folam said. He clapped her on the shoulder, trying to smile through withered lips. Then he turned and hurried down the corridor. His feet sank into the soft mud, squelching.

Gwen suppressed a shudder, but there was some warmth in her heart. It was the first time anyone of the pagan tribes had expressed trust in her, rather than suspicion or outright hatred. And he was right—if anyone should be present at the shrine of the vernal god, it was Gwendolyn Adair. Last of the tribe of iron.

The shrine was nothing like Gwen expected. The ceiling was close and fetid. A tapestry of roots hung from the broken earth, tangling in her hair as she passed. Rivulets of murky water flowed underfoot. Black rocks stuck out of the mud, once part of a henge but now broken into splinters.

The whole room was hardly larger than a modest cottage. Only Gwen could stand up straight, and then only at the center. Their boots sank into the mud, and foul gasses escaped each time they took a step. Their light came from a bare flame, flickering in Noel's palm.

Gwen looked around the miserable space and sighed.

"This hardly looks like a place of the gods," she said.

"Everywhere is of the gods," Noel answered quietly. "It depends on the god, and their madness."

"The vernal spirit has fallen far, pushed away by its followers and broken by its own violence," Folam said. He knelt at the center of the room, running pale hands reverently over the smooth, black stones. "It has laid here undisturbed for generations. Gods bless that we got here before the inquisition's agents."

"I can't believe they would have ever found this place," Gwen said. "No matter who was leading them."

"We found it," Cahl answered. "At the hands of a child."

"The hands of a child and your holy sight, shaman," Folam said. "Noel, I will need more light than that if I'm to do the work of the gods."

"And I will need something to burn," Noel answered. "There's little enough of the god of fire in this place."

Gwen gathered the bindings Folam and Cahl had used to hide their faces, then wound them around a length of root that was sticking out of the center of the space. "It's not a torch, but without pitch or alcohol, it's the best I can do."

Noel took the makeshift torch and cupped her hands around it. Her palms muffled the light, plunging the room temporarily back into darkness. For a handful of heartbeats, Gwen stood in the thick, black air and breathed in the stink. She swore she could feel something moving in the mud, as well as a wind that reached out from the earth and plucked at her ribcage like an instrument. She pressed her eyes closed, but that only made it worse. She was about to bolt for the door when Noel moved her hands and a pyre of bright light came to life in the center of the room.

Gwen breathed a sigh of relief.

Folam laughed.

"A flame of summer, to light the way for spring," he said. "How appropriate."

"It won't last long," Noel said. "Be about your business quickly. The sooner we're out of here, the better."

"Indeed," Folam said. He swung a satchel onto the ground and opened it, drawing out various objects and setting them in a circle around him. "Cahl, take the anchors and place them around the chamber. Noel, keep that fire going."

"What can I do?" Gwen asked. Folam glanced up at her, chewing on his response.

"Watch closely," he said finally, "and stay closer."

Cahl moved around the room, dropping icons of cold iron on the perimeter. Steam hissed from the mud wherever he left an anchor. A troubling sharpness entered the air. Noel's fire snapped in an invisible gale.

"The spirits stir," Folam said absentmindedly. Gwen could feel it, as well. She crouched closer to the voidfather. He glanced at her, then offered her a silvered knife. "There is something troubling you, yes? An uneasiness of soul? The damage done you by Fomharra might be contributing to that. This will ground you."

She reached for the knife, but instead of handing it to her, Folam slashed lightly across her palm, drawing blood. Gwen jerked back with a stifled cry, nearly toppling into the mud. Folam smiled.

"Blood to ground, to trace the spirit, to bind the soul," he said. The voidfather placed the knife on the earth at his feet, arranging it beside a number of other icons. Pressing her palm with the other hand, Gwen strained to see what they were, but the old man shifted his robes, blocking them from her sight.

"I'm sorry for the cut," he said. "As sacrifices go, it's a small thing." He looked away from her, busying himself with the instruments on the ground. "Rub some mud on it."

"Hardly reassuring," Gwen muttered to herself. She palmed a clump of mud and pressed it into the wound, staunching the flow of blood and cooling the pain to a manageable throb. When she looked up, Cahl was watching her closely. He shrugged and went back to laying out the anchors. "What is this ritual supposed to do, anyway?"

"Seal the wound," Folam said. "This shrine has been a seething pit of everic energy since the god was broken. Well-hidden, yes, and well-managed, but still it bleeds. If Sacombre's agents were able to track Fomharra's tomb, there's little doubt they could find this place one day, as well."

"And if they do? Will this ritual somehow stop them from using it?"

"Perhaps. At the very least, it will make accessing the shrine very difficult." Folam lifted the knife to his forehead, pressing mud and blood into the tattooed runes of his skin, muttering something under his breath. The air changed. Whatever comfort Gwen was supposed to have gotten from the cut to her palm, it wasn't working. Her skin seethed with tension.

"It is the best we can do, for now," he said.

"And why wasn't this done before?" Gwen asked. "When the vernal god was broken by its followers? When the tribe of flowers threw down their host, and broke him?" Folam ignored her, so she looked at the other two. Noel was absorbed in keeping her torch lit, the flame flickering madly around, sometimes swirling up, sometimes dying down almost to embers. Gwen turned to Cahl. "What makes this possible now, when it wasn't before?"

"The tribe of the void had not been formed, yet," Cahl said. The big shaman placed the last anchor with care, crouching beside the earthen wall, wiping his hands clean of spattered mud. When he looked up, his eyes were twin pinpricks of light, the reflected fire of Noel's torch. "The emptiness was alone. We did not worship it, nor call its name."

"There was no… no voidfather?" Gwen asked. "I thought the old religion never changed. I thought it's remained the same since the Spirit War."

"Much has changed. Your crusades have seen to that," Cahl said. "We found a need to hide. A need to pour emptiness into our hearts, and into our gods. And so…" He gestured to Folam. "…a new tribe, and a god we had never worshiped."

"Never *should* have worshiped," Noel said briskly.

"Never mind how my kith came to be," Folam said, ignoring Noel and her sudden anger. "At the time of the vernal god's breaking, no one thought it would need to be hidden. It was forbidden, and that was good enough for the elders of that age. But this is a different age, and a different enemy. I am here to serve a blessing of the old gods."

"A blessing," Cahl said stiffly. "One we have paid to achieve."

"We are done," Folam said, cutting off all further discussion. "Now we will start."

"Whatever you have woven into the air, it is making this light almost impossible to maintain," Noel said. "I can't promise anything."

"Never mind that. I have my own tools to hand," Folam said. He raised an arm, breathing a chant. The anchors scattered about the room began to glow. Sparks shot off of them, as though they were under a great deal of pressure, or friction. The pain in Gwen's chest swelled.

"Gods almighty," she hissed, wincing and leaning forward, hand to her chest. "What is that?"

"The vernal god is the manifestation of change. The return of life to a realm of death," Folam said. He stood, his gray head scraping the ceiling as he extended his arms, palms up. "He is a god of wind. He is a god of storms."

As he spoke the wind rose to a howl. A torrent formed in the corners of the buried shrine, turning the dangling roots into streamers. Noel and Cahl, already standing near the entrance to the room, flinched away. At the center of the room, though, there was peace. Peace and the voidfather.

"You better get a handle on this, Folam!" Cahl yelled. "If that god starts to manifest..."

"Have faith in me, Cahl of stones," Folam answered. "All spirits bend to the void."

The eight anchors sparked more and more, as though a giant whetstone ground against them. The mud on which they rested turned hard with the heat. Bright embers flew through the wind, spinning through the room. The wind increased until it shrieked. The ghost-light flickered like lightning, and thunder rolled through the earth.

Noel tested herself against the wind. She wrapped her head in the mud-splattered hood of her robe and pushed into the storm. The wind met her, pressed her, defeated her. She fell backward, rolling until she rested against the wall.

"You're losing control!" Cahl shouted. The storm stole his voice. In the narrow confines of the buried shrine, there was nothing but the mud, the storm, the eerie light of Folam's ritual. Cahl knelt beside the fallen witch, while Gwen cowered at Folam's side, in the tight center of the storm, the pocket of silence at its heart.

"Voidfather!" Cahl looked up, shielding his face with one massive arm. "Break the squall! If you can't harness the spirit, we must end it!"

"We must do nothing, friend," Folam muttered. Only Gwen was close enough to hear him. She turned to him curiously. The voidfather ignored her.

He was consumed by his ritual, but he certainly didn't look like he'd lost control. He stood stiff as a column, hands splayed in supplication, face tilted slightly toward the sky. The wind only barely touched his robes. The tools at his feet hummed with frenetic power. Gwen's eyes were drawn to them.

She knew little of the pagan rites. Her role as huntress allowed only certain weapons of ancient power—the bloodwrought spear, the joined crystals of everic power known as tears of the earth, created to battle those blessed of the celestial church, and little else. Her house had been cut off from pagan knowledge, the better for them to hide among the celestials. So the tools at Folam's feet meant little to her.

Still, they caused her concern.

There was the knife he had used to draw her blood, still smeared with crimson and black. There was a sickle of pewter, its half-moon blade touching the tip of the silver knife. Nestled between the two, a doll of elderwood, simple and crude. The doll was wrapped in hair. Black and crimson, glossy with anointed oil.

It was Gwen's hair, shorn for her disguise.

"What the hell are you doing?" she hissed. The voidfather spared her a glance, but not a word. She pressed closer. "What are you doing, Folam! Why do you have my hair? What is the meaning of this ritual?"

"I am closing an old wound," he said. His voice grated through clenched jaws. "An infected wound that must be burned shut before the infection spreads."

Gwen reached for the doll, but Folam kicked her hand away, shoving her back into the gale. The change in the air was sudden, her breath stolen, her body thrown around like a rag. She stumbled, leaned closer to the ground, then started to crawl forward. Cahl was yelling behind her, but his words were lost in the storm. Tongues of fire flashed around the shrine, snatched from the air and spun by the broken god's wind until they snapped out.

Slowly, painfully, fighting the fury of an angry spirit with each foot, Gwen dragged herself back into the still circle that surrounded Folam.

Too late.

There was a flash of sulfurous light and the storm broke. At the heart of the shrine, caked mud cracked open, and the shrine gave birth. What had begun as a storm came to life, horrible and bright, shrouded in the burning petals of flowers and hail.

The emptiness in Gwen, the strange wound that was stitched into her bones—the place where Fomharra had bound herself to the young huntress—that void opened itself. It welcomed the storm.

The storm rushed in to fill it.

37

IAN WATCHED AS a pillar of wind and ice twisted out of the sky to crush Elsa beneath its weight. The shaman stood at the edge of the storm, hands raised to the sky as the corkscrewing column ground through the remnants of the stables, flicking slate tiles and wooden beams through the air like dust.

Light blossomed in the middle of the pillar, a spear of sunlight at the center of a tornado. Slowly, the storm peeled open, tumbled apart like a colonnade collapsing in an earthquake. Pillars of twisting snow crashed into the courtyard and dissipated. On the ground at the center of the storm, with the snow scoured away, Sir Elsa LaFey lay motionless. The sunlight flashing from her breast flickered out. The storm closed in again.

"Her sword," Ian muttered. He had last seen it by the doma. Without it, she'd never win this fight. He glanced back at the shaman. Still wrapped in the faltering gheist, the man stalked toward Elsa's limp form.

Slowly the vow knight stood.

Their combat started again.

The humble grounds of Harthal continued coming apart at the seams. The stables had collapsed, the tower where he and Elsa were housed had been stripped of its shutters, and the roof was coming loose one heavy tile at a time. The main keep was hidden behind a squall of sleet. The gate banged open and closed, the beams of iron-bound wood slowly working apart with each booming strike.

Only the doma appeared undamaged. Ian ducked back, and began making his way around the courtyard toward it.

As he stumbled through the wreckage, he found the farmers who had been pummeling Elsa moments earlier, now cowering behind barrels and the toppled pillars of the stables. Horses cantered through the storm, their eyes wide with terror. As he went around the keep, Ian slipped and fell on his ass, knocking the breath from his lungs. He was still struggling to breathe when he realized he had fallen in the ruin of some peasant's skull, the man's brains smeared across the cobbles like spilled stew.

Fighting back the bile in his throat, he scampered far enough away that the dead man disappeared in the storm. Then he collapsed into the snow. His ears rang, either from the force of the storm or the frair's blow that had knocked him out. His wrists were chafed from the ropes that still bound him, blood seeping into the hemp, his fingers sticking together. His breath came in short, panicked gasps. The fall left his spine sparkling with pain, jolts of sharp agony that prickled through his hips, his lungs, all the way to his skull.

Ian's arms shook. His whole body trembled.

"Get your shit together, Blakley," he muttered. He pressed his back into the stone of the keep, slowly pushing himself to his feet. "Elsa's sword, and then shelter. Let the vow knight sort it out. Let *her* do the killing."

There was a crash, and Elsa pinwheeled into sight. Her

spinning body toppled a pile of crates that were stacked against the outer wall. Stored food spilled out, sliding to the ground in a scree of salt and shattered masonry. Slowly the vow knight stood again, grimacing as salt ground into her many wounds, then marched back into the courtyard and out of sight.

"Right. The sword," Ian said. The sounds of conflict resumed. He stole a glance around the corner of the keep, saw Elsa and the shaman spinning madly through the snow-covered grounds. Then he dashed to the doma.

There was a hole in the snow, sword-shaped and empty. The ice around it had melted and then refrozen in a flash, burned by the blade's fire and then re-formed by the gheist's storm. The sword was gone, but there were footprints beside it, leading to the doma.

"Oh, damn it," Ian said. He bent to the footprints. Slippered feet, the arches soft in the fresh snow. Not farmer's boots, or the hobnailed soles of a soldier. Slippers. A noble, or a merchant. He looked up at the door of the doma, shut against the storm.

"Or a frair," he muttered.

Ian threw himself against the splintered wood of the door. It rang, his shoulder bouncing painfully off. He crumpled into the snow. That would never work—not without an axe or a ram, neither of which Ian had. His own sword had been taken from him by the frair.

Looking around, he saw only the swirling chaos of the storm, and brief flashes of the fight between Elsa and the shaman. He had to get inside before she fell, or the shaman spotted him and guessed his purpose. So he examined the door. It was braced with iron, the hinges sunk into the stone. From his brief encounter with the wood, Ian was pretty sure it was barred from the inside. There had to be another way in.

Perhaps through the keep, but that would be full of guards, and Ian wasn't sure of Halfic's disposition. Did he know of his frair's treachery? Probably, but if not, now wasn't the time to explain.

He stood and started circling the doma's perimeter. There were no other doors. He looked up. The dozens of shutters that lined the roof had been smashed by the storm. The wooden panels had been pried apart, their sheathes of silver and gold peeled away, leaving small, dark openings. All he had to do was climb up, in the wind and ice, with bound wrists and possibly broken ribs.

Ian turned back to the whirling fight at the center of the courtyard.

"Might be better to face the gheist," he mused. "Might be easier." He looked up the sloping arc of the doma and sighed. "But no, no. This is the thing I'm supposed to do. Right."

The first few feet weren't so bad. Ian was able to hook his wrists around the stone gutters that ringed the lower level of the doma and scramble up the flat surface of the wall. Beyond that, though, things got tricky.

The sloped dome of the roof was closely fitted stone, with the only interruptions being the calendar windows. Most were too small to allow Ian's passage, but he was able to use them as hand and footholds. The spaces between were slick with ice and snow. The wind was relentless. With each foot Ian dragged himself forward, the wind shoved harder and harder. More than once he tore free, balancing precariously or sliding down before catching himself on a broken shutter or ill-joined stone.

The rope between his wrists proved both invaluable and a burden. Ian used it to hook around buttresses, but it prevented him from keeping one handhold while reaching for another. Every move was a commitment. Every jump was a launch across an icy wall, with nothing below but stones.

Finally he reached a window that had been pried open far enough to allow entrance. Gold leaf curled out from the ruined paneling, and the winch that controlled the shutters clattered against the roof, hanging out like the guts of a disemboweled fish. Ian tangled his fingers in the winch's rope, then pulled himself through the slit in the stone. It was a tight fit, and halfway through Ian was sure he'd get stuck, but then he slithered through and nearly fell the thirty feet to the doma floor below.

Only luck and the grace of Strife kept him from falling. His hands, still bound, became fouled inextricably in the winch. He swung through and dangled from the window's mechanism, wrenching his shoulders and leaving his feet fluttering in open air.

He spotted the frair, watching his progress from below. The man stood beside the altar, Elsa's sword gripped uncomfortably in both hands, held like a torch.

"You are very persistent," he said. "Bound, beaten, at the feet of a gheist with no weapons and no hope, and still you live."

"Don't worry," Ian said with a grunt. "I may still fall to my death." He twisted slowly in the air. The pulleys along the wall began to pop free, one at a time. "It would be quite a mess to clean up, though."

"I have to warn you, I—" the frair started. Before he could finish, the remaining pulleys ripped free from their stone moorings, all at once, leading to a jerky, jangling descent that ended among the pews.

Ian lay still for a long time. When he stirred, it was with a moan of pain and quiet regret. He shifted to his knees and then, reluctantly, stood. The room spun around him. Everything ached, but nothing appeared to be broken or ruptured or crushed. Quite gloriously, his bonds seemed to have torn free in the fall, along with most of the skin of his wrists.

"I have reached my limit on climbing," he muttered to himself. "I won't do it again. Not for gods or gold or pretty girls. Bloody awful practice. Nearly as bad as falling down. Gods."

"I have to warn you," the frair said again. He waved the sword stiffly in Ian's direction. "I'm not afraid to use this."

"Afraid? No, I suspect not." Ian limped into the aisle and then hobbled toward the altar and the frair. "Incapable of using it, though. I think that's quite likely."

"I'm not without the blessings of the gods!" the frair snapped. He held the blade in front of him with an angry snarl and spat the words of an invocation. The power of the binding twisted around the sword, the air bending and warping with heat. The runes along the blade sizzled into life, glowing with sudden fire, which then blossomed.

With a yelp, the frair dropped the sword and backed away, his charred fingers blistering, the cuffs of his vestments turning into cinders. He stumbled to the altar and plunged his hands into a silver bowl of holy water.

Ian chuckled. "You'd have been better off throwing it at me," he said. "Or dropping it on my toe." He stooped quickly and, using the torn ends of his shirt, carefully picked up Elsa's blade. It was still warm beneath the cloth, and the smell of burned flesh hung in the air. "Now," he said, "to get this to my lady foul."

The doors boomed, as though struck by a battering ram. There was angry yelling, then they shuddered again. The third time they broke. Sir Elsa slid gracelessly into the doma on her back, hands slapping against the pews as she went. She skidded to a halt in a heap at Ian's feet. He set the tip of the blade on the floor and dipped the handle toward her.

"Sir Elsa," he said. "Your blade."

"Could have used that a bit earlier," she said weakly. "Too damned late now."

At the foot of the aisle, the gheist-wrapped shaman stooped and came through the shattered doors. The storm whipped around his feet, scattering snow and splintered wood. Once inside, the pagan unfolded to his full height. The god of storms filled the doma with its fury.

38

ONCE THEY WERE off the road, LaGaere's path was easy enough to follow. The horses churned a track in the mud, and soon there was a trail of torn brush and trampled shrubbery that ran up and down the rolling hills of the moor. Judging from their stride and the frequent stops, LaGaere and his men did not expect pursuit.

"They're certainly taking their time about it," Martin said. "Stopping to rest frequently, it seems, and the mounts led as often as they're ridden. Do they think we won't chase them?"

"It's not an unreasonable belief," Lucas said. He glanced down at the strange river of silvery water that had led them this far, and which stretched over the next hill and beyond. "Without Fianna guiding us, we would still be beating through the forests and following the roads. Besides, their horses are exhausted. We'll have them soon enough."

"And what then?" Martin asked. "They outnumber us, and even riding only occasionally, they'll be fresher than us in a fight."

"Not to mention your high inquisitor," Fianna said. The witch was dragging. Whatever magic bound her to the water that led them had sapped her energy. Once they found the trail in the mud, Lucas tried to get her to release the binding, but she refused. He wondered if the little river might be the only thing sustaining her.

"We will come upon them unawares," he said. "Sacombre is powerful, but the battle of the Fen Gate reduced him greatly." He turned to Martin. "I have heard great things about your skill of arms, Sir Roard. Surely Warhome and his men will be little match for you."

"Yes, of course. I will simply recite my tournament record, and they will surely cast down their arms," Martin muttered. "Not a worry."

"There's the spirit," Lucas said. They approached another gentle hill, but at its base Fianna stumbled. Lucas laid a hand on her shoulder, but she shrugged him off. "Not long now, witch. We are nearly at the end."

"My end is far from here, priest," she answered irritably.

"What game is LaGaere playing at?" Martin asked, hoping to change the subject as quickly as he could. The thought of putting the witch to trial, even after she had helped them, made him uncomfortable. "You don't think he's another heretic, do you? Secretly serving the pagan gods, or one of Sacombre's conspirators?"

"Heretic? Oh, I think not. I'm sure he had nothing to do with the gheist's attack," Lucas said. "LaGaere likely saw his opportunity and took it while we were distracted. Though someone led that gheist to our camp."

"Could Sacombre be responsible? Even in chains?"

"I think not. There are rituals required, and sacrifices to be made," Lucas said. "Someone must be following us. A troop of pagans, perhaps, or priests loyal to Sacombre's heresy."

"None of mine," Fianna said. "We would not dare stir

the ancient dust of Gardengerry. Not even now, with the hunter gone."

"Then the sooner we are to Heartsbridge, the better. I won't feel safe until those sacred walls have embraced us," Martin said quietly.

"If then," Lucas said.

They crossed another hill, much taller than most, affording a view for miles. The path of churned mud and broken shrubbery disappeared into the distance, and a strap of smoke leaked into the sky from the valley beyond. Night was beginning to fall. Lucas pulled them back from the hill's summit before they were silhouetted against the sky.

"This is as far as you go, for now," he said. "Stay beneath the crest of the hill. If they set a watch, they might have already seen us. I doubt it, but there's no reason to risk it any further."

"If they do have a watch posted and have spotted us, we should strike now," Martin said. "Even with tired horses, as soon as they know they're pursued, LaGaere will push to the coast without remorse. This may be our only chance."

"Perhaps, but if that's the case, we're already lost. We'll never cross those hills in the time it would take them to mount up and flee." Lucas slid to the ground and started to unpack his bags. He unrolled a leather wrap of arcane tools, drawing each one from its sleeve with a mumbled prayer. "I will scout ahead. Perhaps something can be done about those horses."

"You're exhausted, my frair," Martin said.

"I am tired, yes, but I am bound to the task—and what better time for a priest of Cinder to do his work than under Cinder's pale gaze?" Lucas laid the tools in a broad circle just beneath the crest of the hill. He settled into the center of the circle. "Besides, the witch will never make those miles in her present condition. As much help as she has been, I would not count on her in a fight."

"Nor I you," Fianna said. She collapsed to the ground, crossing her legs and leaning her head forward to rest in her palms. "But this will not come to a fight, I think. Not while Sacombre lives."

"Perhaps. Either way, you must guard us both, Sir Roard. Don't let her interfere with this ritual, and if I fail and LaGaere comes for her, you must run. Protect her, and see her delivered to justice."

"I will," Martin said. "Even unto death."

"Even unto death," Lucas said. Then he lay his staff across his knees, closed his eyes, and began the slow, steady process of unraveling his soul from the flesh of his body, spooling it out into the night.

They sat in a tight circle of light, their shadows stretching long and sharp into the moors. Sacombre sat on his campstool quietly, head tipped up to the moon in prayer. The soldiers ate without speaking. LaGaere stayed close to the high inquisitor.

"We should have hunted longer for the witch," one of the knights muttered darkly into his cup. "We could have already seen her to justice by now."

"You would linger too long with her flesh, I think, Sir Sault," LaGaere answered. "Best that we leave her to the inquisition."

"Like the inquisition doesn't dawdle in the flesh," Sault answered. He gave the high inquisitor a sideways glance and a smirk. "Got to stay warm in winter somehow, eh?"

"No," Sacombre said without lowering his eyes from the sky. "We don't."

The men shifted uncomfortably on their campstools. LaGaere waited a long moment, then closed his eyes and sighed.

"Now that we have secured your safety, your holiness, we should discuss what comes next," he said. "The hypocrisy of this hedge priest, dragging you south to face judgment after he stood beside Malcolm Blakley and Colm Adair. It cannot be tolerated." He fidgeted with a bottle of wine. "The ignominy of it. You, the one man willing to expose the Tenerran savages for the pagans they truly are! And to use Lord Halverdt's death as justification…

"Cinder and Strife, what's to be done?"

"What's to be done indeed," Sacombre said quietly. He sat with his shoulders hunched, barely touching the food they offered. His face and hands were crossed with strange scars, wounds that looked very old and deep, but which hadn't been on his flesh during the campaign against Adair. LaGaere wanted to ask about them but, frankly, he was reluctant to broach the subject.

The silence stretched for several minutes.

"Yes," LaGaere said finally. "Sophie Halverdt might be brought around, if we were able to explain what happened to her father. She holds his deep distrust of Tener, as any good and faithful Celestial must, but the duke's blood haunts her. Perhaps now that she has his body…"

"What remains of his body, that is," Sault muttered. There had been little left of the duke of Greenhall following the gheist's attack.

"Halverdt will be no friend to me," Sacombre said. "Not until her mind has been bent in my favor. But she will be no friend to Tener, either."

"Best we leave her out of it, then," LaGaere said.

"The true lords of Suhdra will stand with you, your holiness," Sault said sharply. "We will raise your banner along the Burning Coast, and gather the faithful of Cinder and Strife to protest this miscarriage of justice."

"Enthusiasm suits you," Sacombre said, "but I wonder, Sir Sault, have you been to the Circle of Lords?"

"Of course. I served as my lord's honor guard last Frostnight, and now that his son will take the peaked throne, I hope to render young Fabron the same service."

"Very good. And did you see the throne that sits there, in the midst of the Circle?" Sacombre asked. He turned to Duke LaGaere and smiled. "Or the remains of a throne, at least."

"We all know the history, your holiness," LaGaere snapped. "The church ended the line of kings in the south, and promised to do so again, should we rise against them. But our faith is absolute—it is what has led us to this point, and nothing less!"

"The Celestriarch might not see it that way, should you march against his walls with banners flying and spears raised," Sacombre noted. "No matter how pure your intentions."

"Well, what of Heartsbridge itself? Surely there are allies in the Celestial Dome who will see through this lie?" Sault asked.

"If you mean to take me to Heartsbridge, it would have been better to leave me in the frair's custody. The court of winter will not look kindly on galloping off into the moors, away from the celestially designated escort. Frair Lucas was taking me to my justice." Sacombre raised his bony head and looked at LaGaere. His eyes were the color of fresh snow. "Do you think I would be ill served by the church's justice?"

"Hard to call it justice when—" LaGaere started.

"Cinder's reason is absolute. Cinder's will is pure," the high inquisitor said. "If you truly believe that I am innocent—

that I have been wronged by Frair Lucas, and Malcolm Blakley, and all of Tener—then you should have let these men deliver me to Heartsbridge." He stood, unfolding like a siege weapon to loom over the campfire. "Do you believe in my innocence, Duke LaGaere? Or do you side with the likes of Colm Adair, and name me heretic?"

"If we believed that, we wouldn't have risked our lives to save you," LaGaere growled. He remained seated, though, cowed in place by Sacombre's strange presence. "If half of what they say about you was true..."

"And what do they say? What has Lucas whispered behind my back, to poison the minds of the timid and the broken?" The circle was quiet, the men staring down at their mugs, unwilling to answer. Sacombre studied them each in turn, finally settling on LaGaere. "Do you fear even to speak it?"

"I would not give words to their lies, your holiness," LaGaere said meekly.

"No? Or are you afraid they might be true?" Sacombre asked with a strange grin. He raised one bony hand and pulled back his sleeve. The knotted scars continued down his arm. "You have seen the marks left on me by my battle at the Fen Gate. And you have heard the words of Malcolm Blakley, a man you trusted before he raised his banner in defense of House Adair."

Sault spat. "House Adair lied for generations to protect their pagan god," he said. "They and all the Tenerrans. Why should we take the word of a hound over that of a priest?"

"But what of Frair Lucas?" Sacombre asked, wheeling on the knight. "He is blessed of Cinder, is he not? And he swears I am a heretic. What if he's right?"

"Years in the pagan wilderness have twisted his mind,"

another knight answered. "He made his allegiances clear, there in the Fens, going with the Adair bitch to the witches' hallow. Gods know what happened to him there. What promises he made, or betrayals he committed."

"Yes, but how are you to know *anything* when the priests of the god of reason disagree?" Sacombre asked. "You, mere mortals, benighted by the flesh, driven by the madness of Strife." He turned in a slow circle, his grin cracked wide and wild. "Why, you're hardly more than animals, howling at the moon!"

"Now, just a second," LaGaere said, standing up. "We risked our lives to bring you away from that priest. And we risk our souls defying Heartsbridge. We believe you, man. You don't have to belittle our honor!"

"It is not your honor I am belittling," Sacombre said, "but your wisdom. Think on how this looks. Fleeing into the moors at the first opportunity. Hiding from a priest of the inquisition. If I am not guilty, then I must submit to Cinder's judgment. How am I to do that here?" Sacombre threw his arms wide. The shadows swirled around him, the flickering light of the fire growing sharp against the darkness. The men cowered away from the gaunt form. "What justice is there in the wilderness? Where is the judgment of winter?"

"I am here, Sacombre," Lucas said.

He emerged from the shadows, his form wrought in ribbons of purple light. Some of the soldiers sprang to their feet, drawing steel, while others pushed back with a cry of surprise. "Surrender, and I will spare these men. They cannot continue with us south, but they will be free to return to their homes."

"Mercy," Sacombre growled. "That's something not in the canon of Cinder, Lucas. Perhaps Sir Sault is right. Perhaps you have been too long among the pagans."

"If I have learned anything of mercy, it is from Sir LaFey, and not the gheists that she and I hunt together." He turned his writhing form toward LaGaere. "Be wise, Warhome. I believe you have done this out of faith for the church, but I promise you that this man has left behind the celestial path. Take your horses and your knights and return to your keep. Let Cinder judge him."

"If Cinder's judgment is to come from cowards like you, I'll have none of it," LaGaere said. He drew his sword and took a step forward. "Bring your threats, shadow, and we will see who is favored of the gods."

"Don't do anything foolish," Sacombre said. Raising a hand, he twisted his fingers into a strange knot. The shadows thrown by the campfire took form, creeping across the grass.

Lucas saw this, and started to try to untangle the spell that the high inquisitor was casting. Sacombre continued. "Lucas doesn't want to kill you, obviously. It would look bad if people kept dying at his hand—especially faithful Suhdrin lords. How will Heartsbridge see that, Lucas? If these honest servants of the gods are murdered by your hand?"

"Listen…" Lucas started, but he was too late.

Sacombre's eyes turned dark. Inky tendrils bled down his cheeks, and then he stretched his arms toward the ground. The shadows on the ground grew solid, those nearest the fire shying away. Those at the feet of the half-dozen men who stood around the fire rippled with unnatural life.

They turned to blades and rose up from the ground, piercing foot and leg and chest and skull, a quick spindle of bloody violence that pitted each man like an apple. One man twisted away from the piercing shadows, his feet and legs already locked in place by the barbs, but the tendrils of night crawled slowly up his chest until they reached his head. He let out a scream as shadowy hooks sliced into his mouth, his eyes, piercing cheek and jaw bloodlessly.

Another soldier, who had been watching Sacombre closely, managed to dance out of the way of the first grasping tendril, only to trip across the twisted roots of the growing darkness. He fell and was met by a blossom of shadow that punched through his chest, sprouting from his back in a dozen cruel blades. His fingers trailed across the ground.

The rest died in seconds, their blood sluicing down the shadowed blades of the night to pool on the ground. They hung in the air like corpses left out to dry.

Then Sacombre dropped them. The shadows dissipated, the blades evaporating like fog. LaGaere fell heavily to the ground. Sacombre stood still in the circle of the dead, a smile on his face.

"And now you must explain this, as well, Frair Lucas. To the council, to the celestriarch, and to their families. All of Suhdra will want to hear why you butchered these men." He sat cross-legged beside the fire, folding his hands in his lap. "All of Tenumbra will know of your violence, and your evil."

"You're a devil!" Lucas spat. "A murdering, demon-fucking, godsdamned devil!"

"No," Sacombre said. "I am something much more than that. A prophet, maybe. Or a new kind of god. The kind of god that bends other gods to his will. Yes. Yes, I think I like that." He closed his eyes and leaned forward, as though in prayer. "Now bring your servants, and let them bind me again. Heartsbridge is waiting, after all.

"Heartsbridge, and judgment."

39

IT WAS A long, jagged inhalation. As though Gwen had been holding her breath ever since the goddess of spring abandoned her at the witches' hallow. She was finally able to breathe again, but the air had turned to broken glass, and she felt as if her lungs were starting to bleed.

Whatever it was that came out of the ground beneath the shrine at Greenhall, it was far from holy. A lacework of sick yellow light the color of bile erupted from the mud. It thrashed in the air, whimpering and screaming without a voice, cutting through the darkness. A spindle of it clipped Folam on the shoulder, burning through his robes and sending the voidfather sprawling into the storm. The winds picked up. The air crackled with electricity and sulfur.

Gwen was alone at the center.

She knelt in the mud. Her clothes were soaked from the damp and the unnatural storm that whipped through the chamber. Her bound breasts ached, and her fingers were bloody from dragging herself across the ground against the winds. Then a deeper pain joined the chorus, something stitched into her bones—an emptiness that had carved a place for itself in her spirit, and was only now apparent. She felt herself falling down a steep incline in her soul, toward a cliff that tumbled off into darkness.

Gwen struggled against the fall. She cried out for an anchor, a rope, anything that would keep her upright. For a moment she had it. Her blood stiffened, her veins tightening like steel cord, the muscle of her heart pumping hot and stony through her body. She became hard, but she was already falling, and the vernal god was falling with her. They came together with a crack that split the air and the earth and the stone. It nearly split Gwen, but her blood just shuddered and shook off the impact.

The twisting matrix of yellow light wrapped itself around her.

She rose, and the god of spring consumed her.

Horold woke where Noel had laid him down. His head hurt. His whole body hurt, the way it sometimes did when he hadn't eaten for a few days and his breath would stink and his belt would come loose. It hurt deep.

Then he remembered the blind pagan and the light, and Horold lurched to his feet. He fell straight back down, his joints howling. In the dim light of the corridor, two hands lay in front of his face. He moved, and both hands moved with him. They were his hands, but they were *different*.

He twisted to a sitting position and looked at them, though his vision didn't seem quite right. On the right, familiar skin and bone, the nubs of his fingernails grimy and pink except for the dead nail on his little finger, as black as night.

His left hand was dead. *No*, he thought, watching his fingers wiggle, just like the fingers on his right. *Not dead. Old.* Old and withered, like his grandmother's hand. He stood up, and the pain in his joints came back. The tunnel was choked with debris, as though the ceiling had shaken free a generation of dust and loose trash. Horold shuffled through it, his feet heavy, his legs unwilling to lift. There was light ahead. He went toward it.

The street was crowded with people rushing around. Everyone looked scared. Baskets had tumbled off of carts and lay on the ground, their contents spilled out on the hard-packed stones. Plaster lay like snowdrifts around the buildings. A silver vendor, her face set in a harsh line, was gathering up her wares and piling them into a pouch she had made with the hem of her robes. But no, not the vendor. Horold knew the silversmith who worked this street, and this woman was not her. He came closer, and the woman glanced up at him. Horror filled her face.

"What is happening?" Horold asked. His throat was choked with dust. He sounded like a pauper, his voice rattling drily through his ribs. The woman swallowed hard, dropped one more silver bracelet into her pouch, then ran down the street. Horold reached out for her, but the woman was gone.

The ground shook, and strange gusts of wind puffed out from the broken corridor he had just left behind, along with every window and door along the street. It felt as if the city was coughing. Horold's withered hand came down on a silver plate, and he almost snatched it away before curiosity filled him. He picked up the plate and looked at his face in its reflection.

Half of his face looked like a fruit left to dry in the sun. His hair had gone white, and the sunken pit of his eye was black and glossy. His lips peeled back. Horold's teeth were sharp and long, fitting together like a jigsaw trap. He nodded.

"Of course," Horold said quietly. "A curse. I have been

cursed." He turned his head to get a better look at the wicked teeth sprouting from his jaw. "Cursed by a pagan witch." It all made sense.

A lilting shiver of screams broke from down the street, reaching Horold in echoes. He looked in that direction. A flock of mocking-doves scattered from the rooftops, mingling with the smoke from what appeared to be a large house fire. What was going on?

Snapped out of the shock of his own appearance, Horold spun in place, taking in the view.

Towers leaned like drunken guards, their roofs crooked and on the verge of toppling. Flames licked through the slums downhill, where he had first led the pagans into the Curse. Incense had filled the air ever since Lady Sophie returned from the south, but now it mingled with black, oily smoke that stank of burned trash. As Horold watched, an avalanche of plaster slid noisily down the side of a warehouse. It was followed by bricks, and then the whole building deflated, sending a plume of dust into the sky.

The ground shook again. This time it felt closer, like the street was a harp string, humming under Horold's feet. Behind him, the buildings started to dance together. They were falling.

"Gods in heaven, spare your servant," Horold whispered under his breath. This was the prayer his mother had taught him on her deathbed, the one his father hissed into her grave, the one Horold prayed every high day and low holiday. He took a step backwards, stumbling into the silversmith's wares, toppling the rickety stall and sending priceless platters and dishes and other finery clattering to the ground.

Horold clutched the cheap linen the woman had used to

cover her stall, holding in his tiny fists—one young and pink, the other withered, the color of snow. He willed the prayer out of his forehead and into the heavens.

"Gods above, spare your servant. Spare me!"

Another building split like an egg, then another, then another. A storm hatched from the shattered brick, tearing into the sky like a thunderbolt wrapped in wind. The wreckage of the buildings went up with it, spinning slowly into the air like a wind chime, rotating slowly around a pillar of flickering light.

Then he saw it.

A god stood in the middle of this chaos, its head crowned in lightning. A cloak of endless flowers swirled around it, their petals washing down the length of the cloak to shower onto the ground. Each petal burned, like a curl of charcoal, its edges tipped in bright embers. Among the swirling folds of the flower cloak, Horold caught glimpses of ruby dark fire, churning like the heart of a kiln. The face of the gheist was blank, a silver mask that flickered with the lightning that arced around its body.

The gheist horn sounded from the high towers of Greenhall. The choir, safe in the doma inside the castle walls, began singing the rites of coming dawn, beginning with the one that burns away all darkness. The gheist turned its flowering head in that direction. It walked through the city, its passage heralded by the sound of whispering petals and scouring wind. Lightning played against the castle walls. The horn sounded again, and again, a strident call to battle.

The gates of the castle boomed open and a stream of knights flowed out. Their column bristled with the dull red shimmer of bloodwrought steel. They flew the banner of the gheist hunt, an arcane eye pierced by silver spear, the tri-acorn of House Halverdt fluttering beside. Horold caught his breath at the sight of it.

Abruptly he was shoved aside by the blind pagan, no longer blind, his robes white with dust. Blood leaked down the side of his face, turning the dust there to dark paste. The man didn't spare Horold a second look. He ran down the street, away from the gheist, away from the castle. He ran for the gates.

Horold lay on the ground and whispered his prayer, as the city came apart around him.

Noel fell to her knees. The center of the chamber disappeared in a cloud of dust, carried by the gale force winds summoned by the voidfather. Cahl disappeared into the squall, trying to push his way forward even as the storm took him. Of Gwen and Folam there was no sign.

The archway at the entrance to the buried shrine offered some protection. Noel huddled in its lee, covering her face with the folds of her robe as the storm rolled toward her. There was a brief moment of howling violence, then she was buried beneath dust and debris. The storm's violence continued, but it was muffled and distant.

The weight of the wreckage crushed down on her. The shock of what had happened clouded her mind. Noel lay there, wondering what she should do next. What she *could* do.

Had the voidfather betrayed them?

The thought crept into her mind like a crack in the foundation. Folam of the empty tribe had kept the pagans together for so long, insisting on maintaining communications with the few faithful in the south, wrangling the anger in the north, keeping things from getting out of hand. Maintaining balance. She had trusted him to end this threat, as well. They all had.

The sound outside her little shelter changed. The storm seemed to have passed, to be replaced by a low, throaty rumble. The debris that piled on top of Noel's head began to hum and vibrate. She pushed against it and something shifted. A beam of light fell against her cloak, and she shoved the cloth aside.

She was in open air. The sky above was blue, a thin sliver of sapphire set in a ring of hard iron. Noel coughed, and heard someone call her name.

Cahl stood in the middle of a debris field. It was more than just the collapsed chamber of the hidden shrine. Bricks and mortar, broken cobbles, vast piles of shattered slate tile, as sharp and jagged as swords. There was a clear space around him, held at bay by a shivering ring of everic power. The shaman stood with his hands spread, sweat turning his face pale and bright.

"Again!" he said weakly. "I can hear you, but..."

"Cahl!" Noel shouted. The man's head turned toward her, and she saw how drained he truly was. He shouldered in her direction, his every movement banded by the lines of everic power that he was channeling. A path cleared in the rubble. Bricks and stone shuffled aside like playing cards. Noel pushed toward them, finally stepping free of her bondage, limping toward the shaman of stones.

Once she was close enough, Cahl released his binding and collapsed to the ground. The stones shifted dangerously around them, a few tumbling down to form a scree at their feet, but most of it held. Noel knelt, putting a hand to his forehead. He was burning up. She started to wick the heat away, untangling the weakness from his flesh and bleeding it off into the air. Smoke wafted up from her shoulders.

"What happened?" she asked while she worked.

"Folam..." Cahl gasped. "He... he must have lost control."

"That is not his way," Noel said. "That is never his way."

"I just can't believe he would do this," Cahl said, shaking his head. "Any of this." He looked up at the wreckage that surrounded them. They lay at the bottom of a crater, its sides carved out from the buildings and walls of the city. The castle was perched at the edge of the wreckage. Whatever wards Halverdt maintained, they had been enough to protect against Folam's spell.

"We have to get out of here," Noel said. She pulled her companion to his feet. The shaman was massive, his thick arms nearly limp in her grasp. "Whatever Folam did, it's put us in a shit position."

"Wait... Gwen..."

"Probably dead," Noel said, "and good riddance. She's caused enough trouble for one child."

"No, I saw her fall. The god flowed through her, like a pipe, bursting. I... I think Folam needed her. *Used* her. As a focus," Cahl said. His voice became steadily weaker with each word. He leaned over and nearly passed out. Noel shook him.

"Better that she died here, then," she insisted. "Fomharra's possession changed her, no question. If this is the sort of power that change has wrought, she should never have traveled with the tribes. Folam has demonstrated it well enough." She looked hopelessly around the crater. "She should be at peace, finally. With her family. With her tribe.

She has nothing else to do in this world."

"I will decide that." Gwen's voice came from above them. They looked up, squinting into the light. Gwen was perched on the edge of the crater. Her clothes were ruined, ash smeared from her eyes to the temples of her shaved head. Something glowed through her, a frenetic energy that looked as much like madness as the burn of a fever dream.

"But my time of peace hasn't come yet," she said.

"Did you know—" Cahl started. Gwen cut him off.

"Don't be an idiot. Twice I've placed my faith in pagan elders, and twice I've paid in blood and ash. Folam spent whatever debt of trust I had left."

Noel stood, placing herself between the feeble shaman and Gwen. She started to draw on the spirit of her god, reflected in the fires that spotted the city around them. She lifted her chin.

"Whatever you mean to do to us, best get it done," Noel said. "We knew nothing of Folam's plot. Will you kill us for that?"

"Mean to do?" Gwen asked. "I mean to save you. Before the thousands of angry Suhdrins crawling through the wreckage of their homes realize they have pagans in their midst, and before I come up with a reason to not trust you, either." She reached out to them, everic power crackling around her shoulders. A gale of wind lashed down the debris field, clearing a path through the wreckage.

Noel and Cahl shared a look. Then, limping, they struggled up out of the crater.

The sky was split between startling blue and the swirling madness of the risen god, his wrath etched in lightning and burning flowers. A cohort of knights rode against him. Banners flew, burning through the fields surrounding Greenhall. There were bodies among the pageantry, dead horses and crushed ranks of lesser spears, sacrificed to the fight. Flames danced through the city. The wail of the dying and the lament of the survivors mingled with the choir's song, echoing down from the castle walls.

They turned from it all and fled from it all, passing unnoticed through the chaos. Of the voidfather they saw no sign, other than the chaos he had sown, and the death he had reaped.

Sophie Halverdt was at her meal when the gheist horn sounded. The attending knights, in their doublets of silk and golden chain, stared dumbfounded. Sophie swept to her feet and went to the window.

Beyond the wall to the citadel, out among the twisting streets of the Curse, a storm growled. As Sophie watched, a petal-cloaked god rose from between the buildings. Lightning danced across its body, and thunder shook the sky. She just laughed.

"The Lady Strife has given us a second chance," she said. "I let Sacombre slip through my fingers, and I feared the bright lady's judgment. But instead she has shown me mercy."

Several of the knights crowded behind her. Sir Grier seized the drapes and pulled them aside, to give the whole group a better view. An immediate babble of panic broke out around the table.

"My lady, we must secure the keep," Grier said. "Order the gates closed, and the guard mustered!" Sophie shook her head.

"I will not fail Strife twice, sir. The horn has sounded, and I will answer its call." She turned to the collected knights. "Bring my armor and my lance. See to your blades, and draw the bloodwrought iron from your sheathes. Strife is judging us for our failure, and giving us the gift of trouble. Pray that we die in her service, or live in her glory!"

By the time she had her armor on and her mount caparisoned, the first column of knights had already ridden out. Sophie cursed herself for not being at their head. The people needed to see their lady in their midst, leading their defense, protecting their homes.

She drew the blade her father had not lived long enough to gift her, the sword he had put aside to instead wield the cursed blade of Sacombre's betrayal. It was an ancient blade, older even than Greenhall. Her family had carried in north in the war that earned them their title—the war fought against the pagan tribes.

She raised the blade over her head.

The column that was riding with her, made up mostly of the knights who had been eating with her when the horn sounded, settled into silence. Sophie raised her chin and nodded to the gates of the keep.

"The eternal enemy is before us," she called. "It has worn many names over the centuries, and many faces, but it is always the same. Pagan! Tenerran! Children of winter and of death. Those of us who walk in the light will always be troubled by these bastards." She thrust the sword higher into the air, her voice louder with each word. "And we will always stand against them! Stand in the light. Stand in the majesty. Stand with Strife and your house will stand forever!"

Her call was met with cheers, the glory washing through the crowd, riling them to the point of madness. Grinning maniacally, Sophie lowered the blade and pointed it at the gate. The guards cranked the doors aside, and she spurred her charger forward. The column of knights leapt after her, banners fluttering, in full voice and armor, blades high, spirits higher.

Outside the gates, Greenhall was a warzone. The streets were abandoned, strewn with upturned carriages and barrels of food, their contents scattered across the cobbles. The braziers that stood at every corner still burned, though several had been knocked over. Cinders danced in the air, threatening a wildfire that could bring the city low, but Sophie had no time for that.

Strife was the goddess of fire. If she chose to consume the city, it was a gift Sophie was willing to give. Whatever the bright lady asked, she would surrender.

Her armored column thundered through the empty streets, turning toward the Curse, and the god who waited there. It was hard to get a good look at the gheist. There were glimpses between buildings, a wave of burning flowers, a fist crown in lightning, a face as smooth and bright as a silver plate, reflecting the light of flickering flame. Yet no sooner would she get a look at the gheist than the road would turn, or a cart would stand in their path, or a burning tower would intervene. Finally, Sophie just bent to her charger's neck and urged him to go faster.

Suddenly, they found themselves among broken horses and the discarded armor of knights, choking the road. It was the wreckage of the first column that had charged out of the gates. Sophie had to slow down and pick her way through the carnage. The gore turned her stomach, and the smell of spilled guts and blood made her head swim. She found herself wishing she'd brought the frairwood sachet she kept by her bed.

Beyond the dead, the road opened up into a broad avenue, and then a final turn brought them to an open square. The gheist stood at the center of square, surrounded by the remnants of the first column of knights. Their banners lay on the ground, along with a handful more of the dead and dying. The tight ranks of the column were broken. Individual knights rushed around the creature, giving half-hearted charges, wheeling past to strike whenever its attention was turned away, retreating just as quickly to the perimeter of the square.

There was no rhythm to it, no glory. Their bloodwrought spears tangled in the unnatural flesh of their foe, tearing holes in the cloak of flowers, wounds that trailed bright cinders after the spears passed through. The gheist barely noticed. It struck with lightning-wreathed fists, digging ruts in the ground, as intent on destroying buildings as it was on killing the knights that attacked it.

One of the knights wore a familiar sigil on her chest. It was Sir Lareux, who had attended her in the cloister—sent by her father to protect Sophie, should one of the other lords of the Circle try something clever with the heir of Greenhall. Lareux was gathering the scattered remnants of the column for a final charge. Sophie hailed her.

"Deva! Sir Lareux!" Sophie shouted. The knight's head snapped up. Her armor was dented across the shoulder, and her left arm hung limp against her saddle, but Lareux raised her sword and started toward Sophie's position.

Sophie waved her back. "We must strike together! As one, and from the other side." She pointed to the other end of the courtyard, where a small gathering of knights hid behind the wreckage of a carriage. "Rally those men, and attack on my signal!"

Lareux answered by wheeling her mount, shouting at the knights around her, and then charging to the ruined carriage. The knights there shied away, but Lareux urged them together, striking with the flat of her blade when they balked, circling them like a wolf. Like sheep, the knights clustered together, becoming more afraid of Lareux than they were of the gheist.

"Are all my father's bannermen cowards?" Sophie growled.

"It is hard to blame them for their fear, considering what we face, my lady," Grier said. "They are accustomed to fight steel and flesh, not the storm itself. Give them a spear wall to charge, and they will not balk. Ask them to die in battle with a god, however..." Grier shrugged. "It is difficult."

"Strife asks us to do difficult things," Sophie said. "She asks us to fight, to die, to raise the banner of summer in winter's darkness, to burn rather than rest." She whirled on the men following her, sword gripped angrily across her chest. "I ask no less of you. Do I have your faith, or will I need to find braver hearts to lead?"

"You have our faith, my lady," Grier said grimly. "And our hearts."

"Very well! You ask for a battle, to prove your loyalty? This is the battle I offer." She pointed her blade at the whirling storm of the gheist. "It is not the battle I expected, nor the death I would choose, but it is what Strife has given us, and I do not question the gifts of the bright lady. So come, let us fight, and die, and burn!"

She whirled her mount around and gave it the spur. As one, the riders of the column lurched forward. On the other side of the square, Lareux and her bolstered knights shouted and charged in.

The charge was a wild, rampaging gallop, Sophie's mount hammering across the stones of the courtyard in a thundering tattoo that filled her skull and shook her bones to the core. Her throat was ragged with screaming, the sweat from her brow stinging her eyes. The gheist was in front of her. The rest of the world narrowed into a pinprick, and with each crashing stride of her charger, the gheist got closer. It filled her vision, and then she could only see the closest edge of the storming god. It looked like a squall line, cutting across the square, a whipping wall of wind and lightning.

Closer, and the gale winds struck her helmet, drowning out all other sound.

Closer, and the winds were drowned out by growling thunder.

Closer…

And the gheist was gone.

The tip of Sophie's spear tore a hole in the air in front of her, so that it parted like a curtain before a play. Streamers of flame and ash spun down from the tear. Sophie's shoulders and knees hummed as the flesh of the gheist brushed against them. Her mount thrashed his head madly.

Then the gheist burst like a melon. A wave of light and life washed over them, carried on a wind that smelled of sulphur and loam. Lightning cracked against the nearest tower, sending showers of rock into the courtyard. Another stroke fell, this time farther out, and another, until the sky was alight with streaks of lightning. Sophie screamed and covered her head, but the thunder became one long, rumbling growl that rattled her teeth… and her faith.

A dozen fires started, then a hundred, uncountable. For a brief moment the city of Greenhall burned—even the stones—as though it was being consumed by Strife herself. And then the rain began.

Only a drop at first, splattering on Sophie's forehead as she looked up to watch her city being destroyed. In the next heartbeat the sky opened up, and a torrent such as she had never seen fell on the city. It quenched the fires, soaked the braziers, and turned the streets to mud. The lightning settled, changed to flickering light between clouds, and a low, comfortable rumble, distant and safe. The edge of the storm seemed to spread out beyond the walls of Greenhall, reaching the forest, stopping just beyond the tree line.

Mingled with the rain, half-burned flower petals fell. Of the gheist there was no sign. It was as if its fury had been spent in the storm, as though it couldn't keep a hold of itself, and so dissolved into the rain.

"Inside," Sophie said. She sheathed her blade. The rain was warm on her face, the water soaking into the padded lining of her armor. "Let's get inside, before this thing turns again."

She led her sodden knights back to the keep, passing the already bloating bodies of their companions. Lightning scars danced over the walls, and every tower bore the mark of the gheist's fury. Ruptured roofs, broken windows, cracked walls. The rain leaked in, soaking the castle in the remnants of the mad god of spring.

40

THE GROUND IN front of the Fen Gate was blackened and cracked. The walls were scoured clean by flames hotter than any fire could create. Nothing was left of the barricades that had separated Suhdrin from Tenerran. At the heart of this wasteland there were two figures.

One was small and dead, the other bent and shaking.

The Orphanshield made his slow, shuffling way across the dark earth, leaning heavily on his broken staff. The ironwood, blessed in Cinderfell, consecrated with the spirits of Frair Gilliam's ancestors, had split down the middle as though lightning-struck. The silver icons of Cinder and the inquisition were forge hot, the air around them bending in waves, the sweat from Gilliam's brow hissing when it struck the metal.

Tears cut dusty tracks down his wrinkled cheeks. The inquisitor stopped beside the dead child. He knelt, the ashen crust of the ground crumbling beneath his knee.

Marcel lay on his back. His eyes were open, though they swam with inky vapor, and tar-thick tears of his own ran down the corners of his face. The final wound, dealt by Frair Gilliam, steamed scarlet and ebon at the center of his chest. The horrific gheist that had possessed the young priest was gone. Its host had not survived the confrontation, had possibly been dead even before the gheist filled his bones. It didn't matter. Gilliam would always carry the burden of the child's death. His child. His orphan, and his weight to shoulder.

Gilliam cast his staff aside and dug calloused hands under the boy's body. The hard crust of the ground cut his knuckles, but he ignored it, gathering the dead child into his arms. He rose and looked around. A handful of soldiers stood near him, all of them looking as if they would rather die than draw his attention.

"Who has done this!" Gilliam wailed. "From whom must I take my justice?"

He was answered by silence. The disturbance of clouds that had formed during his battle with the gheist was slowly dissipating. The sun came out. Its heat and light mocked Gilliam's misery. He scowled at the sky.

"Answer me!" He held up the body, turning slowly.

The Suhdrin forces gathered in a huge semi-circle around the castle gates, their ranks motionless. Along the walls of the Fen Gate, those few Tenerrans who remained stood in quiet regard. "One of you knows," he said. "His blood is on someone's hands! Give me that criminal, and spare yourself my wrath." He stopped, facing the Suhdrin ranks. "He came from your camp. Did some twisted Suhdrin heart bow at the heretic's shrine? Must I seek to pay this debt in southern blood?"

"My frair, we would never lift a hand against the sworn of Cinder," one of the men said. He was a peasant, his gear patched together, but his eyes were earnest. Gilliam could always tell an honest man, especially when they were afraid. "He came from outside the camp," the man continued. "From the forest."

"You swear it?" Gilliam hissed, and his voice carried

power and threat. The man broke out in tears, but he nodded furiously. The inquisitor grunted, then turned to the gates of the castle. "And what of you, Tener? I came to sanctify this castle, to root out a heresy that your lord swore to me had passed. Does this look like an end to heresy?"

No one answered. Many along the walls shifted uncomfortably, looking to the spears beside them, weighing the faith of their fellows.

"*Someone killed this child!*" Gilliam roared. "And that same someone brought an abomination, a *devil*, into the world. To wear this boy's flesh." He shook the corpse like a banner, the dead child's arms flopping, his limp jaw clapping shut. The sound echoed off the scorched walls of the castle. "Do words fail you? Fine. Bring me your lord, and let him answer my questions."

"My frair, I saw..." it was a knight of MaeHerron who spoke. She was tall, as though hewn from an oak, her skin fairer than most of the other Tenerrans, and she had no ink on her face. The woman paused and went to a knee. "Lord Blakley abandoned the castle shortly after the gheist horn sounded. I saw him slip out the sally gate, along with most of his loyal knights."

"Houndhallow ran?" Gilliam said. His voice was dangerously low now, dangerously quiet. "Fine. Let him run. I am fit for the hunt. Sir, your faith and that of your house will be rewarded. Yield these gates. It's the time for this game of war to come to an end."

"My frair, I don't have the authority—"

"Yield the gate!" he shouted, and he started marching forward, turning his head to the quiet ranks of Suhdrin troops. "Into the castle, faithful servants of Heartsbridge. Strip the noble of their weapons, fill the dungeon with those of lesser birth. Kill any who resist you." He turned back to the Fen Gate, raising his voice, lacing it with naetheric power until it boomed from the skies like a thunderclap. "Kneel before Cinder and you will be spared! Raise your hand against the true servants of the gods, and your blood will be used in the forges of hell!"

The knight of MaeHerron who had been the first to speak quickly presented her sword, holding it out in her palms. One of the Suhdrin soldiers snatched it away, kicking her over as he passed. A cheer went up among the southerners as their column flooded through the open gates. The Tenerrans were too stunned to resist.

There were a few pockets of violence, the product of over exuberance or stubborn anger. Gilliam saw none of it. The frair marched into the ruined keep and lay Marcel's body on the throne. Then he turned to the crowd of Suhdrins who had followed him inside.

"Find Houndhallow, and bring him to me," he said. "Bring me the lord of dogs! Run him down. Bring him groveling at my feet." They roared in response, and the sound carried into the sky, through the broken walls of the Fen Gate, until it settled in the forests beyond.

The horn sounded. The hunt began.

The waters fell and drained away, taking the dead of Suhdra with them. Malcolm's column of knights stood in stunned silence, watching the unnatural river disappear into the ground.

Sorcha lowered her arms and smiled.

"Easy enough, if you're willing to break the rules of common war," she said.

"My lady, what has happened..." Sir Harrow started. The

woman shuddered as she stared at the duchess, touching fingers to her mouth, her eyes wide. "What has become of you?"

"Not now, Harrow," Malcolm snapped. He turned to his wife, pulling her to one side. "How could you do that? How dare you reveal yourself so, to these loyal knights?"

"How dare I?" Sorcha asked, raising her brows. "Would you rather I let them die in pointless war? Do you not value their lives, Malcolm?" She drew closer to him, as the smile lingering on her lips turned sour. "Do you not value mine?"

"That is not what I meant," Malcolm said. "These men and women are loyal to me and to the church. You have presented them with a decision they cannot make."

"Yes, I suppose I have," Sorcha said. She brushed her husband aside and addressed the narrow crescent of knights tarrying at the edge of the forest. They watched her nervously. "Who will you betray?" she asked them. "Which lord will you turn aside? My dear husband, who has clothed and fed and trained you, to whom you owe your honor and your blades?" She gestured to the sky. "Or the gods above?"

"It was her son what did this," one of the knights said. His name was Sir Flynn, the youngest of an old family, one that listed tribe elders and then earls in its history, before falling humble into the service of House Blakley. His wild red hair spoke to noble blood, despite his new station. Flynn sniffed and looked among the other knights. "Young Blakley brought that witch to us. He broke the old promises. Why are we supposed to take the heretic's brand for him?"

"Ian stood in the broken gate," Harrow said sharply. "Held back the Suhdrin horde, when the rest of us had failed. And he's the son of our lord. He deserves our loyalty, as does Lord Blakley."

"If he's worthy of our loyalty, where is he now?" Flynn asked. He turned to face Malcolm head on. "Houndhallow sent him away, didn't he? Sent him on pilgrimage with that grim bitch of Strife."

"Anyone who speaks that way of a vow knight has little to say to me about loyalty," Malcolm said.

"And yet he speaks so of your son, and let it be so," Sorcha said quietly. "It's no wonder your sworn blades are dithering over loyalty."

"There is little doubt what the church asks of us," Flynn said. "The lady is possessed. The cold reason of Cinder would see her cleansed."

"We will not speak of my wife like an infection to be burned away," Malcolm said. "You have put your faith in me. Have faith that I will make appropriate decisions regarding Lady Sorcha. The church will be brought into this—when the time is right, and the mood has shifted."

"When they won't simply kill her out of spite, you mean," Sir Doone said. The woman who had served as Sorcha's personal guard stood tensely beside her lady.

"When tempers have settled, yes," Malcolm agreed. He took a step forward, addressing the gathered knights who, until now, had known nothing of Sorcha's condition. He held out his hands. "I am not asking you for heresy, or even intrigue. I'm only asking you to trust me. Trust the lord who has led you in war and in peace, around whose banner you gathered on the fields of White Lake. I will see my wife to holy health, with the blessing of the church. I just won't lose her to the inquisition."

The crescent of knights stood still, looking back and forth from Sorcha to Malcolm to their own ranks. Finally, Sir

Flynn took a step forward. He drew his sword. Sir Doone's blade was in her hand immediately, the steel whispering eagerly from the scabbard. Everyone froze.

Flynn smiled at Sir Doone, then went to one knee, presenting his sword in uplifted palms and bowing his head.

"I swore an oath to you, of service and of faith. I will keep that oath. Gods know you've earned it, Reaverbane."

"I rode beside you in the charge at White Lake, and stood by your son on the walls of the Fen Gate," Sir Harrow said. She knelt. "I am not going to abandon you now."

The rest of the knights knelt, one by one, whispering oaths of their own, to the Hound, the hallow. Reaverbane. Even iron in the blood. Sir Doone was the last to kneel, and her sword tipped in Sorcha's direction. Malcolm sighed.

"Would that I were worthy of your loyalty," Malcolm said. "I swear to earn it."

"Your son would be here as well, on his knee with the rest of them," Sorcha whispered. "If you hadn't sent him away with that damned priestess."

"Priestess," Malcolm answered, sudden horror in his voice. "Gods, the priestess!"

She was where Malcolm had left her. Her breathing was shallow, she was still terribly pale, but her wounds had stopped bleeding and some color had returned to her face. Her horse cropped nearby, oblivious to its rider's distress. Malcolm knelt beside her, taking her hand.

"We have to get her to the castle," he said. "Flynn, Doone, give me a hand."

"You will reopen her wounds," Doone said. "Better to bring a medic here."

"The Suhdrin forces will be forcing the gates by now," Flynn said. "The barbers will have their hands full with our own wounded."

"We can't leave her here," Malcolm said. "The Orphanshield will have my skin if one of his pet children dies in my care."

"What were you thinking, letting a priestess ride out with you?" Sorcha asked.

"It wasn't my choice," Malcolm muttered. "She was very insistent, but it doesn't matter now. Flynn, return to the castle and bring one of the inquisitor's people to us. Even a priest of Cinder should be able to stabilize the child."

"Or usher her into the quiet, if we're too late," Flynn said, but he mounted smoothly and rode hard for the sally port. Malcolm looked to his wife.

"You will need to hide, my love," Malcolm said. "We have gone through too much to reveal you now."

"The child already knows," Sorcha said, bending closer. "You know, I could..."

"No," Malcolm said. "The child is better dead than damned."

"Oh? And what about me?" Sorcha asked. "Am I better dead, my love?"

"You aren't yet dead, and far from damned," Malcolm said. "I will see you healed, my love. Have faith."

"Healed? Or fixed?" Sorcha turned squarely to face her husband. Her pale skin flashed with bright light. "Am I a cracked vase to be repaired, husband? So I can be returned to a place of honor on your mantle?"

"Gods, Sorcha, you know that isn't..."

"No, I don't know, actually. What I *know* is that you

have hidden me away since this happened, sent my son into exile as punishment for my condition, imprisoned the woman who saved my life, and now stand on the edge of heresy to keep the inquisition from finding me. You're so damned convinced that I can be fixed, I wonder how you'll react when you learn that there is no solution for my particular problem," Sorcha said. "Or worse, what you will say if I learn the price of my repair, and refuse it?"

"Sorcha..." Malcolm said sadly. Sorcha cut him off.

"These knights have kept their loyalty to you, in spite of your actions. Perhaps you could learn from them. I know I would appreciate it," she said. "I'm sure your son would have, as well."

Malcolm stood quietly, working his jaw. He was about to answer when Sir Flynn returned, riding as though his mount was on fire.

"My lord! To Houndhallow!" Flynn shouted. He dismounted at a run, grabbing Malcolm's shoulders. "The inquisition has betrayed us. Marchand's men have taken the castle without a fight. Your banners are struck, and your men are being marched into the dungeons. We must flee to Houndhallow!"

"Surely there is some mistake," Malcolm said. "Frair Gilliam's writ was to cleanse the castle of pagan influence. He would never take a hand in our battle."

"You overestimate the faith of the inquisitor," Sorcha said sourly. "He will do what he thinks is best. For the church, not Tener—and certainly not for us." At that moment another rider scrambled up, a man they had sent to scout the Suhdrin flank. His eyes were wide.

"Suhdrin banners along the godsroad, my lord," he said.

"They have passed us, and seem to be hunting."

"They seek us, no doubt," Flynn said. "They must think we fled before the battle."

"If the road north is closed to us, we must go elsewhere. Doone, you've spent a month in these woods. Is there another way?"

"North? No," Sir Doone said, shaking her head. "Deer paths lead around the castle, but the Fen is too dense to our north. We might make it through eventually, but we don't have the supplies to support so many riders."

"Then we go elsewhere. We go south. Last I heard, the Reaveholt was besieged but still held." Malcolm gathered the reins of his mount. "Doone, lead us by these shadowed paths as far south as you can. We'll risk the godsroad only once we're well away."

"And what of the girl?" Harrow asked. "Do we leave her for the Suhdrins to find? She may die in the interim."

Malcolm paused. He sighed deeply, then turned to his wife and nodded.

"Do what you must," he said. "Join us when it is done. I would not witness such heresy."

"Of course not, my love," Sorcha said. Malcolm mounted quickly and trotted off. Most of the knights followed him, but Doone and the others who had served Sorcha for the past month remained behind. The duchess knelt beside the priestess and smiled.

"The gods will forgive you for this, my dear," she whispered. "As they will forgive me."

41

THE SHOULDERS OF the gheist scraped the doma's ceiling. The summer chimes, packed away for the season, tore free from their moorings and spun through the roaring winds that cloaked the creature. The sound of it was like a vault of coins falling on hard stone. The pews shifted, the storm plowing down the aisle to make room for the feral god and his attendant shaman.

Elsa sighed. This fight had gone on too long. She was barely recovered from the blizzard. Her own impatience had forced her out of bed, forced her into this situation. If she'd stayed down, the people of Halfic wouldn't have felt compelled to throw her and Ian out of town. They would have left the gates closed, and whatever wards they were employing would have kept this monster outside.

She wasn't the type to stay down, though. Not even now. As the gheist hauled its ponderous form into the doma, she slowly got to her feet, using the sword as a crutch until she was standing. Ian watched her nervously. He had a good heart, she mused.

Pity he was going to die this way.

Maybe Halfic's people would live, though. Those children. Their parents. Maybe they were fleeing from the village even now, out into that storm. It wasn't a good death, but they stood a better chance at living than if they had remained.

"Let's end this," Elsa said. She was weaving on her feet, her legs unsteady, the pain in her bones an endless roar. Channeling the bright lady's blessings was hard on the body. Harder without her sword and the bloodwrought magic it contained. At least she had the sword back. She held the blade in front of her, almost losing her balance as she brought it up. Frustration kicked through her blood, and she fed it into her muscles, bearing down on the weakness with an iron will. She steadied and fell into the familiar balance of a guard stance.

"We've played around long enough," she growled. "Summer is waiting for you, pagan. The dawn will always come."

"Not for you it won't, vow knight," the shaman responded. "Never again." The gheist surged forward, dragging the shaman behind it. A wall of fog blanketed the doma in its wake. At her side, Ian stumbled back, hiding behind one of the lesser shrines that lined the sanctuary. She had a brief flash of memory, being regaled with stories about this boy and how he'd faced a gheist on the fields of Greenhall during the Allfire. He had learned a lot since then.

Thank the gods.

They came together just in front of the altar.

Her opponent struck, and Elsa parried, stepped aside, and was forced to parry again as the feral spirit swung its ice-sheathed fists in broad, hall clearing arcs. Elsa's blade glowed hot, sparks cascading from the edge with each blow. The magic written into her blood and forged into the blade flashed bright, light leaking through her skin from the veins beneath.

The fog swept around them, cloaking the altar and hanging like a tapestry from the ceiling of the doma, but the heat of Elsa's defense burned it away before it could creep any closer. Strands of it hung in tattered streams at the perimeter of the fight.

The gheist fell back. The gray-white mass of its icy fists was fractured, bright white lines cracking through its knuckles. Several of Elsa's ripostes struck true, leaving long scars across its chest. The shaman at the gheist's center bowed in concentration, his hands clenched desperately around the dagger that seemed to be the focus of his power. Around him, the gheist shifted like a cloak that kept slipping from his shoulders.

Perhaps she wasn't the only one feeling the weight of their fight, Elsa mused with a certain satisfaction. Perhaps there was a way out of this after all.

"Your wards are strong," the shaman said. "Your inquisitor taught you well."

"My inquisitor taught me more about soup than wards," Elsa said. "Come, shaman. You tarry too long in this world. I mean to part you from it." She took a step forward. The gheist retreated, flinching back like a shadow in flickering light. Elsa pressed the attack.

"Elsa! The altar!" Ian shouted from the side. "He's trying to draw you away!"

She paused, unwilling to take her eyes off the enemy in front of her. Instead she unfolded her attention, wrapping the room in the focus that usually stayed in her sword. To her surprise, the doma was crossed with magical power. It laced through the air, filling the place and stretching to the walls outside, anchoring wards that Elsa only now sensed, because they weren't directed at her and she hadn't looked for them before.

The entire pattern was centered in the altar behind her. The threads weren't the bright energy that sparked through her blood, but the cool, smooth shadow of the naether. Inquisitor magic. Winter's power. But there was no inquisitor in Harthal.

In the brief moment that Elsa was distracted by the wards, the gheist renewed its attack. Its first blow knocked her from her feet, driving her back to the altar. She only kept a grip on her sword by luck and habit. Now that she was aware of them, Elsa understood that the wards cushioned the blow. She scrambled to her feet, but the bank of fog filled the room, hiding the gheist along with everything else.

"Ian! Can you see anything out there? Do you know where it is?" Her words were muffled by the damp air. She sketched a line of light with her blade, throwing it into the fog like a whip, but the cloud quickly absorbed it. "This is your hope, coward?" Elsa said. "To strike me from behind? Is that the only way you can win?"

"Freedom at any cost. Honor is a light price, and easily paid." The shaman's voice came from everywhere and nowhere, echoing through the close shroud of the fog. "I will see you bleed, summer child."

"I've blood enough to spare," Elsa said. "You must—"

A patch of fog to her right darkened, resolved into the gheist before she could turn to face it. Elsa had only a breath to twist, the forte of her blade coming up close to her body, the full force of her blood pressing the defense. The creature hit her and she fell, scrambling mindlessly behind the altar, the pain roaring through her body as her mind struggled to grapple with whatever fresh injury had been wrought.

Howling, the shaman drove the gheist forward. His grip

on the spirit appeared to be failing, and yet he spurred it on. Another massive fist swung at Elsa, but landed on the stone altar instead.

The altar cracked, and like a net drawn out of the ocean, the wards snapped back into the naether, spinning into the altar's splintered face, disappearing from the world. The shaman laughed hysterically. Whatever nuisance the wards had been, they were gone. His binding of the gheist visibly tightened, the shifting cloak of power cutting trim. He stood over Elsa.

"Another glory for my name," the shaman said. "Another dead vow knight under my fist. You all die this way, bitch. Ashen and hot, like a fire waiting to be stamped out."

Elsa didn't have the energy to answer. She lay behind the broken altar, sword still in hand, but the fight was gone from her. The mists slowly cleared, rotating around the doma like water draining into a hole. As the walls resolved and Ian's shadowy form appeared near the door, Elsa realized it wasn't a metaphor at all.

The fog *was* draining from the room, spinning faster and faster, disappearing into the cracked altar. The shaman didn't seem to notice, but the gheist clasped to his shoulders was caught in the current, as well.

The collapse was sudden. The gheist's fists calved, undercut and drawn away from the main body. Shards of bright ice flew into the altar, and then the very essence of the creature began to dissolve. The shaman realized his grip was failing, but half a breath too late. Power flared through his dagger, veins of light that traveled up his arms and wrapped his skull as he pushed everything into maintaining his control, but it was hopeless.

The gheist fell apart in shrieking horror, its essence

sucked into the altar. Or more precisely, to what lay *inside* the altar. As Elsa and Ian and the stunned shaman watched, a dark shape unfolded from the broken platform, tar-black arms and teeth like hooked daggers rising up, its body shifting like a fountain of pitch. It looked around with an eyeless face, shrieked once, then fled down the aisle and out into the storm.

"Those weren't wards at all," Elsa whispered. "It was a prison."

The shaman, robbed of his might, dropped unceremoniously to the floor, falling to one knee and crouching. Once the night-black spirit scampered past, he wasn't far behind.

"Ian!" Elsa shouted.

"I have it," Ian said, stepping smoothly from beside the door. He held a massive candlestick in both hands. "Best you stopped there."

The shaman ignored him, running faster, looking to dodge past. Ian shrugged, wound up and took a hard swing at the pagan's head.

A blade came from nowhere and blocked him. Sparks flew, and the shaman ducked past and disappeared into the courtyard. A figure, the blocking sword in his hand, stepped out of the shadows of the doorway and watched the fleeing man.

Ian turned on this new threat, ready to strike again. The figure threw his hood back. Ian's face went pale, first in horror, then anger.

The man's face was a horror show. It looked like a clean porcelain mask that had been broken, then fitted to a wax head that then melted, pulling the pieces of the mask apart like a puzzle being undone. The flesh beneath was raw and red, and his face shifted strangely as he talked.

"Peace, Blakley," he said. "We are on the same path, you and I."

"We thought Sacombre killed you at the Fen Gate!"

"Perhaps he did. This feels like I always thought dying would." The man turned to watch as the shaman reached the gate. The snows picked up, and the figure disappeared from sight.

"Why did you do that?" Elsa said. She stumbled toward the door, trying to get a better look at the man with the sword. "Why did you let him go?"

"If you catch him, it will make following him incredibly difficult," Sir Volent said. The former knight marshal of Halverdt glanced at them, smiling. The gesture turned his face into a pinwheel of fractured flesh. "And my hunt is not yet finished. Not by a long shift."

Aedan crawled through the snow. There was blood in his mouth, and the streaks of blackened flesh that ran up his forearms were starting to throb painfully.

Breaking through the wards at Harthal and then binding the gheist of the blizzard had cost him dearly, but it had been worth it. Hunting down the vow knight who was blood-bonded to the Adair bitch, then defeating her in combat... he had done his duty to the voidfather. Aedan had won.

And then he had lost, and he was still unsure what had happened.

Finding the blizzard gheist had been a gift. Some dark spirit moved at the center of that storm. It had taken all of his will to bind it, and Aedan's control of the god had been light, but still he thought he would be able to hold the spirit together. When the altar broke, though, Aedan sensed a hunger like nothing he had ever known, an endless void that took and took and would never be full. The thing hidden in the altar had fed off Aedan's bound god and then, replenished, had fled.

Aedan was lucky to escape. He didn't know the man who had saved him, couldn't even make sense of the brief glimpse he had gotten of his face, but he hoped to thank him someday. Now that he was free, Aedan had to return to the conclave and report his failure. If he lived that long.

He dragged himself to the crest of a hill and looked back down on Harthal. The storm was breaking. Whatever dark spirit had driven the blizzard was gone. There would be pursuit, as soon as the vow knight recovered. The earl of that damned place might even send out his own men. Aedan didn't understand what had happened there, why such a lonely place had been warded so strongly, but it didn't matter.

Aedan looked down at his hands. His flesh was cracked, blood seeping from knuckles and palms, the ache going down to his bones. There were other wounds, deeper and more complicated, suffered when the gheist was taken from him. This must be how Gwen felt—the emptiness, the pain, as though something stitched into his bones had been yanked free. He tried to stand and failed. He lay there for a long time, staring up at the rapidly clearing sky.

"Too far to go, and I'll never get there like this," he muttered to himself. "The voidfather will have to wait." Blood filled Aedan's mouth again, and he coughed it out. Bright red against the snow. Aedan tried to laugh, but the pain was too much. "Ah, Fianna. To see your eyes again. I have carried this as far as I can."

"Perhaps I can carry it for you. *With* you." The voice

came from the shadows, from beneath a holly shrub that hadn't yet bloomed. The sound was silk. Aedan propped himself up on one arm and squinted.

The shadows gathered, pouring out onto the snow like ink. Talons clicked against ice, and head, smooth and black, only a mouth that stretched and stretched, its teeth endless. The thing that had broken free from the altar.

"You are of the faithful, yes?" the gheist whispered. "Not one of those calendar priests. I know the taste of you." Black tendrils slid over Aedan's head, pressing into his mind. He lay there, agape. "Yes, good. An emptiness, and you know of the iron girl. You even… you hate her. Very good."

"What are you?" Aedan asked. He tried to feel out the edges of the gheist, but his thoughts were turned away. He had never known a deeper spirit.

"I am the quiet," the gheist said. "The ending. The darkness at the end of every life, a void never to be filled. Let me carry your burden. Let me take you down the road you wish. To Fianna, yes? And the voidfather."

"Yes," Aedan said. His life was already draining out of him. Why not carry his death with him, as well. "Yes."

The gheist slithered forward, inky and smooth. The binding was quick, like a shadow falling across a field, like the sun falling into night.

3
DEMON NIGHTS

42

MARTIN WALKED NUMBLY through the wreckage of LaGaere's camp. The dead were twisted, their bodies torn open, the wounds smooth and bloodless. The ground was cracked, the tall grasses of the moors burned into ash that drifted in the air. Sacombre lay at Lucas's feet. The high inquisitor was bleeding from the mouth.

The witch would come no closer. Fianna stopped at the edge, away from the charred ground and burned grass. She wouldn't even look at the dead.

"What happened?" Martin asked. Lucas spared him only a glance before returning his attention to Sacombre's limp form.

"He killed them," the frair replied. "He retains more power than I knew. We will have to keep him bound from this moment forth."

"Killed them? The men who were helping him escape?" Martin turned in a slow circle at the camp's center, taking in the destruction. "But why?"

"Because he's a twisted bastard," Lucas hissed. The priest drew a length of graying rope from his bag and trussed the high inquisitor's hands. Black iron icons of the church of Cinder jangled quietly from the bonds. He whispered to them, and runes of violet light flashed in the air. Sacombre moaned. "Help me get him to his feet."

Martin shook himself out of his stupor and moved to Lucas's side. They heaved the old man to his feet. He was thin and light, like a bundle of sticks wrapped in mud, but even so Lucas swayed on his feet with the effort, screwing his eyes shut. Martin touched his elbow, and the priest flinched away. Sacombre slumped between them.

"Are you alright, frair?" Martin asked. Lucas waved a hand, but didn't open his eyes. Martin waved to the witch urgently. She shook her head, but when he signaled again, she came reluctantly. "Take the high inquisitor."

"The bonds..." she whispered. "They burn."

"Then don't touch the bonds," he hissed. The witch took Sacombre by the shoulders, wincing. Martin turned back to Lucas, gripped his elbow, and led him away from the carnage. "You must rest. We'll need to..." he looked around the camp. The horses were dead, along with the rest of LaGaere's force. "None of us will be riding."

"No, Sacombre saw to that. He has forced our hand." Lucas sat heavily in the grass, nearly pulling Martin down with him. "I would rather continue on foot, but we will have to make our way to Gallowsport."

Fianna followed closely, Sacombre on her shoulder. When they reached Lucas's side, she grunted and rolled the high inquisitor to the ground. He fell like a bag of rocks. The impact seemed to wake him, because his red-rimmed eyes snapped open in shock. Fianna sat down beside him, leaving only the young knight on his feet.

"If LaGaere meant to betray us, he may have allies in the city," Martin said. "The earl of the Black Isle was always loyal to the inquisition."

"Cinderfell has given him enough business over the years," Lucas said. "I am still a priest of Cinder. Perhaps his loyalty will extend to me."

"Over the high inquisitor? I would not lay a wager on that."

"The disgraced high inquisitor, traveling to Heartsbridge to be judged," Lucas corrected him. "Don't forget that we're in the right, here. We are bound to Cinder's justice, not Sacombre."

"In the right," Fianna said quietly. "The priests of Cinder are always so sure they are in the right. It allows them to..." she paused, glancing toward the twisted bodies of LaGaere and his men. "It allows them to justify anything."

"Sacombre was certainly willing to bend the truth for his purposes," Lucas agreed. The witch looked at him with fear in her eyes.

"And what of you, Frair?" she asked. "Would you do the same?"

"This was done by Sacombre's hands," Lucas said sharply. "He and I are entirely different." As he spoke, Martin looked between the frair and the witch uncertainly. A heavy silence hung over the trio. Finally, Fianna shook her head.

"As you say," Fianna relented. "His heart is certainly dark enough."

"LaGaere didn't feel that way," Martin said uncomfortably.

"No," Lucas agreed, "and look at the cost he paid."

The young man was silent for a minute. He looked from Lucas to the crowded dead. "Yes," he said. "The price of heresy."

Fianna snorted behind them, drawing Martin's eye. She shook her head.

"I will meet a fine reception at the Black Isle," Fianna

said, "even as your prisoner. The earl of that place only knows one path for heretics."

"It doesn't matter," Lucas replied. "We have no other choice. Neither Sacombre nor I are in any shape to walk to Heartsbridge. Gallowsport is our only choice."

"You could always leave us behind, Martin Roard," Sacombre mumbled. The high inquisitor's voice was dry and his lips cracked, but there was iron in his words. "Go for help. I'm sure the son of Stormwatch would be welcomed in the earl's court."

"No, we all go," Martin said. "I don't trust you alone with the frair."

"Afraid he might kill me, and escape the court's justice?" Sacombre said wryly. "Or afraid that I might slip my bonds and disappear into the night."

"Both," Martin said, and Lucas laughed weakly.

"The boy accounts my taste for vengeance too highly," he said. "We will rest here tonight, and continue in the morning. On foot, Gallowsport is days away, and we haven't enough food to tarry."

"Then we make for Noosehall," Martin said. He squinted nervously at the circle of dead Suhdrin knights not twenty feet away. He didn't fancy the idea of spending the night there, but he also didn't think the two priests of Cinder could go any further without some rest.

So he pushed some grass down into a bed, then curled up. He thought the others had already drifted off until the high inquisitor spoke.

"Die here, die on the road, or die in Heartsbridge," Sacombre said. "Doesn't matter to me."

No one said anything else. There was no talk of watches.

All four of them slept where they lay, Sacombre still in his bonds, Lucas leaning against his staff, Fianna between them. Only Martin kept himself a little bit apart.

In the dead camp, the flames of the campfire flickered until their fuel was gone, then ghosted away into embers and ash. Morning was far away.

The Gallowmoors stretched out before them in soft hills and jagged copses, the lone darkwood pines that gave the region its name towering over the horizon. The winds that swept through the plains and whipped the grasses in swirling waves carried a hint of the sea, though it would be days before they caught sight of the waters of Felling Bay.

Forming a line through the grass, they fell into a rhythm—march and rest, march and eat, march and sleep. Martin led, with Fianna behind him and Sacombre following her. The two prisoners were bound together by Lucas's chiming rope of icons. The frair took up the rear of their column, trailing farther and farther behind with each step. Martin was forced to stop frequently to let the man catch up, tarrying longer among the grasses than he liked, in order to let the man rest.

The sun burned their skin and left their lips cracked and dry. Their food lasted a day, though it was stretched as far as they could manage. Their water lasted longer, but it tasted of silt, leaving a gray coating on their tongues and in their throats. They slept where they fell.

The sun woke them, and the pain in their backs.

On the third day, when their journey had stretched longer than Martin expected, Lucas motioned for his attention and led him to the top of one of the gentle ridges that folded through the moors. The old man looked withered.

"Frair," Martin said carefully as they crested the ridge. They stopped and turned to look down at the two prisoners sitting glumly below. "Is it safe to leave them alone?"

"We are past considering what is safe, and what is wise," Lucas said. His voice was crumbling around the edges. "We must discuss what is to come."

"When we get to Gallowsport?" Martin said. "I'm beginning to doubt that we will ever arrive."

"Yes. We have slowed." Lucas sighed. "I have slowed. I am accustomed to having a knight of the vow at my side, to guard my dreams while I slept. The duty is costing me more than I expected."

"Have I not served as a worthy guard, my frair?"

"You have done as well as you are able," Lucas said, waving off the boy's concern. "This is my burden, son. Sacombre's chains weigh heavy on my mind. I should not have mentioned it. We will get to Gallowsport soon. A day, two at most."

"Longer than two days, and we will run out of more than water," Martin said.

"That will be a kind of justice for the high inquisitor, I suppose. Starvation in the wilds, and his bones cooked to crack in the sun. Summer has its own judgment." Lucas's mind seemed to wander, his eyes losing focus for several moments while the wind beat against the two men.

He shook himself back to alertness. "It will not come to that," he said. "I will not let it. We will make Gallowsport, and then our true troubles will begin."

"Dying of starvation isn't trouble enough?"

"Far from it," Lucas answered seriously. "Know that we are alone, young Stormwatch. Now, and in the city. We don't know what allies Sacombre has among the lords, or even in the church." His voice gathered strength as he talked. "The inquisition is knitted into the fabric of Gallowsport, as much as it is in Heartsbridge and Cinderfell. We depend on the Black Isle to carry out certain sentences, and they depend on us for their trade. There is no question Sacombre has friends there."

"The question is whether those friends would commit heresy in his name," Martin said.

"Heresy is a slippery concept," Lucas said. "We can argue about what is necessary and true, but the gods do not always share their will with their servants. Sometimes faith is justification enough. Other times not." The frair sat down heavily again, as though considering what was to come had at first strengthened him, and then stolen that same strength. Martin stepped forward to offer the frair his hand, but Lucas shrugged him off. "Whatever Sacombre's allies do, they will believe they are doing the right thing. That's what makes them dangerous."

"You're worried someone will come for him? I thought we would be able to reach out to the church once we were in Gallowsport. Get an escort, at least, if not another vow knight to see us safely to Heartsbridge."

"The vows are spread throughout Tenumbra, in preparation for winter's season. The gheists have come early this year, and hard. As for my brothers of the inquisition," Lucas shrugged. "I would have trusted the likes of Frair Allaister with my life, if I had not met him in battle in the Fen. After LaGaere's betrayal, I don't even feel comfortable seeking help among the lords of Suhdra. Strange times, Stormwatch. Strange and dangerous times."

"So what will we do? There's no way we pass unseen

through the port. Sacombre is known—both his station and his treachery—and the witch..." Martin sighed, nodding down at the prisoners. Fianna was still in her forest clothes, rough leather and tribal icons, but even in Suhdrin clothes she would have stood out. "There will be no disguising what she is. Especially bound in an inquisitor's chains."

"We will stay in Gallowsport long enough to regain our strength and supply our bags, and then we continue south along the coast."

"Not by ship?" Martin asked. "Surely that would be faster, and speed is becoming an attractive alternative to trudging through the wilds."

"We will be spotted in Gallowsport. Once that happens, Sacombre's allies will assume that we travel over the water. The ports from here to Godsmouth will be watched, and the canals, as well. We will have no chance of arriving in Heartsbridge unheralded." He gave Martin a meaningful look. "Stealth is more important than speed, for now."

"Still, once we don't arrive on any of the expected ships, surely—"

"I am not here to discuss plans with you, Martin," Lucas said abruptly, the last of his strength mustered. "You have proven yourself a worthy friend, and a fine sword, but the high inquisitor's transport is my charge, and mine alone. We will follow the coastal road until the high ridge, and then turn toward the mountains. I know certain roads among the hills that will not be closely watched."

"Those mountains belong to Marchand," Martin said. "Most of his army sits in siege around the Fen Gate. If any lord cannot be trusted..."

"I am familiar with those mountains," Lucas said sternly.

"Perhaps more familiar than Highope himself. We will pass safely to Heartsbridge by those roads. I promise."

"As you say. And what of our prisoners?" Martin asked. "Will they behave once we are in the city? It will only take a word from the high inquisitor to draw attention. Without an escort, we will be hard pressed to protect them from a mob."

Lucas was silent for a long moment. Martin thought he had drifted off again until the frair stretched his arms and rolled his knuckles together. In that brief moment the old man looked like a pit fighter. When he spoke, his voice simmered with undisguised anger.

"It will be a difficult thing, my friend," the inquisitor said, "but sometimes Cinder asks us to do difficult things. That is the nature of winter. Winter, and the gray lord's will."

43

AS SOON AS the fight ended, the storm passed. The gray fury had hammered the walls every day since they arrived at Harthal, but now it lifted and a clear blue sky moved in to replace it.

Less than an hour after the combat concluded, the sun turned the fields of snow into brilliant ivory. A slow melt began, creating a thousand singing streams of water trickling down the stones of the keep. The people of Halfic's tiny realm emerged from hiding. Even the children, maimed and horrific.

Elsa burst out of the doma, slamming the already-broken doors against the stone. The earl followed meekly in her wake.

"Do you know the business of a vow knight, Harthal? Are you familiar with our duties?" Elsa snapped. "Have I come far enough north that oaths of the Lightfort have been forgotten?"

"No, my lady," Halfic said. The earl was the color of sour milk, and he kept his eyes averted when Elsa whirled around to face him. When she said nothing, he ventured more. "The order of the vow is respected in my halls, my lady. As it is in all the north."

"And yet, when you had a gheist infesting those halls and a vow knight to hand, it never occurred to you to seek that knight's aid," Elsa said. Behind the earl, Ian crept silently out of the ruined doma. Elsa ignored him. "Instead, you sought to deceive me. When discovered, your people attacked me, and your frair *led* that attack. Tell me why I shouldn't try you for heresy right now, Harthal? Tell me why I shouldn't draw this blade and pronounce judgment on you and every godsloving idiot in this castle?"

Halfic didn't answer at first. He was quiet, his shoulders slumped, his hands knotted at his waist. Elsa's fist grew restless on her scabbard. She was about to draw and ask her questions again when he spoke.

"They were defending their children, sir," Halfic said. "We all were." He looked up, a resigned frown on his face. "People do foolish things for their children."

Elsa stood quietly for a long moment, her shoulders heaving with the fight that had so recently ended, the blood still on her lips. She flexed her fingers around the grip of her sword one more time.

"Very foolish things, Harthal," she said. "Very foolish, indeed."

"Leave the man in peace," Volent said. He was still in the doma. All she could see of him was the fractured mask of his face, and his shoulders, broad and dark.

"You stay out of this," Ian snapped. The prince of Houndhallow stood just outside the door, his arms crossed, face creased in a furious frown. "Since when does the Deadface argue peace?"

"That is a broken name, and one to which I no longer answer," Volent said. He came into the light. His maimed features made it hard to read his emotions, but the man spoke gently. "This is the north, LaFey. Vow knights have earned a reputation for slaughter."

"That's rich, coming from you," Elsa said stiffly. "The knights of the vow are sworn to protect these people from the gheists. What sort of reputation do you mean?"

"You just threatened to murder every person in this village because their lord lied to you," Volent said. When Elsa didn't answer immediately, he continued. "Why do you think the people of Gardengerry abandoned their homes, the places where they and their parents and their grandparents have lived and done business for generations? For fear of the inquisition—and don't get precious with the difference between an inquisitor and a knight of the vow," he said, cutting her off before she could speak. "They both come wielding the church's justice. To these people, there is no difference."

"You don't understand the danger of what was done," Elsa said. She was largely ignoring Halfic now, her attention entirely on Sir Volent. "This man, untrained in the naetheric arts, shrouded this place in wards. That alone could have destroyed this village and created a blight on the landscape that would have taken generations to scrub clean." She turned to Halfic. "Did you know that, my lord? The wards of naether can draw the gheists just as easily as repel them? The consecration of holy ground is a skill best left to the inquisition."

"I only wanted to keep my people safe, and the books..."

"The books. Gods save us from curious lords and their books," Elsa said. "Speaking of which, I will be taking those with me. Or, no, they should be burned. Either way, you had no business with them."

"Of course, sir," Halfic said. "I will gather them."

"No," she said, and she gestured. "Ian, go to the earl's chambers and collect everything made of paper. See that nothing is left behind." She turned back to Halfic. "Go with him. Demonstrate your good faith by turning over any scrap that might be heretical. You have lied once to a vow knight. Do not make me ensure you are incapable of lying ever again."

Halfic bowed and rushed away, his robes shushing through the snow.

"What of the frair?" Ian asked.

"Find him, if you can, but see to the books first," she said. Ian nodded and slipped off after the earl. Volent watched her closely.

"You won't find the man," he said. "Unless he has a death wish, that priest will have gone over the wall the moment the altar cracked."

"I will still hunt." She waited until Ian and the earl were well gone, then turned toward him. "Young Houndhallow asks a good question. What are you doing here? Shouldn't you be at Greenhall, learning the will of your master's heir?"

"Tomas Halverdt was my master, and a poor one at that," Volent said. "I will not answer to his child, nor to any other master, ever again. As to how I came here, that is simple enough. I followed you, because you were following her."

"Gwen Adair," Elsa said. Volent nodded.

"The same. Though what led you to this cursed hall is a mystery to me." Volent looked around at the ruined courtyard, the stables already crawling with workers salvaging horses and wood. "Gwendolyn isn't here. She has never been here. Your hunt has gone astray, sir."

"That thing, the gheist that came out of the altar… that was it. The gheist Gwen dragged to the witches' hallow. The one your high inquisitor bound to his soul. The god of death." Elsa loomed closer to Volent. "That it is what drew you, Volent. You have always been drawn to death."

The knight smirked and pushed himself away from the doma. Though his blade was sheathed, Elsa subconsciously shifted her guard, ready to defend herself against an attack. He ignored her, strolling out into the middle of the courtyard, where he tugged his gloves off and fastidiously tucked them into his belt. Volent's hands were a jumble of scars.

"Look what they make us do, sir," he said quietly. "The church. The gheists. Our masters. Gardengerry abandoned, its priests murdered by angry peasants who were led there by a priest of your inquisition. Tener and Suhdra at war, and my lord dead at the hand of the god he loved most. The steps we dance, all to their song."

"The world isn't a dance, Volent," Elsa said. "It's not some kind of pageant, and if we don't like our part we just throw away the pages. The church is harsh, yes, but rightly so. The people fear us, but when the gheist comes, those same people sound the horn and stand aside while we ride to battle. To save them." She set herself firmly between Volent and the doma, hands on hips, cloak thrown back so her armor glittered in the newly revealed sunlight. "That is what the church asks of us, and I answer its call."

"As did Sacombre," Volent said. "Look where that got him."

"I never thought I'd hear heresy from a servant of Greenhall. What would Duke Halverdt say to that?"

"My lord is dead," Volent said sharply. "By Sacombre's will, and still Suhdra raises a flag of war in his name. The lords of the circle know that they were deceived, but pride keeps them fighting, and for what?"

"Sacombre will see justice," Elsa said. "If any priest can

bring the high inquisitor to trial, it is Frair Lucas. Have faith in that."

"In the man, perhaps, but not his god," Volent said.

Elsa drew her blade. Volent turned around, the faintest amusement framing his broken face.

"That brings your sword out? After everything the earl has done, and his frair. With a shaman freshly fled into the wilds and the wayward son of a Tenerran lord in your company, the thing that tips you into violence is my unwillingness to bow to a god whose servants murdered my lord and manipulated this land into war," he said. "That's a tricky faith you have, sir."

"Why are you here?" Elsa demanded, grinding her teeth. She moved closer.

"As I said. I am pursuing Lady Gwen."

"But why? It was Sacombre who betrayed your lord. House Adair has fallen. What good is the girl to you?"

Volent squared himself to the vow knight, tilting his head back. His fingers brushed the hilt of his blade, though he made no move to draw.

"I have my reasons," he said. "Same as you."

"I would know your reasons," Elsa said.

Henri Volent was very still for a long time. When he moved, it was as quick as wind and just as quiet. In a blink his sword was in his hand.

"Do you think to judge me, Sir Elsa? To decide if my actions are justified, to shackle me if I am out of line, and to aid me if I am in the right?" His words were quiet, reminiscent of the still voice he spoke with in the past, when his face was dead. "By what authority do you claim that right?"

"I am sworn to the gods. I took a vow to see Strife's light

shine in winter." Elsa dropped into an easy guard, her sword stretched in front of her, knees low. The snow around her glistened with melt water as she wove summer's invocations into her blade. Volent laughed.

"You will need to threaten someone else, LaFey," he said. "I do not recognize that authority. Leave me to my hunt, and I will leave you to yours." As quickly as he had drawn, Volent sheathed his sword and turned away. He walked to the keep, disappearing inside despite the protests of the servants. Elsa remained in her guard position in the center of the courtyard until he was gone, then slowly lowered her sword, still scowling.

That night the fire burned brightly. Halfic had a healthy collection of naetheric tomes, gathered from around the island over a great many years.

To be safe, Ian gathered up every book of folklore, pagan medicine, and tome of mythology he could find in the earl's extensive library. He took them down to the courtyard, and set flames to them, the old paper and leather bindings curled into embers, floating up to the join the stars above. Halfic did not attend the bonfire, but watched from his rooms above.

"Was this really necessary?" Ian whispered. They stood apart from the workers who tended the fire. The maimed children watched from the shelter of the doma's stoop, the light flickering off their twisted forms.

"It is," Elsa said. "They could have done great harm to themselves. They may have, already. The earl possessed these long before that gheist appeared." Her eyes flicked up to the window where the earl was watching. The man's face was mournful. "He was up to something. Whatever it was, he may have drawn the gheist inadvertently. When this is all over, I will return to Harthal. Have a conversation."

"Dreadful," Ian said. He looked up from the fire, blinking into the darkness beyond. Volent rested just inside the gates. The man had brought his horse inside the walls at some point, and now fed the beast from his hand as he watched the fire. "What are we going to do about the Deadface?"

"A simple choice. We can travel with him, or we can have him following us from a distance." Elsa shrugged. "Which would you prefer?"

"Neither. Can't you send him away? Send him back to Greenhall?"

"I have no authority over him," she said. "Short of killing the man, I don't see a way around it."

"Then do that," Ian said. "He murdered all those children at Tallownere, and started the war. Isn't that reason enough?"

"The church does not involve itself in the crimes of mortal flesh," Elsa said quietly, as though reciting something nearly forgotten. "I hunt the gheist. Nothing more."

"That man is half gheist, I swear it," Ian muttered. "Gods, what happened to his face. It was bad enough before, but now—"

"That is no reason to kill." Elsa shifted, tension draining out of her stance. "Those children did nothing to deserve their condition. Would you have me take the sword to them?"

"Something will need to be done," Ian said. Unconsciously he scanned the little faces watching from the doma's shadows. Young eyes, broken bodies, their expressions creased in fear. He looked away. "Gods have mercy. Something."

"Cinder knows nothing of mercy," Elsa said, "but I am of Strife. They will live. Though it won't be much of a life.

Even so, I wouldn't take it from them."

"It's almost more of a mercy to end their suffering," Ian said. Elsa tensed up again, turning sharply to stare down at him.

"Your mother would disagree," she said. Ian was about to answer, then bit down on his tongue and returned his gaze to the fire. The flames crackled, the pages burned. The memories of the old gods disappeared into cinders, and their histories went with them.

Only the gheists remained.

44

THE VILLAGE WAS abandoned, the residents driven away either by drought or the firestorm that stretched across the eastern horizon. Gwen didn't care. She had been breathing smoke and drinking ash-choked water for days. All she wanted was a clean breath. All she wanted was to escape.

They had gotten out of Greenhall well enough, their flight masked by the chaos of the vernal god's ascension. The gheist tore its way through the city walls, leaving Gwen, Cahl and Noel a clear route out of the city.

Once they were in the surrounding villages, however, word of the tragedy spread quicker than the panic. They were spotted on the outskirts of Daewerry. Halverdt's hunters were on them before the night was out, followed by enough knights to start a war. They were cut off from the henge that had brought them south. All they could do was run and hope Halverdt's spears lost the trail.

Then the feral god caught their scent.

Gwen wasn't sure what attracted the spirit, the unspoken fear was that it was following her. For the first day it was a dark storm on the horizon, prehensile lightning lashing the sky, its voice flickering through their thoughts—waking or asleep.

On the third day the feral god manifested as fire. The

drought-starved forests west of Greenhall kindled in a flash, and the smoke that rolled down on Gwen and her companions was as black as boiled pitch, and nearly as hot. Their food was already spent, and the water they drank tasted like ash. It left their tongues and throats coated gray.

Still they ran.

Gwen stood at the top of a gentle hill, looking down at the abandoned village. Cahl loomed next to her, one arm wrapped around Noel, the other gripping a broken log he was using as a staff. All three of them looked like burn victims. Their clothes and skin were smeared with soot, eyes bloodshot, tears streaking down their cheeks. Noel still limped from whatever injury she had picked up during the flight, and whatever magic Cahl was using to guide them left him drained. They were close to their end.

"This is the place?" Gwen asked. "Doesn't look like much."

"It has to be," Noel said. "We've seen no other sign of civilization."

"Ancient pagan sites are rarely found in places of civilization," Gwen said. "Not in my experience."

Noel started to answer, but a fit of racking coughs seized her. She fell against Cahl, who grunted and also nearly collapsed. When she was finished, Noel's only response was to shake her head sadly.

"I can check," Cahl said. He shifted Noel like a baby, propping her against a tree, then started to kneel. "The ley lines are tangled this far south, but I should..."

"No," Gwen said. "There's no point in it. Either we've found it or we haven't. You'll need to save your energy for the casting." Cahl didn't answer, but he grunted again and hobbled down the hill. Noel watched him go for a moment, then visibly gathered her will and followed.

"What are we looking for?" Gwen asked as they entered the village. "Would it be the doma? The meeting hall? Somewhere in the surrounding fields?"

"It doesn't look as if this place rated a doma," Noel said, glancing around. She was right. There were only a few buildings, chief among them a meeting hall of fitted staves, along with an empty silo and three other smaller structures, apparently houses. "If it's not in one of the buildings, we'll have to tromp around looking for the graveyard or something."

"We won't have time for that," Gwen said. She glanced back the way they had come. The fire was close and getting closer, crashing through the trees like a bull. Among the flames, the voice of the feral god echoed, and the sky was crowned in lightning that flickered between the ash clouds. She turned to Noel. "Can you do something about that? You're of the tribe of fire, aren't you?"

"I've been wicking off the flame's power since it started, but there's only so much I can do," Noel said.

"Well..." Gwen grimaced, looking around the village. "...I've never fancied burning to death. If it gets to us, can you make it quick? I'd rather not smell my own flesh roasting."

"Yes, *that* is within my power," Noel said. "You will feel nothing."

"Enough of that talk," Cahl said. "Search."

They split up. Gwen went straight to the meeting hall, while the others searched the outbuildings. This place had been empty for a long time. The hall was empty, the stones of its fire pit scattered, the ashes blown across the floor, and the roof had leaked. But Gwen could find nothing of pagan gods or ancient power.

She paused in the middle of the room and tried to clear her thoughts. She wasn't sure how Cahl did it when he sensed the ley lines, so she just tried to think positive thoughts and let herself drift. She stretched her soul thin, to taste the air.

Smoke. Smoke, and she was hungry, and whatever tiny part of her wasn't hungry and choked with wood fire was angry at Folam and the pagans and Sophie Halverdt, and she missed her parents. And her brother, and all those dead Suhdrins who had done nothing but woken up in Greenhall on the day a god decided to tear their city apart.

Before she knew it, Gwen was crying, great heaving gasps and shuddering tears that smeared down her face. She curled into a ball, balanced on her heels, arms wrapped around her knees and face buried. She cried and howled and retched out the smoke and bile that had been choking her heart ever since her parents died.

There was so much pain.

So much, and Gwen found it all.

When she was done, when the pain had bled out onto the floor, not enough but as much as she could bear to let go of right now, Gwen stood and walked out of the meeting hall. Out into the inferno. Cahl was waiting for her.

"We found it," he said, then he looked closely. "Are you okay?"

"Fucking great," she said. "Show me."

Noel was in the silo. The wide doors had fallen off their rotten hinges. The walls were wood, but the pillars that held up the roof were stone. Stone, and roughly hewn, with a few wooden columns to complete the structure. Cahl ran a hand across the face of one of the stone pillars, wiping away decades of chaff. There were runes beneath.

The smoke was so dense in the air that it resembled a thick, dark fog. Breathing became more difficult by the minute.

"A place of the gods, in a silo of grain," Gwen said. "Who would have thought?"

"Whoever built this place knew what they were doing," Cahl said. "Knew what they were hiding. If they kept it filled, the inquisition would never find what lay behind these walls." He dusted off his hands, peering at the markings. "Maybe the villagers forgot, and thought nothing of their silo, and what it contained."

"Where does it go?" Gwen asked. "Will we be able to use it?"

"Away. It goes away," Noel said. "That's all that matters now."

"Enough of the old bindings remained for me to be able to find it," Cahl said. He went to the next pillar, and the next, cleaning them and reading the runes beneath. "We should be able to activate it."

"But where does it go?" Gwen asked again. "I don't want to surface in the middle of Heartsbridge or, gods forbid, the Fen Gate."

"It doesn't matter," Cahl said, agreeing with Noel. "If we stay here we'll be cinders by morning." He threw off his cloak and started moving faster around the hidden henge, whispering to the stones and drawing in the dirt of the floor. "Noel, I will need whatever power you can provide. There is too little stone in this ground for me to act alone."

"Gwen should do it," Noel said. "If she's able. All I have is the flame, and if I draw it..."

"Gwen doesn't know how to control her spirit," Cahl snapped. "It has to be you."

"But..."

"I know what I'm asking, witch," Cahl said calming. "Prepare yourself. I will let you know when I am ready."

Noel bowed her head, but drew her cloak tight around her shoulders and went to stand in the doorway, looking out. Cahl began working more frantically behind her. In the distance, the roar of the forest fire grew louder.

"What can I do?" Gwen asked. They both ignored her, though, so she folded herself to the ground in the center of the room.

"Cahl," Noel called from the doorway. "Soon."

"Yes, soon." The pillars were clear, and a steady hum vibrated through the ground. "I have only to..."

"No," Noel said. "I can not hold this any longer. It is here." The witch flinched back, and the light outside grew much brighter, a stark red and black that reflected off of the thickening smoke and washed out all other color. "We must go now."

"It's not quite ready," Cahl said. "You must hold it for a moment longer."

"That will not happen," Noel said. Gwen stood and went to stand beside her. The ridgeline they had crossed moments earlier was a wall of fire. The flames washed around the village, consuming the forest that surrounded them, but it had not yet found its way to the buildings. Noel glanced at Gwen. Her face was pinched tight, the stress clear on the witch's face.

"Cahl!" Gwen shouted. "She's not kidding. This has to happen, now, or we're dead."

"If we go without properly aligning..."

"Now!" Noel howled. Sweat rolled down her face, and when she opened her mouth to speak, glowing red sparks danced along her teeth. She turned to look at Gwen, pleading, terror in her eyes. "I can not hold it. I can not!"

Suddenly flame roared out of the witch's mouth. Her eyes rolled back in her head, and a cloak of fire rose from her skin. Then Noel went limp. Like a windchime cut from the branch, she fell.

Gwen grabbed her, not thinking about the spirit that flowed through her veins. The flames wrapped around her. The pain hesitated for a second, then came rushing through. She screamed, but dragged Noel inside the henge. Cahl shouted something, but Gwen couldn't hear him over the blood thrumming through her head. She collapsed, and Noel rolled away from her.

The meeting hall boomed as the forest fire consumed it. The thousand staves that made up its walls cracked and split, the roof erupting in a twisting lash of cinders and smoke. The first sparks danced across the interior walls. Bright light shone between the cracks in the roof. Smoke rolled through the door, crawling up the walls to form a billowing cloud above them. It was over. The spirit of storm and fire had caught up to them.

Noel opened her mouth, and the tongue of flame speared out of her. It danced into the air, then bent and flowed gracefully to each of the five pillars of the henge. Cahl began chanting, weaving the fire's power into the stones. Old runes began to glow, the dust sizzling off the rock. Part of the silo wall collapsed, showering them in embers.

Gwen's clothes began to burn. The smoke stung her

eyes and cut holes in her lungs with each painful breath. She covered her mouth and huddled next to Noel. The witch's eyes and mouth were open, but she was breathing in short, sharp gasps that rattled her chest. Cahl stood among the flames, drawing them together, reaching out into the everic realm, seeking the path that would save them.

The silo collapsed with a crash. The roof fell in, pouring hot cinders down on the henge. The stones cracked with the heat, and the sound was like a thunderclap. The mad god howled in the sky above, lightning wreathing his head, his voice shaking through flame and ember until it seemed to fill the whole world.

45

SORCHA AND THE priestess sat on a hill, their light mingling with the stars. The two had spent much time together since their flight from the Fen Gate. Heads bowed close, whispering, hands on the other's arm as they turned away from the others. Malcolm watched from the pickets. Sir Doone approached him.

"They should come in soon," she said. "If nothing else, that light will draw attention."

"I will speak to them," Malcolm said. He took a step, but Doone grabbed his arm and pulled him back.

"No," she said. "No. Let me. The lady..."

"Is still my wife," Malcolm said, but he made no move. Doone waited a heartbeat then shook her head.

"Doesn't matter," Doone said. "They've made their own way down."

The priestess led the way, Lady Sorcha trailing just behind, their fingers entwined. Sorcha smiled at Malcolm as she approached the picket.

"Husband," she said. "You look concerned."

"It worries me when you go unguarded," he said. "These lands are no longer friendly to Tenerran blood."

"The guards are for you, Malcolm. For your peace of

mind. I am safe enough without them," Sorcha said. "Have I not proven that by now?"

"The less you draw on that spirit, the more of you that remains," Malcolm said. "Let my steel protect you, when steel is all that is needed."

Sorcha smiled. "You are very determined, Houndhallow. It's admirable." She patted Malcolm on the cheek, then slipped by, nodding to Doone as she passed. The knight muttered her farewell to Malcolm and followed Sorcha into the camp. He watched them go, frowning.

"She is the same woman, Houndhallow," Catrin said, as if reading his mind. "Nothing about her has changed."

"Nothing?" Malcolm asked. "You are wrong, priestess. I remember the girl I married, the mother to my children, the wife of my heart. That girl did not glow beneath her skin, or summon the gods of water, or kill a column of Suhdrin knights."

"Nor did she have wrinkles around her eyes, or hands that ached in the rain, and her hair was golden, not gray. Or had you not noticed those changes, my lord?"

"I... that's not..."

"And still you love her. Or has that love waned because age has touched her skin, and bent her hands?" Catrin asked. "Is the girl you married still behind those wrinkled eyes?"

Malcolm sighed. "That is different. Of course she's the same woman, but those things are natural. They're expected."

"You speak as if you're the same man she married. Should the girl who fell in love with the hero of Bassing's Ferry find another, when the boy she married becomes a grumpy old man, more concerned with his title than he is with his son?" Catrin took Malcolm's hand. His knuckles were knotted with age, the skin of his palms as rough as a saddle, scarred, ruined. "These are not the hands that slipped against hers on her wedding night. Why should the man be any better?"

Malcolm snatched his hand free. "You should watch what you say, child. You have no place."

"Don't I? You are cold to her, not because of age or reason, but because you fear she has offended the church. Not by her actions, but because of what she is. Well," Catrin took his hand again, clasping it in both of her own, "I speak for the church, or for a part of it, and I say that she is the same woman. She is still your wife. Just as you are still her husband."

"You speak as though we have changed equally, she and I. Time changes us, yes," Malcolm said sharply. "And war, and hatred, and love, but the god inside her… that is nothing to do with me. That is different. That is something I can not overcome with memories and pleasant thoughts."

Catrin drew back, dropping Malcolm's hand. Her face grew stern.

"You are right, Malcolm," she said. "There is no god in you. And there won't be, as long as you hold on to that difference."

Without tents and proper supplies, the Tenerran camp was little more than a circle of beaten down grass and dying fires. Malcolm lay near the center, hands folded on his chest, staring up at the stars. Catrin's words tumbled through his head.

"Should the girl who fell in love with the hero of Bassing's Ferry find another, when the boy she married becomes a grumpy old man?"

They didn't understand. That was the problem. Sorcha and Ian and the priestess, they didn't understand what it took to be lord of a duchy. Not just a duke, but the duke most trusted in both Suhdra and Tener, the man who had joined the countries together against the Reavers, hero of countless battles and true servant of the celestial church. The pressures he faced, the standard to which he was held, both by his fellow lords but also by the priests, the inquisition, the gods themselves... they could never understand.

Catrin especially. A child, that one. She was just a child. How could she know anything about him?

He turned angrily, curling up on his shoulder. Sorcha lay across from him, close, yet far enough away to be distant. She rested so peacefully. Light crawled through her veins like quicksilver, a slow brilliance that was almost beautiful. No. It *was* beautiful. She was beautiful.

What had he done, pushing her away? Malcolm told himself that it was best, that the church would not tolerate a duchess of Tener twisted up with pagan magic. He had hidden her away to protect her from the inquisition.

But had he? Had he made a mistake with her?

Had he made a mistake with Ian?

As he looked over his wife's face, with the gentle glow of her blood leaking up like mist off a morning pond, he noticed another radiance. Subtle at first, it mingled with her light, but the colors were somehow... different. *Strange*, Malcolm thought. Then he heard a shout from the other side of the camp, and sat bolt upright.

Suddenly the forest beyond the camp was shot through with brilliant light. It looked like sunrise seen through stained glass, beams of rainbow reflected off of twisting fog. The trees shivered and the ground shook. Malcolm jumped up. Without thinking, he put himself between Sorcha and the light.

"You nearly stepped on me," Sorcha said from underfoot.

"Apologies, my love," Malcolm said.

She stood and looked around, not just at the light but at their camp, the sky, the dark forest that surrounded them. She put a hand on Malcolm's shoulder.

"Get the priestess," she said, "and then run."

Then she was gone, calling to the knights of Malcolm's company. They were slow to respond, sluggish to answer her call to arms. Those who had served as Sorcha's guard formed a loose circle around her. Frair Catrin stood beside her, and the two women spoke quickly in low tones.

"Everyone, form up," Malcolm snapped. The dim light of the remaining campfires could not compete with the new illumination. His knights squinted and peered into the distance, trying to track whatever threat might have appeared. "Stop staring and arm up, you idiots!" he bellowed. "The Hound! The hallow!"

That roused them. A column formed at his side, most of them unarmored, a few still rubbing sleep from their eyes. It was an embarrassment.

"Oh, there," Sir Harrow said. "I see it now. It's quite pretty."

"Stop admiring and prepare to fight," Malcolm said.

"There will be no fight," Sorcha called to him. "The calendar is wrong. We approach the low point of Lady Strife's power."

"We should run," Catrin said to her. "I can do nothing to protect you. Even if I were trained as a vow knight, which I am not."

"And you, wife?" Malcolm asked.

"Not enough," she said. "It is not of the river. It is… gods know what this thing is, but it does not answer to my call."

"Then stop calling it," Malcolm said. "Before you catch its attention. Everyone, gather your things and make for the horses. Make sure you save the waterskins, and whatever food remains. Gods know how long we'll be in the saddle." Better to be prepared for a long pursuit. "But be quick about it. If it notices us..."

"It already has," Catrin said urgently. "We should go now."

There was motion in the distance, among the trees. Along the road to the north the forest rose up and knit itself together, forming into a dome. While they watched a spinning, crystalline light coalesced over the dome, then dove inside. Brilliant colors beamed out of it—reds and blues and an amber glow that rivaled the finest gems. It was like an explosion of jewelry in the murky night.

The dome wrinkled and started to move, making and unmaking itself as it walked, caterpillar slow, toward them. It seemed to absorb the forest as it came, leaving the shivering remains of trees in its wake.

It sped up until it was moving fast. Crossing the road it turned, and started to roll like a ball along the forest's verge in their direction. Malcolm grabbed his pack and a few provisions, then ran to the horses. His mount was unsaddled, but there was no time. He threw his leg up, twisted his fingers into the beast's mane, and gave her spurs.

He nearly tumbled off the back as the destrier bolted forward. After a few terrifying moments of bouncing, the animal slowed and Malcolm was able to look around. Most of the company rode beside him, with Catrin and Sorcha leading the way. Sorcha looked completely comfortable on her unsaddled mount, but the rest of the riders swayed alarmingly, hanging on for dear life.

"We can't go far like this, my lord," Sir Harrow muttered. She looked straight ahead, as though even a glance to the side would unseat her. "If the gheist comes on us, I'd rather fight on my feet than die like a fool."

"Aye," Malcolm said. "If it comes to that."

"Hold," Sorcha called from the front. She held up her arm, but few of the riders had enough control of their mounts to slow, much less stop. "Hold and turn!"

Malcolm rode past her and quickly realized why she had been calling for the halt. A river, swollen beyond its banks and frothy with current, swirled on the trail ahead. He jerked back on the horse's mane, but that only caused the beast to spin wildly. Fortunately it slowed, coming to a stop knee deep in the swirling waters.

Sliding unceremoniously off of the mount's back, he crashed into the river, sputtering as he came up for air. The other riders hemmed and hawed along the banks, tumbling into mud or falling to the solid ground. One knight—Sir Connor, perhaps—clung madly on to his mount as the beast charged full-on into the water. They were swept up in the current and disappeared downstream, mount and rider screaming.

"We'll fight here," Malcolm said. It wasn't much of an order, as they had no choice in the matter. He trudged to the shore, drawing his feyiron blade and bellowing commands to those who could hear him. "Harrow, Darcy, form a line along the bank. Doone, I leave the flanks to you. Sorcha, can you do anything about this water? I'd like to have an escape available, if possible."

"The madness of spring is upon it," Sorcha said. She slid

easily from her horse, bare feet squishing in the mud. "It will fight, if I ask it, but gods know who it will strike."

"Best leave it out, then," Malcolm said. He turned to the priestess, who had tarried and was only now coming over the hill. "Frair Catrin! If my men fall, I will leave them to your care."

"That may not be necessary," she said. "The gheist has turned."

"Turned?" Malcolm said. He walked up the bank to the priestess's side. Sure enough, the light from the gheist glittered on the horizon, lighting up the sky. It progressed slowly south, keeping to the road. "It bypassed our camp, at least, but where is it going?"

"I think I know," Catrin said. She pointed, and Malcolm was able to see a scattering of campfires in the distance, directly in the rogue god's path.

"But who..." Malcolm didn't finish his thought. The gheist reached the lights and stopped moving. The dome sealed shut, until the only light came from a collection of slits along the side. At this distance, the gheist looked like a doma, dropped into the middle of the woods, illuminated by candles through stained glass.

Moments later the screams began.

They didn't stop for several minutes. Once the night was silent again, the gheist came apart and disappeared.

They gathered their saddles and fitted them in silence. Sir Connor's gear was split among the survivors. Once everyone was ready, they rode to where the gheist had been. The road was quiet. Not even the campfires remained.

The wreckage was simple. Dead bodies—men and women

and horses—all dressed for war. The gheist had not come on them unawares. Swords lay broken in the mud. Supplies were thrown about, and the half-dozen fires of the company were smothered under a blanket of fine ash. Malcolm stirred the remnants of the nearest fire with his toe. A sweet smell rose up, like incense.

"They were burning frairwood," he said. "For all the good it did."

"I have never seen a gheist move with such intent," Catrin said. "It was as though it hunted them. As though it was drawn to this place."

"You have been too long isolated in Heartsbridge," Malcolm said. "The feral gods move and hunt as they will. Without the vow knights and the inquisition, the whole north would be like this. Snuffed out."

"That's hardly true," Sorcha said quietly, but Malcolm ignored her. The men moved somberly among the dead, looking for survivors.

"These are Suhdrin," Doone said. She held up a tabard. Red, with a golden heart. "Galleux. They marched with Halverdt."

"Aye. So they've extended their search south," Malcolm said. "I was hoping they would focus to the north, toward Houndhallow. They must know we slipped free."

"Or these men were coming north, as part of a reinforcement for the Fen Gate. Few enough of Galleux's men fought at White Lake," Sorcha said.

"That would mean that the Reaveholt has fallen, or been enveloped," Malcolm said. "Either way, we'll be too late to find shelter there." He fell silent. The knights lost interest in the dead, drifting back to their horses. Malcolm followed them, mounting up and peering to the north. "What of the gheist?" he said. "We should see where it came from. What drew it into the world."

"I think that's best left a mystery," Sorcha said. The duchess looked pale, even against her own internal light. She leaned wearily against her horse's neck, trailing fingers through its mane. "We should not have come here. They will see us, now."

"Who will see us?" Malcolm asked, but his wife fell once again into her strange reverie. He glanced at Catrin, but the priestess could only shrug. "Very well. Either the Reaveholt has fallen, or we are racing Galleux's men to reach its gates. Either way, we should be on our way."

"The calendar has turned against us," Catrin said quietly. "The nights of gheists are here, and then it will be winter. Lady Strife is far away."

"If she will not come to us, then we will ride to her," Malcolm insisted. "Quickly now. South, before the old gods find us again."

Leaving the Suhdrin dead behind, they reached the godsroad and beat their way toward Reaveholt, riding fast until the dawn brought them some warmth. Though a fog had set in, there was something comforting about daylight, that made it seem as if the gheists would leave them at peace, at least until night fell again.

The eyes that watched them from the shadows of the forest were of mortal blood. A dark form, armored in black and riding a pale horse, stood watch on a hill overlooking the road. It had trailed the gheist on its hunt, like the master follows the hound. The form noted Malcolm's haste, and Sorcha's light. It counted the Tenerran strength, and it smiled as it recognized Catrin's pale form.

Once the Tenerrans were gone, the form whispered to its horse and turned north, riding for a dozen steps before blurring into shadow and fog. It disappeared with a whisper.

46

THE FIRST IAN saw of the old god was a wall of fog that moved at the edge of the campfire's flickering light. The bank of swirling mist scudded between the trees, gray on black on shadow. The others were asleep, and he thought he might be dreaming, so he stayed silent. Stayed silent, and watched.

The gheist brushed against a lonely pine, and a shower of needles shook free of its limbs, dusting the god's back in debris. The beast flexed iron hard muscles beneath tangled fur, and threw the needles off. The sound was like the jangle of pins on glass, even though the pine was green and the ground soft with autumn mulch. Ian stood and drew his sword. The gheist snapped like a banner in the wind, then disappeared among the trees.

"What was that?" Volent asked. Ian looked back to see that the Deadface had rolled to his feet, his vivid eyes staring into the woods.

"Nothing," he said. "Fog, I think." Even as he spoke, two bright eyes appeared in the distance, the color of storm clouds just before the tornado whips down. A rolling growl curled through the forest. Ian edged back. Volent seemed to not have heard the sound, or seen the eyes.

"Fog," Volent answered. "Fog hides many things in the north."

"It's just fog," Ian insisted. "You're jumpy." He sheathed his sword and sat back down on the log, his back to the fire so that he could continue to watch. The forest grew quiet again, and he began to think Volent had gone back to sleep. Then the knight marshal loomed suddenly out of his peripheral vision, sitting heavily at Ian's side. "I still have the watch, Volent," he growled. "Get some sleep."

"Sleep is no friend of mine," Volent said. He uncapped a bottle and handed it over. "Nor yours, I think. I haven't seen you sleep since we left Harthal."

"I sleep," Ian said, waving the bottle away. Volent pushed it toward him again, and Ian took it, reluctantly. It was just water. "And I'll go back to sleep just as soon as my turn at the watch is over. Sooner, if you want to take over."

Volent didn't answer, but sat quietly, drinking and staring out into the woods. Ian cleared his throat and started to stand. Volent grabbed him.

"Don't think I don't see, Blakley. Your pet tails us like a bad scent. If it weren't for your lady fair, I would have dragged you into the woods and cut your pagan heart out days ago." Volent didn't look up as he spoke, the slack mosaic of his face turned toward the darkened woods. "You have the vow knight fooled, but not me. Never me."

"I don't know what you're talking about," Ian said, snatching his arm away. "But know that if it comes to murder, you will need to take me unawares. I'm more than a match for a broken old knight like you."

Volent snorted, then waved at him dismissively. "I've put down my share of young pups. You won't be the last. Go to bed, Houndhallow. Dream of the glory you will never earn."

Ian spun and stomped back to his bedroll, curling around

his sword so that he faced Volent's back. The Deadface didn't move, just sat silently on the stump, watching the woods. Then Ian glanced over at Elsa, to see that the vow knight was staring at him. Her face was still and calm. She looked from him to Volent, then breathed a long, shuddering sigh and closed her eyes.

The Hound, he thought to himself. *Why is it following me?* Ever since his family's ancestral totem had urged him forward on the road to Harthal, Ian had felt the creature's presence in the back of his mind. Nothing terrified him more than the thought of Elsa finding and slaying the gheist. *What would I do?* he wondered. *Would I try to stop her?* The idea pressed at him, yet he had no answer.

Best not to think about it. Best not to worry.

Ian fell asleep much later, and his dreams were troubled.

They rode at a steady pace, each leading a spare horse acquired from the ruined stable at Harthal. Their days were strained by silence and the imminence of violence. Ian tried several times to convince Elsa that they should leave Volent behind, but she was insistent.

"Whatever he is, Volent is no enemy of the church," she said. For his part, Volent watched Ian closely. More than once, he caught the two in close conversation. Ian spent his nights trying to come up with some way to convince Elsa that Volent couldn't be trusted. He started to worry that Volent was doing the same thing.

After Harthal, the pagan's path led them north and east. Beyond the Fen, Tenumbra opened into a landscape of rolling hills, sharp granite cliffs and sudden valleys that cut deep into the earth. The mornings were wrapped in fog that lifted slowly into the skies, to become low hanging clouds and rain. The grasses that swept from horizon to horizon were brilliantly green. The air was cold, and when the winds blew across the granite hills, the mists that scudded around them cut like knives.

"Are we sure we're going the right way?" Ian asked. "I don't know how we could track anyone over these moors."

"Have you lost your faith in our dear Sir Elsa?" Volent asked. "Surely the goddess of summer won't lead us astray."

"This *feels* like astray," Ian said. He huddled deeper into his cloak, any pretense of northern pride abandoned. "What sort of reach does summer have in this place?"

"This place?" Volent asked. "You talk as if this is a foreign land, Blakley. Aren't those the Grayeyes?" He nodded toward a line of jagged mountains to the east, barely visible among the clouds. "And this the reaveroad? We should be dreadfully close to Houndhallow."

"I am long from home, you're right," Ian said. "But that is your fault, not mine. It was your master's war that roused my house from their hearth. I would still be hunting boar in the gray wood, if not for you."

"And all the duller for it," Volent said. "Think of all the adventures you've had! The battles you've fought, and the friends you've made. Why, if not for my master, that heretic Adair would still be scheming on the Sedgewind throne, and your mother still sleeping well at night."

"I have had enough of your taunting, Deadface," Ian said. "Halverdt got the death he deserved, buried as a pawn of a corrupt inquisition and used as an excuse for unjust war. Why couldn't you have died at his side, like a good monster?"

"Some monsters don't die when they're meant to,"

Volent said. He looked away, and his voice grew distant. "Some aren't meant to die at all."

"I would love to settle this with a duel or something," Sir Elsa said sharply. "So the two of you could kill each other, and maybe I could get some holy work done. Failing that, I must ask you to settle into your leashes and serve the church's will."

"This one's not fit for a leash," Ian muttered.

Volent snorted. "As if I would…"

"Silence!" Elsa roared. Her voice echoed over the moors, startling a flock of crows into the air, sending them cawing toward the distant mountains. "I can accept that you have your differences, and your history, but that is not unique. It doesn't make you special. When I entered the Lightfort, I was one person. When I left, I was someone else. Someone better.

"And so I ask a simple question," she continued. "We are here on the church's business. Will you serve that task, or are you determined to complain every inch of the way?"

Ian and Volent were silent for a few moments. Ian blushed bright red, while Volent's face went the color of ice, and his jaw was set. He spoke first.

"The last priest who spoke to me that way was Tomas Sacombre," Volent said. "So you will forgive me if my service is not freely given."

"What the servants of Cinder asked of you was unforgivable," Elsa said. "But let's not pretend you were coerced into violence, Deadface."

"Do not call me that, sir," Volent said, "and do not speak of Cinder as though he is foreign to you. The difference between Cinder and Strife is a polite fiction. Heartsbridge moves the pawns of Tenumbra as it pleases them, and if any defy their will, we are thrown to the gheists. It's little wonder the north rises against you."

"It's not the church that we rise against," Ian said tightly. "It's gods damned southern dukes who think the church gives them free rein to take our lands and burn our fields in the name of crusade. If it weren't for Halverdt's paranoia..."

"Or Adair's heresy—" Volent cut in.

"Gods save us from stiff-necked soldiers of glory," Elsa snapped, interrupting the exchange. "Forget the past that has brought you here. You are both exiles from your houses, shunned by your lords and abandoned by the war that set you against each other. *Forget* those things." She drew in front of them, turning her mount in their path and bringing them to an awkward halt.

"We are on the trail of a god. Brought into this world by a man of my church, yes, and an enemy to us all. If we are lucky, that god will lead us to Gwendolyn Adair, and perhaps a greater understanding of the things that have broken our world apart." She threw back her cloak, revealing the blade of her office. "I do not ask for your loyalty or affection. I only ask that you not kill each other, and *maybe* argue less—at least until we've seen to Gwen Adair. You're making it very difficult to sleep at night."

"Difficult to sleep?" Ian asked. "This man has threatened to drag me into the woods and cut my heart out!"

"Yes, well," Volent said, "justice and all that."

"The man who murdered the village of Tallownere shouldn't seek justice," Ian said. "He might not like what he finds."

"That was different. That was... I was... different," Volent said. Ian thought he could sense the slightest timidity in the man.

"Fine," he said. "Our histories will return to us, but not today, and not until we've seen an end to this hunt. Agreed?"

"We all seek the same thing," Volent answered. "For different reasons."

"Different reasons, but one road," Elsa said. "The death god, and Gwen beyond. So let's walk in peace, if we can."

"If we can," Volent agreed. "Which brings us back to young Blakley's original question. Are we sure this is the correct path?" He peered out onto the moors. The fields of green and granite stretched unbroken. "How can we know you've led us true?"

"There are no tracks to follow, and no distant figures to hunt," Ian said. "There are endless places to hide, and few enough locals to guide our way. The pagan could be watching us from a cave right now, and we'd never know."

"We're going the right way because we're following the same road as our quarry," Elsa said. "We are merely restrained by how fast we can go."

"How fast? We have horses, and spares, and a steady supply of food and water," Volent said. "That man was on foot, and injured. We should run him down before nightfall."

"Certain pagans travel by more than road or river," Elsa said. "This one showed enough proficiency with the old gods, that I must assume he knows of these hidden roads. Ley lines, beneath the earth, concentrations of great power. If properly trained, the servants of the gheists can move along them very quickly."

"Then how are we *ever* supposed to catch him?" Ian asked.

"Because as Volent says, he is injured, and such travel takes much from the practitioner. Also, the man must be going somewhere. To someone. Either for help or healing, or simply to warn them that we still live." Elsa closed her cloak and turned back to the path they had been following. "He will not run forever."

"And when he stops, especially if he reaches allies? One shaman nearly proved the end of all three of us," Ian said.

"Because we were unprepared. Because we didn't know what we were facing," Elsa said. "It's not a mistake I will make again."

"Very well," Volent said. "Let us ride together toward death, and unquestionable glory. Maybe enough glory that the storytellers will forget all the terrible things we've done."

"The terrible things *you've* done," Ian said. "I've nothing to hide from history."

"Children," Sir Elsa said sharply. "Don't make me give the speech again. I've grown tired of trying to convince you with words and clever arguments. That was always Frair Lucas's job, anyway."

The silence lasted until they topped a moor and stopped to eat, only guessing at the time. The sun was little more than a lesser grayness in the sky, and the steady misting rain soaked them through. Elsa tried to tease flame out of their limited supply of dry wood, hoping to make some tea before their afternoon ride, when Volent drew their attention south.

"I see spears," he said, pointing along the reaveroad. The broad, flat path that wound its way south was masked with fog, but dark figures could be seen in the murk. Ian joined him, squinting into the distance.

"Dozens of riders," he agreed. "I can't make out their colors."

"They ride openly along Tener's roads," Volent said. "Unlikely to be bandits, even in those numbers."

"Nor pagans," Ian said. "Horses and spears don't have a place in their service."

"They're Suhdrin," Elsa said. She was balanced on a rock, her runic armor glowing gently with some sort of invocation.

"Impossible," Ian said. "The Fen Gate is still in Tenerran hands. My father would never let such a large host pass unharassed."

"Unless the Fen Gate has fallen," Volent said. "And your father with it."

Ian was silent for a long moment, staring down at the column as it approached. Soon there was no denying their Suhdrin colors. The black spear and golden rose of House Marchand flew at their head. Volent turned to look at the young prince.

"Still willing to forget your history in the service of the church?" he asked.

"In the hunt for Gwendolyn, yes," Ian said sharply. "Besides, Houndhallow has exiled me. My fight is not with Suhdra, or Tener." He turned to his horse and prepared to ride. Volent snorted.

"Yet still you flee their approach?" he asked.

"Not at all," Ian said. "Whoever those spears are, they will be loyal to the church. Where we're going, we could use the steel." He threw a leg over his saddle and mounted. "We must speak to them."

"And if they try to take you?" Elsa asked.

"Then I must trust to your help, sir," he replied, "and yours, Volent. Or were your words of aid as empty as your face?" Volent shrugged and turned to Elsa. The vow knight sighed. She tossed aside the tinder she had been struggling to light and went to her horse.

"Let me do the talking," she said, "and the fighting as well, if they draw steel."

"I make no promises," Volent said. "At least this should be interesting, though."

47

GALLOWSPORT WAS A place to die. A cradle of ink-black stone formed the port's harbor and climbed in sharp blocks to the moors above. The harbor itself was choked with the iron-bound barques of the inquisition. The city lay between, stone walls hewn from the surrounding quarries, the homes and towers of House Bourreau as dark as night.

Out in the bay, churning with the strong currents of the Felling Sea, lay the Black Isle. It perched among the dark waters like an anvil on which the souls of men could be broken. The grim banner of Bourreau snapped in the coastal winds—noose and eye, red for blood and black for the inquisition's justice.

"I have stood on this road and seen this city a dozen times," Sacombre said quietly. "To oversee an execution or deliver a prisoner. Never did I think I would be traveling here in chains."

Frair Lucas looked exhausted, having become more and more tired with each day of their journey. Fianna worried the man would die before he delivered the high inquisitor to trial. She couldn't decide which she feared more—her own trial in Heartsbridge, or Lucas dying and leaving her alone with Sacombre and the boy.

"We are only passing through, for now," the frair said.

"You will see Gallowsport again, however, when the sentence has been given and your execution arranged."

"Gods pray our stay is short," Martin said. "We have enough to worry about without getting stuck in this hellhole."

"Keep moving," Lucas said, prodding their captive. "Don't speak, not even to answer questions. Cause me any trouble and I'll cut you down in the street." He looked from Sacombre to Fianna, his tired eyes as hard as steel. "Either of you. Trials and consequences be damned."

"You've brought me too far and at too great a cost to kill me now, Lucas," Sacombre said lightly. "You have your precious justice to pursue. Threats won't change that."

"I've put no trouble into this at all," Martin said. "No skin off my knuckles if you don't make it to Heartsbridge. If the frair can't bring himself to see it done, I'll be happy enough to spill your guts, Sacombre."

"Oh, well… brave words from young Stormwatch. Do see that you keep them," Sacombre said. "I'm sure Lucas will have no trouble explaining to the celestriarch how he let a Suhdrin prince murder his charge in cold blood."

"This is not my trial," Lucas said heavily. "Not yet, it isn't." He grabbed Sacombre by the shoulder and pushed him down the road. A rope tied her to the high inquisitor, and it jerked Fianna forward, causing her to stumble. Lucas ignored her.

"No, Lucas, not yet," Sacombre said smugly. "We will get to that."

They marched down the switchback road toward Gallowsport. The sounds of the city—the clanging brass bells of the mournvendors, the cries of women and children lined up along the gallows wall, the steady moaning from prisoners chained along the penitent's harp—all mixed together into a soft dirge of human suffering. Even the drunken song of sailors drifting out of a tavern carried a sorrowful air to it.

"I never liked this place," Lucas muttered.

"Justice does not need affection, frair," Sacombre said. "Better that it's feared."

"Better still that it's unnecessary," Lucas answered. They joined the stream of priests that crowded the city's streets, blending easily with the traffic. Not even Fianna looked out of place, as there were dozens of men and women in pagan garb being led through the city, prisoners and penitents on their way to judgment. Only Martin stood out, his noble features and fine armor at odds with the rough steel of the guards who patrolled the streets.

"Unnecessary," Sacombre spat. "And how will you accomplish that? End the law? As long as there are rules to follow, mortal hearts will find a way to defy them. It is their nature. They steal, they lie, they ruin lives and take what belongs to others. It is our nature to enforce those laws."

"By lying, stealing, and ruining lives, Tomas?" Lucas said testily. "That has become your way, hasn't it?"

"Cinder is not a god of emotion, frair," Sacombre answered. "Perhaps you are wearing the wrong color."

"Perhaps *you* are," Lucas said. "Perhaps a god of judgment is better served by a man of mercy."

Sacombre snorted but didn't answer. Fianna was glad for his silence.

After a great deal of what seemed to be walking in circles, Lucas led them to an out-of-the-way inn, its roof paved in slate and the stone of its walls settling into the soft mud of the bay. It was an old building, perhaps one of the original structures of the port, going back to before the inquisition's reign. The innkeep seemed to know Lucas, though if he recognized the high inquisitor, the pudgy little man gave no sign. Lucas got them rooms, then followed them up the winding staircase. The room he gave the prisoners had no windows, and the door locked from the outside.

"You will leave me in here with this witch?" Sacombre asked. "Is that wise?"

"I worry more for her than for you," Lucas said. He glanced at Fianna. "To be honest, I'm not that worried about her. I have the feeling Fianna can take care of herself. Better than you can, old man."

"And where will you—" Sacombre started.

"Elsewhere," Lucas said sharply. Then he slammed the door, bolting it quickly. With the door closed, there was only the dim light that leaked through the sill. Muffled footsteps clumped down the hall. It was still early enough in the day that the inn wasn't crowded. The only sound was Sacombre's heavy breathing, and her own heartbeat.

"So," Sacombre said. "What do you make of this?" The room was close, but still his voice sounded far away. Fatigue, or perhaps theatrics. The high inquisitor had always valued the appearance of mystery, especially in his dealings with her. She heard him thump against the wall nearest the door, then slide down to the floor.

Fianna closed her eyes, then folded into a sitting position without touching the walls to steady herself. After a few deep breaths, she answered.

"It is according to the plan, yes?" she asked, then added, "My master."

"Yes," he said. "Yes, it is."

* * *

Martin watched from the end of the hall while Lucas had a short argument with Sacombre, then slammed the door and bolted it. The motion had the look of long practice and familiarity. As the frair approached, Martin pushed himself off the wall and folded his arms.

"What now?" he asked.

"Now we wait," Lucas said. "For them to kill each other, or for someone to try to rescue them."

"You're sure this is smart?"

"No, not at all, but I think it's going exactly according to plan," Lucas said. "Now, I need to find something to eat, and maybe a bed."

"We aren't sleeping here?" Martin asked.

"Gods, no. Who knows what those two will do to the place?"

Martin gave the bolted door one last look, then retreated down the steps. When he reached the bottom of the stairs, he could already hear their voices echoing through the floorboards. The innkeep gave him a frightened look, but Lucas was out the door, humming to himself.

"Lover's spat," Martin said to the innkeep, shrugging. "What can you do?"

The man looked less than comforted as Lucas and Martin disappeared into the streets, melting into the river of black-robed priests and mournful prisoners that swamped the city.

"You're serious?" Fianna said. "This is your plan? This is the grand scheme you proposed to my father—the blow that would unite the north, and bring the church tumbling down?"

"That is not what I said." The high inquisitor fidgeted with his robe, tucking it under his bony legs, his outline only barely visible in the dim light of the room. "To your father, at least. Those were not my promises."

"Oh, of course not. More accurately, those were not your *lies*," Fianna said. "Don't try to deny it. The voidfather knows when he's being lied to, Inquisitor. You never wanted to end the church. No more than you wanted to free Tener from Suhdrin oppression. Nevertheless, my father saw what he could get out of this, and he took it."

"My words were honest," Sacombre said, "if not complete. The war I promised would have pulled the church out of the north by the roots. The Tenerran lords would have done the job themselves, once I was exposed. If you'd only let me finish the task at hand."

"And what did I have to do with that?" Fianna's voice rose, but she didn't care. Most likely the priest expected them to fight, regardless. "My business was with Blakley's son."

"What came of that? Eh? Where is my tame princeling, witch?"

"Where he needs to be. On the path he needs to walk," Fianna said. "Alone."

"Oh, but he isn't alone, is he? The vow knight is with him, and if you think Frair Lucas is formidable, you've seen nothing of Sir Elsa LaFey!"

"Every road contains hazards," Fianna said shortly. "Every test must have a solution."

"Enough of this," Sacombre said. The old man stood, shuffling across the room to stand in front of Fianna. Even bound with the frair's icons, Sacombre wielded some of his old power. "Your people did not hold their end of the bargain," he continued. "Where were the gheists, to disrupt the Suhdrin lines? Where were the druids, burning farms in the homeland while Marchand and LaGaere and his companions were away at war? What of the loyal Tenerran lords, who would declare for Adair once he was exposed? None of this came to pass."

"None of it ever would," Fianna said, letting the words hang in the air for a beat before she added, "Master." Sacombre drew back, confusion on his face.

"Betrayed, eh? That's what you hope to accomplish? You feared my inquisitors, and so you thought to play a game with me? Hoped to instill in Tener a little mistrust for the priests of Cinder? Well, I hate to tell you this, but that will never work. Lucas will see me hang. I'll be shown for the heretic I am, and then it's the Black Isle for me." Sacombre paced back, putting some distance between himself and the witch. "You will follow shortly after. Blakley's witch, hung for her faith."

"I was never Blakley's witch, and I was never yours, either," Fianna said. She stood, and the light in the room flickered. Sacombre edged farther away. "You can see me, yes? You still have the inquisitor's eyes?" Sacombre didn't answer, but the look on his face told the story.

"Good," Fianna said. "Keep them open. Watch closely, priest, and see who you truly serve."

She changed, and the air changed with her.

48

THEY RODE IN numb silence. The forests were dark even at noon, crowding down on the godsroad and urging Malcolm and his company forward. Catrin and Sorcha stayed close to each other, glaring into the trees every time the column stopped to rest the horses, or eat from their dwindling supplies.

Their progress was slow, and the days were becoming shorter than the nights, the moon hanging low in the sky even during the daylight hours.

"Cinder watches our path," Catrin muttered over breakfast one morning, a week into their flight from the Fen Gate. Malcolm wasn't sure if she meant it as a threat or a warning.

"Let him watch," Malcolm answered. "Let him judge. We will need *all* the gods, if we're to live through this."

"All?" Sorcha asked quietly. "Or only those locked into calendars?"

Malcolm didn't answer, but when he stood a few minutes later to call the riders together and prepare for the day's journey, he paused at the roadside shrine that kept the path safe from gheists. Sorcha watched him closely.

"That man's faith will be the end of us," she muttered.

"Or the beginning," Catrin answered. "Everything has a beginning."

* * *

It was cold, even at noon, the shadows growing quickly from the verge-side trees as the afternoon slipped into night. Dusk was purpling the sky when one of the outriders appeared from the forest and approached Malcolm.

"The way oxbows ahead, my lord. There are scouts watching over the road from the bluffs, and a camp near the Hallingsrun bridge."

"How many?"

"Hundreds in camp. More roaming the forests," the man said. "I put it at nearly a thousand, all told."

"Whose are they?" Malcolm asked.

"They fly no banners, but their fit and form is Suhdrin."

"Damn it," Malcolm muttered. "We'll have to circle back and follow the trampled mud of the Suhdrin army to White Lake. If we can get across before the storms set in, we should…"

A horn sounded behind them, and was quickly answered from the flanks. A wave of nervous chatter went through the company. Catrin and Sorcha joined hands and started to pray. Malcolm signaled to Sir Doone.

"Form a wedge, my wife and the priestess in the middle," he said. "Fly the colors. When we sight their line, sound the horns and ride hard. We need to get through before they close ranks."

"If they were expecting us—" Doone started.

"They weren't. This isn't an ambush. We've just stumbled into their lines."

"How did we get so close without being seen?" Doone wondered.

"By coming from a direction where they weren't

expecting resistance, perhaps," Malcolm said. "Though that's strange for a Suhdrin force. Regardless, we must take advantage. Form on me, and ride!"

He trotted down the road, letting the column coalesce around him before picking up the pace. He glanced back once, to make sure his wife was safely in position. The two fey women were still clasping hands and chanting their prayer, though it was beyond him how they managed that at a canter.

The first scouts appeared on the bluffs, blowing horns, silhouettes against the dying sun. They were armed with longbows, but none of them loosed quarrels in Malcolm's direction. The horn from behind sounded again, farther away as the company pushed forward, and then for the first time was answered from ahead. If the bridge was already blocked, it would take nerve and luck to break through.

Malcolm spurred his mount forward, the column flowing easily into his wake. The long, slow curve of the road gave way to the bridge's approach. Smoke rose from the bluffs on Malcolm's right. The bridge came into sight, a low stone span over a narrow gorge. The river was low, but steep banks and a wide course guaranteed that they wouldn't be able to ford it, at least not here.

The bridge, though, was clear. Their path was unobstructed, but a brace of riders was rushing down the bluffs, riding hard to cut Malcolm off. It was going to be close.

He bent to his horse's neck and whispered encouragement, then offered the spur. But the beast was already at the end of a long ride, and had nothing else to give. Malcolm glanced back at his column and saw that they were lagging behind, their own mounts failing them. They weren't going to make the bridge before the Suhdrin force.

Malcolm sighed, then drew his blade.

"The only way out is through!" he shouted. "Blades, blades, brace for charge! Spears to the fore! Blades and shields!"

"The Hound!" his men responded. "The Hallow!"

"The Hound!" Malcolm answered, and raised the dull black edge of his sword toward the Suhdrin host that was forming at the mouth of the bridge. "The Hallow!"

The Suhdrin force made hasty preparation. There weren't that many, but they were knights of spear, all in armor and prepared for battle. Perhaps they had known Malcolm was coming this way after all. He glimpsed bright color among their ranks, a single figure in red and gold who dismounted smoothly and strode a few feet down the road toward Malcolm.

A knight of the vow. Malcolm searched the rest of the host and found the knight's companion, an inquisitor in dark robes, weaving naetheric shadows into the air. The rest of the Suhdrin force fell back from the pair—all but one man, who was digging desperately through his saddlebags.

"Are we going to ride through a vow knight?" Sir Doone shouted.

"If we must," Malcolm said. He glanced back at Catrin, but the priestess was in a fugue state, her eyes closed and face lifted to the sky. It was a mystery how she hadn't toppled from the saddle. He turned back to the bridge. Strange lights began forming around the vow knight, a circle of gold that twisted up into the air, forming a dome.

The knight's armor crackled with power, and her blade was a splinter of the sun given form. Malcolm squinted into the brilliance, and couldn't help but wonder if this was how he was meant to die. It seemed strange, to face down Sacombre's heresy and Adair's betrayal, only to fall at the hand of a servant of loving Strife, the only god he seemed to understand anymore.

Well, Malcolm thought, *if this is what the goddess asks of me, it is what she will have. Sacrifice, and glory.*

A shadow passed in front of the vow knight's glare. Malcolm shielded his eyes, peering at a lone figure who had ridden in front of the light. It was a man on a horse, waving some kind of rumpled banner. The fool was going to be trampled.

The light changed, and the banner became clear. Malcolm signaled the halt. In the glaring light, it took Doone and the others a while to realize they were stopping. The column slid around Malcolm before stomping to the canter and finally stopping completely. He rode through them, easing their worry and ordering swords into sheathes before he emerged from the churning chaos of his troops. He rode toward the man with the banner.

"Redgarden," he called. "I did not think to find you so far north."

"Nor you, so far south," Castian Jaerdin answered. Behind him, the vow knight spun down her invocations, the lights winking out one by one.

Malcolm rode to Jaerdin's side. They clasped hands. He nodded toward the vow knight and inquisitor. "Visitors from Heartsbridge?" he asked.

"We came upon them on the godsroad. They were recalled from their hunting to the north to handle matters in Greenhall. Is your wife..." Jaerdin craned his head, his eyes widening when he picked Sorcha out of the column. Lady Blakley's head was crowned with light, and her eyes shone like stars. "Ah," he said.

"Yes," Malcolm said, staring down the inquisitor.

The man marched down the road, stern face scanning the Tenerran force, fists clenching a mace as big as his head. "Ah, indeed."

Jaerdin's force had joined with sympathizers from the south, Roard and Bealth chief among them, to form a small army. They tarried in southern Tener following their expulsion from the Fen Gate, but mostly because the way south wasn't clear.

"Surely Sir Bourne would let you pass," Malcolm said as they rode up the bluff to Jaerdin's camp. "Your stand at White Lake is well known in Tener."

"Bourne has no say in the matter," Castian answered.

"So the Reaveholt has fallen, then," Sir Doone said. "Gods pray Bourne gave them hell in the process."

"No, no, the 'holt still stands, but it is surrounded. Bassion has marched north with enough force to circle around White Lake, hold the fords and the Redoubt, and cut Bourne off from both directions." The camp was alive with activity. Jaerdin signaled to the guards, letting them know to stand down. "This is as far south as we dare to go. Any further and we may draw Bassion's attention. We've been expecting an attack for days."

"From Bassion? Here?" Malcolm asked. He looked around. They were on a war footing—even the pages and cooks were wearing loose chain shirts and carrying swords awkwardly at their sides. "Why would Bassion attack you?"

"Because of you," Castian said, "and because of Greenhall."

"That was months ago," Malcolm said. "By now Frair Lucas will have delivered Halverdt's body and told the story of Sacombre's treachery."

Castian slid from his horse, handing riding gloves and rumpled banner to a page. Malcolm followed suit.

"Come see for yourself, Houndhallow," Castian said.

The pair made their way through the camp, to the southern picket. The bluff here was slightly higher than the rest of the grounds, providing some cover from the southern approach, as well as a superior lookout. Several rangers sat casually along the line, nodding to Jaerdin as he approached. None of them moved to stand or salute. They wore no house colors, and had the look of bandits.

"You've become lax in your recruiting standards," Malcolm muttered as they passed the men.

"Any blade in a war, Houndhallow, and this is truly a war."

"It has been for some time," Malcolm said.

"Yes," Castian answered. "But now..."

He paused at the tip of the bluff and motioned to the south. From this distance, the Tallow was a winding shadow in the grasslands, the Reaveholt a flat black disk at the intersection of road and river, the air above it smudgy with wood smoke. An army camped along the northern road, and another to the south. Their banners hung in the lazy air, the colors of Suhdra.

"I have seen many armies since this all started, Redgarden," Malcolm said. "This is another one, no larger than most, and no smaller. It certainly doesn't equal the force currently camped around the Fen Gate."

"Not in number, but in composition, it varies greatly." Castian produced a looking glass, unfolding it and handing it to Malcolm. "Look closer, Houndhallow. See what is arrayed against us."

Malcolm took the glass and sighted down the valley. He recognized the banners and ranks of Bassion, Marchand, and other southern houses, all arranged in classic military order. They were prepared for a long siege. But he saw nothing extraordinary about their disposition. He was about to hand the glass back to Castian when a shadow loomed across his vision. He quickly pulled back, found the dark void in his view, and refocused on it.

A group of inquisitors stood in a loose circle, outside the boundaries of the Suhdrin camp. They were engaged in some sort of ritual, their hands and minds joined by lines of naetheric force. The space between them shimmered in blackness. A creature loomed out of the void and the background darkness vanished, like a window snapping shut. The inquisitors quickly fell on the beast, lashing it to the earth with bonds of naether, sealing it into the waking world.

Malcolm dropped the glass. His mouth was agape.

"Yes, Houndhallow. Exactly. The house of Cinder has sworn to the enemy. They have put their vows aside, and joined the Suhdrin crusade against the north," Jaerdin said. His face was grim. "And they have brought their god with them."

49

THE HENGE NESTLED among a peaceful copse of trees, tucked deep in the forest. The stones were old and worn, but their roots reached all the way to the bedrock, their power true. It was a forgotten place.

Despite the bright autumn sun, fog began to form between the stones. At first it was just a gray whisper, but slowly it gathered, thicker and thicker until dark mist billowed up from the mossy rocks, forming a cloud that engulfed the henge. Cinders licked through the fog in curls of light that sparkled in the mist. Then, with a thunder that shook the dry leaves still clinging to the trees, a column of ash and ember crashed out of the henge and washed through the forest.

Gwen was the first to emerge. She stumbled out of the fog bank, her eyes pressed closed, arms outstretched, face smeared with soot. Bits of her clothing were on fire, and the short stubble of her head was singed. Her fingers brushed a lichen-shrouded tree and she stopped and looked around.

"We made it," she called. "We're somewhere else."

"Quietly," Cahl cautioned. "Until we know where we are." The big shaman loomed out of the mist, Noel on one arm and a broken log in his other hand. He limped into the open. The witch settled into a coughing fit, then blinked up at the sun and smiled.

"A gracious sight," Noel said. "I thought I'd never see the sun again."

"We're farther north, for sure," Gwen said. "Gods pray far enough."

"Well, there's no smoke in the air, and this henge is in good enough repair." Cahl put a hand against one of the stones. "We are away from Suhdrin influence, at least."

Noel disentangled herself from his arm and limped to a nearby stump. She sat and began rubbing her eyes. "So what now?" she asked. "I'm assuming this henge can't take us anywhere else?"

"Gods, no. It barely got us here," Cahl said.

"We will need food and shelter," Gwen said. "Water, and then we have to get back to the conclave. They must know of Folam's betrayal."

"We don't know—" Noel began.

"Gods *hell* we don't," Gwen snapped. "I've had enough of you defending that man. I expect it of Cahl, but you, a Suhdrin born and raised... you should know better."

"There are so few friendly voices in the south," Noel said sadly. "It is hard to find betrayal in the north, as well."

"Yet betrayal found us," Cahl said. Wincing in pain, he limped up a nearby hill and looked around. "Grace Steading," he called down. "North and east of the Fen. North of the hound's lands, as well. The conclave is not far."

"Do we return to them?" Noel asked. "If Folam has already reached them, there is no telling what lies he has told."

"And there was already little love for me in their ranks," Gwen said. "He won't have to weave a strong tale to convince them of my betrayal." She sat down heavily beside Noel. The witch put a hand on Gwen's shoulder and rubbed it.

"Even if he's there first," Cahl said, "we have to warn them. If you don't want to take that risk, I won't ask it of you. But I must go."

"I'm not staying here," Gwen said, "and there's nowhere else for me. Besides, the bastard used my hair and blood in the ritual. Used my body to summon that gheist." She drew her knife, then slid it under her shirt. A short time later her hand emerged with the linen she had used to bind her chest. "It seems like my debt to pay. At least in part."

"There is no debt among the gods," Cahl said. "Nevertheless, your company would be welcome."

"Fine," Gwen said. She stood, then helped Noel to her feet. "To the conclave, but we'd best be on our way. Gods know how Folam travels, and we'll be walking."

"No," Cahl said. "You did not hear. We are on the hound's border, and I have walked with his heir." He closed his eyes and raised a hand, his palm cupped. A drop of blood nestled in his hand, like a crimson bead. "Ian owes me this much at least."

In the distance, something howled.

The pack was a fury through the trees, moss-gray trunks whipping past so quickly that Gwen lost count, speeding by until their arching canopies blurred into a long, sun-dappled tunnel that shifted overhead.

She lay across the creature's back, its spine flexing beneath her belly, ribs scraping her legs, her fingers tangled in a mat of fur so thick it seemed like iron chain. The smell of the beast filled her lungs with musk. Whether these creatures were gods or spirits or merely wild, Gwen didn't know. They carried her through the forests like a wind.

They skirted distant Houndhallow, the pack falling toward the sanctuary of their grounds like a stone, only pulling away from it at Cahl's urging. Gwen briefly glimpsed the black stone walls of the castle before they were swept away. The sun moved but didn't move.

When they came to a halt, it was dusk, and the valley below them sparkled with campfires.

"I can't believe Blakley would tolerate such a gathering so close to his walls," Noel said. The witch sat on her mount comfortably, as though riding feral dogs through the forest was a regular exercise for her.

"The lord is away, and his eye does not reach far into the woods," Cahl said. "Even so, this is a little close for my comfort. Something must have driven them here."

"Fear, perhaps? Or rage. Are they hunting something?" Gwen asked. "We left them in some disarray."

"All part of Folam's plan, no doubt," Cahl said. He slid from the hound's back, running a hand through the creature's fur and scratching its ears. The beast curled back a lip and let out a bone-shuddering rumble that might have been pleasure or rage. "The conclave will be on edge."

Noel laughed and shook her head. "They talk so much of sacrifice and faith, but put them within a day of a doma and the northern elders shake like children in a thunderstorm. You would think the smell of frairwood burned their precious noses."

"The inquisition does not hunt in Suhdra as they hunt here. You have only to wear decent robes and learn the words to the evensong to pass undisturbed, Noel," Cahl said. “These people live in fear of being dragged from their beds and hanged in the village square. It is not the same.”

“So you say,” Noel answered quietly, “but I have seen my share of hangings—for a word spoken wrong to a neighbor, or the fortune of having a child not fall ill when the rest of the village takes sick. Even cooking a decent loaf of bread when your neighbor’s burns can bring the church’s attention. We may not have as many inquisitor’s, shaman, but we have gossips, jealousy, and spite.”

“So how do we approach the conclave?” Gwen asked, brushing the conversation aside before it could get out of hand. “Do we know an elder who can be trusted? Someone who won’t have fallen to Folam’s spite?”

“Morcant will be too involved with his own people to listen to the voidfather, though he may not listen to us, either,” Cahl said. “Aedan is consumed with his hatred for you. Anything Folam says that aligns with that hatred, the elder of the hunt will lap up. Tammish and Vilday will wait to see what the others do, though Tammish might be moved.” He turned to Gwen. “His tribe was close to your family, before the crusades. As elder of the depths, he may be willing to welcome the last child of the tribe of iron into his fold.”

“I’m not looking for political alliances, nor friendship,” Gwen said. “I need someone I can trust to stand against the voidfather. Against the elder of elders.”

“I have a name,” Noel said. They turned to her, and she shrugged. “Honest enemies make honest allies.”

“Judoc,” Cahl said. “Elder of bones.”

“If we can’t trust the dead,” Noel answered, “who can we trust? They have nothing to hide, and less to gain.”

“Very well,” Cahl said. “Judoc.” He turned to the forest,

his limp barely noticeable now in his long stride. "I will speak with him."

"Let me," Noel said.

"He will trust you?"

"No." Noel bent and whispered to her hound, and the beast loped toward the campfires below, still carrying the witch. She turned back to them. "But he will do as I ask. If only to see me ruined."

She returned some hours later, without her mount. Judoc walked beside her, his cloak of bones clattering like birdsong. He and Noel were engaged in deep conversation, their heads bent close, their hands gesturing madly. Cahl waited until they were close before he cleared his throat. Judoc jumped.

"Gods, elder. Did you lose your way in the woods?" Cahl asked with a smile.

"I have lost my way with this woman, perhaps, but that is nothing new," Judoc said. The grim elder of the tribe of bones settled onto a stump, folding his legs and hands awkwardly, until he looked like a vulture waiting for someone else's death. "Elder Cahl. We thought we lost you in Greenhall."

"So Folam has returned to you," Gwen said. "What has he been saying?"

"Folam is dead. Following the failed ritual in Greenhall..."

"That was not—" Gwen started. Judoc raised a hand to stop her.

"...following the failed ritual in Greenhall, he returned to us, gravely injured. He said you were betrayed by men of the hound, conspirators who dined with Lady Halverdt and walked the streets with inquisitors," Judoc finished. "Noel has had much to say about your time in the voidfather's company. I would not trust her with my death, but I would never accuse her of trying to undercut Folam's command, at least not without good reason. Still, I would rather have it from Tenerran lips. Cahl?"

"There were no conspirators in the city. No men of Blakley, nor inquisitors," Cahl said. "If anything, the place has become a refuge for Lady Strife, despite winter's approach."

"And the only betrayal was Folam's," Gwen said. "He tricked me into helping summon the vernal god. He tricked us all." Judoc listened to Gwen's accusation, then turned to Cahl for confirmation. The shaman nodded sharply, and the elder of bones sighed.

"His tale didn't feel right," Judoc said. "Several of the others rallied to his side, though, mostly of Fianna's kin. They wanted vengeance. Folam hesitated at first, but eventually agreed to lead us here."

"He led you to Houndhallow?" Gwen asked. "But to what purpose?"

"They intend to attack House Blakley," Noel said, her face drawn. "They think they will find evidence of Houndhallow's complicity in Sacombre's plot. The Duke of Greenhall died in his company, after all. If Greenhall falls, and Adair with it, Blakley would have claim to much of that land. Especially as a spoil of war."

"That's ridiculous!" Gwen said. "Malcolm Blakley is the man who drove the demon out of Sacombre's flesh! Without his deeds, the high inquisitor could well have killed the defenders of the Fen Gate, and overrun the strength of Tener. If anything, the pagan lands owe Blakley a debt of gratitude!"

"Perhaps, but once we were here, Folam went out to scout the castle. He and his whole party were taken." Judoc paused, looking meaningfully at Noel. "Killed by inquisitors. A dozen, if there was one."

"The inquisition doesn't move in groups like that!" Gwen said. "I've worked with them my entire life. They travel alone, or with a knight of the vow. The only reason to gather in any kind of numbers..."

"Would be to wage war," Judoc said. Gwen hesitated, then nodded.

"Yes. For war, and nothing else."

"And the others? Do they still intend to attack Houndhallow?" Cahl asked.

A horn sounded in the distance, harsh against the peaceful night air. Judoc didn't answer, but turned to face the distant walls of the 'hallow.

"We have to stop them," Gwen said. "Blakley's strength is at the Fen Gate, along with his wife and son. Only the child remains! Young Nessie will have no idea how to lead a castle's defense."

"We will do what we can," Noel said, "but it will be like trying to turn the tide. The elders are decided."

"I'll go," Cahl said. The shaman started clearing the ground at his feet, finding bedrock stones, feeling out the path to the battle line. "The rest of you will have to catch up."

"None of you are going," a voice said from the woods. Dark shapes surrounded them, emerging from the trees as though they stepped out of shadows. They wore dark purple and black, the chains of their belts worked in silver. Inquisitor robes, but corrupted somehow, as though the vestments had been turned into soldier's uniforms.

Cahl stood and faced them. The small company came together, standing back to back. Judoc's bone cloak rattled.

The priest in front came closer. He threw back his hood and smiled. It was the first time Gwen had seen Folam smile.

It was an ugly sight.

50

THE COLUMN OF knights was in tight formation, shields facing outward, their spears bristling overhead. Their horses banked skittishly beneath their rider's spurs, following the road like a snake, slithering forward. There weren't as many of them as it first appeared. Their core was hollow, their strength arrayed in long columns to hide their numbers.

They slowed when Elsa came around the corner, her companions slightly behind. Ian rode with his face in shadow. Volent's hood was thrown back, the ruin of his skin bold under the sun.

"Halt," the company's sergeant called. The column came to a sporadic stop, some thinking the man was addressing Elsa, others obeying the command for themselves. The column stretched out along the road, drawing harsh words from the sergeant. Finally he turned to Elsa again, making his words clear.

"Riders approaching, halt!"

In the confusion, the trio rode close enough to count the straps on the sergeant's cassock. Elsa nodded to her companions, and they ambled to a stop. She sat her mount with one hand on the reins, the other pressed into her thigh, throwing her cloak over her shoulder and revealing the gold and crimson of her tabard.

"You're far north for Suhdrin souls," she said, "and too far west to be headed for Cinderfell. Are you lost, or foolish?"

"Hunting," the sergeant said. "The traitor Malcolm Blakley has fled the Fen Gate, but not before seeding it with pagan gods."

"Oh? The man who exposed the heresy of both Adair and Sacombre has turned feral overnight?" Elsa asked. "That will come as some surprise to his wife."

"The stories of his heroism are overstretched," the sergeant said. Elsa's eyes strayed across his company. Other than the banner of House Marchand, none of them wore house colors or carried crests of the southern lords. They could be bandits, though bandits never rode in such force, or with such discipline. The commander continued, his voice sour with contempt.

"There are many questions about Sacombre's deeds, but all agree that Blakley was involved with Adair. Why else would he rush to stand at the heretic's side, and offer his blood in defense of a pagan's castle? As for his battle with the high inquisitor, well," the man waved a dismissive hand. "Tall tales and fabrication. I was there. I saw Sacombre drive the gheist out of Adair's castle, only to be struck down by Houndhallow before he could finish the demon off."

"Brave words, and foolish, for one so far from home," Ian growled. The sergeant squinted at him, but Elsa edged closer, drawing the man's attention.

"The words of better witnesses than you tell a different story, sir," she said.

"As I said, I was there…"

"As was I," Elsa answered. "In the keep, and at Blakley's side. I saw Colm Adair fall, and Sacombre rise. I saw the god of death in his eyes, and witnessed Houndhallow's feat of will." She held out her hand, as though offering a drink from her palm. "Or do you question the word of a vow knight, as well?"

The column shifted uncomfortably, the sergeant backing away, though his face was set in stony silence. Finally he looked over at Volent, who had thus far escaped his attention.

The sergeant recoiled. "Sir Volent?" he gasped. "But you were... they said..."

"I live," Volent answered. "If anything, I am less dead than I was—in spirit, if not in flesh. Which lord claims your loyalty, sir?"

"That is not, we were..."

"Stop stammering, man!" Volent snapped. "We are three and you the dozens, and still you act like you're facing off against an army. You are a military force, on military patrol, and yet I see no colors on your chest nor sigil in your ranks. Are you ashamed of your lord? Mine led us into false war, and died a fool's death, and yet I would never forsake his name. What coward do you serve, that you lack such pride?"

"Our orders are to ride without colors, so as not to startle Lord Blakley, should we come upon him. It's also thought..." the man paused again, glancing at the vow knight. "It is believed that the gheists of this land are drawn by Suhdrin crests, as commanded by their witch lords."

Elsa let out a laugh so brisk and loud it startled the horses all down the line, and set off a few moments of panic as the riders tried to bring the beasts back under control. When they were calm, she spoke again.

"As a priest of Strife and an agent of the celestial church, I demand to know your loyalty. Whose colors do you fly?"

"Douglas Marchand, Duke of Highope and lord of the

southern range," the sergeant said. He bowed his head only briefly. "And I am Sir Harold Tombe, sworn to his service."

"Sir Tombe, your lord has led you far north, perhaps farther than he has a right to claim," she responded. "But in asking that you cast off your colors, he has made a grave mistake. One I am afraid I must rectify."

"Sir?" Tombe asked with some trepidation. "We are agents of war, not bound by laws of chivalry."

"I would never accuse you of being bound to chivalry, sir," Elsa said sharply. "No, in surrendering your colors on the field of battle, you have brought your loyalty into question. You may turn your coat, or worse, flee the field entirely."

"We are not on a field of battle," Tombe said with a harsh laugh.

"Are we not?" Ian asked, drawing his sword. Tombe stared at him with disbelief, but Ian did not yield. Tombe kept looking between Ian and Elsa, occasionally glancing at Volent.

"What is this?" he said. "Has Strife thrown in with House Blakley?"

"Quite the opposite," Elsa said. "Blakley has thrown in with Strife. His loyalty is to the church, as is the loyalty of all holy men and women of Tenumbra. He has renounced his household, and answers now only to Heartsbridge."

"More like his father has thrown him out on his ass," one of the knights murmured. Ian bristled, but Elsa held him back with a glance.

"This is my question, men of Marchand," she continued. "I have need of you. We are following a pagan of great power, and a gheist of dire intent. I ask you to renounce your Suhdrin loyalty, and answer to the call of Strife. Ride with me, and rid these lands of the gheist." She nodded to her companions. "As have Ian Blakley, and Henri Volent."

Tombe was silent for several moments. He glared at the vow knight for a long time before shaking his head.

"I will not ride with such company," he said.

"We should take him," one of the group growled. It was the knight who had spoken earlier. "Take them both. Highope will pay well for Blakley's whelp, and surely there is a ransom in the Deadface's blood. Gods know he's done crime enough."

"You take them only through the shedding of my blood," Elsa said, "and you will find that hard to accomplish." She didn't touch her blade, but the violence in her voice was enough to cut stone. Tombe didn't move.

"I'll ride with you," one of the knights said. He rode forward, breaking formation and trotting to Elsa's side. He was old, his weathered face calm under a helm of steel. "Lady Strife never has to ask me twice."

"And I," another called. He was joined by a half-dozen others, each man and woman pulling out of formation to stand beside Elsa. Ian smirked at Tombe's growing rage.

"You will be reported," Tombe said. "All of you. Your families will hear of this."

"Gods pray my family serves the church as well as it has served me," the weathered knight said. "This news will be met with favor back home."

"This is a mistake. You're all making a terrible mistake," Tombe insisted. His reduced column drew tight, collapsing on the gaps in their ranks. They looked much smaller, as though a stiff breeze could send them running.,

"You should go," Volent said. "Before my service to the gods includes knocking you off that damned horse."

Tombe hesitated as long as his nerves could manage, but not as long as his pride would want. Then he turned and led his column back the way they had come, moving quickly, if not with greater poise.

"That will be trouble," the weathered knight said quietly. "Tombe always had more pride than sense."

"The world is little else but trouble these days," Volent answered. He turned his horse back toward the moors. "I've stopped letting it bother me."

"And what of you, young Blakley?" the knight asked. "Does it bother you that your father has broken, his numbers scattered to the winds?"

"That is not my fight," Ian said. He turned to follow Volent. "Not anymore."

They rode in relative silence for most of the afternoon. The eight Suhdrin knights who had joined them stayed together, speaking quietly on occasion, the young deferring to the weathered knight whenever there was disagreement.

Ian and Volent rode ahead, knee to knee, never looking back. Elsa negotiated the distance between these two groups, only speaking when they strayed from whatever invisible path led to the pagan god.

They found traces of its passing. The skittish herds of silver deer that roamed these moors stayed well away from them, but more than once they crossed a corpse torn apart by human hands, the wounds seared in ash, only the heart and lungs consumed. Elsa stopped long enough to breath a prayer into the dead creature's flesh. The Suhdrin knights grew quiet, and began to ride closer to the vow priest.

As the afternoon waned, the weathered knight broke free

from his companions and rode to the front of the column. He brought his mount even with Volent, keeping the Suhdrin between him and Ian. After a few quiet moments, he turned and addressed the broken man.

"You are not what I assumed you would be," he said.

"The stories of a man travel farther than the man himself," Volent said, "and often change in the going. Even so, I am not the man the stories were told about." The knight seemed satisfied with that, nodding curtly. He offered his gauntleted hand, not in a handshake so much as a benediction.

"I am Sir Bruler, recently of House Marchand, but..." he smiled, his face cracking into a thousand wrinkles, the lines around his eyes light with joy. "I seem to have broken that commitment. Do you think this makes me a holy man, perhaps?"

"It makes you a strange man, at least," Volent said. "Why did you answer Sir LaFey's call?" Bruler shrugged, an elaborate gesture that encompassed his entire body.

"She seems a dangerous sort," he responded. "The sort that is worth getting into trouble with. I have followed worse lords for lesser causes."

"You're not a zealot, are you? I have never trusted zealots."

"No? That is unusual, coming from you—but as you say, stories travel, and men change." Bruler blew his nose. "I am not given to great enthusiasm for the gods, if that is what you mean. For anything, really. That itself makes me unusual these days."

Volent turned and looked at the man, up and down. He tilted his head.

"How do you mean?" Volent asked.

"There is something wrong in the south. In all of Suhdra,

and Tener besides, I imagine, though perhaps they have merely caught it from us." He glanced back at his seven companions. "They will never know it, the way things were during the Reaver War, when our lands stood united." He glanced past Volent, addressing the still silent Ian. "When your father rode with us. When the banner of the hound flew at the head of our battle line, and the blood of Tenerran and Suhdrin flowed together."

"That was apparently not enough to save him at the Fen Gate, sir," Ian said, his head buried in his hood.

"No. No, it was not," Bruler said, shaking his head sadly, "but when the priests tell us that House Blakley has fallen to heresy, that the Reaverbane is colluding with pagans and his son has taken up with witches, well... that is a story I have trouble believing."

"Stories change," Ian said. "Men change."

"They do, and so when this golden lady came to me at the end of a long and thankless journey and offered me the opportunity to know for myself, to see and judge the son, and perhaps learn more of the father, I could not turn it down." Bruler spoke out over the moor, his eyes roaming the grassy hills and peering into the mists that clung to the horizon. "I could not believe what I was told, so I determined to follow the church's call, to know for myself."

"It's not often that unbelief leads to service with the church," Volent muttered. This brought another laugh from Bruler, a hearty sound that seemed to cut through the fog and bring a little sun to the grassy hills.

"No, it is not, but that is my path," Bruler said. "That is the road I must travel, and you will travel it with me, Sir Volent. Sir Blakley. We will arrive at our destination together, or not at all."

"Are you always this talkative?" Volent asked. "Or can we look forward to brief moments of silence?"

"Brief, yes," Bruler answered, "but never dull."

Without untangling what that meant, the three continued down the unmarked path, Elsa nudging them north or south as they wandered, the young knights following quietly after. Bruler continued his stories, and Ian his silence.

51

"WHAT THE HELL are we doing, frair?" Martin asked sharply. The flow of traffic slowed momentarily, as the passersby in gray and black frowned at Martin's abuse of a priest. He ducked his head and rushed after Lucas. So easy to lose the man in this crowd, one more gray-hooded frair among multitudes. When he caught up to Lucas, Martin forced him to the side of the road.

"Lucas? Have you lost your mind?"

"Hardly," Lucas said. He reached down and gently pried Martin's fingers away from his chest, then nodded amicably to the dozen or so priests and guards who were watching them nervously. "It may be better to take this conversation inside."

"And we're just going to leave them there?" Martin said, pointing angrily back to the inn. "Just like that?"

"Enough talking," Lucas said with a sigh. He led his companion into a bar. The room was dark and dingy and full of desperate drunk sailors, none of whom noticed their entrance. Lucas hurriedly closed the door behind him, then went to the shuttered window and peered out between the cracks. "Hopefully they'll have followed… yes, here we are."

"What? What's going on?"

"You're going to excite the clientele, and this lot doesn't

seem in the market for excitement," Lucas said. "We have been followed, sir. Since the Fen Gate, I suspect, but certainly since Gardengerry. Attacks like that don't just happen."

"You said it was a rogue gheist. That you should have searched more closely."

"I did search more closely. I blanketed that city in wards, but each and every one of them was looking outward. Which either means our attacker was already waiting for us in the city, or..." he drew Martin closer, whispering in the boy's ear as he pointed outside. "Quietly. Our hunter was already in our midst."

Through the narrow crack in the shutter, Martin was able to see a slice of the road outside. Most of the traffic blurred past, gray robes and dingy armor, shot through with the grim faces of the residents of Gallowsport. The only solitary figure was a man in black and silver, his garb not too out of place, but it carried the dust of the road, and the chain mail that peeked out of his shirt was clean and well-oiled. Before he could speak a second figure appeared.

Martin recognized her immediately.

"She's dead," he whispered.

"Apparently not," Lucas said. Out in the street, Sir Horne spoke briefly with the lookout, who nodded to the door of the bar in reply. Another few words and the scout directed her to the inn where Sacombre and Fianna were waiting. She set her face into a scowl and marched off in that direction.

"No," Martin said. "You misunderstand me. When I get my hands on her, she's fucking dead."

Fianna changed, and the room changed with her. Sacombre fell back against the far wall of the room. The high inquisitor held up his hands, shielding his face from the creature. From the god.

The witch stood slowly. She held out her hands, still bound by Lucas's bonds, the rope entwined with icons of silver and steel. They were glowing with the effort of restraining Fianna's presence. Water poured from her wrists, soaking the strands of the binding until they dissolved. Slowly, what was left of the rope unraveled.

Fianna's skin turned to quicksilver, parting at wrist and throat to bleed light. Her eyes changed to fog, the empty sockets filling with clear water that poured down her cheeks in small cascades, falling in slow motion, spreading out in a silver lace that covered her shoulders and continued down her chest. The water that fell from her body formed a pool at her feet, eating away the surface until Fianna stood over a bottomless well of dark liquid that churned with inky shapes.

"You will not frighten me, witch!" Sacombre snapped. He drew himself upright, gathering the pride he had so recently abandoned, his back stiff as a spear. "The powers of the north are considerable, but they are nothing in the face of true winter!"

"Call to your frozen god, priest," Fianna said. "I have played your game long enough. Let's be done with this charade."

"Played my game? Ha! Without my help you and your damnable father would still be praying to mud and digging berries out of your hair! You lot are all the same." Sacombre clenched his fists and tugged at his bonds, the skin of his wrists tearing open, blood running down his fingers. "It was a mistake trying to raise you up. Tener will never be Suhdra's equal! The gods are wasted on you!"

"For a man of the church, there is so little you

understand about divinity," Fianna said. She lifted her right hand, touching fingers together, tapping her palm. The water beneath her stirred, then rose in thin ribbons, corkscrewing into the air to dance around the hand. She wove the strands of water as if on a loom, patterns emerging in the beaded light that flickered through the liquid.

"The gods are wasted on us?" she said. "No. They are not a resource to be mined, nor a gift to be squandered. You celestials have everything backwards. You measure Cinder and Strife in days and hours and weather, and think that all gods can be made to march to your calendar. You push, and the gods move, and so you blame us for not pushing." She clenched her fist, and the pool of water rose up in a column that twisted around her like a cloak. "The gods move, and we move with them. The gods rise, and we rise at their side."

"And when your gods fall at my hands, it will be your death!" Sacombre howled. He closed his eyes and the dim light from the door disappeared completely, leaving only Fianna's silvery illumination. The shadows in the corners crawled along the floor, gathering at Sacombre's feet, slowly crawling up his robes, turning the dirty gray linen black as midnight. Fragments of moonlight shone behind his eyelids. The darkness gathered in his flesh. Then it reached the bonds Lucas had tied. There it sputtered, and died.

Sacombre sagged against the wall, his energy spent. The icons on his bonds flickered quietly, the force they absorbed slowly cooking off into the air. He took a long, shuddering breath.

"Trouble, Sacombre?" Fianna said. Her voice came through the cloak of water, echoing in Sacombre's skull like a dream. "The god of winter obeying the laws of winter, after all? How do you like feeling abandoned? Alone?" Sacombre didn't answer, bleary eyes staring at the ropes around his wrists, lips mumbling wordless curses in the darkness. "Don't fear, Tomas. It will be over soon enough."

Fianna surged toward him, a flood wall of glowing water and fury. The floorboards beneath her creaked with the weight, the room twisting and wood shrieking as the building distorted. Still Sacombre didn't move.

"Lord Inquisitor!" The woman's voice came from the hallway. Someone was hammering on the door, trying to force open the twisted frame. "Sacombre! Can you hear me?"

"Abandoned?" Sacombre muttered, raising his eyes to Fianna's shocked face. "This is my season, pagan. I am never alone."

The door finally burst open, shattering into splinters. The hallway beyond was crowded with inquisitors. No, not inquisitors, their robes were too dark, the trim of their armor too fine. Silver chain mail and dark blades drawn, no naetheric armor or spells in the air around them. They were not of Cinder, but they answered to the high inquisitor.

And Fianna's gheist answered to them.

The woman in the doorway raised her hands toward Fianna. Her palms were etched in dark runes, smeared with ash and blood. A wave of force washed out from the runes, clearing the shadows and striking the column of water like a hammer blow. The gheist ripped free of Fianna, tearing away from her and slamming into the far wall. It flattened in a rippling blanket of living liquid. Fianna dropped to the ground with a gasp. The light of her skin faded.

"Sir Horne," Sacombre said as he dusted off his hands and straightened. "I thought we'd lost you on the moors."

"Frair Lucas dampened your aura, my lord," Horne

said. She stood with arms outstretched, as though she were holding up the wall of water with her will. "We followed the obvious route, but sent riders to search elsewhere, just in case. We will recall them as quickly as possible."

"Good. We will need their strength." Sacombre strolled to Fianna's side. With his toe he pushed the witch onto her back. "You see, my dear? A wolf is dangerous, but it is only an animal. It can be hunted, beaten, muzzled. It can be tamed. Your gods are no different." He motioned to the figures in the hall. They flowed around Sir Horne's extended arms and went to the gheist—who shimmered, pinned against the wall. At Sacombre's signal, they drew dark blades and plunged them into the writhing spirit.

The gheist squealed as it died. Tattered rags of living water broke free from its body, floundering on the floor, spraying mist before losing shape and washing formlessly between the boards. Some of the water splashed onto Sacombre's robes. He shook it off, grinning. Sir Horne lowered her hands, then drew a blade, went to Sacombre, and cut him free of his bonds. The high inquisitor nodded, rubbing his bloody wrists.

"And like a wolf, their throats can be cut," he said. "Messy. Unfortunate, but sometimes necessary."

Fianna stared at the dead gheist, now nothing more than damp wood and a quickly dissipating fog that clung to the air. Sacombre marched out of the room, followed by the rest. Only Horne stayed behind.

"Who are you?" Fianna asked finally, her tear-streaked eyes focusing on the Suhdrin knight. "And what have you done?"

"We are the inheritors of your wasted power, witch," Horne said. "And we have ended you." With that, Sir Horne bent down and drove her knife into Fianna's heart. The witch's last thoughts were of the dying god, and the silence that waited beyond.

Lucas wanted to be sure the conspirators were gathered at the inn before he struck. Martin stood impatiently in front of the tavern's door, twisting his sword in his hands and generally making the other patrons nervous.

When the frair gave him the signal, Martin burst out the door, thinking to bull rush the lookout while Lucas hurried on to the inn to capture Sir Horne and whoever else had shown up to rescue Sacombre and the witch. He made it through the door and halfway across the street before he learned the error of this tactic.

The man watching them from across the street threw open his cloak, revealing a void, a yawning chasm, lined with teeth and stretching into an impossible distance. Martin slowed just long enough for a tongue to flick out from that chasm, bowling him over into the mud. While he scrambled to his feet the man threw off the cloak, dropping it to the ground and fleeing down an alleyway.

As it fell, the cloak unfolded and unfolded again, a gheist of teeth and hunger growing in the middle of the street. The crowd of priests—most of them book keepers and administrators of the prisons of the Black Isle—flinched away. That initial flinch quickly became a rout. Even the guards threw down their weapons as the gheist rose, towering above the buildings. Soon, Martin found himself alone in the street, staring up at the gheist.

"You will need to do something about that," Lucas said from the shelter of the tavern. "Quickly, I would think."

"Me?" Martin asked. He stood slowly. The gheist

thrashed back and forth, unfocused, as though it was just waking from a long sleep. "What am I supposed to do?"

"You're a hero," Lucas answered. "Do something heroic." He picked up one of the discarded swords and tossed it to Martin. It stuck in the mud at his side. The blade was black, runes along the runnel, the edge pitted with age. Feyiron.

"And you?" Martin asked. He grabbed the blade, testing its weight, cursing the poor quality of the hilt and the clear lack of maintenance in the pommel. The tang shifted under the wooden handle, biting into Martin's skin. Still, it would have to do. "Is there a reason you can't, you know, help me with this?"

"This is a distraction," Lucas said. He slipped from the tavern and hurried down the road. "Sacombre will be getting away. Gods be with you!"

"Yeah," Martin said. "A distraction. Great. *Very* distracting."

The gheist shifted, settling into a body of teeth, the last scraps of the man's cloak fluttering away from it like peeling dry skin. Its massive head swung back and forth, snuffling nostrils sucking dust off the slate roofs before it turned to Martin and grinned. Teeth, teeth, nothing but teeth and bright bone.

Martin dropped into a guard, holding the poor and ancient blade in both hands. The gheist roared, and the street shook.

52

CAHL WAS THE first to move. He drew a spear from his quiver and threw it at the voidfather. Gwen thought the aim was true, even hissed as the steel head of the spear passed through Folam's cloak, seemingly headed for the man's heart. But there was a flicker of motion, the slightest bending of light and air, and the spear fell to the ground in pieces.

"Always quick to violence," Folam said. "You would have served us well, Cahl of stones. My daughter was right to take you as her shaman."

"You wear Suhdrin clothes, and stand with Suhdrin thugs. I think you may have lost your way, voidfather," Cahl answered. Gwen glanced at the dozen or so figures that surrounded them. He was right. Fair hair and fine features, Suhdrin men and women, all—and while the robes Folam wore looked like a priest's vestments, there was something different about them.

The voidfather laughed. "We make sacrifices to the gods, Cahl. The company we keep, the clothes we wear." Folam drew a blade of dark steel, tipping the point in Cahl's direction. "The friends we murder."

Noel spat and drew her gheist into the world. She stepped away from the tight group of Judoc and the others, to avoid burning anyone as the air around her flared into light. Flames wreathed her shoulders as she rose off the ground, a pillar of smoke and ash that screamed as it sucked the oxygen out of the air.

One of the dark-clad figures stepped forward and raised his hands. The skin of his palms split, blistering in strange patterns before a rune of ash emerged from the wound. The wave of force that followed knocked Noel to the ground, and snatched her gheist from her flesh. She knelt, gritting her teeth, hanging on to the burning spirit. Flames snapped from her skin as though they guttered in a strong breeze. The ground under her hands turned black. The Suhdrin pressed at the air, as if he were pushing a great weight up hill, blood flowing freely from his hands.

For a moment they were frozen in silent conflict. Then with a shriek, Noel slumped to the ground. The gheist disappeared, swirling up into the air, singeing leaves as it went. The witch lay there, eyes open, breathing shallowly. Judoc stepped over her, his hands held at the ready, darkness surrounding him.

"No more," he said. "They have given enough."

Cahl and Gwen froze, turning slowly to face the elder of bones.

"Judoc?" Cahl asked. "You are with the voidfather in this?"

"You accused me of leading the inquisition to the witches' hallow," Gwen said. "And Noel, as well. Then when the time came for answers, we sought you out. Why?"

"The calendar is turning," Judoc said. "The buried potential of the witches' hallow was lying fallow, and the north is ripe for harvest. It was time to do something."

"Something?" Cahl echoed. "War with Suhdra, and another generation of children dead in battle. Is that what you mean by *something*?"

"All die," Judoc said with a shrug. "Some die with meaning."

"Godsdamned elders and their self-important..." Gwen trailed off, her rage too much for words. She whipped a knife out of her belt, grabbed Judoc by the collar, and brought the blade to his throat. They faced Folam.

"Let us go, or your damned ally gives his blood to your cause," she said. Folam watched her with a bemused smile. He shook his head.

"Judoc knew the price of betrayal," Folam said. He nodded to the elder of bones. "Do you still think they've given enough, Judoc?"

"We all have," Judoc said. "This was meant to be clean, voidfather. Halverdt overthrown. Blakley raised, and the witches' hallow tapped. The old gods brought back to Tenumbra, the domas leveled, and Suhdra returned to the ancient ways."

"There was always going to be blood—or did you think House Adair would give up their secrets without a fight?" Folam stalked closer, sword in one hand, his other caressing the iron pendant of his station. He grinned at Gwen. "Your family is dead, Gwen. You are the last of your tribe. What more do you have to fight for? Surrender, and this will be over quickly."

"You have a lot to learn about negotiation," Gwen said, pressing the knife into Judoc's throat, drawing the tiniest bead of blood. "The tribe of bones won't bow to you without their elder's command."

"It doesn't matter," Judoc said quietly. "He has what he

needed of me. Eldoreath is free, by my hand and his."

"True, my friend, and thank you for that," Folam said. Then he slid forward and drove his sword into the elder's heart. Judoc went to his god without a sound, sliding bonelessly from Gwen's grasp. "And now, Gwen Adair, we must settle things between us."

Gwen released Judoc's dead body, holding the bloodwrought knife in her hand at a guard position. This was the same knife she had used to raise Fomharra. It would certainly do to kill the voidfather.

"You never had a chance, Gwendolyn. If only you could have been brought—"

She lunged at him. Folam snapped his mouth shut with a clack, raising his sword to block her attack. He was inexperienced with the blade, though, and she easily brushed it aside. Out of the corner of her eye, Gwen saw Cahl try to help, but three of the shadowy forms pounced on him.

In front of her, Folam backed up. There was a long slash on his sleeve, and a trail of blood that wound between his fingers and dripped onto the ground.

"Very well," he said, raising the iron pendant above his head. "The hard way."

"I have no hidden god to be battered by your trickery, voidfather," Gwen said. "This will be settled by steel and blood. Mostly your blood."

"Anything can be made empty," Folam said. The air around his clenched hand growled, churning around the pendant, and then a wind of mad power sprung out of nowhere, battering at her. Gwen fought against it, but through the rising gale she could hear Folam's voice. "This is how it ends, Gwendolyn. Your tribe, your house, your name and your life. Wiped away by the void."

The pressure against her face was grating. She pressed back, but quickly found that it was not something that could be fought. The air left her lungs. Her eyes dried in their sockets. Gwen's blood sang beneath her skin and then, slowly, began to peel free of her body. Crimson lines trailed from her mouth, running languidly down her cheek, dripping past her ear. Tiny wounds opened on her skin, her arms, her hands, her back.

Iron in the blood, Gwen thought morbidly. *And the god of iron to be cleansed.* She stumbled back, crying tears of blood, staring in horror as crimson wings unfolded from her back, hanging like molasses behind her, suspended in the wind of the void. Her fingers, numb, dropped the knife. It fell to the ground. She tried to reach it, but her body felt like it was moving in slow motion.

The hounds remembered her, and the debt they owed.

In a blur of motion, a tide of gray fur sprang from the forest, landing on Folam's outstretched hand. The voidfather yelped loudly, and the sound of breaking bones split the air. At the sound of the crack his servants, hands full with Cahl, turned distracted heads.

The horrid fury of the pendant flickered out.

Gwen dropped to the ground.

Her blood, hanging above, fell with her. She was drenched in it, bright red against her pale skin, the slick-gore running down her face and fouling her shirt. Her fingers closed on the knife.

Folam threw off the dog that had attacked him. He searched the ground for the pendant. His injured hand hung backward, fingers curled in on themselves, bright bone peeking out from the sleeve of his robe.

Gwen stood and took a shaky step toward him. She had lost so much blood. A dark ring began closing around her vision, her brain shutting down.

"In steel," she muttered. "And blood."

A hound whipped out of the forest and knocked into her, its arm-length jaws closing gently over her belly. She tried to push it away, but the fetid smell of its breath overwhelmed her. She went limp. The hound craned its head and lay Gwen on its back. Without thought, her fingers twined into the creature's fur. Her blood matted the blackened curls of its coat.

The last thing she saw before the hound leapt away was Cahl, throwing off the last of his attackers. He stared in horror at her...

And then she was gone, the forest moving past so quickly that the trees blurred, became gray, and then her exhausted, blood-weak mind drifted into nothing. Gwen did not feel the rivers of blood on her skin as they coiled tight against her flesh, crimson turning to rust, and then to iron.

Nessie was the daughter of a duke, raised in warm furs and plentiful food, with strong walls to protect her, and stronger guards to watch her every day.

She woke with a start. There were loud voices in the hallway. No one had stoked the fire in her room yet, so it had to be very early. She pushed aside her blankets, shivering at the cold air, then rolled to the edge of her wide bed and lowered her toes to the stone floor. Father didn't allow rugs, especially in winter, but sometimes when he was away mother would have the servants lay a runner from Nessie's bed to the hallway. Now that both of them were gone, Nessie had them roll it up. She preferred the stone.

The light that came from the shuttered window was strange. It flickered, and was too dim for sunlight, but too orange for the moon. It seemed like a campfire. A thrill of fear went through her. Nessie shuffled across the floor and threw the windows open.

Thankfully, it wasn't the castle that was on fire. A starfield of bright lights flowed down the hills that surrounded Houndhallow, wave after wave of torches, outlining dark shapes. Yipping shouts drifted on the wind. Nessie craned her neck, looking up at the moon.

"It's not morning at all," she whispered to herself. "It's only just night. Hm."

She closed the shutters and went to the door. She was nearly there when Master Tavvish threw it open. His stiff hair hung around his head like a halo, and the chain shirt and leather sash he always wore were askew. He stared in horror at the empty bed, switching to the unlatched window with increasing panic.

"Dear gods!" he said. "Dead gods above!"

"Master Tavvish?" Nessie asked. He turned on her with a start, hand on blade, eyes wide. Nessie fell back, a little startled. "Are you alright?" she asked.

"Lady Ness!" he barked, then he swooped into the room, securing the window and rushing around her chamber, staring at shadows and mumbling to himself. Eventually he slowed and turned back to her. "Lady Ness!" he repeated.

"Tavvish," she said calmly. "What is happening?"

"The castle is under attack, my lady," he said. "A host of pagans is at our wall."

"Pagans?" she asked. "Not Suhdrin knights? Father said

it would be Suhdrin knights, if he didn't come back."

"Your father is coming back, my lady. He always comes back."

"If you say so," Nessie answered. "I suppose if it isn't Suhdrin knights, you might still be right." She went to the door, pulling a quilted robe from her closet and slipping it over her head. "Well, sir. What are we waiting for? I must see to the walls, yes?"

"The walls are in order, my lady, but we need to get you to safety," Tavvish said.

"If the walls are in order then I am perfectly safe. And if they are not in order, then I must see to them. Mustn't I?"

"But, my lady..."

"Enough of this, sir," Nessie said. The howls of the attackers could be heard through the shutters, and the light of their torches was as bright as the sun. Nessie waited patiently until Tavvish relented with a sigh. She moved into the hallway, and he followed.

53

THEY MET ON a hill overlooking the fields of the Reaveholt. The Suhdrin army, fully aware of Malcolm's presence, detached a portion of their strength to shore up their flank. The sky above was flat and gray, and the fields were the weathered brown of late autumn. Malcolm wrapped himself in a borrowed cloak and huddled close to the fire while the others talked.

"It is not a question of tactics or even will," Castian Jaerdin said. "It is a matter of numbers. Of math. We are vastly outnumbered here. There is no way to overcome Bassion's advantage of numbers!"

"I say her numbers are a disadvantage," Sir Harrow countered. She stood like a titan over the hastily drawn map at the center of the table. The wind that buffeted the hill blew the walls of their tent close, shrinking the space. If anything, it made the woman look larger. "Bassion is scared of being trapped on this side of the Tallow, so she tries to hold the fords at White Lake, all while placing forces to cap the Reaveholt at the north and the south. If any one of those groups is routed, the other two will come running."

"Come running, and send us into a rout when they arrive," Jaerdin countered. "Even if they are so greatly separated, we haven't the spears to face even one of them."

Harrow thought for a moment, her face creased in stubborn concentration.

"The outrunners who patrol the moors between White Lake and the Reaveholt are few enough. We could..."

"Oh, gods, yes, we could kill their messengers!" Jaerdin said. "All that would do is irritate them. Maybe rouse them enough to come up here and kill us all." He stomped around the table in frustration. "To say nothing of the consequences at home. When this was a talking war, and a matter of honor, I had no reason to worry about my family—but now that blood has been spilled—"

"No," Malcolm said from his corner. "That is not what bothers you."

Jaerdin froze, turning slowly. "I beg your pardon."

"That is not why you are worried about your family, Redgarden." Malcolm unfolded, his stiff bones protesting the cold, the weeks in the saddle, the endless jarring of hard rides and harder beds. He went to the table but didn't spare the map even a glance. "Blood was spilled at White Lake, and again at the Fen Gate, but you did not waver. Even after the Orphanshield kicked you out of the castle, you did not rush home to see to your wife. Only now do you protest."

"I am not wavering, Houndhallow! I merely present the facts of our situation. There was a time when you would do the same."

Malcolm watched his friend for a long moment. Long enough that the other people in the tent grew uncomfortable. Eventually, Jaerdin dropped his eyes to the map.

"It's the inquisition," he said quietly. "Bassion, Marchand, even Halverdt... I can handle them in the Circle of Lords. They would never set foot on my lands. But the gray priests…"

"Yes. This I understand, Castian. They could come into your home, take your children for testing, claim your cattle as tribute, and put your wife on trial for a whim. They are a force worthy of fear, even from strong dukes and stronger blades." Malcolm nodded slowly, looking down at the map for the first time, then taking in the rest of the room. He and Jaerdin were the only lords present. Everyone else was, at most, a knight. Most were merely soldiers, experienced enough to earn an invitation to the battle plan. Nearly all were Suhdrin. "How many of you live in that fear? That the inquisition may visit your homes while you're away? Take what is yours, and give it to Cinder?"

The averted eyes gave Malcolm his answer. Only Sir Harrow, as Tenerran as her braids and her blood, met his gaze.

"Now you know what it's like being us," Malcolm said. "Now you understand the fear of the inquisition. And the hate. Now you are truly one with us. So, let us win this fight together. For our homes."

There was a murmur of assent that moved around the room, assent and courage, bolstered by his words. When he turned back to the map, Jaerdin was the first to speak.

"There are still the numbers, Malcolm. How do we face so many?"

"You are asking the wrong question, Redgarden," Malcolm said. "Your estimate ignores the Suhdrin's greatest strength. The priests. They could have five squires and a broken down mule. As long as a column of the inquisition marches at their side, we could not stand against them."

"That is hardly encouraging," Harrow said.

"No, but it gives us our question. Why now? Why have

the priests joined this fight now, when they have held back for so long?" Malcolm asked. "Sacombre marched with Halverdt, but did not lend his strength to the battle. He was there only as a blessing, as well as a goad, and we all know him for a heretic. That makes it doubly strange. You would think the inquisition would be particularly careful to appear nonpartisan, following their leader's betrayal of both Suhdra and Tener."

"For that matter," Jaerdin said, "Bassion would have to think twice before accepting that assistance. She knows what happened to Gabriel Halverdt."

"Yes, well, the gheist at Greenhall explains some of it, I'm sure," Harrow said. "Perhaps the inquisition is tired of screwing around with pagans who are willing to summon gods in the middle of Suhdrin cities."

"And yet Sophie Halverdt has not joined her army to Bassion's cause," Malcolm said. "Why is that? What game is the inquisition playing?"

"What are you getting at, Houndhallow?" Jaerdin asked.

"I'm not sure," he said, then he gestured at the map. "However, once we have that answer, I think we'll have solved this problem, as well."

The meeting broke up an hour later, with none of them closer to an answer. The columns of Suhdrin spears marched in the fields below, the slow roll of their drums echoing off the hills. Malcolm hurried down the hill, anxious to be back in his own tent, and a bowl of decent stew. There was a lot to be said for Suhdrin cooks.

Most of the crowd that dissipated from the commander's tent wore armor, but one figure was dressed in white silk and gold. Catrin DeBray, priestess of Strife and somehow linked to Malcolm's wife since nearly dying outside the walls of the Fen Gate, slipped from the press and hurried after Malcolm. He walked faster, trying to outdistance her.

"Houndhallow!" she called. Malcolm quickened his pace, but his old bones were no match for her youth. She paced along beside him effortlessly. "I may have an answer to your question."

"Which question is that, my lady?"

"Why the inquisition has joined Bassion's force, and why Lady Halverdt has not," she said.

"I did not know you were in that meeting," Malcolm said. "Tell me, what qualifies a junior priestess of Strife to attend a battle plan?"

"Well, at the moment, I have the answer to the question you seem to think may untangle the whole war," she said at a trot. "So I guess I have *that* qualification."

Malcolm sighed heavily, finally slowing enough to allow her to keep up at a walk. His legs couldn't have gone much farther, anyway—not at that pace.

"And what is this answer?" he asked. "Why didn't you speak up in the tent?"

"Because this is not for every ear," she said. Catrin glanced around the camp. "In fact..."

"Yes, yes, privacy. We will find privacy. An easy enough thing to do in a crowded war camp, where all the walls are made of linen and the lion's share of the soldiers are from an opposing country."

"I have the place," Catrin said. "Your wife won't mind helping."

* * *

The river was set in a narrow gorge, the banks steep and rocky. Malcolm peered down its length with trepidation.

"I would have been a fool to try to cross this elsewhere, especially at the gallop," he said.

"You would have found a way, my dear," Sorcha said, taking her husband's arm. "It is your nature." Malcolm nearly didn't flinch at her touch, and the cold of her skin, and the unnatural light. He smiled and laid a hand on hers. Nearly the same as it had been.

"This will do," Catrin said. She looked up at the camp in the distance, then turned. "My lady?"

Sorcha bowed slightly and carefully picked her way down to the stream at the bottom of the gorge. Catrin nodded Malcolm forward, then followed him. By the time the two of them had reached the water, Sorcha was already knee deep in the stream, her eyes closed. The water moved strangely.

"Where did she learn to do this?" Malcolm muttered to himself. Sorcha heard.

"Where did you learn to breathe, Malcolm? Or the bird to fly? This is part of me. Something the witch did. It was meant to come out, when she was done healing me, but you got in the way of that. And so it remains, and gives me these gifts. She's dead, by the way."

"What?" Malcolm asked, startled by the change in subject.

"The witch. Earlier today. I'm not sure how, but I felt her leave us. Like a limb I didn't know I had, and can only feel by its absence." Sorcha bent to the water, her palms inches above the splashing current. "A quick trial, it would seem."

"Yes, well," Malcolm said, but had nothing to add. Catrin watched quietly, as Sorcha lifted her hands, and the water came with it. The stream backed up, flowing into a dome that Sorcha shaped over her head. She opened her eyes and looked at her husband. "Quickly now."

Catrin gave him a little push, and together they walked across the dry river bed. Once they were beside Sorcha, she dropped the dome of water over them, then spoke a few words and closed her hands. The bubble of air around them quivered. The surface of the water shimmered like a mirror. Malcolm stood staring up at it.

"To anyone watching, the stream is undisturbed. We're just a bubble floating beneath it, no bigger than a breath. But we should hurry," Sorcha said. "I can't do this forever."

"It's amazing," Catrin said. "And you can travel like this?"

"With the current, yes. Maybe faster, if there's a need. I have never done it, but—"

"I'm sorry, we couldn't have just talked by the stream's edge?" Malcolm said. "We had to invoke pagan rites?"

"It's important this remain private," Catrin said, "and frankly, when she described it I was a little curious about this phenomenon. I've heard stories, but they weren't so... beautiful."

"Glad to have satisfied your curiosity with my wife's freakishness," Malcolm hissed. "We have an inquisitor in the camp who might take an interest in this, if we're found out. So best you say what you must and let us get back to work."

"Of course," Catrin said, ignoring Malcolm's frustration. "That's precisely why we must meet in private. You see, there is a schism inside Heartsbridge."

"Naturally," Malcolm said, "and nothing new. Strife is of summer, Cinder of winter. Their priests have never seen eye to eye. That is how the gods intended it."

"More than that. There has been talk in the celestial dome of replacing the celestriarch. That he should have been aware of Sacombre's heresy, and should stand accountable for his fall." Catrin's eyes were bright with excitement. "Some say the High Maiden will stand for election!"

"I'm not sure replacing the celestriarch with the chief priest of the Lightfort is going to do anything but make more trouble," Malcolm said. "If the church shows that it can't trust the inquisition, what will the lords think? Gods, what will the people start to believe?"

"What *do* the lords believe, Malcolm?" Sorcha asked. "Why did you hide me from the Orphanshield? Surely you trust the inquisition?"

"It isn't the same. This is..." he motioned helplessly at his wife. "This is different. You're different."

"But I'm not," she said. "The fact is, you knew you should have turned me over to Frair Gilliam when he arrived at the Fen Gate, and you didn't. You knew what would have become of me. How can you expect your people to feel any differently?"

"This is all beside the point," Malcolm said. "I have never loved Cinder, but I have served him. The gods do not ask us for love."

"Strife does," Catrin said quietly. "It's all she asks."

Malcolm made a harsh sound, disbelief and frustration mixing in equal measure. When neither of them said anything more, he shook his head. "What would you have me do? Throw the church aside, just because my wife has... because of this?"

"There is more," Catrin said quickly. "Stories from the south, from soldiers of Jaerdin who came north before Bassion cut them off. Lady Sophie has rejected Cinder."

"Because Sacombre killed her father," Malcolm said. "What do you expect?"

"It is deeper than that," Catrin said, frustrated. "You brush off everything, out of hand, as simple human emotion. Sophie is right to end her worship of Cinder, and not merely because of Sacombre's sin. You need to stop thinking of the high inquisitor as an exception to Cinder's reign."

"What are you saying? Are you even listening to yourself?"

"Very clearly," Catrin said. "Are you? Cinder is the god of winter. Of death. Of judgment, when there should be joy. Cruelty, when Strife would give compassion. Why do we worship Cinder? Why would anybody?"

"Because the world is hard," Malcolm said. "He sacrificed his flames to give the world the peace of night, but the price was great. Without him, humanity would still be living underground, in caves, while the surface burned to ash. We owe him that worship."

"He asks too much," Catrin said, becoming angry.

"He asks what he is owed," Malcolm argued. "Cinder's judgment makes us strong. He tests us, winnowing the weak, stiffening the strong. The world cannot be eternal summer, child. There is sadness, if only to sharpen the joy." He drew closer to the girl, taking her shoulders in his hands, staring down at her. "There must be night, to quench the heat of day. Give everything to Strife, and we would burn into ash."

"Cinder is evil," Catrin said. Her face was stiff with anger. "He is darkness, and death, and every wrong thing in the world. He does not deserve our worship."

Malcolm hissed and pushed her away, as though her heresy would rub off on him. The bubble of air wasn't large, but Malcolm stalked to the edge of it and stared out into the shimmering water. A light grew behind him. Sorcha's hand came down on his shoulder, which twitched.

"There was a time, my husband, that we celebrated our love. My touch was not something you flinched from. My eyes were a pool you would fall into." She turned him around and rested her head against his chest. This time he did not react. "Why can't we worship love? Why must we suffer this chasm between us? I am not the one pushing you away. It is Cinder. It is winter's hold on your heart that separates us." She pulled away just far enough to look into his face. "Please, love, stop running from me. Please."

Malcolm collapsed, from heart to lips. He pulled his wife close, squeezing his eyes shut, holding her and mingling his tears with the soft water of her skin. She was his, she had always been his. How could he have been such a fool.

The shimmering wall of water collapsed, drenching them in the cold stream. Malcolm came gasping to the surface, still holding his wife, the two of them sitting up to their armpits in the biting current. When he had his breath, Malcolm looked wildly around.

The inquisitor stood on the bank, his vow knight at his side. The look on the man's face was all Malcolm needed to see, to know that he was ruined, and his wife with him. He stood.

"No," he said, and drew his feyiron blade.

54

THE CREATURE SLITHERED across the street, its constantly changing body of teeth and shadow clicking loudly off the stone walls of the tavern. The tiles of the slate roof cracked under its touch, sliding down to shatter on the street below. Martin shielded his eyes with each impact, tiny fragments of broken tile stinging his hands.

"A city of priests and prison guards, and I'm left to face this thing," Martin muttered to himself. The wave of screaming that marked the retreat of those guards and priests echoed as they slipped farther away. Surely someone would answer the alarm, at some point. He just had to hold the demon back long enough for the cavalry to arrive, or for Lucas to get back. He glanced in the direction the frair had run, but there was no sign of the man.

Martin sighed and twisted the ill-fit feyiron sword around in his hand.

"These things are priceless, you know," he said to the gheist. "You can't mine the damned metal anymore, much less smelt and forge the blades. Church claimed most of them as spoils of the crusades. Malcolm Blakley wouldn't have inherited his if the man didn't have a ducal throne and generations of faithful service to back it up. It's a damned crime this one is in such bad shape."

The gheist shifted, growing wide as a broadcloth sail before collapsing down into a seething ball no larger than a casket. Martin held the sword out, almost as if presenting it to the gheist. "And yet, here's a feyiron sword, plucked up out of the mud like a beggar's coin."

The beast didn't seem interested. Instead, it growled quietly in the middle of the street, its hundreds of talon-like teeth chewing through the stone. Really, it didn't seem malevolent, or even willing to fight, any more than a thunderstorm seeks to cause a flood. Martin had seen shamans bind and control gheists—it was the stuff of legend when he was a child—and yet something that happened over and over since the start of this strange war. This creature acted nothing like those spirits. Even the snake-god that chased them out of Gardengerry showed more intuition than this monster.

The feral god squirmed and growled and broke whatever was close to it, but it did not pursue, neither the screaming crowd of priests, nor the man who stood in front of it with a sword. Not even Lucas, who might be the only frair in the city both willing and able to stand up to it.

The dark-clad man who had summoned it disappeared without giving it direction. Like a man dropping a lit flask, then slipping away before the flames spread.

"This isn't a god of war," Martin said. "Nor of murder. Though it's frightening enough to cause flight, it seems to want nothing." He looked down at the ground beneath it. A shallow pit was forming where its hundred mouths tore apart the stone and formed a ring of scree at the edge. Martin was no mason, but he could easily believe the scree was enough to fill in the pit. It was eating but not consuming.

He took a biscuit of hardtack out of his pocket, saved back from his days of near starvation on the road. He tossed it at the gheist, but missed the throw and watched as the biscuit landed short.

"Great," he muttered. "Now I just need to dive in, kick that forward and pray you don't—"

The gheist moved before Martin could finish his thought. A pod of darkness slipped free of its body and landed on the biscuit, then the rest of the gheist flowed forward like spilled oil. It settled over the food. The sound of its growling changed briefly. Then it returned to eating and shitting stone.

"Ok," Martin said. "Result. And maybe I don't have to try to kill you with someone else's shitty blade." He searched his pockets, then remembered those days of starvation and realized he was out of food. So he turned back to the tavern, kicked in the door, and disappeared inside.

Curious, the gheist followed.

The inn was physically unchanged, but something had happened to it. Lucas could feel the difference somewhere deep in his heart. The distant screaming of the crowds echoed eerily off the empty streets. He expected more of his fellow priests, but he wasn't really surprised. The faithful of Cinder had become comfortable in the courts of law. Too few ventured out to the hunt, leaving that duty to the vow knights and the relatively small ranks of the inquisition. Fear was their tool, but their greatest weakness, as well.

Lucas slipped in the front door, drawing on the naether to let him see in the dark interior. There were strands of deeper darkness threaded through the room. The whole place felt dead. The innkeeper and a few patrons lay slumped over, their ragged souls drifting free of their flesh, fluttering tethered to their bones. There was no sign of violence, as though their lives had ended as suddenly as a candle snuffed by the breeze from an open window.

"I'm sorry, old friend," Lucas muttered to the innkeeper. He paused long enough to shrive the man's soul, freeing him into the quiet. The others would have to wait. There was noise from the stairwell, footsteps that banged like a drum through the empty building. He faced the stairs. Whoever was coming down the stairs, they weren't alone. Maybe a dozen feet, maybe more.

"Corner the pursuers, let them release the high inquisitor and the witch, face them alone while on the verge of starvation," Lucas said quietly. "I've had better plans."

The first man came around the corner at a run. He might not have been expecting Lucas to be standing there, but he adjusted quickly enough. His cloak of black leather flickered out like a whip, concealing his arm and the knife. A blade flashed through the air, thumping into Lucas's shoulder. The frair, expecting some kind of spiritual or demonic attack, fell to steel, keeling back on his heels, stumbling into a table, and then falling heavily to the floor.

The man slowed down, standing menacingly between Lucas and the door to the street. Another half-dozen figures, similarly dressed, fanned out through the room. They looked like an honor guard, thoughtful in their station, alert to every corner. Behind them, two figures hurried past. One was Sir Horne, her hand protectively on the other person, the other curled into a fist that was bleeding profusely.

The second figure was Tomas Sacombre. The high inquisitor was drained of color, limping, face turned down.

He looked broken, but his bonds were cut. As he disappeared into the street, Sacombre caught Lucas's eye. The high inquisitor nodded, and was gone.

Once Sacombre was out of the room the guards drained out, as well, one at a time. Before he left, the first man walked over to Lucas and twisted his knife out of the frair's shoulder. He leaned down to whisper in Lucas's ear.

"The gods will forgive you, frair," he said. "If you live long enough." His voice was rough, but beneath that his accent was deeply Suhdrin, court-born and careful. He nodded once, then followed his fellows into the street.

Lucas stood carefully. The pain in his shoulder was intense. Blood poured down his arm, dripping heavily from his fingers, staining his robes. He limped slowly to the door. There was no sign of the high inquisitor or his rescuers. Lucas teetered on the door frame, watching his life blood pool at his feet.

With a grunt he climbed the stairs and found the witch. Her body was already dead, though her spirit clung stubbornly to the flesh. Lucas tried to sit beside her, but lost his balance and collapsed gracelessly to the floor. The blood was his—Fianna had died cleanly. There was a knife in her chest, but the skin around it was puckered and dry. Lucas lifted a hand and realized it was soaked, not with blood, but water. He pushed up onto one arm.

Fianna's spirit hung over him.

"So," he said. "You made a play. You took your chance, and it got you killed." The spirit didn't answer.

There was something twined around Fianna's soul that writhed and gushed. Lucas took a deep breath, then shifted until he was kneeling over the witch's corpse. He rubbed his hands together, covering them in his blood, then gripped Fianna's skull.

"I am sorry about this," he said, "but I have to know."

With the small power of his blood and the latent energy of the dead witch's passing, Lucas reeled Fianna's soul back into her body. Her corpse stiffened, back arching and eyes peeling back, as the spirit spun slowly down into its departed flesh. The dry skin around her wound turned to ash, and fresh blood pumped out of her chest, staining her robes and mixing with the cold water on the floor. She took a long, terrible breath, a wretched scream from empty lungs, and then the witch's eyes fixed on Lucas.

"Why?" she coughed. "I was with them. Give me peace. Give me that, at least."

"Who are they?" Lucas said urgently. "The ones who killed you. How did they do this thing?"

"A knife should be no mystery to you, Inquisitor. A blade buried in a heart does not require a ghost to explain," she said. Her whole body shuddered, and the fingers clawing into Lucas's shoulder went soft. "Now leave me to the ever."

"That is not what I meant. You have been playing a game with me, Fianna. I have seen inside of you. What is that thing bent around you, that it holds your soul in place?" Lucas asked. Fianna didn't respond, so he pulled her face closer, pushing her eyes open with his thumbs. "My bonds never held you, did they? Did they, witch?"

"It was good to have a leash for my pet priest," she said quietly, her words slurring, eyes flickering shut. "Made it easy to keep track of you."

"And those who killed you! If you are what I believe, if a gheist rode these bones, then how could they do it? Who were they? What art did they wield?" He shook her limp body, but no response came. He was about to lay her down when Fianna's eyes snapped open.

"Older than you, winter's son," she said. "Older than us. There was a war before this one. I thought it was over, but no. They are still there. Waiting."

And then she died, and whatever remained of her soul fell apart. The peace she sought in the everam was denied, not by death, but by the stubborn life Lucas demanded of her. He had an answer, but it cost the witch her heaven.

Martin appeared at the quay's edge, carrying a basket of apples in his arms. The young prince looked frantically around the docks. Prison barges, mostly, bound for the Black Isle that dominated the harbor, but on the end there was a fisherman's trawler, just coming in from the harvest. He ran to it. The sailors aboard watched him with curiosity.

"Do you have a catch aboard?" he yelled.

"Aye, and enough to feed a rank, if you've men to provision, my lord," the owner of the boat responded. "Two silver a barrel, and the service of a fine smoker if you're bound to march north. A deal at twice the—"

"Get out!" Martin yelled. He was practically hopping from foot to foot. The fisherman squinted nervously at the young lord, noticing for the first time that the fool had dropped a trail of apples that extended back into the city. "Get out of the boat!" Martin said again. "I'll buy the lot, my name is worth that much at least, but I don't think we'll be needing a smoker. Now get out of the boat!"

"My lord, we must pack and prepare..."

Something came out of the city, a black shadow hanging

with loose horns. The men on the ship shouted in horror, the lads on the oars who had been bringing them in to dock reversing their motion. The owner stood in horror as the demon lunged from discarded apple to core, slithering ever closer to the prince of Stormwatch. Martin's mouth dropped open, then he took the basket and threw it onto the trawler. The remaining apples spilled out across the deck.

"Godsdamn you, my lord," the owner shouted, then he jumped ship. His men followed moments later.

The gheist reached the end of the quay and hesitated. Swollen arms of tooth-lined shadow tested the waters, splashing almost playfully in the harbor. It brushed against an apple bobbing in the surf, consumed it without thought, then hurled itself across the narrow gap between quay and vessel.

Moments later wood splintered, and the holds of silverback trout burst open. The gheist busied itself in consumption and the butchery of cold, scaly flesh. Martin grabbed a boat hook and pushed the boat away from the quay. Its sails were still deployed, so when a fortunate wind caught the sheets they billowed out, dragging it further into the harbor. The sound of severed fish and cracking scales diminished, until the only sign that there was something wrong with the boat was a huddled mass of shadow on the deck, and the unnerving sight of teeth scenting the air.

The owner of the vessel dragged himself from the water and, sopping wet, loomed over Martin.

"What have you done?" he asked.

"Saved the city, I think?" Martin answered. "We'll leave it to the priests to decide. For now, at least, we should find someone to tug that thing out to sea. Pray it doesn't try to eat its way back to us."

"But... but..."

"I'm sorry to interrupt, but"—Martin pointed out to the boat, bobbing on the water—"Is it getting bigger?"

The man turned and stared with horror. "No, I don't think so." He turned back. "Now what are you going to do to compensate me, sir?"

But Martin was gone, slipped back into the city, which was rapidly filling up with priests who had finally come out of hiding. The sound of their educated chatter filled the air with speculation and prayer.

55

THE ANCIENT WALLS of Houndhallow were raised over generations, built around the shrine that had been holy to the tribe of hounds, and the doma that was raised above it. The traditional throne of the Blakleys was a grand castle. During the crusades, armies of both the north and south broke themselves against its stone. Reaver bones were buried at its foot, and feral gheists dared never ascend its height.

It was a tower of strength, guarded by steel, blessed by the gods of Suhdra and held by Tenerran might.

The pagan army overwhelmed it in one night. The river that flowed around the castle walls swelled and then became still, allowing the shamans of the old ways to walk across. Archers from the towers were baffled by swirling winds, their flights scattering like matchsticks to fall harmlessly on the attacking horde. Wherever there was bedrock stone inside the castle walls, ink-eyed shamans and their witching wives emerged to secure hallways and kick open doors.

Their victory would have been absolute if not for the strange figures who countered them. Like a fisherman letting the hook settle in his victim's mouth, the counterattack came once the walls had fallen and the main gate thrown wide. Blakley's spears had fallen back to the keep when the first mysterious shadow claimed its victim.

It happened in the shrine, once holy, now a relic of forgotten faith.

The black-pit eyes of the iron hound guttered with flaming pitch, and the low wall that served as cistern and kneeler cast sharp shadows across the floor. A slow trickle of water started in the cistern, pushing aside dust that had gathered for generations, turning black with muck before finally reaching the gutter and flowing out onto the cobbles. The trickle became a stream, the stream grew into a pool, and then a hand splashed out of the water and scrambled for the cistern's wall.

A man emerged. He pulled himself up onto the floor, shook off like a dog, then reached back into the shallow pool and drew a woman with him. The pair sat huddled in the dim light, staring with reverence at the statue of the hound.

"Not in a hundred years have pagan eyes witnessed this hallow," the woman whispered. "We should make a sacrifice."

"We'll make sacrifice enough in the blood of Blakley heathens, Kara," the shaman answered. He stretched, making his absolution to the hallow before drawing twin knives and creeping to the door. "Come, eventually they will think to secure this room. We must strike while their backs are turned."

"Morgan and Sammath will have their attention for a while," Kara said. She stood and turned slowly. "I never thought my life would come to this."

"Standing in the hallow of the tribe of hounds?"

"No, Marik, though that is strange enough," she said. "I never expected to be striking out at House Blakley. They are kneelers, of course, and shelter the church as much as any lord of Suhdra, but they are Tenerran. They have the ink, and our blood. No matter what they did, I thought those things would overcome their mistrust of our faith."

"All the worse," Marik said. "They knew the gods and abandoned them. We should have struck long ago. Maybe some of this could have been prevented."

Kara didn't answer her shaman. Instead she went to the hallow and brushed a finger against its iron cheek. "I wish Fianna were here."

"She isn't," Marik said sharply. "She has been taken from us, by the master of this house. If you wish to mourn, take your grief out on him."

"You were always borne by the tide, Marik. Rising in anger, sinking into silence when it is calm," Kara answered. "You would have been better served by the tribe of fire. Water does not suit you."

"The river rages, wife," Marik said. He nodded impatiently to the door. "Now stop delaying. You have brought us here. Let's be about the task the gods have given us."

Kara closed her eyes and nodded, smiling mournfully as Marik went to the door. Before the burly shaman could turn the handle, the door opened and a strange man in black and silver stepped through.

"That is far enough," he said. "A sweet parting. I hope you will not regret it."

He struck before Marik could move. A column of ash twisted out from between the man's palms, blood and darkness mixing to slam into the shaman. Marik turned away from it, but the plume enveloped him. Kara heard him cry out once before she felt the death in her bones. She stumbled back, falling into the cistern, still in midair as she reached out to the water and undid the binding that had brought her to the hallow in the first place.

When Kara struck the water, she fell through it, as though a great depth were contained in the shallow cistern. She sank in slow motion. The light of the shrine reflected off the surface of the water, flickering oil lamps and the dispersing cinder from the ash cloud that had killed her love. The bare outline of the black-and-silver figure appeared in the water above, leaning against the cistern's edge, staring down into the depths. Kara watched him as she fell, deeper and deeper, until the portal to the hound's shrine closed.

Then she turned and swam hard against the current. She had to get back to the camp. She had to warn the others. The Blakleys had inquisitors with them. They had been prepared.

The house of Cinder was waiting for them.

Nessie watched the destruction from the central keep. Master Tavvish insisted she wear a chain shirt, but it was so big on her that it looked like a silver dress. She had belted it at the waist, and tossed aside the helm and greaves.

"Mother has one of these, but it fits better," she said, holding out the hems of the skirt. "It's very heavy."

"Yes, well, we were supposed to have you fitted for one this spring, but your father didn't allow it. He did not want his daughter going to war," Tavvish said. The man stood awkwardly behind her, one hand always on her shoulder, replacing it each time she shrugged it off. "That seems to have been a mistake."

"Why are they attacking?" she asked.

"They are pagans. They follow the call of their gods, and

the madness of their blood," Tavvish said. Nessie shrugged off his hand, and he laid it once again beside her neck. "They've never needed a reason to attack in the past."

"That doesn't seem right," Nessie mused. "Father always said that the pagans are just like us. Trying to worship their gods, only their gods don't come to doma or follow the calendar. And some of them are crazy—the gods, that is, not the pagans." She rubbed her nose on her sleeve, forgetting about the chain shirt and hurting her face with the cold, slithery metal of its links. This caused more of her face to itch. She shook her hands free of the over-long sleeves and rubbed her face with both palms. "He always said we were safe enough, long as we didn't evoke them."

"Provoke," Tavvish said. "Your father never wanted to provoke the pagans. He never wanted to provoke anyone. Always making peace, making friends. Never acting alone. Gods know what good it did us."

"Father always said it's better to greet a man as a friend than to treat him like an enemy," Nessie said quietly. "That's what he said."

"Yes, well." Tavvish clapped her shoulder, pushing down on sore muscles, already exhausted from the chain shirt. "That advice would not serve well tonight."

Nessie didn't answer, because for her whole life, her father's advice had served well enough. She couldn't believe he wasn't right, even now, even tonight. Then again, father wasn't here, and these men and women didn't seem like friends, no matter which way she looked at them.

The walls were a patchwork of fire and smoke. The scaffolding that usually served as guardwalks and archer platforms had taken to flame, which prevented the Blakley guards from defending the heights and hindered the pagans who had scaled the walls. Men fell to their deaths every few minutes. They looked like bottles that had been tipped off, spinning end over end until they smashed into the courtyard.

Nessie wished her brother were there with her. Ian had always been better at the sword stuff. She liked her dogs, and her dresses, and the silly songs Friar Daxter used to sing on the Allfire. She wondered where Frair Daxter was. She turned to the doma, and immediately wished she hadn't done so.

Daxter and all the celestes had been dragged out into the courtyard. Their clothes were bloody, and most of them were lying down. Daxter stood over them, hands bound behind his back, arguing with one of the pagan men with the dark eyes. Even at this distance, Nessie could see the man's face looked like a tree of leaves. They were both very angry.

Then the tree-faced man hit Daxter, and the old frair went down in a heap. There was blood. Nessie was okay with blood, except when it was her blood, and then she didn't like it. She decided she didn't like it when it was Frair Daxter's blood, either. She liked his songs. She liked the way he smiled during his services, especially in summer. Frair Daxter lay on the ground outside his doma.

"What are we going to do?" she asked. Tavvish didn't answer, so she turned to look at him. His face was streaked with sweat and tears, his eyes reflecting the flames from the walls. She tugged at his arm, the one he had clapped firmly against her shoulder, and he jumped.

"It'll be fine, dearie," he said, barely taking his eyes off the fight long enough to look at her. "Everything'll be fine, soon enough. Your father will sort this. Or Ian. It'll all get sorted out. Eventually."

"That's a shit answer," she said. Master Tavvish looked almost as bothered by her profanity as he was by the wholesale slaughter of the men and women in the courtyard below. "My father might do a lot of things in this situation, but stand on the tower and wait for someone else to fix it? No, that's not one of them."

"Yes, but, my lady... your father is the Reaverbane."

"He didn't become that by waiting around," Nessie said. She slipped a knife from her belt and cut free the straps that held her chain shirt in place. "Do you think the castle is lost, Master Tavvish?"

"I don't... I think, maybe, if we hold here we can stop them. But if not..."

"If not, we're all dead," Nessie answered. "Who remains of our strength?"

"Those here. A sizable number in the great hall below, waiting for the main hall to be breached." Tavvish gestured hopelessly to the courtyard. "Some scattered few, holding out in whatever bolt hole they could manage."

"I will not have my father's men stranded like rats in a trap," Nessie said. "We will open the doors, and we will save them."

"But, my lady, the pagans..."

"Will die if they stop us. Or they will kill us," she said. "That is the nature of war.

"Father always said."

Gwen woke in motion. The long, rolling stride of the hound beneath her was like a wave through the forest. She lifted her head and was surprised to find her face stuck to the beast's matted fur. When she pulled free, a tangle of dark fibers on her cheek writhed briefly in the air before laying flat against her face once again. They felt like fingers closing over her cheekbone, a part of her and yet not. She reached up to touch them and found cold iron, as much a part of her body as her veins and hair.

She glanced down at the hand she was using to explore her face and jerked away. She was wearing a gauntlet, roughly forged, the fingers as narrow and nimble as her own, the wrist spiraling into smaller and smaller rings until it burrowed into her flesh. Black iron, glinting with rust red, so like her hair that Gwen had to touch it again to convince herself that it was hard and cold as stone.

Her attention was snapped away from her strange condition by the battle going on around her. Small gaggles of shadowy figures struggled among the trees, fighting with fire and sword, others lying dead on the ground. The beast shifted suddenly, nearly knocking Gwen from its back. She grabbed on and saw that it was dodging away from one of these small skirmishes. A half-dozen pagans, dressed in the green and leather, faced off with a pair of black-clad strangers. They looked like priests, but weren't.

They were the voidfather's followers.

Gwen hauled on the hound's neck, turning it back toward the fight, finally convincing it to stop while she watched. The void priests were outnumbered, but the pagans were holding back as though they were scared. At some unseen signal the pagans rushed forward. The priests stood firm. The nearest pagan began to manifest some kind of spirit, small tongues of flame wreathing her head and hands. One of the priests gestured toward her, and Gwen saw another of those blood-smeared runes on his palm.

The wreath of flame grew. Her arms caught fire—not her

clothes, but the flesh itself. The pagan started screaming, a mad, panicked, animal sound that tore at Gwen's heart. The other pagans stepped back, staring in horror at the living pyre of their companion. The priest stepped forward, waving his hands, each motion shoving a chunk of burning skin off of the burning woman and hurling it at her companions. The fire spread quickly, hot enough to scorch stone. The pagans scattered.

The void priests turned their eyes to Gwen. The hound beneath her started to growl, low and deep. She bent to its neck.

"Get us out of here."

The hound hurled away into the night. There were dozens of fires in the forests all around, and the air smelled of scorched flesh and boiled blood. Gwen held on with all her might. She strained to reach the hound's ear.

"To the castle," she said. "To your home."

56

THERE WAS A moment of surprise on the inquisitor's face. Malcolm stood in the middle of the river, water flowing around his knees, sword held at the guard. Sorcha and Catrin stood behind him, hands twisted together. On the bank, the Suhdrin force stood in a loose crescent with the inquisitor and vow knight at their center. No one moved.

"Think before you speak, Houndhallow," the inquisitor said. "You have been faithful to the church, as has your family going back for generations. The peace of Tenumbra depends on that faithfulness. Would you throw that away for—?"

"Yes," Malcolm said simply. "I would. I should have, long ago. This is not a peace worth holding."

"I knew Adair for a heretic, but I would not have expected that of Blakley. Not after all you have done for Heartsbridge." The inquisitor shifted, leaning his darkwood staff against his shoulder and taking something out of his sleeve. It was a rag, just a scrap of linen he used to wipe the sweat from his face. "When the celestriarch needed a Tenerran lord to argue the peace, High Elector Beaunair personally recommended you. And now, this."

"Leave us in peace, frair. This war is none of the church's

business. You should not be involved. In the war, or in my family," Malcolm said.

"All business belongs to the church," the inquisitor answered. "The celestriarch speaks for all of Tenumbra!"

"But you do not speak for the celestriarch," Catrin said sharply. The girl came around Malcolm, her fists balled at her side, the white linen of her robes soaking up the stream's cold water. She was shivering. "You have murdered enough of these people, frair! You and your ilk have taken their children and their lands and sacrificed them on winter's cold altar! Leave them in peace, or leave in blood."

"Such words from a child of the church," the inquisitor said. He was a large man, soft in all the ways Malcolm was firm, but a cold fury burned in his eyes. Not much of a fighter, but the battles fought in Cinder's name were rarely won with physical might.

He shifted slightly, his attention split between Catrin and Malcolm. "But heresy comes from all quarters these days. Have you fallen in with them, Catrin DeBray?"

"This man saved my life, and this woman, my spirit," Catrin said. "So if I have to give both again to protect them, it will be a debt justly paid."

The inquisitor laughed, a deep, rolling sound that didn't get close to joy. He signaled to the Suhdrin guards at his sides.

"See that the girl is not harmed, but do not let her interfere in this. I do not wish to explain to the Orphanshield why I broke one of his pet vagrants."

"That is the problem with the faith of Cinder," Catrin said. "It must be forced with steel. The truth of Strife never has to be shoved down anyone's throat."

"We can't all worship debauchery and madness, child," the frair said evenly. He took a menacing step forward, his staff held in front of him, the iron tip radiating. "Now, Houndhallow, a final warning. Cinder can forgive, but he is not inclined to forget. Surrender now, and we will end this nonsense. Without blood."

"I cannot do that, frair," Malcolm said. "I must stand with my wife. If that means standing against you, and the whole celestial church, then I shall."

"Very well," the frair said. "The warning was given."

The inquisitor leapt forward with speed that belied his build, his boots splashing into the water as he attacked. Naetheric light swelled around his shoulders, cloaking him in steel-hard shadow and wind. He drove his staff toward Malcolm. The duke of Houndhallow parried, the ancient metal of the feyiron sword dancing off the barb of naetheric power. The footing was unsure, and both men stumbled through the current, their weapons spinning.

"You could just kill me, frair," Malcolm said through gritted teeth. "I have seen it done. Surely you have the skill."

"Not all priests are as bloodthirsty as Tomas Sacombre," the man said. "I will not bend my god to your death. Not yet."

They exchanged blows again, Malcolm stumbling under the frair's assault. The spear of energy that swirled around the priest's staff cut cleanly through Malcolm's tabard, but the steel of his shirt turned its barb.

"You have done this before," Malcolm said.

"Dueled? My life before the church was one of honor, Houndhallow, but honor did not pay my debts, and I went to the church to even the account."

"I have never known a debt that honor could not settle,"

Malcolm answered. "Nor did I know that the church was accustomed to giving gold for their vows." He swung in, the dark edge of his blade skittering across the supernatural armor of the priest's shoulder, the ancient iron cutting into the shadows and drawing blood. The inquisitor laughed, grasping the wound and shaking the blood from his fingers. Malcolm retreated, measuring his opponent.

"There are debts that demand more than honor and gold. Know the gods, and you may one day understand." The frair dealt a series of arcing blows, his staff spinning in dark circles overhead, Malcolm only barely keeping upright. The attack pushed him to the far bank, where he sat heavily on the muddy shore. He glanced up at Catrin and Sorcha.

"The two of you are just going to stand there, I take it?" he asked.

"You heard the frair," Catrin said. "We are to remain unharmed."

"Well, sure. You wouldn't want to force the issue, would you?" Malcolm pushed himself up, grimacing as mud squished through his fingers. "Is this really the fight you want, frair?"

"No," the man said, "but it is the fight the gods have given me, so I will not shirk from it." He lunged forward, nearly spitting Malcolm on the twisting energy of his spear. Malcolm only barely escaped, and then gracelessly. He splashed back into the creek, nearly falling. Sorcha watched her husband closely. Malcolm was sure he could feel the water stiffen under his feet, keeping him sure.

"That bloody honor again," Malcolm said. "What were you before a priest? A knight? Some lord's personal trainer?"

"A brigand," he said. "A thief and a murderer. Only the right people, of course—those who earned a cold murder in their beds, or a notch taken out of their purses. Still the spirits of my crimes stalked me for a long time before they hunted me down. When they did, it was only Cinder who could save me. Cinder, and no other."

"So you escaped judgment once, and for that you have sworn to see others held accountable for their sins," Malcolm said. "Typical Suhdrin thinking."

"Better than expecting endless tolerance," the frair answered. "Besides, as I said, Cinder has forgiven me, but he has not forgotten the debt."

"Forgiveness without love," Malcolm said, buying time while he sucked air into his lungs and steadied his legs. "What god is that?"

"The god who gives justice without mercy," the frair said. "The unblind god." His next attack was earnest, a concentrated effort that took all of Malcolm's will to resist. The two spent several minutes in frenetic action, naether and steel spinning, clashing, countering, whistling menacingly inches from flesh and then coming back around to strike again. The sound of their battle rang out through the creek bed. The watchers edged slowly away, afraid of being struck.

When they separated, both men stood wearily, their lungs heaving, arms weak.

Malcolm smiled.

"A good fight," he said. "If this is how I'm to go, you've made a good show of it."

"Thank you, but I ask again, Houndhallow. Surrender. Even if you defeat me, the inquisition will find you. You can not stand forever against the whole church."

"It is not the whole church he stands against," the vow knight said quietly. She was a slight woman, hardly larger than Catrin. The sword she held was of Suhdrin design, narrow and fine, the pattern of bloodwrought runes running down its blade a wavering script of great beauty. Her other hand rested on a main gauche, the dueling dagger still seated firmly in its scabbard. Like most vow knights, her hair was short, though hers shone with an inner light. The inquisitor hesitated, turning slightly toward her.

Malcolm took advantage of the moment and drew in gulps of air, gathering himself for the inevitable resumption of combat.

"What the hell do you mean, Trueau?"

"What are your brothers doing in that camp, frair?" the vow knight asked. She ambled down the steep shore, stepping lightly into the water. "Why has Cinder raised his banner against the north? Are we crusading, again? Is that the vow I swore?"

"That has nothing to do with me," the frair said. He gestured to Malcolm. "That has nothing to do with *this*."

"Doesn't it? Would the faithful duke of Houndhallow rebel if the inquisition doesn't lead an army against his friend, Colm Adair? Heretic or not, they were bound by blood and honor. Two things you know enough about."

"That was Sacombre's war! It still is. As for Adair..."

"Yes, a heretic, and known to all," Trueau said. "But he is dead, and yet a Suhdrin army is still camped around his castle. Another stands siege at the Reaveholt, just across that ridge. Why haven't they gone home?"

"You would have to ask them, sir," the frair said. Slowly, the three of them moved to form a triangle. "That does not change our duty to free these lands from the threat of the gheist."

"I see no gheist here," Trueau said. She nodded to

Sorcha, who was watching from the banks. "Yes, the lady has a strange cast, but she seems no threat. We have passed by gheists who have stabilized, either by pagan rite or their own nature. Our task is to protect, not to kill. Not even the gheist. So by what right do you fight this man, now?"

"He defied the celestriarch's will," the frair insisted. "He hid this woman, from us and apparently from the Orphanshield as well. Sheltering a gheist, Trueau, what do you call that?"

"Protecting his love," Trueau said. "As Strife would will it, and as I am vow-sworn to protect."

The inquisitor shrank back, his staff now held in guard. "I will not fight you, sir. That is not what the church would want."

"Your church," Catrin whispered. She swept at the man from behind, her knife sliding easily between his ribs, just beneath the pit of his arm. The frair went rigid, clenching his arm close, trying to strike behind him with the staff. His body became unhinged, the shroud of naether failing as he went to one knee.

Catrin twisted the blade and the frair's face bunched up in pain. His scream was quiet. The strength of his lungs was gone. He toppled forward into the water, and was still.

"Your church," Catrin repeated as she leaned closer to him, pulling her knife free. "Not mine."

The crowd stood in stunned silence. The Suhdrin guards edged away. At least one drew his sword, while several others looked to their fellows for guidance. Malcolm studied them and shook his head. He walked to the inquisitor's floating body and sighed.

"I never learned his name," Malcolm said.

"Frair Albet Montris," Trueau said quietly. She sheathed

her sword, then bent and said a prayer over the dead priest. "He was a good man. A better man that this."

"This shouldn't have ended with his death," Malcolm said. "I'm sorry."

"It did," she said, "and you aren't. But that is where we are in this world. Sorry for things that shouldn't have happened. That might not have happened, if we lived in a better time."

"What will you..." Malcolm started. Sir Trueau waved him to silence. The vow knight marched up the creek bank, then on up the slope until she disappeared among the trees. The silent party watched her depart.

"What now?" Catrin asked.

"You should have considered that before you murdered a priest of Cinder," Malcolm said. "It's a miracle Trueau didn't kill us all in a fit of rage."

"She is not given to rage," Sorcha said, still staring in the direction the vow knight had disappeared. "Though if she ever finds that well, she will drink deeply."

"I meant with the body," Catrin said. "What are we going to do with the body?"

"Bury it," Malcolm said. "We're standing in a river. Sorcha, I assume that's something you can manage?"

"Yes," she said, "but not before you are out of the current."

"Yes, yes," Malcolm said. He sheathed his sword and then scrambled slowly up the muddy incline. Catrin hopped out after him. He looked the guards over, weighing them. "This is a change, I know," he said, "and you are not sworn to me, but the war is changing in ways we can't understand. Not yet. So until we know why Cinder has joined with Bassion, you must keep faith in your lords, and in their wisdom."

"Redgarden knows nothing of this," the man with his sword still drawn said. "And I will not lie to him."

"Nor would I," Malcolm said. "And if he judges me guilty, and my wife, or this priestess, he may order you to take me prisoner."

"That order has not yet been given," the man answered. He lowered his blade, nodding. "Gods pray that it never is."

"You are young, and many," Malcolm said with a smile. "Surely you can take me, if the time comes."

"You are the Reaverbane," he said. "Many have made the attempt."

Malcolm shrugged, then turned back to the stream. Sorcha stood there, her hands uplifted, her eyes closed. A gentle swell of water grew at her feet, quickly rising as it flowed forward, until a white-capped curl towered over the narrow banks. When it reached the dead priest's body, the wave crashed down, swamping the corpse. The sound was tremendous, but the wave dissipated as quickly and mystically as it had formed. Gentle ripples splashed against the shores.

The body was gone.

"Very well," Malcolm said, turning back toward the camp. "Let's go speak to Lord Jaerdin. See if I need to be tried for heresy. Or murder. Possibly both."

57

THE FAMILIAR WALLS of Houndhallow loomed before them. The courtyard was burning. The forests all around were shot through with lesser fires, like veins of ruby in black marble. Ian had known where their path was taking them, as soon as the road turned south. Still, it was a shock to find himself home.

"Things have changed, I take it?" Volent asked gruffly.

"Everything, yes," Ian said quietly. The sight of Houndhallow burning struck him strangely. He expected to be furious, or afraid, or maybe shocked—but in truth, and cold horror filled him, a horror that left him numb. "Everything has changed."

Elsa brushed past Ian as he stared, and hurried her mount down the hill.

"Are we just going to let her go?" Volent asked. "She'll be killed on her own."

"I'm not sure about that," Ian said. "More likely that we'll be killed without her to aid us."

"Gods help us, but I think the boy is right," Bruler said.

Volent gave Ian a nervous look, then rode after the vow knight.

"Sir LaFey!" he shouted as they descended. "There seems to be a battle ahead!"

"What better place to fight, Sir Volent?" she yelled over her shoulder. "What better place to die?"

"Well, yes, true, but I'd like to know who it is I am killing," he said. They rode side by side, with Ian trailing close behind. The Suhdrin knights rode in a loose crescent in their wake, Bruler at their center. Not even a dozen, and yet they rode to battle. "Whose banner do we rally, and whose do we fight?"

"There are few enough banners, sir," Elsa said. "We are not here for the battle. I seek one man, and the gheist he has conjured."

"You have your pick of pagans," Ian shouted. The numbness was wearing off, and it left a wound of rage behind. His fingers twisted over the hilt of his blade. He wanted to sink steel into flesh. "How will we know we have the one we seek?"

"Process of elimination," Elsa said. She drew her blade and spurred forward, carefully drawing power from the wild flames that surrounded them, threading just enough of Strife's energy into her blade and armor, without cooking the flesh of her mount. The destrier snorted nervously at the sudden change in temperature. Still she surged ahead of the others, eager for blood.

"There must be a better way," Volent mumbled. He looked over at Ian, whose full attention now was on the castle. Blakley banners still flew from the keep, but it was clear the walls had fallen. There was a hint of red hair among a crowd at the tower's peak, and thoughts of Nessie crowded to the surface of his mind.

"What do you say, young hound?" Volent pressed. "Where should we hunt?"

Suddenly Ian jerked. "She's here," he said, and he tore

his eyes away from the sight of his sister. "Gwendolyn. She's here. Somewhere among the pagans."

"How can you know?" Volent asked. Ian just nodded, and the knight marshal heard a sound, picked out from among the chaos, easy to miss. It echoed through the forest. The baying of hounds.

"Your dogs are loose?"

"Not my dogs," Ian said. "The gods. The gheists. The hallow itself."

Volent grunted. Ahead of them, Sir Elsa dived into the woods, riding hard and disappearing from sight. "Best keep our bright friend away from them, then."

"It won't come to that," Ian said. He sawed his reins to the side, pulling them off the road and coming to a stop. "She's going to attract too much attention. We will find another way in."

Volent stayed with him, and they watched. Nothing happened for a time, then suddenly the area where the vow knight had vanished burst into a column of sparks and light, pluming over the trees.

Still Ian did not move. Elsa, he decided, could take care of herself.

Though he had only been gone for part of a year—not even a full turn between Allfire and Frostnight—the forests of his childhood were strange to him. These trees and trails seemed like a dream. It was more than the fire and the gheist-wielding pagans scattered through them. His memories, of hunting, riding with his father, exploring with sister and brother, all were overlaid by change.

Some part of him had assumed he would never return, but no part of him thought he would return in the company he now kept.

Was it his castle now? His throne to defend? There was no word of his father. Malcolm Blakley might have gone east. He might have smuggled south with his friend Castian Jaerdin, or he might be dead in a creek, the cold water running like blood through his flesh. Anything was possible.

He couldn't think of that now. Couldn't think about anything beyond the task ahead. His home was under attack, and gods be damned if he wasn't going to defend it.

Yet the way had grown crooked, and his goal less clear. Seeking Gwen had become seeking this gheist, the god of death, and somehow that brought Ian back home, to find that home in flames.

Why were the pagans attacking? *Who* were they attacking? House Blakley had done nothing to draw this sort of army, nothing more than stand by Adair's side when he was accused, then to condemn the man when his heresy was uncovered.

"Something's wrong with this," Ian muttered to himself. He pulled up short, scanning the approach to the castle walls. The gates were thrown wide, the way there choked with fighting. Small groups, their shadows flickering with the burning forest, some adding new flames to the darkness. "Why is there fighting outside the walls?" he asked no one in particular. "Why would Tavvish have ordered a foray?"

"These don't look like your father's spears," Volent said. Bruler rode up beside them. The Suhdrin knight looked nervous.

"They aren't spears of any house," Bruler said. "These are pagans, all. Heretics murdering each other, near as I can tell."

"He's right," Volent said. "Whatever remains of your house guard, they are inside the walls."

"So what is this?" Ian asked.

"In Heartsbridge, I think they would call it a schism,"

Bruler said. "Not sure what the witches would say."

"I need to get to Nessie," Ian said. "I need to know that my sister is safe."

"How will your guards feel about a force of Suhdrins riding through their front gate?" Bruler asked. "Accompanied by the Deadface, at that."

"Better than a pagan god, I suspect," Ian said. "They will recognize their master's son. I hope."

Elsa burned through the night. The pagans fell away from her like fog from the morning sun and, even though it was near the end of Strife's cycle, she felt invincible.

There had been so many questions leading up to this day. Should she have stopped Gwen? Had Ian Blakley been corrupted by his time with the witch? What could she have done to prevent the tragedy at the Fen Gate? What did the gods want of her? Or she, of them?

It didn't matter now. The battle was here, and Elsa was forged for battle. Yet the battle wanted nothing to do with her. The first group of pagans she charged fled from her, offering no resistance. She could smell the strange echoes of everam—the last vestiges of gheists summoned and killed—but the air seemed flat, as though the spirits had been wrung out of the earth, like stale water from a rag.

There were dead bodies on the ground, their flesh twisted and broken, but still no signs of battle. No arrows among the fallen pine needles, no blades in the hands of the dead. Their wounds were charred and vicious.

This was a different kind of fight. This wasn't a battle of flesh, but of spirit. These weren't warriors at all. So who were they, and who was killing them?

Elsa dismounted. The tension from the flames coursed through her veins, too much for her to contain. She was afraid she would slip and kill her horse, so it was better to abandon it. Once she was on foot, Elsa let the power flow, forming a nimbus of flame and light around her. The undergrowth crisped at her approach, turning to ash and floating away on the troubled currents.

She entered a clearing and went to the dead bodies to examine them. Pagans, all. The ink on their faces, the fetishes in their braids. Elsa was used to finding a single icon, hidden in the depths of robes or buried in hearths. These victims wore their faith openly and profusely, whole necklaces jangling with iron and stone, the runes as old as the hallows. She had never seen such things, not even on Fianna.

"Elders," she muttered to herself, realization dawning. "These are the elders of the pagan tribes." She stopped and looked around, catching glimpses of similarly dressed figures darting through the night, running toward the castle or away, their movements confused by the flickering light. "This is a gathering of the pagans," she added, louder now. "*All* of them."

"The important ones, at least," a voice said from the woods. Elsa turned toward it, but saw only an inquisitor, dressed for war. No, not an inquisitor. The robes were wrong, and the armor. "I see your confusion. Don't worry, Sir Knight. Your vow will be honored tonight."

"Who are you? What's going on here?" she asked.

"My name is Folam. These people called me the voidfather, though I have grander titles." The man walked forward. His arm was wrapped in leather, and he held it carefully as though some great injury had befallen him. His eyes were cloudy with remnants of shock, but his stride was steady. "You must be Sir Elsa LaFey."

"How do you know me?"

"Aedan spoke of you, and Allaister as well, before he died. Your doing, I think?"

"Allaister was a heretic," Elsa said. She rounded on the man and brought her sword to the guard. "If he spoke of me, it was with fear. As you shall learn."

"Of course," Folam said. "It is your duty to kill me. Yet that is not why you are here, I think."

"I am sworn to kill a gheist and bring its pagan to justice," Elsa said. "I think your death falls within the essence of my mission, well enough."

"Aedan brought you, as he was meant to," the pagan said. "I had little hope that he would be your end, though by the look of him, it was close. Plus the added gift of returning Eldoreath to our ranks..." He shook his head. "It was more than I could hope. And young Ian? He is in your company, I trust?"

"There's no way you planned all of this," Elsa said. "We've traveled too far. You couldn't have known we would be here."

"No?" Folam said. "As you say, and yet here we are." He held out his hands. "Shall we end this? Or shall I simply tell you how it must end?"

"I have been in a thousand battles, friend. While I don't know you—or what you planned, or how you imagined this ending—I can tell you this." Elsa opened herself to the flames, drawing spiraling skeins of light into her spirit, the aura of her power growing and growing until the heat of it scorched the canopy of trees that surrounded the clearing. "I will not fall to an elder of the pagan faith. I have killed your gods. You are no threat to me."

"Ah, but who are my gods?" Folam said. He raised the arm, and she saw that it was a stump. The dark leather swirled with inky shadows, and then a plume of ash erupted from the end. "And who are yours?"

The wave of burning ash rolled toward her, twisting like a snake through the air, its head folding open as it approached. Instinctively, Elsa opened her senses, seeking the source of this power. There was nothing in it.

It was nothingness, and the screaming void.

She burned bright, throwing an arc of Strife's holy light against the ash. It cut through, scything the column open like fire through wheat, but still the ash rolled forward, curling around the flames, smothering them. The closer it got, the more Elsa felt as if she was standing on the edge of a precipice. She fell back, cutting the air with her blade, drawing holy sigils in light. The ash swam around them, surrounding her. It blotted out the sky. Only a narrow dome of air remained, pushed back by her nimbus of light.

"The gods answer to me, Elsa." Folam's voice echoed through the ash. "All the gods."

The ash fell on her, choking out the light.

58

"IRON TO THE doors! Flame to the fire! Pagans at the gate! "Pagans among us!"

The streetcaller was young, and the fear in his voice cracked like lightning. He hurried past Martin and Lucas, clanging his silver bell as he ran. The crowds he passed were already in a panic. The priests of Gallowsport weren't used to such excitement, their stock in trade being somber. Lucas pulled Martin to the side of the road, keeping his robe pulled tight over his face. The wounds the frair had received at Sacombre's hand were still bleeding, and his flesh was as pale as snow.

"You may have to go on without me," Lucas whispered. His voice was rough.

"I can't," Martin said. "I wouldn't even know where to go. Are you sure he's gone?"

"Horne was ready. She knew we would be waiting. Probably drove us here and simply waited to spring her trap." Lucas coughed, and it became a grinding hack that bent him double. "At the very least, she would have prepared an escape. There's no way she's still in the city."

"Then we have to get moving!" Martin urged. "Every moment we tarry here is another mile the high inquisitor puts between us and him."

"It's hopeless. Horne could have him on a ship heading south, or north, or even out to the Black Isle. Gods know how deep this goes. She could have stuffed him into the back of a wagon and ridden halfway to Dunneswerry by now."

"I will start with the docks, ask some questions. See if they chartered a ship. They closed the port after I anchored that gheist in the harbor mouth, so it's not like there are a lot of possibilities," Martin said. "And if that proves fruitless, I'll get us some horses. We'll find him. We have to try."

"Martin, listen to me." Lucas took the boy by the shoulders. "He's gone. Sacombre is gone. It was a fool's errand to think the two of us could get him to Heartsbridge. I should have sought help. In Greenhall, or here, or at the Reaveholt. I was too stubborn." Lucas's hands fell to his side, and the old priest wavered on his feet. "It's my fault. I should have… anything. I should have done something more."

"You did the best you could, given everything that's happened," Martin said. When he touched the frair's shoulder, Lucas nearly jumped out of his boots. "But you're right. You need to rest. Let me handle this."

"There will be a doma… a doma nearby," Lucas said. "It will be safe. Gods know what Horne's people have released in the city. Wouldn't do to come this far only to get eaten by a god."

Martin took Lucas's arm and led him down the street. The city's guards were reestablishing control, now that the most obvious gheist was gone—or at least had been contained to the harbor. He tucked his cloak over the pilfered feyiron blade, unwilling to surrender it. They were passing an alleyway when Lucas pulled them to a stop. Martin looked at him quizzically.

"Down there," Lucas said. "Something among the

rubbish." Martin looked in the direction he was pointing, and saw a figure huddled beside a pile of crates. "That's a body."

"No doubt the city is full of bodies right now," Martin said. "Including yours, if we don't get you somewhere to lie down."

"Nonsense," Lucas said. Weakly he pushed Martin away, then walked down the alleyway. Martin waited in the street, looking from side to side until it was clear that no one was paying them any mind, then followed. Lucas knelt beside the body.

"Throat cut. No struggle, not even a look of surprise."

He tilted the corpse's head back, and it nearly fell from his shoulders. The flap of his neck was bloodless, though there was a rusty stain on his shirt. The hood of his robe was lined in fine silk and silver beads. Lucas grunted.

"An elector of Cinder. Either he was in town for a judgment, or Gallowsport will need to find a new leader," Lucas said. He lay the man's head back down, then started going through the dead man's robes.

"If we're seen..." Martin said nervously.

"We will have an excuse. I am an inquisitor," Lucas said. "I am inquiring." He held up the man's limp hand. "Look here. Pale as snow. I'd be surprised if there's a drop of blood in this man's veins."

"Yes, but what—"

"And here." Lucas stood, tottering further down the alleyway. "The ground is smeared in ash. These planks look burned, but it's only a hair deep." He scratched at the wall and snorted. "The wood beneath is unharmed. Horne did this. Or one of her friends."

"So she could be nearby?" Martin asked.

"Yes, or no. I still don't think she'd be so foolish to stay in Gallowsport, but we might find some evidence of where she's gone." Lucas looked up and down the alley. "What is this building? A doma? An inn?"

"There aren't a lot of wooden buildings in this city," Martin said. He went around the corner and looked up at the signage. "It's a coach house."

Lucas's brows went up. "Well," he said. "Well then. That's something."

Inside they found an agitated man in black, busily polishing a leather harness. His face was heavily scarred, and when he walked to the shop's counter, his leg bent in an awkward limp.

"What can I do for you?" he asked, then spied Martin's tabard and face, and decided he should amend his greeting. "My lord?"

"You rent carriages?" Lucas asked.

"Did," the man said. He continued to address Martin, though. Perhaps he was used to ignoring priests in a town like Gallowsport. "Most are out. Couple of people came in a few minutes ago and bought my last. Heading to Dunneswerry, they said."

"Well," Martin said, glancing at Lucas. "We can be sure they aren't headed to Dunneswerry, then." He turned his attention back to the proprietor. "Were they dressed as priests?"

"More or less. Perhaps more less than more," the man said. Martin was still untangling that in his head when Lucas shouldered his way back into the conversation.

"So you're out of carriages," the frair said. "Do you still have any horses?"

They negotiated a price, claimed the horses, and rode out of Gallowsport as quickly as the crowds would let them. The mounts weren't meant for riding, their broad backs and thick legs more suited for farm work than a gentle country stroll.

A short distance from the city they stopped to acquire some supplies. Food and water lent Lucas some renewed energy, and once they were on the road again, they rode hard. Though not fast, the horses made up for it in stamina.

The frair led them south.

"If we eliminate Dunneswerry, and assume they can't return to Tener without risking the Reaveholt or whatever horror is stalking Greenhall, then south is the only option," he explained. "It's a long trek, but if they have a planned route through the Harper's Teeth, they could be in Galleydeep before winter truly falls in Suhdra."

"Perhaps they learned about the harbor closing, scuttled that plan, and are hoping to catch a ship somewhere along the southern shore," Martin suggested. "There are other ports."

"Yes, that's possible, and we will pass through those towns. None are large enough to hide an entire group of priests, especially dressed as Horne and her friends. Even the high inquisitor will attract attention. If that is their plan, we will hear word of it." Lucas sat high in his saddle, looking better than he had in weeks. "We may have struck gold, young Roard. We may catch up with Sacombre after all!"

Their day was quiet. Traffic out of Gallowsport was minimal, and the only travelers they passed were prison trains and their grim escorts. Few were interested in talking, but then they passed a lonely messenger on his way north, and learned that a carriage matching their description had been seen on this road, riding hard and looking mean. Perhaps a half-dozen riders with it. When hailed, they had not slowed.

Hearing this, Lucas drove them faster. Whatever fatigue

he felt in the streets of Gallowsport was replaced with a fever of rage. He rode in silence, Martin at his side.

Sometime late in the day, Martin looked over and saw that the frair was muttering to himself. Worried his companion was slipping slowly into madness, the young prince rode closer and tugged at the frair's robes. Lucas jumped, but kept his eyes on the road ahead.

"Talking to yourself?" Martin asked.

"Just going over the witch's words. 'Older than you,' she said. Older than us, and then something about a war before this one."

"There have been plenty of wars," Martin said. "The Reavers, the crusades, the endless settling of debts. Even in the south we've had our share of disagreement. Which one do you think she meant?"

"We have had plenty of wars, but for the pagans there has only ever been one conflict. To the faithful, this is just a continuation of the crusades, of the Suhdrin migration," Lucas replied. "One long, endless war of lost henges and new domas and murder, stretching back to the first landing of Suhdrin settlers on Tenumbra. So she must have meant something before that."

"A war between the tribes, perhaps?" Martin asked. "Seems likely. Give people space, and they'll find a reason to fight over it."

"Between the tribes, maybe. Or against them. She said she thought they were gone, but no, they were still there. Waiting."

"Who do you think 'they' could be?" Martin asked. "Other pagans? Some group who lived on the island before the tribes?"

"The Tenerran's oldest legends claim the island was

uninhabited when they arrived, a gift from the gods, prepared by the spirits and waiting to be taken."

"So a war with the gheists themselves?"

"I don't know," Lucas said, and he sounded frustrated. "We know so little of those days, and what we have is kept hidden, for fear the pagans would find a way to use it against us."

"Well, either way, if they're killing pagans, perhaps they aren't our enemies after all," Martin said.

"That elector was no pagan," Lucas answered, "and neither am I."

"Well." Martin shrugged. "They didn't kill you, at least."

Lucas settled into silence, his eyes fixed on the road ahead. They rode until dusk threatened. Then a shadow loomed by the side of the road. Martin saw it first.

"Frair?" he said. "Is that..."

It was a carriage, broken open.

"Godsbless," Lucas said under his breath. They pulled up, Lucas dismounting stiffly, Martin following suit, drawing his stolen feyiron sword with one hand, palming a knife in the other. They crept forward as quietly as they could. There was no sound from the wreckage.

The horses were still in their harness, cropping contentedly at the side of the road. All the doors of the carriage were thrown open, and the leather travel satchels that lined the box hung limp and empty. The driver, if one had been employed, was nowhere to be seen. The passenger compartment was empty, though a faint stench of sulphur remained.

Lucas circled the carriage once, then kicked at something among the grasses, causing a jangle of metal. Martin reached down and picked it up. Chains, hot to the touch.

"That's what the elector's blood would have been for.

Bloodwrought shackles, freshly formed and very powerful, but why would they need them?" Lucas asked, peering around. "And where have they gone?"

"If we're right, and the business in the harbor disrupted their plans, perhaps this is as far as they needed to go to get back on track," Martin said. "They came here, met some co-conspirators, and rode off into the forest."

"If so, then they're truly gone. But why here? And why these," Lucas asked, taking the shackles from Martin and examining them. "Worse, why did they stop needing them?" As he pondered, Martin looked across the landscape.

"What's down there?" he asked, pointing. The moors to the east rolled gentle and featureless to the horizon, but to the west, in the direction Martin was pointing, the land descended quickly toward the distant coast. There, among the crags and sharp crevasses of broken stone, was a twist of smoke.

"Very good, Sir Roard," Lucas said. "Perhaps they haven't fled yet at all, but are only resting."

"Without setting a guard, and leaving the team and carriage unattended?"

"Yes, well. It does seem unlikely, but *something* is burning." The frair tossed the shackles to the ground. "Let us take a look... carefully."

They made the descent, though any hope of doing so quietly was shattered by the rattling scree that tumbled ahead of them. Whoever waited around that fire would know they had company. The trail of smoke emanated from a narrow ravine that was sheltered from the road. As they got closer, the origin of the smoke became clear. Lucas sniffed the air.

"Flesh," he said. "Dinner or tragedy. Which do you think, young Martin?"

"Given the last few months of my life, it would be a startling change of pace to learn that it is dinner, frair."

Lucas didn't answer, but when they approached the ravine he pulled Martin back, taking the lead with his iron-tipped staff. He braced himself at the entrance, drawing naether into his robes and building a shield of shadow-dark power. When he stepped forward, it was with a rush, his motions aided by Cinder's might. He hovered at the entrance to the furrow, staff at the ready.

He stopped, and remained perfectly still. When nothing attacked him, Martin pushed past. It took several blinking moments for his eyes to adjust to the gloom of the ravine. When he understood what he was seeing, he gasped and stepped back.

"It would seem Tomas did not escape after all," Lucas said. He lowered himself to the ground, dispelling the intricate naetheric rites of his armor.

The husk of Tomas Sacombre stood in the middle of the narrow ravine. He was propped up by a picket, hands tied behind his back, feet secured to the stone floor. The high inquisitor's head was thrown back, mouth open, eyes staring sightlessly to the sky. Smoke trailed lazily from between his teeth. For all practical purposes, that was all that remained of him. The rest of his body had erupted, chest split in a single fissure that ran from neck to hips, continuing down his right leg. The shell of his skin was as shiny as coal, a char buffed clean of impurity.

Inside, Sacombre was hollow. Even his ribs were gone, somehow burned away. The ground in front of the body was scarred and dusted with soot. Long wounds criss-crossed the stones, scrambling up the steep wall until they disappeared.

59

THE SHRINE SANG to her heart, thrumming through the hound's spine and into the matted blood on her skin. Gwen's body felt like a bell that had been struck, and the chaos of the battle was the sound it gave.

Her bones shivered. Her soul rejoiced.

Houndhallow rose above her like a mountain, limned by the bonfires that had sprung up on the grounds around the castle, in buildings, and on the walls. The gates were open, and a heavy skirmish had developed on the approach. Three separate groups were killing and dying in the churned mud of the road.

Most of the dead wore the black and white of House Blakley, but there were pagans who died, as well. Only the strange void priests seemed to have suffered no losses. The swirl of combat added to the confusion. The Blakley troops formed a tight knot at the center of the road, the pagans surrounding them yet held at bay by a ring of spears. The void priests lurked unseen at the edges, striking at the other two parties without reprisal.

"Closer in," she whispered to the hound. "Get us to their flanks." The beast obeyed, but as they approached the battle, it stopped and settled into a lurking crouch, sticking to the trees. Gwen tried to urge it closer, but it refused.

"We can't do anything from here," she whispered. The pagans were constantly surprised when one of their shamans keeled over with darkness bubbling out of his mouth, or the spirit of a feral god fluttered and disappeared. Each time they struck, the priests fell back to the forest, and the confusion in the pagan ranks gave the Blakleys courage to venture out from their ring of steel. This drew the pagan attention back to the spears.

Frustrated, Gwen gave the hound a kick.

"We have to get in there!"

The beast craned its massive head around, staring at Gwen with an eye the color of murky water. It huffed at her, a massive gust of wind that flapped its lips, baring teeth the size of daggers. Gwen blanched and tried to pull away, but discovered that the matted iron-hard blood from her wounds had pinned her in place. She ran a hand down its jaw.

"It's alright," she said. "Peace, peace. We'll find a way."

The hound stared at her a moment longer, then turned back to the battle. Three more pagans had fallen, but some action had forced the void priests into the shadows. They were nowhere to be seen, and at least one body on the verge of the road wore the strange black and silver armor of their ilk.

"They are few," Gwen muttered to herself, "and they spend their blood dearly. Good to know. Now, can we interfere in this slaughter?"

The hound grumbled assent and started to lope forward. Hoofbeats hammered down the road in their direction, and the hound hesitated. Its ears flickered to attention.

"The Hound! The Hallow!"

Ian Blakley charged into the pagan host with two riders

at his side and a small gaggle of mounted knights in his wake. The circle of pagans ducked away, parting like a wind-blown sea of grass, letting him reach the Blakley faithful. However, those spears didn't lower at his approach. The prince of Houndhallow pulled up short, his horse rearing and kicking in protest.

This wasn't the child who rode out of Houndhallow's gates six months earlier, and far from the boy Gwen had last seen years ago. Her memories of the battle of Fen Gate were filtered through the Fen god's vision.

There was a confidence to him, in the way he sat his horse, the look he gave the men arrayed before him. His clothes were nearly pagan, scraps of traditional lordly gear scattered among hunter's leathers, silk and chain shirt under a cloak of leather autumn leaves, as was the tradition among Tenerran shamans. She briefly wondered by what right he wore that cloak, and what Cahl would think of a Tenerran lord wrapped in pagan glory.

To further complicate matters, the men who followed him were Suhdrin knights, wearing the colors of several different lords of the south. They rode close together, knee to knee, each mount feeling its rider's nervousness and mincing delicately side to side. A cadre of Suhdrin knights led by a pagan lord.

It was no wonder Blakley's men didn't recognize their master's son.

"Down your spears, friends," Ian said. "There is no danger here."

"Pray forgive, sir," one of the spearmen responded, "but there's been blood enough today. We'll judge the threat."

"Tenny Knox! Who gave you a spear? Last we spoke, you were wielding a fishing pole and getting whipped for catching crawfish in the village well."

"Lord Blakley? My lord, we didn't recognize you! Or your… host," Knox said, looking over Ian's shoulder. "A friendly face has been rare enough, these days."

"Strange days, stranger friends," Ian said. "I must speak to Tavvish, and see to my sister's health."

"Of course," Knox said, but still neither he nor his fellow Tenerrans lowered their spears. "What of your companions? The day hasn't dawned when I would stand aside for the likes of them."

"You'll have to trust me," Ian said. He gestured to his closest riders. "They are not the same men you knew. Especially this one."

Gwen turned her attention to the two knights flanking Ian. One was a grizzled man of Suhdra, wearing the yellow tabard of Marchand, the paint on his shield heavily chipped and worn. He kept his eyes roaming between the pagans and the Blakley force, unsure of which presented the greatest threat. The other rider looked strange, his face a ruin of red and white. Gwen stared at the man for a full breath before his name snapped into her head.

"Volent," she hissed. The hound sprang forward without her willing it. A swirling mass of pagans solidified around her, falling into step in the hound's wake, the strangeness of her appearance and the size of the hound marked her as part of the ancient and faithful.

The knight of Marchand noticed her first, sucking in his breath and barking a warning to the others. The Suhdrins flowed into a defensive stance behind him, leaving Ian and Volent stranded between the Blakleys and Gwen. Ian turned to look at her. He didn't seem to recognize her.

"It's me, Ian," she said. "It's Gwen Adair."

"Lady Gwen," he said, his face lighting up. "I suspected you would be at the center of this." He flicked his reins and brought his mount around to face her, but made no motion toward his sword. "Would you care to explain?" Volent seemed nonplussed, though it was impossible to read emotion on his broken face.

"What explanation do I owe you, Blakley?" Gwen said. She turned to Volent. "Deadface."

"I do not answer to that anymore," Volent said. His features shifted awkwardly, the misfit pieces of his face shuffling together. "Though if any of us owe an explanation, it is I."

"So," Gwen said. "Explain."

Volent shook his head slowly. "Now isn't the time. I would say you wouldn't believe me anyway, but,"—he gestured at her—"You seem to be wearing armor made of your own blood, and riding a dog the size of a small horse. So my story may seem dull."

"Strange times," Gwen said.

"Stranger friends," Volent answered.

"Why are your people attacking my home?" Ian demanded.

"They aren't my people," Gwen said. "Any more or less than they are yours, Ian of the tribe of hounds. As for the attack..." She glanced back at the pagans who had fallen into step behind her. "...I believe they have been deceived."

"The Blakleys attacked us first," one of the pagans said. Gwen remembered seeing the man at the conclave of elders, though he had none of the braids of a shaman. He was dressed in bones, marking him as a member of the tribe of the dead. One of Judoc's faithful. Would he know of the betrayal? Was he party to it?

"The voidfather was escorting us through the forests," the man continued, "when a patrol of inquisitors fell on us. They were flying the hound! We weren't even in Blakley lands."

"That's a right load of shit," young Knox said. "This lot appeared out of nowhere and started killing villagers. Master Tavvish ordered folks inside the walls. They burned most of the outer farmyards and granaries before their main force arrived. It was a slaughter."

"Your people burned their own houses as they retreated," the pagan said. "Not that we need your damned walls. The forest gives us what we need, as it always has. Typical Suhdrin bullshit."

"Now you take that Suhdrin shit back," Knox said. He surged forward menacingly, courage plucked by Ian's presence. "We won't have any of that shit."

"You don't have to say shit with every sentence, Tenny," Ian said quietly. "It gives less steel to your words than you think." The boy fell back, his face blushing. Ian smiled and raised his chin to Gwen. "What do you say to these accusations? I know nothing of this voidfather, but if he's been taken captive, I'm sure I can negotiate his release. If it will end this conflict."

"Folam Voidfather is not in your dungeon, nor was he taken by your father's men," Gwen said. "I fought him just now, in the forests overlooking this castle."

"I was with him," the young pagan said. "I saw him taken." He glared at her with hatred in his eyes. "Aedan was right about you. The huntress of Adair is not to be trusted."

Some of the pagans edged away from her, others stood

closer. The rift in their ranks was clear. Spears started to turn inward, the Blakley threat temporarily forgotten.

"Peace, peace, godsdamned *peace*!" Gwen said loudly. "We traveled with the voidfather to Greenhall, to mollify the vernal god." She shot a look at Ian, who appeared to have heard of events at Halverdt's castle. His brows were up, and his hand was resting on the hilt of his blade. "Folam betrayed us. Nearly killed the three of us, and brought terrible ruin to the castle."

"That's not the tale he told," the man said. A murmur of agreement went through the pagan ranks. "Noel Summerdaughter, the Suhdrin, murdered Cahl and the two of you tried to kill the voidfather, as well. Then you tried to summon the vernal god and failed to bind it to your will. As you did with the Fen god, Gwen Adair, at the high inquisitor's will."

Ian and Gwen laughed together, a sound that sent the nervous Suhdrin knights into a murmur. But it was Volent who spoke.

"Whatever I know of Sacombre, it is this—his madness was of Cinder born, and not of the old gods. That lesson he taught me well enough, whether he meant to or not," Volent said. He looked around at a sea of doubtful expressions. "Though I imagine my word is little currency in this company."

"That's an understatement," Gwen said. "I still don't know why you're here at all."

"Looking for you," Volent said.

"That still doesn't solve this problem," the grizzled Suhdrin knight said. "We are all at spear-ends, with the ranks of the dead all around us, and I haven't heard a reasonable explanation as to why."

"Folam," Gwen said firmly. "He deceived you. Faked his

capture, led the conclave here while his compatriots planted the seeds of war. It was his priests who burned your farms, Blakley, and his faithful who posed as houndsmen to give the pagans reason to fight. Now that the battle is joined, his void priests strike at both sides, to feed the flames."

"Where is your proof?" the young pagan said.

"There," she said, pointing to the dead void priest at the verge of the road. "One of his men, uncloaked."

"That's an inquisitor," the pagan said. "The same ones who attacked Folam in the first place, and who even now help defend Houndhallow."

"No," Ian said. He dismounted and walked over to the corpse. Taking the body by the nape of the neck, he turned it over, holding the dead man's face to the gathered pagans. "I know no inquisitor like this."

The void priest's face was stitched in pagan ink, the patterns branded into his skin. Unfamiliar runes had been added to the traditional forms, covering his eyes and running down his cheeks. The man's braids had been shorn.

"His clothes are not that of a priest of Cinder, though they are similar," Volent said. "Perhaps Sacombre's heresy goes even deeper than we thought."

"This proves nothing," the young pagan said. "A Tenerran converted to the celestial faith. There are few enough true to the old ways!"

"You are stubborn in your violence," Gwen said. She turned the hound sidewise to face the man, holding herself stiff. "What do you say of me? Am I of celestial mien? Do I look like a Tenerran converted to the celestial faith? Is my word worth nothing to you?"

"The voidfather—"

"Has betrayed us all," Cahl announced. The shaman limped onto the road, holding his side. Blood leaked out from between his fingers, and each step brought a gasp to his lips. "Do not doubt the last daughter of the iron tribe. She speaks true."

A murmur went up among the pagans, at the sight of the man they thought dead. Some pulled back from the confrontation, while others remained unconvinced.

"So we are to just accept this? The word of this girl, a Tenerran lord accompanied by Suhdrin knights, and the Deadface?" a young pagan asked. It was the one dressed in bones.

"Judoc is dead, friend," Cahl said. "Your elder has passed from this world. You must trust someone." He stopped and stood straight. "Trust me."

"Yet what of Folam?" the tribesman hissed. "What has become of the voidfather!"

They were answered by an echoing scream—a grating, piercing howl that pushed the trees aside like grass, and filled their bones with terror. They turned to face the forest.

There among the trees was a god made of emptiness.

60

THE RANKS ARRAYED against them were vast. Bassion's army represented the slow accumulation of political favor, the mustering of the deep resources of the southern lords, and a noble will to lead that harkened back to the days of Suhdrin kings and queens. The attached might of the priests of Cinder only underscored that will.

Generations ago, the celestial church had shattered the royal lineage of Bassion to replace it with the holy rule of the celestriarch and the subservient role of the Circle of Lords. That Cinder's faithful would march beside this army said much of Duchess Helenne's political power, and more about the celestriarch's waning influence in Cinderfell.

Malcolm sat on his horse atop a hill, overlooking this force. He had scant hundreds at his side, and nothing that could oppose the might of Cinder. Beyond the Suhdrin lines, the iron walls of the Reaveholt stood, containing several thousand Tenerran spears. Perhaps enough to hold out until help came, but of no use to him.

"This is a fool's errand," he muttered. At his side, Castian Jaerdin snorted.

"It has been since the beginning, Malcolm," he said. "Sent to Greenhall by one side of the church, just to be betrayed by the other. Forced into war by Halverdt, only to see him fall to Sacombre's trickery and our own gullible faith. Sworn to protect Adair—the only *genuine* heretic in your midst—and now we face Bassion, whose only ambition seems to be ambition itself."

"And Cinder," Malcolm said. "The court of winter itself fights us, and gods only know why."

"I doubt the gods have much to do with it," Castian said. "Whatever happened at Greenhall has the south in a fury. I would be surprised if there's a single Tenerran priest in their ranks."

"I've learned to expect little of surprise," Malcolm said. "Days come and go, and the wonders of my life pile up. It's become a bit tiring."

"There must be a hint of heroism left in you, friend," Castian said quietly. "Else we would have already fled the field, and spared these faithful few their lives."

"There's nowhere to run," Malcolm replied. "Bassion before us, the hunting ranks of Marchand at our back, and whatever remains of the pagans somewhere in between." He sighted along the length of his arm, estimating distance to the front ranks of the Suhdrin force. His eyesight was failing, along with everything else. Little matter now. "If I were to release them, they would only live a few weeks on the run, eating mud and sleeping on stones before they were driven to ground by some Suhdrin errant.

"At least I can give them a better death than that."

"They ask for no more," Castian said. He sat quietly for a long moment, the distant sound of Suhdrin drums echoing down the countryside. "About the priest..."

"I will hear no more of that," Malcolm said. "It's done. Our lot is cast. If I die today, my soul will not travel to the house of Cinder. That is a blessing and a curse. Winter never held much love for me, anyway."

"The men are worried. They fear the inquisition," Castian said. "They fear the wrath of winter."

"Let them take comfort in the promise of summer," Malcolm answered. "Lady Strife promises warmth, even to those who die in winter's arms. That is our hope." A great shout broke free of the Suhdrin army, and the drumbeat changed. The ranks of spear and horse began their slow march forward. "Our *only* hope, it seems."

Castian reached over and grasped Malcolm's arm. The duke of Redgarden met Malcolm's eyes and smiled.

"It has been my greatest honor to march at your side, Houndhallow. When my children tell this story to their children, it will serve my name well to know that I stood with the greatest, bravest man of my generation."

"Your name, perhaps, but not your soul." Malcolm returned the clasped hand with his own stiff smile. "The honor has been mine, Redgarden. If all in Suhdra and Tener could love as we love, this war would never happen."

"A wishful thought," Castian said, then he turned and rode off to see to his ranks. Horns and drums started to sound from Malcolm's company, the meager lines drawing up to face the certainty of death.

"You look like a statue, husband," Sorcha said as she rode up. "As if they've already made the memorial of you, and cast your flesh in bronze."

"This would be a good place for it, should ever they decide to do such a thing." Malcolm looked around, gesturing to the rolling hills. "No lords to bother my final resting place, and no children to piss on my marble."

"I hate it when you're morose," she said. He turned his horse to slide closer to hers, their knees touching first, then their hands. He clasped her fingers, twining them together. She smiled. "I would blame the weather, but it seems not even the sun could stir your smile."

"I've lost so many days, my love," he said, looking firmly into her eyes. "Days I could have spent with you, with our son, our daughter. Chasing things that have no weight, and titles that will be forgotten once I am dead."

"You never chased your titles, Malcolm," she said. "'Duke' you were given by your father and your blood, though you came to it too early to know its weight. 'Reaverbane' came because you refused to stand by and let your lands fall into ruin. You did not seek glory, my love. That is why it fits so comfortably on your head."

"The only title I would have is husband, and I have not earned it," he said. "Sorcha, love, I'm sorry I treated you so poorly. I could not see the woman I married, and let my fear sweep away the promises I made. You should not have lived a single day in darkness. Not one."

"Oh, silly," Sorcha said. "You make a girl of me again."

"That we were," Malcolm said. "Girl and boy and nothing else. Free to leave this behind, and live our days together."

"We have lived our days together," Sorcha said. "All the days the gods have given us, and now we're here." She untangled her fingers and took his jaw in her hand, pulling it close, kissing him lightly on the lips. Malcolm pressed his forehead against hers, and they breathed together that way, until the world pulled them away.

A great shout broke out from the valley. Malcolm didn't move until Sir Doone shook him, and he realized she had been trying to get his attention for several moments.

"My lord," she said urgently. "There is movement among the Suhdrins!"

"Yes, yes," he said, withdrawing reluctantly from his wife's embrace. "Let us march now, and die... and so forth."

"You misunderstand, my lord," Doone said, her eyes wide. "They are breaking in half. Their ranks are scattering to the winds, and their banners with them!"

Doone spoke true. The vast wedge of the Suhdrin army was splintering apart. A confusion of horns sounded over the valley, and their drums fell silent. Malcolm peered at where Bassion's command platform overlooked the field, but the banners there swayed dangerously, unsettled by the pressing crowd.

The platform itself was abandoned. Among the ranks, spears stuck awkwardly, becoming tangled, the files pressing together or breaking apart. Men threw down their weapons and ran across the fields. A scattering of cavalry rode them down, trampling their companions in their haste to get away.

Only the company of Cinder held firm. The sky above those banners was a little darker, a little heavier, but they were still on the field, rank upon rank of black-clad spearmen and their attendant priests, a rock amid the currents.

"What the hell is going on?" Malcolm asked.

"We know not," Doone answered. "The horns stopped briefly, and then we heard... I swear to you, we heard screaming from their camps. The ranks broke shortly after."

"What does our vow knight say?"

"She has not emerged from her tent," Doone said. "Trueau refuses to be a part of this battle."

"I can't blame her, but fetch the woman. See if she

understands Cinder's patience, or knows what unseen force might have put the fear into Bassion's army."

"I am not at your beck, Houndhallow," the vow knight said, striding up. She wore her armor, as well as a white lace mourning veil that covered the open face of her helm. Only a hint of her eyes could be seen through the pattern. "But I felt the change. What is happening?"

Malcolm pointed to the opposite side of the field. Cinder's ranks had shifted, though they seemed intent on repositioning themselves, rather than marching directly toward his force. A steady drum sounded, and more dark-armored figures joined their ranks, small detachments that seemed to be coming from the surrounding woods.

"They have reinforcements?" Doone asked. "Or..."

"There is a motion of gheists among the hills," Trueau said sharply. "The... the ley lines themselves are shifting."

"What the godsdamned hell does that mean?" Malcolm asked.

"It means that something terrible has happened," Sorcha answered. Malcolm looked at his wife and saw the alarm written on her face. "Yes, I feel it as well. As though a storm has found a way into my heart."

"My lord, the Suhdrin army is coming to us," Doone reported. "We must decide how we intend to greet them." A full half of the force had thrown down their weapons and were now running with no thought to their own defense or safety. It would have been easy enough to ride them down, to cut them down with bows, or spit them on spears, or break them with a solid charge of heavy horse.

It would be easy to win the day, Malcolm realized, but at what cost?

"Open ranks, let them in," he said. "And when those knights reach us, bring me whoever among them seems capable of explaining themselves."

He didn't need to wait long. The first riders slowed as they approached the lines of Malcolm's company, as though they might halfheartedly give charge, but when the men of Redgarden peeled apart and opened a path, they sheathed their weapons and couched their spears into parade formation. They rode in as honorably as could be managed, considering they had the blood of trampled spearmen on their caparisons.

One man spotted Malcolm and turned in his direction. Doone growled and drew her sword, but the knight made no motion to attack.

"What is the meaning of this, sir?" Malcolm asked. "What the hell is going on over there?"

"The priests, my lord! The inquisitors of Cinder. They started killing one another. Without blade or spear, simply opening their skulls with words of ancient power. And then they started killing us!" The knight threw aside his sword and stumbled from the saddle, going to one knee. "I beg amnesty, Reaverbane. I beg your protection!"

"Protection? Why do you think I can protect you from an inquisitor?"

The man looked up at Malcolm, tears streaking his face, tear of ash and blood. Something had touched his mind, leaving a scar of madness.

"I was at the Fen Gate, and saw your battle with Sacombre, and the spirit that rode him. That spirit has returned! It is the god of death who leads them, my lord! No man has faced him but you!" The man grabbed at Malcolm's belt, breaking down. "Gods above, save us, Houndhallow. Save us!"

61

THE GOD OF nothing stood before them. The forest keened at its presence, as though a sharp wind blew unseen through the trees. Ian shielded his eyes from the emptiness that lapped at his vision, drawing in sight until only blindness remained.

"So this is his plan," Gwen whispered. "Crush the strength of the north here, and let the remnants fight among themselves over who's to blame."

Ian glanced over at her. If she had not named herself, he would never have recognized the daughter of House Adair. She sat in rags, a thousand tiny cuts across her flesh, but from each one a scale of iron hung. The mask that gripped her face made it look as if someone had poured molten metal over her head, letting it run in beads across her cheeks before it cooled. For all the blood and iron, however, she seemed relatively unharmed. Indeed, she seemed *strong*. He was still looking at her when Gwen turned in his direction. Ian realized he was staring, and looked quickly away.

"What do you think, Ian?" she asked.

"Of what?" he stuttered.

"Of what? The gheist, of course. Do you think we can take it?"

"Oh, well, no," he said. "I mean, maybe. I don't really know. Aren't you the expert in these things, huntress?"

"That's a title I have long abandoned," she said. "But no, I don't think the iron has been wrought in blood that could kill this god. Nevertheless, there must be something we can do."

The emptiness moved closer, brushing aside trees and people as it came. The remnants of the pagan force—those few who remained outside the walls—scattered like the wind. Only those inside Houndhallow remained.

"Is this what it was like, when I fell on the Fen Gate?" Gwen asked with wonder in her voice. "Was it this hopeless?"

"It was worse," Ian said. "There was a Suhdrin army beating down the door, and Sacombre channeling the god of death."

"And how did you succeed then, Ian?" she asked, with a hint of humor. "You talked me out of destroying everything, didn't you?"

"Aye," Ian said, "though you weren't terribly interested in listening."

"Somehow I don't think that's going to work on this voidfather fellow," Volent said from the side. The knight marshal of Greenhall squirmed uncomfortably in his saddle. "Still better than facing Sacombre again."

"I don't think any of us will need to do that, ever," Ian said. "Speaking of which, where is Elsa?"

"I lost sight of Sir LaFey when we met this lot," Bruler answered.

"Gods protect her, then. Or perhaps the gods should protect whoever she's fighting," Ian said earnestly. "What are we to do?"

"Pray to the gods and die heroic," Volent said. He hefted his lance and checked his nervous horse's skittering. "Point me to this voidfather. I will settle him, once and for all."

"No," Gwen said. She put a surprisingly gentle hand on Volent's shoulder, stilling him. "He is the master of the emptiness, and I sense a void in you as well, Sir Volent. Our wounds speak, one to the other."

Volent hesitated, but when he looked at Gwen and nodded, Ian saw something he had never seen on the man's face.

Fear.

"Sir Volent and I are useless in this task, I'm afraid," Gwen said to Ian. "Folam has too much power over us."

"Too much... but how is that possible?"

"Another time, Sir Blakley," Gwen said. "This falls to you."

"If only Elsa were here," Ian said. He had an uncomfortable feeling in his heart, a twisting that he suddenly realized was worry. Surely Sir Elsa could handle herself, he thought, but something about the way the god of emptiness growled across the horizon made him wonder.

He was afraid for her, he realized. Afraid.

"The gods cannot help us, here," Gwen said firmly. "Whatever power he wields, Folam can cast the blessed into darkness, and the shadowed into light. This battle cannot be won by arcane power." She nodded at Ian's hand, still gripping his simple sword. "This must be done with blood and steel."

"Blood and steel, and the sweat of honest flesh," Bruler said gruffly. The old knight lowered his visor and bowed respectfully in his saddle. "That's as it should be. Lead on, Blakley. I'm willing to die under the banner of a son of Tener."

"Gods bless we live through this, but if we die, let us die as sons and daughters of Tenumbra," Ian said. He shook aside his worry for Sir Elsa, and the resounding terror that struck him on seeing the walls of Houndhallow on fire. "Let's not let anything else divide us." He twisted in his saddle and stared at the shimmering gheist. It towered over the castle walls. "So how are we to begin?"

"I will direct whatever forces I can gather in an assault against the gheist," Gwen said. "As long as Volent and I keep some distance, we should remain effective. I don't think we can destroy it, but it must be faced. To keep it from the castle, at least. To save what lives we may." Gwen stretched her neck, peering among the trees. "However, you must strike the fatal blow, Ian, and it won't be at the gheist itself. Folam is out there, somewhere, driving this thing on. That is your only chance."

"My place is in Houndhallow," Ian said. "Standing with my sister."

"I will see Nessie safe," Gwen said. "Volent and I will die before any harm comes to her." Volent looked surprised at that, but after a moment he nodded.

Ian hesitated, his eyes lingering on the tower keep. He thought he could see a flash of red hair among the battlements, maybe even hear his sister's voice. Yet Gwen was right. He tore his eyes from the tower. It took all his will, and left a bitter wound in his heart.

I will return for you, sister.

"Very well," he said. The Suhdrin knights, the remaining spears of Blakley, and a handful of pagans stared at him in disbelief. "Are you with me?"

"The Hound!" Tenny Knox shouted. "The—"

"Tenumbra!" Ian howled before the boy could continue. "Tenumbra, and the gods!"

They charged into the night, and the forest swallowed them.

* * *

Nessie Blakley was worried. Master Tavvish had stopped answering her questions an hour earlier, and shortly after that had gone down into the tower and never returned. Her personal guard was dwindling away, with spears disappearing into the stairwell, whether to check on Tavvish, add their strength to the fight below, or simply to flee.

Only Sir Hague and Sir Clough remained. Hague was a grumpy old fellow, and he smelled like cabbage whenever he had had too much to drink the night before, but he stood grimly by and watched the castle burn without flinching. Sir Clough, on the other hand, was hardly older than Ian. Her hands seemed more fit for the harp than the spear, but as the world fell apart around them, Clough didn't bat an eye.

"They're in the keep," Nessie said to no one in particular. The sounds of fighting echoed up the stairwell like distant drums. She wondered if they'd break her things on the way up, then wondered why she cared about that at all. If the pagans reached the roof, she would be dead, Clough and Hague notwithstanding.

"Yes, my lady," Hague said, "but have no worry. Tavvish will be back soon, and then we'll start the counterattack.

Nessie didn't answer that. She knew better, but if it made Hague happy to believe that she didn't, Nessie could play along. She went to the edge and peered down. The gates were open, and a strange mix of people gathered just outside, talking."

"That's Sir Volent," she said.

"Oh, it cannot be the Deadface," Hague said simply. He shifted uncomfortably in his armor, and a plume of cabbage drifted across the roof. "Gods know where that coward is, but it's certainly not here."

"She's right," Clough said simply. "That's Volent, or I'm

the iron hound. And there's a whole cadre of Suhdrin knights with him."

Hague made a disbelieving sound, but limped to the edge of the tower and peered down. He was still muttering to himself when Clough spoke again.

"Pagans, too, and that... gods be damned if that isn't Master Ian."

"Where?" Nessie asked, failing to keep the excitement out of her voice. "Where is he? Where is my brother? Show me!"

Clough pointed, but it took several moments for Nessie to connect the wild-looking figure below with the brother she remembered. Then he tossed his head toward the tower, and the gesture was unmistakable. Nessie crawled up on the rampart and started waving her hands.

"Ian! Ian, we're up here!" she shouted as loudly as she could. The sound dropped into the courtyard and disappeared among the smoke and screams of dying men. "They're going to get into the tower, Ian. Help!"

Beyond the walls, the sky opened, and something empty poured into the world.

Minutes later—long, quiet minutes that Nessie spent staring at the gheist bearing down on her home—Ian gave a single look at the tower and then rode off into the forest. Nessie watched until he was gone. The smoke stung her eyes.

"He didn't see me," Nessie mumbled through her tears. "He didn't see."

The forest air stung with smoke and trailing cinders. Ian could barely see the path in front of him. He sawed his reins back and forth to drive his horse past trees that sprang out of the choking miasma in front of him. The going was slow, and behind him Ian could hear stones breaking and people dying.

Nevertheless, he pushed on.

Bruler rode close. The old man's expression was calm, but his knuckles gripped the reins like the last knot on a fraying rope. Ian called over his shoulder.

"Did you think it would end this way?"

"At the side of a heretic's son, hunting some kind of pagan god?" Bruler asked. "More or less, but I don't think this is the end. Not for me, at least."

"No? Old man like you, and you've got no fear of dying?"

"I've had plenty of chances to die, young Blakley. Missed every one of them. Now keep your mind on the path."

Ian grunted as a fallen timber rushed at him, scraping over it by mere inches and coming down in a bramble. The horses chomped their irritation, but once beyond the tangle, the air seemed to clear. The forest thinned, and here most of the flames had burned out.

"Think we're close?" Ian asked as they passed over the remnants of a fire.

"Closer than this lot," Bruler said, staring down. They were stomping through a charnel floor of bodies, all burned to a crisp. Ian reared back, but there was so little difference between body and ash that the horses didn't seem to take notice. Moments later, the brace of Blakley spearmen flowed over the bramble, flanked on both sides by pagan hunters. Each group kept a guard against the other, watching their new allies out of the corners of their eyes.

"Spread out," Ian called. "Folam has to be around here somewhere. It doesn't seem as if he could accomplish anything in that haze, not properly, so he's probably up high, somewhere the wind can scour. That would give him a good view of the battle, too."

"He's probably along a ley line," the pagan of bones said quietly. Ian rode closer.

"What's your name?"

"Hassek," he said, "but you'll do well to forget it after tonight. It's the last time we'll be talking."

"Very well, Hassek. What's this about lies?"

"Ley lines," Hassek said scornfully. "You celestials have forgotten so much of the true ways, it's hardly a wonder the soil rebels against you. The rivers of the earth. Henges string them along, or focus them. There are no henges here, other than the dog shrine, but the lines survive."

"Henges," Bruler said. "The pagan north is supposed to be filled with 'em. Shouldn't be hard to find one in this mess."

"Not true," Hassek answered. "Suhdrins and their precious priests came through and tore them down. 'Pulling the teeth of the old gods,' they said, but all it did was loosen their bonds. Give them freer rein in the world."

"He's right," Knox said. "There's not a standing stone in a hundred miles of this place. Church tore them all down, and sanctified the earth."

"Not all," Ian said with a smile. "Do you really believe he'll be at a henge?"

"Can't imagine doing a summoning of that power without tapping into a line," Hassek said. "Do you think he's in your shrine, houndsman?"

"No. There's another place," Ian said, turning his horse. "Follow me."

* * *

The doma stood harsh against the sky, the colored panes of its windows dull with the absence of the shining sunlight. The forest all around stood silent, black trees against grim sky, the soft loam of the ground swallowing their footsteps.

Inside, however, there was singing. The words were foreign, strange, like the broken rambling of a madman. The air above the doma twisted slowly, debris floating in the air like a whirlwind seen in slow motion. The sight of it made Ian's stomach queasy.

"Many of the domas were built on henges," he whispered as they approached. "Places the priests couldn't make holy, or where the power of the gods was so clearly present that the sanctity lingered, even with the gheists expelled. Ley lines, I suppose."

"Godly churches on pagan ground," Bruler muttered. "I will never understand the north."

"Your churches, too," Ian said. "They were all pagan once. They were all profane."

"Not sure how I'm meant to feel about that," Bruler said, "but it makes me uncomfortable."

"Good," Hassek whispered.

Ian held up his hand, and the scattered murmuring of their party disappeared. They were on foot, having left the horses below. There were no good roads up to this doma, only a winding path that clung to the rocky hill like a vine, switching back and forth up the steep side. The doma was a shrine used by pilgrims to meditate, or passing youth to dabble in adulthood. The priest who worked and lived there claimed the place was blessed of silence, and the undisturbed hour.

His body hung outside the door, neck snapped and throat cut. His fat belly, naked, was smeared with blood. Bruler whispered a prayer as they passed.

The door was broken. Shadows skipped over the windows, the dancing forms of a dozen or more of the void priests. Ian paused beside the entrance, bracing himself. Bruler watched him.

Ian nodded, and they rushed in.

62

THE MEN AND women guarding the voidfather were not priests, or Ian's attack would have failed before it began. The feeling of sickness that had seized him when he first saw the doma grew sharper with each step. The moments before he and his men stormed the building, the ground shimmered under his feet. Ian's shoulder slammed into the wooden doors, throwing them wide, and he stumbled inside.

The interior was nearly empty. The pews and altar had long been removed, but even the scattered furnishings that Ian remembered were gone. Scraps of cloth skated along the perimeter, caught in the wind that rushed in through the open door. A dozen figures sat loose-limbed around the room, surrounding a lone form at the doma's center.

They were dressed in black, chain dulled with thick oil that muted the light from a dozen lanterns, and they carried short spears with wicked blades, the hafts bound in leather and steel. As one, they stood and faced the intruders. There were both men and women among them, some tall and thin like Suhdrins, others staring out from the tattooed faces of Tenerran tribesmen.

At first Ian thought they had been singing, but the voices

continued even though none of the figures spoke. The song was coming from the air, rising from no mortal throat, sung by no mortal tongue.

The last figure was Folam Voidfather, huddled at the center of the room, his forehead bent against a crooked spear that pointed to the sky. Traces of light sparked along his wrinkled cheeks, following the pattern of ink that covered his face, drawn up the shaft of the spear and into the air. The sparks threw more light than seemed possible, casting shadows against the walls that shifted as they spun up toward the ceiling. The whole effect was dizzying, and Ian took a long breath to steady himself inside the door. Bruler, Knox and the others stood at his side, waiting for him to move.

"I see the son of hounds has found me," the voidfather whispered. His voice carried through the doma like smoke, quiet but everywhere. "Very well. Let's see what my daughter taught you."

"Daughter? How would I know your offspring, pagan?"

"Oh? She never mentioned it, I suppose." Folam nodded thoughtfully. "The witch Fianna is my blood, Ian of hounds. She was sent to you. I understand she made quite an impression, and you certainly seem to have been an able student."

The Suhdrins shifted nervously, turning some part of their attention to Ian. Bruler looked at him with a hint of accusation in his expression.

"I need nothing of the pagan craft to end you, Folam," Ian said, shaking free of the confusion that had gripped him. He motioned to Bruler, and the men spread out behind him, lining the wall. "You made a mistake in attacking Houndhallow."

"I never attacked you, Ian. Even now, as you stand before me with blade bared and Suhdrin dogs at your side, I hold back." The pagan guards shifted uneasily, like wolves on the leash, impatient to blood their jaws—but they came no closer. "My daughter led you safely through the Fen, and saved your mother when none other could. If I wanted you dead, you would have ended in the river, given to the water."

"Is that why you lay siege to Houndhallow? I had nothing to do with her arrest."

"Think who your allies are, Ian of hounds," Folam said. "Think more on what the church has asked of you, and the trouble it has brought."

"I'm not here to match words with you," Ian snapped. "Release your god, or yield to me. Do not make me take your surrender in blood."

"I have surrendered more than blood to this struggle," Folam said. "I will not yield now."

"You heard the man," Bruler muttered. With hardly a wasted move, he slid forward and attacked the nearest pagan guard. Despite the obvious threat, the man seemed shocked at the assault, and barely got his spear up in time. The wrapped haft of the weapon absorbed Bruler's blade. The counterstrike came quickly.

For a breath, Bruler and the pagan were the only figures moving, locked in a desperate battle of swing and riposte, the bright blade of Bruler's sword cutting hunks out of the leather, blocking the wicked strokes of the spear's head, both weapons ringing off stone as their masters danced around, whistling through the air and filling the doma with their song.

"Tenumbra!" Ian shouted, and he leapt into the fray. The rest of his followers were a half step behind. They joined with the pagan guards in a clash of steel and shouted battle cries.

Young Knox fell quickly, staggering back to the far wall,

only to be saved at the last second by one of the Suhdrin knights. Ian found himself across from a pagan girl barely old enough to carry the spear. The sides of her head were shaved, and the top bound in narrow plaits. She wore no ink on her face, but had smeared her eyes in a band of ash that made her look feral. She sidestepped his best attacks, pricking his chest with light strikes from her spear that failed to pierce the steel of his chain. They knocked the wind from him, though, and bruised his ribs, as well as his pride.

She smiled at him fiercely as they danced.

"Not as fast with your blade as you are with you tongue, hound?" the girl spat. "A pity. Brother Aedan failed to kill your vow knight, but I will not fail to kill you."

"I have faced gheists and gods," Ian said. "I won't fall under a child's hand." The girl grimaced, but answered with renewed fury. Ian was hard pressed to defend himself. He was about to retreat when Bruler, his sword already bloodied, stepped behind the girl and put the flat of his blade across the back of her head. She stumbled away, rolling behind her brothers before Ian could strike a fatal blow.

"This is no time for flirting," Bruler growled. "Kill them or kiss them, but not both."

"You could have killed her," Ian said.

"Aye," he said. "That I could have."

Then they were pressed again, pagans swirling around them like the sparks that still floated up from Folam's spear. The two men stood back to back, defending themselves from the onslaught. Slowly they worked their way to the wall, joining half their number in defense of the door.

"Weren't there more of us than them?" Bruler asked. Knox had rejoined the fight, though the boy's face was pale and blood spotted his shirt. "They fight like bears, half starved from their winter's sleep, and angry."

"Gods bless they don't raise a gheist against us," Knox said.

"I don't think they can. By Gwen's word, the power of the vow and the inquisition are useless against Folam Voidfather. We must meet him with steel. Perhaps the other pagans are just as limited," Ian said. He paused as a group of opponents fought their way closer to the door, as though they meant to break out, but just as the door was in their reach, the black-garbed guards fell back to the voidfather's side.

Bruler snorted in frustration.

"We take the word of one pagan heretic, to aid us in our battle against another pagan heretic," he said. "Gods help us if the inquisition tries to untangle this one. We're probably being played by both sides."

"I do the will of the gods," Ian said, though even he was unsure of which gods he meant, or how he was supposed to know their will. "They keep falling back. Why?"

"They mean to hold us here," Knox said. "Distracted."

"Distracted from what?" Bruler wondered. He glanced at the door, but immediately had to turn his attention to a new assault. Moments passed—moments spent dodging spears and dancing across the smooth stone floor of the doma. When that attack had been repulsed, he looked again to the door.

"There's something outside," he said.

Before Ian or the others could react to Bruler's words, the stained windows of the doma shattered, and pagans poured through the gaps. The door buckled and flew open. Beyond the walls, the night-shrouded forest was filled with torches.

"Forward!" Ian shouted. "We're not here to live! We're here to fight!"

"We've got to get to their leader," Bruler responded. "For Tenumbra!"

Ian led the charge, and his men formed into a narrow spear behind him. They punched through the pagan defenses, pushing past the ring of spears that protected the voidfather, overwhelming them just as the pagans thought the battle won. It was a suicidal effort, abandoning any hope of retreat in their press to strike.

His sword crashed through spear haft and chain, spattering blood and splinters in his path as he charged forward. Yet the closer to the center of the room he got, the more the sickness returned, until the floor was pitching under his feet and the air hung fetid with sickness.

Like a sailor in a storm, Ian stumbled forward, keeping his feet moving even as the world spun around him. Even the pagans seemed caught in the illness, standing stunned as Ian brushed past them, offering little resistance. He knocked them aside with his blade, sparing lives when he could, taking them when he had to.

The girl's face floated past him, eyes wide in the streak of ash, her hands empty. He pushed her down and stepped over her limp body.

Folam hadn't moved—*wasn't* moving. He was the only solid point in the doma. The room spun around his spear, a top balanced on the iron point of the blade. Ian took another step and the world settled into silent balance. All around him the battle continued, but it seemed as though he stood at the center of a storm, just his blade and the voidfather.

He swept his sword high over his head and stepped forward.

"Far enough," Folam whispered, his voice again drifting

through the air as though the stones themselves had spoken. The singing stopped, and the world slowed. "You have done well, child. Now. Come with me."

Folam's spear tilted toward Ian, and the doma fell into darkness.

He stood blinking in the new darkness. The doma's walls were still there, but it seemed as though they existed on the other side of a confounding dusk, the sparks from Folam's spear settling into a night sky of constellations.

The smooth floor underfoot bent into a bowl, cobbles curving toward the horizon like distant mountains. Folam sat at the middle, a hood hiding his features, his spear stretching to the sky. Ian felt as if he was floating in a dream, the gauze of sleep wrapping tight against his head.

"What would you do, Ian?" Folam asked with surprising calm. "What did you come here to accomplish?"

"I'm here to stop you," Ian said. He shook the gauze from his head and strode forward. The priest looked enormous, yet far away, as though the space between them stretched to the horizon. No matter how quickly he walked, Ian didn't feel like he was getting any closer.

"I'm here to end this, Folam."

"I would have you end it. End the work my daughter started in you. It is a seed, and the time has come to harvest it." The voidfather stirred, his eyes cracking open beneath the voluminous drape of his hood, bright lights in the shadow. "What can be drawn from your flesh, to feed my furnace?"

"You and Sacombre are too alike for my tastes," Ian growled. "Talking, and threatening, and looming against a shadowy horizon. It gets old." He stopped walking and bent his will against the voidfather's illusion. If this man was truly Fianna's father, then Ian knew the nature and depth of his power. Suddenly, the distance between them snapped short, like a rope yanked against its tether. The sparks of light still floated around them, but they no longer looked like stars.

"All show, no fire."

"I have fire enough," Folam said. The old man unfolded, standing gracelessly, old bones seeming to protest the effort. For an instant he reminded Ian of Frair Lucas, frail of flesh but hard of spirit. He tightened his grip on his sword.

"Where are we, pagan?" Ian demanded. "What have you done with my people?"

"We are tangled in the god, now. The god of nothing, so *we* are nothing, I suppose. Twisting in the void." Folam coughed into his hand and winced. "Nowhere, really. Best not to die here, if you can avoid it."

"I'll do my best," Ian said. Then he stepped forward and thrust his blade into the voidfather's chest. The steel passed easily through, cracking ribs and parting flesh. Folam looked down at the blade and started to laugh.

"You misunderstand. Dying cannot be done. Not in that way, at least," Folam said. He gestured with his hand, and the blade left his body, squeezed out like a splinter. The wound it left hung raggedly open, bloodless. "Walls within walls, Ian. The empty god is immune against the weapons of Cinder and Strife. Pagan, as well, and my body is proof against steel. Long have I dwelt in the house of the empty god, and I am not going to fall to mortal devices."

Ian stood holding the sword, looking down at the tip of the blade. It was clean, as bright as though newly forged.

He recalled something Elsa had said. "Every gheist has

its rules, voidfather," he growled. "This one has its limits—I simply must find them, and break you against its walls," he said. He raised his sword and sliced, wincing as the steel met bone, drawing it back again and again to hack and chop at the old man. Wounds opened in Folam's flesh, but they neither bled nor healed. The bones poked through the severed skin like jagged teeth.

Folam trembled, but stood fast.

"This god is the limit of all other gods, the boundary of their power, eternal and unbroken. The pagan elders bow to my rule. Do you know why?" Folam produced a pendant from his robes, dangling on the end of a leather thong. It looked heavy, as though the entire room tipped toward its weight. "Mine is the god that can not be filled. The end of every ending."

"It hurts, though. Doesn't it?" Ian said. "Your voice betrays that much." He swung to cut the thong, and Folam flinched aside. The blade cut into his arm, leaving it puckered and white. "Yes, it does. If I can't kill you, then I can make you regret living."

"No," Folam said, and fire filled the wounds. Some internal heat singed the voidfather's flesh, flames jetting out to scorch the stone and drive Ian back with their heat. "Emptiness has no regrets. It has no pain."

"Then you aren't empty," Ian said. "I know rage when I see it. Rage enough to sacrifice your daughter to the church, and throw away whatever love you held for Tenumbra, all to serve your bloody vengeance!"

The heat began to parch his skin, even through the leather and steel of his vambrace, and he covered his face with his arm, chopping blindly again and again. Folam howled, and a gout of flame lashed the ceiling, causing Ian to flinch. When he looked again, a brilliant light was erupting out of Folam's ruptured chest. The man's hood was wreathed in smoke.

"There's fury still, and fury can be cut, even if it's wedded to the void!"

"You keep fighting us, Ian—you and your father—but you have no idea what you're fighting! You act like this is a war, and you're the hero of some great ballad. But this is no war! It's a fire, and you are nothing more than fuel!"

"Yet it seems as if the flames have just about consumed you, voidfather," Ian said. "So let's put an end to your guttering!" He pushed against the waves of heat and brought his sword down on Folam's head. The blade passed easily through his skull, the bone crumbling like ash, and sparks blossomed into the air. The sword continued down, parting ribs, belly, leaving the body at the hip and not stopping until it struck stone.

There was a flash of light, then sharp pain in Ian's shoulder. He stumbled back.

Folam's arm came with him, the dead man's fist holding the pendant. The tip was as sharp as a knife, and it stuck in Ian's shoulder. As he stared down in horror, the pagan's arm crumbled into dust, cracks that filled with flame and then collapsed, until only the pendant remained.

The pain was blinding. Ian went to his knees, dropping his sword among the ashes of Folam's body. He clawed at the pendant, but the stone was hot to touch, and burned his fingers. Finally he hooked a finger into the trailing thong and wrenched it free. Though the wound was shallow and the stone smooth, when it pulled out it felt as though barbs had been buried deep in his flesh. Ian gasped in pain and nearly passed out.

He stared down at the wound. It hung open, bloodless, empty, the flesh inside as empty as the void.

With a crash, the battle of the doma resumed around him. Ian knelt over Folam's body, the voidfather's flesh a ruin of torn flesh and punctured bone. Blood soaked the floor beneath him. Folam still held the pendant, and a smile faded from his lips as he died.

The wound in Ian's shoulder hung like an open mouth, screaming silently without blood, without pain, a hole in his flesh that would not close.

EPILOGUE

HOUNDHALLOW WAS A ruin.

Groups of men and women moved through the forests, picking corpses from the ash, cutting down trees that were cinder and stacking stones that had once been houses. It was an exhausting task, and every person who joined in the effort remained forever scarred by the experience.

There remained three nobles of Tener. Gwen Adair, Ian Blakley, and Nessie Blakley disappeared into the keep to nurse their wounds, and try to figure out what had become of their world. Sir Volent stood guard outside the great hall, with Sir Bruler his constant companion. There was an air of quiet about the place, as though the mortal world was still trying to figure out how to cope with the presence of the gods.

The great hounds remained. They emptied the kennels without the master's permission, breaking the locks in their great jaws and leading the duke's packs out into the forests to hunt. The one Gwen had ridden led the way, his fur of matted iron glinting between the trees whenever the pack was near. Their howls carried through the night, though no one seemed to mind. It was as though an old song had been remembered and sung anew, bringing comfort to those who had forgotten the words.

At the end of the first week, one of the crews ranged far from the village. They came across a pillar of ash, vaguely in the form of a woman. She stood with a sword above her head, feet spread wide, mouth open. Curious, one of them took a hammer and cracked the shell. A splinter of ash fell away, and then another. A woman tumbled out. Her hair was burned away, and the color of her eyes had dulled to verdigris. She went to her knees and took a long, dry breath. When she spoke, it was around a mouthful of dust. They couldn't understand her words, because these were simple men, who knew nothing of the hidden rites of the Lightfort.

Sir Elsa muttered the summoning prayers of Strife, but nothing came. No light, no warmth, no fire. Summer had left her.

Her god had left her cold.

ACKNOWLEDGEMENTS

SECOND BOOKS IN a trilogy are interesting. A writer often has a clear vision of how a story begins, and how a story ends, and several important steps along the way. The first draft of this book was a good book, but it wasn't the second book in a trilogy, or even the second book in a series. It was only through the wise and steady advice of my agent, Joshua, and my editor, Steve, that the book you're holding makes any sense within the context of the rest of the series. It's an open secret that good writing is really done in revision, and great writing is done in the re-revision of the rewritten third draft. If that's true, then this is going to be a tremendous book.

Through it all, my wife has stood by me, making sacrifices of time and financial comfort that shouldn't be necessary. She's the best. She's better than the best. She's exemplary.

I would say more, but I have a third book to write. And re-write. And revise.

ABOUT THE AUTHOR

TIM AKERS WAS born in deeply rural North Carolina, the only son of a theologian, and the last in a long line of telephony princes, tourist attraction barons, and gruff Scottish bankers. He moved to Chicago for college, and stayed to pursue his lifelong obsession with apocalyptic winters.

He lives (nay, flourishes) with his brilliant, tolerant, loving wife, and splits his time between pewter miniatures and fountain pens.

The Hallowed War series represents more than a decade of scribbling and late night musing, not to mention years and years of actual writing, revising, and rewriting. If he's done it right, you won't even notice it took that long.

His website is http://www.timakers.net/

ALSO AVAILABLE FROM TITAN BOOKS

THE PAGAN NIGHT

Tim Akers

The Celestial Church has all but eliminated the old pagan ways, ruling the people with an iron hand. Demonic gheists terrorize the land, hunted by the warriors of the Inquisition, yet it's the battling factions within the Church and age-old hatreds between north and south that tear the land apart.

Malcolm Blakley, hero of the Reaver War, seeks to end the conflict between men, yet it will fall to his son, Ian, and the huntress Gwen Adair to stop the killing before it tears the land apart. *The Pagan Night* is an epic of mad gods, inquisitor priests, holy knights bound to hunt and kill, and noble houses fighting battles of politics, prejudice, and power.

"A tale of religious conflicts and cleverly drafted characters, a must for all epic fantasy fans."
Starburst

TITAN BOOKS

ALSO AVAILABLE FROM TITAN BOOKS

DUSKFALL

Christopher Husberg

Pulled from a frozen sea, pierced by arrows and close to death, Knot has no memory of who he was. But his dreams are dark, filled with violence and unknown faces. Winter, a tiellan woman whose people have long been oppressed by humans, is married to and abandoned by Knot on the same day. In her search for him, she will discover her control of magic, but risk losing herself utterly. And Cinzia, priestess and true believer, returns home to discover her family at the heart of a heretical rebellion. A rebellion that only the Inquisition can crush... Their fates and those of others will intertwine, in a land where magic and daemons are believed dead, but dark forces still vie for power.

"A great new fantasy epic."
Library Journal

TITAN BOOKS